Polly swept her ga
full view of the str
driveway.

She saw the cowboy boots first. They totally set the tone for what was to come—jeans, denim shirt over broad shoulders. From what she could see in the shadow of the brim of his dark brown cowboy hat, he had a likable face, not too handsome, not too rugged, and a subtle but earnest smile.

"I was passing by on my way home, saw you lying in your driveway under your car and I thought, well, either A, you had run over yourself, in which case you'd have a story I couldn't miss hearing." His smile took on a hint of teasing. "Or B, I thought maybe you could use a hand."

"B, definitely B." Polly smiled.

"Sam Goodacre." He took her hand in his.

Their eyes met and held. She had been in town for all of a few hours and already met a guy who made her heart race. So much for taking things at a slower pace here...

A New Beginning

Annie Jones

&

USA TODAY Bestselling Author

Margaret Daley

Previously published as *Triplets Find a Mom*
and *The Nanny's New Family*

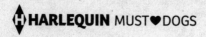

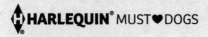 HARLEQUIN® MUST♥DOGS

Recycling programs
for this product may
not exist in your area.

ISBN-13: 978-1-335-50629-0

A New Beginning

Copyright © 2020 by Harlequin Books S.A.

Triplets Find a Mom
First published in 2012. This edition published in 2020.
Copyright © 2012 by Luanne Jones

The Nanny's New Family
First published in 2015. This edition published in 2020.
Copyright © 2015 by Margaret Daley

For questions and comments about the quality of this book,
please contact us at CustomerService@Harlequin.com.

Harlequin Enterprises ULC
22 Adelaide St. West, 40th Floor
Toronto, Ontario M5H 4E3, Canada
www.Harlequin.com

Printed in U.S.A.

CONTENTS

Winner of a HOLT Medallion for Southern-themed fiction and named the *Houston Chronicle*'s Best Christian Fiction Author of 1999, **Annie Jones** grew up in a family that loved to laugh, eat and talk—often all at the same time. They instilled in her the gift of sharing through words and humor, and the confidence to go after her heart's desire. A former social worker, she feels called to be a "voice for the voiceless" and has carried that calling into her writing. She lives in rural Kentucky with her husband and two children.

Books by Annie Jones

Love Inspired

April in Bloom
Somebody's Baby
Somebody's Santa
Somebody's Hero
Marrying Minister Right
Blessings of the Season
"The Holiday Husband"
Their First Noel
Home to Stay
Triplets Find a Mom
Bundle of Joy

Visit the Author Profile page
at Harlequin.com for more titles.

TRIPLETS FIND A MOM

Annie Jones

For Emma Dobben and Alleyah Asher and whoever comes along after—I am looking at YOU, Rob and Melissa—to share our love and grow our family in God's promises!

If your gift is serving others, serve them well.
If you are a teacher, teach well.
—*Romans* 12:7

Chapter 1

If you can't beat 'em...run away.

The finality of the moving truck trundling off made the last thing her sister had said to her loom large in Polly Bennett's thoughts. Too exhausted to move, she stood hip-deep in the stacks of boxes in her rented two-bedroom cottage five hundred miles from everyone she knew. She eased out a long, satisfied breath and smiled. For once in their twenty-six years on this earth, Esther, Polly's identical twin sister, was wrong. Polly hadn't run away from anything; she had run *to* something.

Polly had run *to* the place where she would build a life, pursue a career, make a difference in people's lives. She closed her eyes to form a short, silent prayer that this would be the place where she would meet a great guy, fall in love and raise a family—where she would make her home.

"Amen," Polly whispered, her heart light and her head swirling with a million things she needed to get done. She moved around the boxes that held the contents of her life, boxes marked Kitchen and Living Room and Fragile. She took a deep breath, tugged open the uppermost one and immediately recognized a series of paper-wrapped rectangles. The newsprint packaging rattled as she uncovered a set of four sleek silver frames. Her shoes squeaked on the polished wood floor as she went to put the series of family photos on the mantel of the painted brick fireplace.

"Giving y'all the best spot in the house to watch over me…" she murmured in her soft Georgia accent. First she placed the photo of her brother and sister-in-law and their two kids, who looked as if they'd stepped out of a catalog of perfect families, then added, "But not be able to tell me I'm doing it all wrong."

Next she settled in the photos of her mom and her mom's new husband, and her dad and her dad's soon-to-be next wife, on either side of the first frame. The second she did it, she felt a cloud of heaviness in her chest, so she moved them both onto the same side. That did little to ease the ache in her heart over her parents' split, even though it had happened almost sixteen years ago. Finally she arranged the pictures so that if you stood in just the right spot and gazed at them at just the right angle, you would see the two faces of the parents she loved so dearly side by side. That helped.

A little.

One last frame to unwrap. Polly tugged it free and let the paper tumble down over her ratty tennis shoes. Her eyes lingered over the image of herself and her sister seated on either side of a wrought-iron table under a red-and-white-striped restaurant awning. Unlike the others, it was not a professional portrait but a shot taken the day her sister had accepted her job as first assistant chef. That same day Polly had decided to quit working as a permanent substitute teacher and find her way in the world, wherever that quest took her.

Esther's hair was pulled back so tight that if it were blond instead of jet-black, she might have looked bald. Polly had to peer closely to see the slip of a ponytail high on the back of Esther's head. In contrast, Polly's unruly black hair, which was only a little bit shorter than Essie's, fell forward over one dark eyebrow. It flipped up at the ends against her shirt collar and stuck out on one side.

While Essie's makeup was simple and perfect, Polly had chosen that day to try something dramatic with eyeliner, making her dark pupils look almost black. And despite the fact that Essie worked preparing food in a hot and hectic restaurant kitchen all day long, she looked crisp and cool. Polly was the one with an orangey cheese snack smudge on her shoulder, from where one of her students had hugged her.

She shook her head and sang under her breath, "'One of these things is not like the other…'"

Deeper in the box, she found the big envelope containing her letter of acceptance as the newest second-grade teacher at Van Buren Elementary School. She took it out and hugged it to her chest, filled with gratitude for the last-minute decision by an older teacher to retire that had resulted in Polly getting the chance of a lifetime.

Outside, the rustling of bushes, the snap of a twig made her pulse kick up. She checked out the curtainless window in the front room. The long shadows of late afternoon made it impossible to see much, but the neatly kept houses settled cozily on the treelined street left her with a sense of well-being she had never really known. Renting it sight unseen after her video interview had worked out, after all. She couldn't help but smile at the sight. Even though she hadn't been in this town since she was six years old, she had known this was where she belonged.

"Baconburg, Ohio." She held out the envelope and trailed her fingers over the town's name on the return address then over the cancellation stamp dated July 15, just a little over two weeks ago. To the average person the letter was simply the confirmation of her last-minute contract offer. But to Polly? A flutter of excitement rose from the pit of her stomach and she gave a nervous laugh. "This is my ticket home."

Her whole life since that childhood move she'd felt as if she was at odds with…well, everything. She'd never found peace in Atlanta, Georgia, where her parents had moved to make a better life for their family.

Polly shook her head and sighed, but that did not even begin to unravel the knot in her chest that the memories of those early years in Atlanta always brought. *Better?*

Richer. Faster. More driven, maybe. But better?

Polly didn't see it. The fighting between her parents had started not long after that move and escalated with the driving pace of their lives in the city. They tried to hold the family together, and Polly tried to accept things how she'd been raised—that everything presented an opportunity to be seized, a competition to be won.

But the truth was that Polly just loved kids. Teaching them, guiding them, watching them grow and learn and embrace life in their own unique ways seemed like the greatest ambition anyone could have. Her family did not get that. Sometimes Polly felt her own family did not get her.

They especially did not get her longing to return to Baconburg.

"But here I am—" she swept her gaze over the unpacked boxes in her small house "—on my own. Alone."

The rustling under her front window interrupted her musings again. She set the envelope aside, went to the shallow window seat and peered out. Nothing. She sank to sit on the window seat. The rays of the late-afternoon sun slanted across the gleaming hardwood floor. So she was done running. Now what?

Her stomach grumbled and that seemed like the answer—eat something. She started to head toward the kitchen, then realized she didn't even have any food in the house.

If she were back in Atlanta she'd just hop in her little hybrid and scoot over to her sister's restaurant or over to her mom's house to raid the fridge. She certainly didn't know anyone well enough to do that here. She didn't really *know* anyone here. And the only restaurant she knew of in Baconburg was a fast-food spot out on the highway.

This time the noise outside sounded like a low whine. Probably a corner of one of the shaggy bushes scraping against the glass or the metal gutters creaking. A car pulled up in the drive across the street and two children came scrambling down the walk to greet the man climbing out from behind the wheel. Her stomach rumbled. The people went inside. She glanced over her shoulder at her family's photos on the mantel and it all hit her.

She had no one here. A wave of loneliness swept over her. Real loneliness. She always carried her faith within her and with it her connection to God and to all her friends and family, who routinely held one another in prayer. So it wasn't a matter of being completely abandoned. But…

Finally a clear whimper at her front door made her catch her breath. She shut her eyes, hoping again that she had only imagined it.

Another whimper.

Tension wound from between her shoulder blades through her body to tighten into a knot in the pit of her stomach.

She had seen that little dog hanging around her yard as she moved boxes in. She assumed it belonged to one of the families on the block and forced herself not to try to gather up the sweet-faced little animal.

You never get a second chance to make a first impression. Polly could practically hear her mother schooling her in an attempt to get the imperfect twin to be more like her sister. It must have sunk in a little because Polly had not wanted the first impression she made to be that she had stolen her neighbor's pet.

This time a series of three short whimpers, then a snuffle moved her to action. She went to the front door and opened it slowly. She'd just steal a peek and—

A soft golden-brown muzzle poked into the crack between the door and doorframe.

"Oh! No, puppy." She reached down to push the animal back outside. "This is not your home. You should go back where you belong."

A small, cold nose filled her palm followed by a soft warm tongue. She glanced down and her gaze met a pair of huge, soft brown eyes.

Polly was lost. She had always been a pushover for brown eyes. And these? Looking up at her from the sweetest little face of a doggy who, like her, wasn't sure if he would be welcome in this new environment. Oh, yeah, she was lost for sure.

"Okay, I'll take you in for the night, but starting tomorrow morning I am going to do everything I can to find your real own—" She'd hardly started to pull open the door when the animal nudged his way inside.

He had the elongated body and uncapped energy of a dachshund. The long ears and short, stocky legs of a basset hound maybe, but with the coloring, brown eyes and nose of a golden retriever. Tongue lapping and tail wagging, he jumped on her and threw her off-balance. She sank to the floor and the little guy squirmed into her lap, laid his head against her cheek and sighed.

For one fleeting moment her loneliness eased—until she realized she couldn't allow herself to get too attached. Her first responsibility to this little fellow was to get him back to those who loved him. Much like her duty as the town's new second-grade teacher was to encourage children to learn and grow and then to move on.

"Okay, let's get some food." She stood and brushed the dog hair off her clothes, snapped up her purse, then went to the door. "Tomorrow I'll run up to the school and get whatever I need to make some flyers."

She'd brought paper, markers, glue, scissors and other supplies with her from Atlanta because she didn't know what she'd find in Baconburg. "Then I can take a picture of you, scan it into my laptop, make a flyer and post them around town. But for *now?*" She opened the front door and motioned for him to follow. "Wanna go for a ride in the car?"

Apparently he did not.

"Come out from under there!" Gingerly, she poked her nose under the back end of her car where the dog had darted after she had stepped outside.

The puppy whimpered.

She recognized the sound of a car engine cutting off, a door opening and falling shut again. She couldn't stop to think about what kind of first impression she was making on some neighbor. Despite her thoughts on wanting to leave her competitive upbringing behind, she couldn't help herself—she was determined to win this little battle of wills. A battle not for her own benefit, but this time to help the frightened animal.

"Just a little closer…" Her cheek flattened against the cold bumper. She stretched out her hand, straining her fingers to try to reach some part of the animal. "I wish I could make you understand that this is for your own good. Can't you just give a little bit, too?"

"I know people who name their cars. Even some who give them pep talks or good swearing outs, but trying to guilt your car into running? That's totally new to me."

Polly gasped at the deep, masculine voice. She wasn't

frightened so much as mortified to be caught in this awkward position.

"Uh, hello, I wasn't… That is… Hang on a sec…" She knew it would take her a minute to work her arm back enough to get leverage so she could free herself. Maybe she should say something about how silly she looked to make him chuckle, but nothing sprang to mind.

"I, um, I was just… I wasn't talking to…" Heart racing, she finally got herself out from under the car, banging the back of her head on the plastic bumper as she did. That slight injury—more to her ego than her noggin—did not explain her reaction when she swept her gaze up to take in the full view of the stranger standing in her driveway.

She saw the cowboy boots first. They totally set the tone for what was to come—jeans, denim shirt over broad shoulders, a relaxed, open stance that instantly put her at ease. From what she could see in the shadow of the brim of his dark brown cowboy hat, he had a likable face, not too handsome, not too rugged, and a subtle but earnest smile.

"I was passing by on my way home. Saw you lying in your driveway under your car and I thought, well, either A, you had run over yourself, in which case you'd have a story I couldn't miss hearing." He used his left hand to tip his hat back. No wedding ring. His smile took on a hint of teasing. "Or B, I thought maybe you could use a hand."

He would have laughed if she'd said something about her silly situation while backing out and she sort of wished she'd done it now. There could be worse things than planting herself in this guy's memory. She swept back the fringe of her shaggy bangs, and stole a peek at the man's hunter-green truck parked at the end of her driveway with the painted logo Goodacre Organic Farm. The Farmer Sows the Word. Mark 4:14.

"B, definitely B." Polly smiled. A farmer and a Christian—who better to deal with one of God's creatures? "I could use some help, thank you."

"I'd be happy to take a look." He squatted down, sweeping his hat off as he did. Suddenly they were at eye level. And what warm brown eyes they were.

"I have to admit I don't know a lot about fixing cars, but I'm willing to give it a go." He settled the hat on the drive, then ran his hand back through the shortish waves of sandy-brown hair. "What's the problem? Loose muffler? Oil leak?"

He bent down low to peer under the car. A cold nose thrust forward, a flash of tongue.

"Scared dog," Polly said, her timing just a bit off.

"Hey!" The man whipped his large hand across his chin and nailed Polly with a stunned look. "There's a dog under there."

"I know. *That's* who I was talking to." Hadn't she made that clear? The second she'd laid eyes on her champion farmer she'd had a hard time following the conversation. "Can you help me coax him out?"

"Does he bite?"

"He hasn't bitten me." She pressed her lips together to launch into a more thorough explanation, but he didn't give her time.

"All right, I'll give it a try." He clapped his hands together.

A soft woof came from beneath the car.

Polly sucked air between her teeth. "Thanks, I really appreciate your coming to our rescue. I guess this is one of the benefits of small-town living."

He opened his mouth to say something, but instead a woman's voice called out, "Hey, Sam! Need any help?"

"Got it under control, thanks!" The man, whose name was Sam, it seemed, waved back. He gave Polly a wry look, clearly not quite put out, not quite thrilled with the attention they had drawn. "Another 'benefit' of small-town life—wherever you go...there you are."

Polly gave a light laugh at the oversimplification of his frustration with being spotted.

"More precisely, there your friends are, or your family, or your pastor." He gave a shrug, then nodded to the car tag sporting a frame from an Atlanta auto dealer on the back of her little red car. "Not the kind of thing you have to worry about where you're from, I guess."

"Or here, actually. I'm Polly Bennett, by the way." She held out her hand.

"Sam Goodacre." He took her hand in his.

Their eyes met and held. She had been in town for all of a few hours and already met a guy who made her heart race. So much for taking things at a slower pace here. She drew in a deep breath of fresh summer air. "It's good to meet you. I just—"

A pathetic whimper from under the car kept her from launching into her story.

"Why don't you go around to the other side of the car in case he heads that direction?" Sam directed her by drawing a circle with one finger.

Polly nodded and hurried around to the other side

of the car and started to get down on one knee, but before she could, Sam's head popped up over the roof of her small vehicle.

"Got him." He lifted the dog up. Floppy ears and tongue flapped out, all landing in Sam's smiling face. "Yeah, yeah. No need to get all mushy about it… What's his name?"

She gave a big sigh at the overload of adorableness, then shifted her gaze to the pup. "I don't know."

"What?"

"He's a stray," she admitted, twisting her hands together. "I just saw him around earlier today. Then when I opened the door to check on him, he ran inside, then back outside and now I can't… I just… I couldn't…"

"Don't tell me. You've fallen in love with him already."

"Don't you believe in love at first sight?" Okay, that was way too flirty to say to a man she'd just met. Still, Polly tipped her head to one side and waited for his answer.

"Believe in it?" He lowered the dog out of face-licking range and gave a resigned kind of smile, his brown eyes framed by the faint beginnings of laugh lines. "I think it's unavoidable."

Her pulse went from racing to practically ricocheting through her body.

"Especially when you're talking about a little lost dog as cute as this." He looked down and rubbed the dog behind the ears, then came around the front end of the car to bring the animal to her.

"Of course." Polly let out a breath she hadn't even realized she'd been holding. "I still want to try to find who he belongs to, of course, but if nobody claims him…"

"He's a lucky dog." He bundled the dog into her waiting arms.

"I don't believe in luck." She ran her fingers along the dog's smooth, silky ear. "I believe in God's blessings."

"I've had a few of those in my life." He nodded but didn't offer any further explanation, just turned and headed for his truck.

"So…" Polly looked up and down the street, not sure what to do next. Her gaze fell on the truck. "Oh! Do you know… I mean, it's about food."

"I have been known to eat food, yes." He patted his flat stomach even as he slowed his pace slightly and spoke to her over his shoulder. "What do you want to know?"

I want to know that everything is going to work out fine. I want to know if I made the right choice moving here. I want to know when I'll see you again. "I don't have any dog food in the house, so I was going to take him with me to grab a fast-food burger. Do you think it would be okay if he ate one of those?"

"I think it would be okay if *you* ate one of them." He shook his head and scratched his fingers through his thick, light brown hair. "But there's a gas station with a little fresh market near the burger place. You can get a can of dog food there—for him. You should probably stick with the burger."

She laughed. "Thanks, and thanks for your help."

"Glad to do it." He started toward his truck again,

tossing off a friendly wave. "Nice to have met you. Both of you."

"You, too, from both of us." She took the dog's paw and waved it.

He opened the driver's side door to climb in, then paused and leaned inside the cab, as if looking for something.

"That right there—" she whispered with her cheek pressed against the animal's head "—is the whole reason I came back to Baconburg."

She didn't mean the man. She meant the man's willingness to take time out of his own schedule to help a stranger. Okay, Polly could not lie, even to herself—maybe the man…a little. Or a man like him. What Polly really wanted in Baconburg was the life she had always dreamed possible, and that included a good man and her own family that would stay together no matter what.

Before she could shuffle the little dog into the backseat of her car, the animal dashed around the back of the car. Polly glanced back and there was Sam walking across her front yard, heading back toward her. And he had his hand up in a wave. She raised her hand as the dog returned and ducked into the back of the car.

"Wow, maybe I do mean *that* guy is the reason I came here," she whispered to her canine companion as she took in a sharp breath. "He sure seems like he isn't ready for me to go yet."

The dog paced back and forth over the seat. If she kept him, she knew she'd have to invest in a safety restraint but thought for now this was safer than leaving him in her house or outside.

"Maybe I should see if he wants to join us for burgers." Polly gripped the door.

Sam came to a halt in her yard. His raised hand fell to his side.

She smiled and worked up the courage to say, "Hi, it looks like you're thinking what I'm thinking…"

He cocked his head and narrowed his eyes. "That your dog has my hat?"

"Your… Oh, no! You set it on the driveway, didn't you?" She glanced back in time to see the animal give the hat a shake. "No!"

Sam put his thumb and forefinger to the bridge of his nose. Probably unable to look at what the dog had done.

"I am so sorry." She hurried to the back door, reached in and grabbed the hat by the brim. It took a firm tug to rescue it, but she held it out to him.

He looked down, his expression guarded.

Polly stared at the damp brim and the crown the dog had shaken into a shapeless wonder. "I'm so sorry," she said again. Her voice was barely a whisper.

"What's done is done." Finally he put his own hand up and turned his head to one side as if to say, *I don't want it now.* "It's okay. Don't feel bad. It was just an old Christmas gift from my wife."

"Wife?" Now she felt careless and a bit silly. "I didn't think you were—"

"My *late* wife," he clarified. He frowned down at the mash up of brim and crown. "Hmm. Well, okay, then. I guess that's the end of that."

He flicked it with one finger as if to say, *Goodbye, old friend,* then raised his hand in a sort of salute to her, turned and headed for his truck.

"Your taking this so well only makes me feel worse," she called after him. "Isn't there something I can do with it?"

"Maybe we can cut ear holes in it and let the dog wear it." He didn't look back.

Polly climbed into the car and looked her only friend in all of Baconburg in the eye. Poor little thing. Of all of God's creatures, he could understand her fear, sadness, embarrassment and loneliness when she said, "Maybe Essie was right. Maybe running away isn't going to be the big solution to my problems that I thought it would be."

Chapter 2

"So, let me get this straight." Sam's sister, Gina, slipped off her computer glasses and aimed her sharp-eyed gaze at him. "You just left your hat in her hands and drove off?"

"Hey, it wasn't like I was going to wear it home." Sam moved around the kitchen table gathering up the three empty bowls where a few minutes ago his daughters had been eating ice cream. He stacked Juliette's "sprinkles, please, Daddy, and no nuts" dish inside Hayley's "chocolate on chocolate with a side of chocolate" one. Finally he took up Caroline's "whatever you give me is fine, Daddy" dish, held them up and said to his sister, "Anyone who thinks those girls are completely identical has never had to feed them."

"Don't try to change the subject on me." Gina wriggled in the high-backed oak chair, then kicked it up on

two legs, bracing her hiking shoe against the table leg
to stabilize herself. "Marie gave you that hat."

"I am well aware." Sam plunked the bowls into the
sink. He turned on the water to rinse them out and said,
loudly enough to be heard over the splashing, "By the
way, if Mom were here she'd tell you she didn't care
if you are the owner of this place now, you keep both
your feet and all the chair legs on the floor, young lady."

Gina rocked the chair slightly and crossed her arms
defiantly, not even flinching when her long, dark blond
braid got snagged under one arm. "Tell me again who
this woman is."

"Mom?" He faked surprise to cover his determina-
tion not to prolong any discussion of Polly Bennett. "I
know she and Dad have been living in Florida for a few
years now, but—"

"You know who I mean. The mysterious woman who
got you to help rescue a dog. A dog, Sam. That's huge
for you."

He finished washing up the dishes, then moved to
drying them off with the towel that usually hung from
the handle of the oven door. "I don't dislike dogs and
she's not mysterious. Her name is Polly Bennett from
Atlanta, Georgia."

"New in town?"

"Didn't say." He put the bowls up and shut the cabi-
net, wishing he could finish up this conversation that
easily. He wouldn't normally have even mentioned any
of this to Gin, but she had asked if he had left his hat
at work when he'd come home. And when she didn't
get an answer had wondered aloud if he had left it in

her truck and she'd have to get it out of there later. She wouldn't let it go, even several hours later.

"You don't suppose this Polly Bennett is the new schoolteacher?" Gina asked.

"Thought of that myself." But he'd dismissed it almost instantly. Polly Bennett, with her wild, dark hair, her fresh face and pint-size stature, didn't look like any grade-school teacher he'd ever had. "But then I remembered you said word on the grapevine was they'd gone with someone born here in Baconburg."

"That's right." The chair legs came clunking down. She shifted her laptop around on the table as if she was about to get back to work promoting the farm's upcoming fall pumpkin-themed festival, the Pumpkin Jump, online. Instead she looked up at him again. "And you just left your hat with a stranger?"

"Stop this ride." He held up his hands. "I am not going around again."

"Fine." She leaned in over her keyboard and put her fingers over the touch pad. But always one to want the last word, she said, "You know, they say if you leave something at a person's house, it's a subconscious way of giving yourself an excuse to go back."

"Then *they* don't know me because I don't *go* back." He headed out the kitchen door into the hallway.

"Walking away is not the same as moving forward, you know."

"I'm not walking away. I'm going to check on the girls and tell them good-night." He paused at the bottom of the stairs.

"Good luck with that."

"I don't believe in luck. I believe in God's blessings." He wasn't sure why he'd said it, but the words, and thinking of the woman who had said them, actually made him smile.

"Fine, go say good-night to your little blessings. Remember they're all wired up about getting their classroom assignments tomorrow. I hope you're ready to deal with the fallout."

"I was born ready." Whatever came his way, Sam met it, wrestled with it, made it his or left it behind. Nothing slowed him down. Full speed ahead. Farm kid. College football hero. Hometown business owner. Husband. Father. Widower. Single dad to three six-year-old girls.

He moved forward, always forward, tackling every new role with his faith to uphold him. When he made up his mind, applied his experience and attitude, he could handle anything.

Except second grade.

Sam took a deep breath, stepped into the doorway of the room shared by his daughters and made one loud clap of his hands. "Big day tomorrow, girls! Second-grade registration and we find out who your new teachers will be."

"There's only *one* new teacher," Hayley, the most outspoken of the three, reminded him.

As if he needed reminding. Three second-grade classes at Van Buren Elementary, three Goodacre girls aching for a chance to be teacher's pet to somebody who *hadn't* known them since they were toddlers. A school with a policy not to put multiples in the same classroom, and one new teacher. He didn't have to be a math whiz to know he was going to have a couple of upset girls tomorrow, maybe for a big part of the whole school year.

"Okay, let's not borrow trouble." Especially not triple trouble, he thought. "We'll deal with whoever gets the new teacher the way we deal with everything. And how's that?"

"With grace and with gratitude, with a never-give-up attitude." The trio repeated in unison another line from the bedtime stories their mother had created, stories that they each knew by heart.

He thought of Marie saying those same words, and on the heels of that, he thought of the cowboy-hat Christmas gift she'd given him as a joke. No one expected him to wear it. Which was why Sam had put it on the day they moved out to the farm, a month after Marie had died. He'd worn it every day since. It was his way of making himself embrace change. Now...

In the blink of an eye, his mind went to Polly Bennett. *Polly.*

What a great name. Fit her, too. Upbeat. Fresh, yet maybe a little old-fashioned. And a good heart. He'd seen it in her from the moment their eyes met until she looked at him with true regret over ruining his hat.

Unpredictable, too, just like that crazy hair of hers. Sam had had to clench his fingers tight a couple of time to keep from brushing it out of her eyes. Then that whole deal with that little lost dog...

That thought snapped Sam back into the moment. He shifted his boots on the old farmhouse floorboards. His mind did not usually skip the tracks like that. He had to get ahold of himself. "Actually, I meant that we'd meet the problem head-on and not look back because..."

"The rest of our life is ahead of us." Hayley and Juliette repeated one of the many mottoes Sam had taught them. Caroline just looked at him, saying nothing.

"That's right. Never look back." He didn't just talk the talk in this case. Sam had made these past few years about demonstrating those traits to his girls. People had told him he kept the girls too busy and spent too little time making a new life for himself.

He knew what they meant by that. They thought Sam needed to fall in love again. What those people didn't understand was that he had made up his mind that all his time and energy had to go into his girls, into making sure they did not miss out on anything because they were missing their mom. Maybe one day he'd be able to let up a little and meet…someone. But that certainly wasn't going to be tomorrow. Tomorrow presented its own problems. "Now say your prayers and go to bed."

He reached along the wall and flicked off the light, but instead of turning around and leaving the girls to do what was expected of them, he lingered to listen as they thanked God for their day, their home, the food they ate and then began the list of the people they loved.

"Bless Daddy." Always the leader, Hayley's request came clear and firm.

"And bless Uncle Max," Hayley's carbon copy, Juliette, chimed in to add the youngest of Sam's siblings.

"And bless Aunt Gina." Caroline tacked on a request on behalf of Sam's sister.

"And also, if You don't mind…" Hayley started again, her tone uncharacteristically tentative. "If Mommy is close by to You in heaven right now…"

Don't look back… Sam wanted to plead with his child, *Let your mother go and don't dwell on the loss.*

A lump rose in his throat, which he pushed down again. He turned away. No point in standing there having his heart tugged toward a past he could not change. His life…more importantly, his daughters' lives, lay ahead of them and he had to keep fixed on that and never stop moving forward. It was the only way they could survive.

"If Mom is there with You," Juliette took over for her sister, her tone bright and cheerful, "give her a hug from us."

Sam froze in the dim hallway.

And finally Caroline added softly, "And tell her we will never forget her."

Sam dragged air into his lungs, ignoring the dull ache that still caught him by surprise even two years after his wife's death. Maybe *pain* was the wrong word. *Emptiness? Sadness?* He didn't know anymore. He'd made his peace with his loss, accepted it as God's will and got on with normal life for his girls' sake.

That's why he had moved them from the house he and his wife, Marie, had owned in their small town out to the family farm his sister had taken over from their parents. He did it to show the girls how life was about change and growth. What better place to show that than a farm? Were they not getting it? What more could he do?

"And bless the new teacher, whoever gets her." This time Hayley led off. "I hope she's fun and smart and nice."

Again a twinge of emotion, only this time it was not grief but a mix of misgivings.

"And it wouldn't be bad if she also thinks triplets are cool. And also if she's pretty—" Juliette turned her head enough to peer over her shoulder through one half-opened eye "—and not married."

It hit Sam like a sucker punch. This was why he needed to stop listening in on his girls' prayers, because he did not want the girls using their prayer time to try to make a point to him. It didn't matter if the teacher was pretty or single—all he cared about was how she would help whichever daughter landed in her classroom to have a successful school year.

"What did you say?" He put his hand to the side of his head to remind them he was standing right there within earshot.

"Amen," Hayley concluded.

"Amen," the others agreed.

"Go to bed," Sam muttered, his hand on the doorknob. Just before he pulled it closed, he leaned in to add, "And tomorrow don't make me remind you of my own personal set of no-no's."

"We know. Dad, we know all about your no-no's." Hayley sighed, got to her feet and threw back the covers on her single bed. "No dogs."

That sounded particularly harsh all of a sudden after helping Polly Bennett wrangle that sweet little lost dog. But they had imposed enough on his sister's time by moving in. To add pet care while he ran and remodeled Downtown Drug and while the girls were in school, and dance classes and tumbling and T-ball…just wasn't fair.

"It's not the 'no dogs' rule I'm talking about," he reminded them. "No…"

Juliette and then Caroline rose, each flipping back the covers on their own beds, too.

Three little sighs and three sets of eyes—probably rolling in irritation as they climbed into their beds.

"And no…" he prompted one more time.

"No matchmaking," they all said as one. Then one, two, three, they pulled up their covers in a way that made Sam think of cartoon princesses flouncing off in a huff.

"That's right. Good night, sweethearts." He gave them a nod and turned to shut the door at last, but just before he pulled it closed, he heard one of those little princesses mutter an addendum to his hard-and-fast no-matchmaking rule.

"For now."

Ready? Had he thought he was ready? Oh, no. He was not ready for this. Not ready at all.

Chapter 3

Early that next morning, Polly hurried to the school, still feeling badly about the whole hat thing. With that weighing on her mind, she didn't even feel like chattering out loud to her canine passenger as she drove the four blocks from her house to the place where her street, Mills, met Main. At the intersection, governed only by a four-way stop sign, she took a moment to read the official signs.

"Baconburg Business District." She glanced toward the road that she knew wound around toward the highway where a chain hotel, a couple of fast-food places and a mega grocery store dotted the landscape.

She took a peek down at a patchwork of buildings that told the story of a town that had known growth spurts and setbacks. Polly smiled. "Baconburg Historic District, which means the cool stuff is thataway."

But Polly was headed straight down Mills to the school and she couldn't linger any longer. She sighed. "Too bad there isn't a hat-blocking place back there."

Oblivious, the dog bounced right to left, then right again. In a few minutes she pulled into the school parking lot. The only other cars seemed to belong to the staff.

Today was the day the students would be finding out whose classroom they would be assigned to. The principal had okayed her coming in to collect some supplies but had asked that Polly not stick around to avoid "complications." Polly understood the code word for school politics. She knew that as a fairly new teacher—just three years out of college—and totally new to Van Buren Elementary, some parents would have misgivings about their kids being assigned to her. Others would demand to have their children in Miss Bennett's class, thinking she would have fresher perspective, all the latest approaches and no preconceptions about which were the good kids and which were the "problems." Though Polly couldn't really imagine how much of a problem your average small-town second grader could be.

"No more problem than you right now, mister." She whirred the window down a few inches, got out and shut the door. She started to turn toward the front door of the single-level blond-brick building, then suddenly felt compelled to explain, "You just have to stay here for two minutes while I run into my classroom here to get some paper. I can make up flyers there so we can find your parents, okay?"

The thick tail thumped against the back of the seat and he whimpered softly as if to tell her he understood.

She tapped the window. Did she really have to make flyers today? She had moved here to learn to take her time, relish the past and not be so anxious to press forward, after all.

A silvery-blue minivan came gliding up past her car and pulled up to the curb in front of her.

Parents were beginning to arrive. She had two choices. Go inside and get what she came for and get out. Or run away.

The passenger door of the minivan swung open and Polly couldn't help taking a peek.

One little girl with a bright red ponytail, dressed in canvas-colored overalls over a lime-green camp shirt scrambled out onto the sidewalk with so much energy that she almost fell over herself. No, that wasn't herself she had fallen over. It was…

"Twins!" Polly couldn't help it. She whispered the word in a rush of excitement to the little dog.

The second child emerged. Her red hair was woven into a gorgeous French braid tied with a pink ribbon. In fact, everything she wore was pink. Pink top, pink skirt, pink sparkly shoelaces in pink sequined tennis shoes.

Polly laughed out loud at the sight. "A set of identical—"

A third child climbed out.

"Triplets," Polly murmured.

This one wore tennis shoes, too, plain white ones. With faded jeans and an ill-fitting gray shirt. Her hair was caught up in pigtails, the right one a good two inches higher than the left.

That was the one that got to Polly. She felt a smile start that grew beyond simple amusement to recognition of a kindred spirit. All three girls turned and looked at her, their eyes wide.

Polly wondered if she should say hello. It seemed wrong to just get in her car and rush off now. Maybe she should wave and say, *See ya soon, I hope.* Or should she ask their names? Before she could speak or move or even make up her mind, the driver's door swung open.

"I told you girls we were leaving too early. I don't know if the doors are even open yet." A large, weathered cowboy boot hit the concrete followed by more than six feet of tall, muscular man.

Polly leaned back against the car, a bit for support, a bit to give her room to take in the whole view. "You!"

"Me!" Sam grinned as he shut his door and started toward her. "So, you have a kid in this school, too?"

"Too?" Polly looked at the children, then at the van and realized nobody else was getting out.

He pointed toward the girls each in turn. "Hayley, Juliette and Caroline."

"Those are…*your* daughters?" Sam Goodacre had identical triplets. Some women might have wanted to run from a situation like that, but for Polly, just seeing these girls made her feel less homesick for her own twin.

"Yeah." He held up three fingers. "All mine. And you…"

Three high-pitched squeals tore through the quiet air of the summer morning.

"You…brought…a dog." They all sang out a variation of almost the same thing.

"I don't have any kids, Sam. I'm not even married." Polly moved closer to him to speak softly enough that the girls wouldn't hear as she whispered her confession, "I'm the new teacher."

"Of course you are." He shook his head. "You are the single, new teacher with an adorable, homeless puppy."

In a flash of red curls and giggles, the girls ran up to the car. The puppy rushed to the side and licked the place where the small hands pressed against the glass.

"You say 'new teacher' like it's a bad thing." She ducked her head to try to meet his lowered gaze. "It's because of the hat thing, right? It's the hat?"

"Forget about the hat. That's the past." He waved his hand as if actually pushing it behind them. "No, it's more complicated than that, starting with the fact that my girls are starting second grade this year. This is Hayley. That one is Juliette." He pointed to each girl as he spoke. "And that is Caroline."

"Oh." Polly whipped around and saw the girls in another light—not as fellow multiples but each a potential student.

The one Sam called Caroline gasped, her eyes grew wide and in that second there was a light in her to rival her other sisters' natural vivaciousness. Caroline turned her head to tell Polly, "I like your dog."

"He's not mine, really." She slipped away from Sam and went to the children. "I found him hanging around my house. I'm going to put up flyers to see if I can find his real owners."

"You don't have to do that. *I* know his real owners." Caroline jerked her head around to fix her huge, pleading eyes on her father.

"Me, too." Juliette ran to the car to peer inside.

"Me, too, too," Hayley said with sweetness but conviction.

Sam strode forward from the parking lot to the sidewalk, motioning the girls away from the car. "Okay, girls, you know the rules."

"We weren't matchmaking, Dad," they all protested together in perfect harmony, a trick only identical multiples could fully pull off.

"Matchmaking?" Polly laughed, a bit too nervously for her own comfort. What was this all about? Sam had a rule against matchmaking?

Sam scowled. "I meant the rule about dogs."

"Oh, so we *can* matchmake?" Hayley rushed forward.

"No." He spread his hands wide as if calling a runner out at home plate.

Polly felt a blush rush from the constriction in her chest to the tips of her ears. She didn't know if she should say something or get out of there fast.

"You know we can't have a dog right now. You have too many activities. Juliette, you want to give up ballet?"

The girl opened her mouth, but before she could actually give an answer, the man moved on, intent on making his point quick and clean. It was a familiar means of "communicating" in her family and it made Polly tense up.

"And, Hayley, you have your hands full with your 4-H projects, right?"

Hayley put her shoulders back and didn't answer—a means of getting her message across that Sam did not seem to notice.

"And, Caroline…well, when school starts I'm sure you'll find some things to keep you busy. We're all busy. Bringing a dog into our lives now wouldn't be fair to your aunt Gina having to care for it, or to the dog not getting our full attention."

Caroline glanced back and the dog. "But…"

"We don't even know." Sam tried to glower at the girls then at the dog, but he didn't quite pull it off. "This dog may belong to someone."

"He does belong to someone, Daddy, to *us*," Caroline insisted in such a plaintive voice that Polly could feel the longing in her own bones.

"No." Sam's insistence told a story of something more going on than his simplistic explanation. "He is not ours."

"He should be ours," Hayley said firmly.

"He could be ours." Juliette spoke a bit more tentatively.

Caroline fixed her eyes on her father and added, "If Mama was alive, he *would* be ours."

Sam pressed his lips into a thin white line.

Maybe she was overly sensitive because she'd been so lonely last night, or because she felt so guilty about Sam's hat, or maybe because she honestly liked Sam and felt a connection to his daughters. Whatever the reason, Polly couldn't stay quiet another minute. She hurried to the driver's side door, her keys jangling in her hand.

"You know," Polly said as she rushed to his rescue and put the key in the lock, "I think I'll just take care of him until we find out if someone is looking for him. Right now I've got to go. The teachers aren't supposed to be here when the kids and parents start to show up. Bye, girls, it was so nice to meet you."

The girls all groaned.

Sam mouthed a thank-you that made her feel good and a little sad at the same time. How she longed to point out those missed clues with the girls. Why wouldn't he allow them to have a dog? And the no-matchmaking deal?

Suddenly instead of seeing a funny, kind man of faith she perceived the hurt he hid even from himself.

As she drove away from the family scene, her gaze fell on the hat that she had left in the car last night. She couldn't talk rules or matchmaking with Sam, couldn't interfere with his parenting, but she could help him out here. She could do everything within her power to get this puppy back to his real home so that she could give the dog and the girls a happy ending. But to do that she had to act fast.

"You know, for someone who came to Baconburg to slow down the pace of her life—" she told her passenger, who woofed softly in response "—I sure have been in an awful big hurry ever since I met that Sam Goodacre."

"So?" Sam's younger brother, Max, called out the second Sam came blowing through the back door of Downtown Drug.

He had taken the girls back to the farm after they'd gotten their class assignments. The whole process had taken longer than he'd expected and he was late getting in to open the store. The girls had actually taken their assignments pretty well. Hayley and Juliette patting Caroline on the back as a kind of congratulations, even, and saying they didn't mind. Until they learned just who the new teacher was.

Sam had met the cries of "unfair" and pleas for him to go to the school and let them all be in Miss Bennett's class with his usual "let's not let this slow us down" answers, which hadn't helped much. Maybe it was because for the first time in a long time, he hadn't really believed his own proclamations. In finding out Polly had this connection to his children, it wasn't just the two girls in the other classes that felt just a little bit cheated.

"So?" Max's voice rang out again. "Just how cute is this new teacher?"

The first thing Sam encountered was the last thing he had the time or patience to put up with.

"I spoke with her for five whole minutes in front of the school this morning." Sam slipped the long white lab coat he kept hanging on the door of the pharmacist's station over his street clothes. He strode farther into the old store where his little brother, Max, stood amid a disarray of power tools, how-to manuals and a row of still-crated restaurant-grade appliances. "Do not tell me it's all over town already?"

"Hey, you belly crawl across the new lady in town's driveway one evening, then get spotted talking to her in front of the school the next day?" Max grinned his famous cocky grin, and gave an unconvincing shrug. "People are gonna talk."

"She's Caroline's teacher." In Sam's mind that was the end of the discussion. He moved on toward the front door, flipping on display lights and setting things in their rightful spots.

"So?" Max called after him, not budging so much as an inch to help prep the place for the coming day.

So. Max had a way of asking something that Sam had no way of formulating an answer to.

"Look, it's Baconburg. Everyone is somebody's teacher or scout leader or church youth-group leader or cousin or… You get it. As long as you keep things on the up-and-up and don't give anyone reason for concern vis-à-vis the whole teacher-as-a-role-model thing, I think you could manage a few dates with the lady."

Sam gripped the door's ice-cold metal handle until the chill sank through all the way to his fingertips. He clenched his jaw and looked out at the town where he had grown up, the place that had cheered him in his youthful triumphs and embraced him in his time of deepest grief. He had fully prepared for his faith and this town to sustain him as he raised his girls and they grew up and had their own triumphs. That had been his sole priority.

Then he'd seen Polly Bennett trying to rescue that stray dog from under her car and for a split second his whole life hit Pause.

"She takes in strays," he said loud enough for Max to hear, but not so much for Max's benefit. "Raggedy, sad-eyed, not-too-great-smelling strays."

"Great. That means you might actually stand a chance with her."

"Very funny." He glanced back and laughed at the brotherly jab. Max had always been the ladies' man of the Goodacre boys, so Sam could understand why Max's mind would immediately jump to the romance conclusion. "But really, how could I ever get involved with someone who wouldn't hesitate to take in a lost dog, an animal she might have to give back if the real owners showed up? I can't put my kids through that."

"Then let them have their own dog, like lots of kids their age do." Max sifted through the plans and pencils scattered on a makeshift table in the soon-to-be lunch-counter area of the store.

Sam's throat constricted just enough to strain his words as he shot back, "Lots of kids their age haven't suffered the kind of loss my girls have."

"Did you ever think it might be good for them to have a dog to take care of, not to mention a nice lady in their life—in your life?" Max took up a pencil and tucked it behind his ear. "It might help them find a new kind of normal."

"There's a piece of the puzzle you're not seeing." Sam turned and headed back through the store. Time to get this subject and this day back on track. "This dog she's found could be the model for the dog in those bed-time stories Marie used to tell the girls."

"The ones Gina has written up and wants to publish?"

"The triplets have grown up with an idealized version of an adorable little dog who never gets sick, never gets old, never…" Sam gave a thumbs-down gesture rather than say what he meant. He met Max's gaze and gave his final word on the matter. "No dog could live up to the one in their imagination. It wouldn't be fair to the animal."

Sam headed back to the pharmacy.

Max moved around the work space, putting himself in a place to make sure Sam could hear him as he folded his burly arms over his broad chest and asked, "Have you noticed, big bro, that every time you give an excuse for not letting the girls have a dog, it changes a little?"

"I have work to do." Sam stood still for a moment, aware that Max had a point but that he also didn't have any say in Sam's life. "You have heard of that, right? Work?"

Max withdrew the pencil and a tumble of his shaggy, sun-streaked hair stuck out over his tanned ear. "Hey, I'm working on this."

"If that were true we'd have an operational lunch counter by now." Sam didn't mean to sound mad, but he'd reached his limit on this subject today. No dog. No matchmaking with Polly Bennett. Why couldn't anyone get that? "You know they call it a lunch counter because people expect to come in, sit at the counter and get served a hot, quick lunch, right? Not because everyone is counting the days until this project eats your lunch and you take off again."

"You know you sound like a grouchy old man, don't you?" Max laughed. "Go count pills."

"I will. And while I'm doing that, can you handle taking care of the store? I do not need to be disturbed any more today."

"Any more? You're saying something…or someone… has already disturbed your tightly wound little world, bro?" Max chuckled. "Good for her. If she's as cute as they say, good for you, too. It's about time."

Chapter 4

Getting her supplies from the school wasn't going to work for her flyer project. Polly had taken her wriggling little wet-nosed charge back to her house and settled him in, then headed out to try to find a place to buy more paper. When she found herself at that crossroads between the Historic and Business districts of Baconburg again, she didn't hesitate.

A few minutes later she was strolling down the sidewalk, soaking in every small detail of the lovely old historic buildings. Nothing was going to hurry her along again today. Brass fixtures, ornate cement trimwork, even the names of the old establishments spelled out in colored tile in the entryways leading to the doors. Try as she might she could not recall any of this from her childhood. She strongly suspected that her parents preferred to do their shopping someplace shiny and sophisticated, upscale and urban. She paused just outside her destination, a sweet little throwback to an earlier time, Downtown Drug.

She blinked at the image of a black-haired, dreamy-eyed young woman reflected back at her. She could easily imagine herself in a pillbox hat and gloves, proper Miss Bennett, grammar-school teacher, strolling downtown circa 1950. How could her family have not loved this town? How could they have run so fast and so far away from it?

If Polly didn't look just like her sister, Essie, who so clearly belonged with the Bennett family, Polly would have wondered if she had been switched at birth. All of historic Baconburg, right down to the blue-, white- and silver-painted plateglass windows of Downtown Drug put a whole new spring in Polly's step. She crossed over the threshold of the front door and felt as if she'd walked into another time, a sweeter time, a time when people made time for one another.

She stole a moment to take in the black-and-white-tiled floors, sunny-yellow walls and shelves filled with every sort of thing a person might need. The old store still had a gleaming wooden checkout stand, with a shiny computerized scanner and cash register attached. That didn't dampen Polly's enthusiasm for the quaintness of the old place. She could just imagine how for so many years people in Baconburg must have come here for the things they needed—medicine, candy, school supplies and who knew what else.

"Welcome to Downtown Drug. We've got whatever your little heart desires." A warm, deep masculine voice called out from somewhere unseen in the store. "If you need help finding it, I'm back here at the lunch counter."

"A lunch counter." Polly sighed. "This I've got to see!"

She wound her way back toward the friendly voice, expecting to find a nice paunchy, slightly balding middle-aged man wearing a white bib apron getting a big grill ready for the day's business.

"Hello?" she called out. She rounded the end of a row of shelves and stopped inches from a pile of red vinyl benches and tables that must have once been booths. Beyond that a bright yellow strip of plastic, the kind she'd seen around crime scenes marked off an area filled with power tools, sawdust and chaos.

Middle-aged? Maybe if the average life expectancy was around sixty. Balding? Not even slightly. Her gaze moved from the shoulder-length waves of light brown hair topped with sun-washed blond streaks to his tanned face and two- or three-day growth of beard. He wore a chain around his neck with a cross on it, and a faded T-shirt rolled up at the sleeves to reveal bulging biceps.

He smiled. "Hey there, pretty lady. You got a question? I don't actually work in the store, so I'm not sure where you'd find that. If you'd like, I can ask the old man."

He raised his voice on the last two words and directed them toward the raised platform framed in black-painted wood with sliding glass-panel windows and *Pharmacy* lettered in gold.

In response, one of the panels slid almost closed.

The man in front of her burst out laughing. "They do get cranky when they get old, don't they?"

"I like older people," Polly said in the unseen man's defense. "And I like older places. I think it's a shame you're tearing up this wonderful old piece of local history. Please tell me you're not going to install one of those fast-food kiosks like they have in quick markets and all over the airport in Atlanta."

"Atlanta! You're..." He pointed at her and his face lit up like a kid's at Christmas.

"I'm what?"

"From Atlanta," he said as if that was what he had been reacting to—and fairly unconvincingly, too.

What did this construction worker in surfer dude's clothing know about her? Should she be uneasy or flattered?

"Maybe I should talk to that *old man*." She turned and skirted sideways, keenly aware of the smiling carpenter's eyes on her. Even when she heard the squeak of a door, she did not turn toward the pharmacist's station. Her gaze locked on the other man, she raised the piece of paper. "I have a list. I just need to get in, get out and get back to getting this little dog I found back where he belongs."

"I thought you were keeping the dog."

Polly gasped at the sound of Sam's voice. The slip of paper with her supply list on it slid through her fingers, flipped in the air and fell between her feet and Sam's cowboy boots.

"I can't... That is...*you* convinced me..." Polly looked at him, her mouth open. Sam Goodacre. The guy who showed up in her driveway. Then at the school. Now... "I can't believe we keep running into each other."

"Welcome to life in a small town. The upside is that you tend to make a tight-knit circle of friends and associates who are always there for each other. The downside is that you have a tight-knit circle of friends and associates and they're always *there* for each other, whether you want them there or not."

She thought of her life in Atlanta where she barely knew anyone in her building, or even her church. Where her job meant she rarely worked with the same people more than a few days in a row, and even so, half the time they rarely had time to make eye contact. Of course, not everyone in the city was like that, but that had been her experience and so... "I didn't say I didn't like it."

"Oh?" He tipped his head to one side. "I guess sometimes it *is* kinda nice."

Her heart fluttered. She took a breath and held it just long enough until she noticed her head felt light. She let her words rush out in a whisper, "What are you doing here?"

"I own the place. Bought out my father-in-law when he retired last year." He stuck his thumb under the name tag on his white lab coat, closing the already-too-close distance between them with the starched white fabric.

Polly pressed her lips together to keep from actually reading the tag aloud as she tried to ignore how this man's nearness made her so aware of everything from the rasp of his coat over his shirt to the pounding of her pulse in her temples.

"You're..." She glanced over her shoulder in the direction of the lunch counter. "You're the old man?"

He chuckled softly. "I see you've met my brother, Max."

"Your brother…" Suddenly the guy seeming to know something about her made sense. It also made her wonder if it was Sam who had told his brother about her, and just what Sam might have said. Never in her life had she had this kind of instantaneous reaction to a man. Just being around him filled her with anticipation and the expectation that something good was coming her way. She liked that. Liked him. A good guy. A good dad. A Christian and…

"I thought you were a farmer."

"Close. I'm a pharmacist." He walked over to the raised platform and slid the glass back to reveal a plaque with all his credentials engraved under his name. "I just live on a farm."

"But the truck I first saw you in…"

"Belongs to our family farm. My sister and I trade off depending on our cargo. Her organic produce gets the truck, my redheaded progeny get the minivan."

She couldn't help smiling. "Those girls seem like pretty precious cargo to me."

"Yeah, they are." He nodded as if he really appreciated her saying that, then suddenly his brow furrowed. "Did you come in here for something special?"

"Oh! My list!" She bent immediately to retrieve the list.

"Let me…" Sam did the same.

They both reached out. Polly clenched her jaw, bracing herself for that dull, painful, embarrassing head clunk. Surprised when it didn't come, she jerked her head up.

He was standing there, his face inches from hers. In

the space of a heartbeat she lost herself in those caring brown eyes.

"I'll just get…" she murmured.

"Here, let me…" he said at the same time.

Both bent slightly forward, hands extended and faces
close. Static electricity in the very air drew a strand of
Polly's hair toward his. For a split second, if anyone had
caught a glimpse of them with those words on their lips
and their gazes entwined, they might have thought they
were just about to kiss.

"Um, I have to go." Polly jerked her body upright
and raked her curled fingers through her hair, pulling
it back into place. "I left the dog and…I have to go."

She didn't wait for an answer, just spun on her heel
and ran. For an instant she listened for his footsteps
behind her, or for him to call for her not to leave. Not
a sound, not as she fled with her face flushed and her
throat tight, not as she hit the door and pushed her way
out onto the sidewalk.

In the glass storefront she no longer imagined the
daydream of prim Miss Bennett but saw herself. Polly,
who wanted to find her place in the world but who never
quite fit in had just met a man who made her feel as if
anything was possible—except a match made between
the two of them.

Sam couldn't get the near kiss out of his mind the
rest of the day. Thoughts of Polly Bennett popped up
uninvited in the seconds between the phone ringing and
his answering it. Could it be her calling about whatever
she had come in to get from the store?

Her image formed slowly in his thoughts as he

walked by the spot where Polly had stood. When he caught the whiff of sawdust and bubblegum, the scent in the store surrounding them earlier. So it pulled him up short when, shortly after four, his sister came in to deliver the triplets to him and his brother simultaneously made an announcement.

"All right! Gina's here." Max clapped his hands together, then swung his legs over the tarp-covered lunch counter. "I'm off."

Hayley clambered up onto one of the dozen stools planted around the covered counter. Juliette went on tiptoe, gave a twirl and took the seat next to her. Sam reached out to help Caroline climb up to another stool, frowning at his brother as he asked, "Where you going, Max?"

"To pay a visit to that pretty new teacher."

"Why?"

"Because she came in here this morning with a list of things she needed and after two minutes in your presence she ran out of here without getting any of it." The small rectangle of paper caught between Max's fingers crackled. "So I thought I'd do the neighborly thing—fill her list and take it over to her."

"We want to go." Hayley spoke for all three girls.

"I have a motorcycle, girls. One of you can ride behind me and one on my shoulders, but the other one…" He squinted at Sam. The girls understood this was just another example of Uncle Max's outrageous humor, but Sam recognized the challenge in his younger brother's tone. He was baiting Sam. "You got a skateboard and some clothesline in this place?"

"Very funny." Sam met that challenge with his feet

planted firmly in front of his daughters, on the floor of his place of business. He wasn't going to let his younger brother goad him into getting riled up about Polly Bennett. That no-matchmaking rule did not just apply to the triplets.

Max made an exaggeratedly casual shrug, ending with both hands held out as if weighing the two options. "Somebody's got to stay here. Somebody needs to take these to the lovely Miss Bennett."

"Dad can do it," Caroline volunteered, because they clearly all knew Sam wasn't going to speak up for himself.

Max gave a big ol' self-satisfied grin. "Why didn't I think of that?"

Sam opened his mouth to launch into an explanation of his special set of rules to Max, then reconsidered. It wasn't as if Max ever listened to the rules, anyway.

"How about Gina?" Sam fixed his gaze on his sister, who had paused long enough at the counter to drop some change into the drawer and sell herself a pack of gum. "It would be perfect. You take the girls and deliver this stuff to—"

"Sorry." She leaned down, rummaged around under the counter, then popped back up holding Sam's spare truck keys. "I have an appointment with a seed catalog."

As soon as Gina reached the door, she pitched Sam the keys to the minivan. "See you tonight."

The keys hit the floor with a metallic clank.

Max bent down to scoop them up and dangled them in front of Sam. "I can hold down the store while you pay a visit."

"I don't want the girls getting attached to that dog,"

Sam muttered through clenched teeth, not from anger but from trying to disguise the sentiment from his daughters.

"Fine. They can stay with me." He pressed the cluster of keys into Sam's palm. "I could use the girls' help picking out paint colors."

"Green!" Hayley jumped in the air.

"Pink!" Juliette gave a twirl.

"Can you use wallpaper?" Caroline squinted at the wall as if already taking mental measurements for the job.

The girls threw themselves into the assignment with the kind of enthusiasm that only a chance to do an end run around their dad's no-matchmaking rule could inspire.

What was he going to do about it? Haul the girls over there and risk their falling in love with that little lost pup? Or send his brother over to Polly Bennett's house and risk her falling in love with his hound dog of a brother? That shouldn't matter, but…

He sighed, snagged the bag with the goods gathered up by Max and headed for the door. "I'll be back in an hour. I'm going to make a delivery."

Chapter 5

Sam pulled the family minivan into Polly's driveway, took one look at his surroundings and groaned. They'd done it. Right under his nose. Despite all the so-called rules he laid out and his own insistence he wouldn't be falling for any of their shenanigans, Sam had played right into the matchmaking hands of Max and the triplets.

"I can't believe I fell for that," he muttered quietly, realizing now that Max had never even asked where Polly lived.

He chuckled softly at the ingenuity of the foursome, even if their matchmaking mission was doomed to failure. He was making a delivery. That was all. He focused on the task at hand, getting these things to a customer, to Caroline's teacher. No distractions, no complications.

"No problem." Sam couldn't believe the words coming out of his own mouth not ten seconds after he had knocked on the door and Polly had asked him to come around to the back of the house, go down through the basement door and up into the house because she didn't want the little dog to run out the door again. He should have just hollered back through the closed door that he'd leave the things on the front porch, have a nice day, see you around, something like that. Instead he took the long way around, into the basement, up the stairs and through the door that let him into the small, sunny kitchen.

The impact of what he had just done hit him. Kitchens were generally considered the heart of the home, weren't they? He was in the heart of Polly territory. And he liked it.

Of course, the same neighbors who had seen him on his belly in Polly's driveway might just have taken notice of his going around the back way and letting himself into the new schoolteacher's…make that the pretty, single, new schoolteacher's…house. He wasn't just standing on the porch as he usually would do for a delivery. He wasn't even standing in the front room where the two of them could be seen through the big front window, not that the people of Baconburg were prone to spying on one another. But new-to-town pretty ladies and widowers whom everyone thought should have started dating again made for pretty interesting viewing, especially in late summer when there was nothing good on TV.

He took a breath to holler out a hello when his gaze fell on his cowboy hat. He couldn't count the times he debated if it was time to put the hat away for good but something always stopped him.

His stomach coiled like a fist twisting in his gut. He stared at it for a moment. Another deep breath. "Miss Bennett? I just brought over the things on your list. I'm going to leave them on the kitchen table, if that's…"

The kitchen door swung inward and there stood Polly.

"…okay with you," he finished quietly as he settled the bag on the old oak table without taking his eyes off her once.

Her hair looked as if she'd just stepped out of a whirlwind, and her cheeks were pink. She was barefoot, had a muddy paw print on her neck, dirt on her nose and was wearing a big black garbage sack as a kind of poncho that didn't quite hide her rolled-up pink sweatpants and tie-dyed T-shirt.

Sam wouldn't have been more impressed, or surprised, if she had walked into the room in a sparkling ball gown. He grinned. He hadn't wanted to grin, or intended to grin, but one look at her and his mouth just sort of had a mind of its own.

"Sorry it took so long." She patted a wild strand of her hair down against her forehead, then heaved a sigh and sent that same wayward lock sailing upward again. "I've been wrestling with the native wildlife."

"Lucky wildlife." Yes, his mouth most definitely had a mind of its own around Polly Bennett. He cleared his throat. "I mean, I hope you won."

"Not yet I haven't. I did manage to get Homer in the bathroom, though." She went over to the sack he had just set down and began rummaging around. "I'm calling the little dog Homer for now because everything needs a name, don't you think? Anyway, then your brother called—"

"My brother? Max? Called you?"

"Yeah." She gave a nod, then turned and motioned for Sam to follow her. She hit the swinging door with her hip and paused long enough for him to shuffle by her, not seeming one bit slowed by his hesitant confusion. "Got my cell number from the principal, which in Atlanta would have made me uncomfortable, but here? That's like half a dozen kinds of small-town fabulous in a bucket, don't you think?"

"I might have to see that bucket first," he muttered as she hustled around in front of him and headed down a dimly lit hallway.

"Anyway, like I was saying, I had just wrangled him into the tub when your brother called." She opened the door to a small bathroom.

There in a big claw-foot bathtub sat the saddest-eyed, soaking-wet little puppy Sam had ever seen. It peered over the tub's edge at him and whined softly.

"Ta-da!" Polly threw her arms open wide in a triumphant flourish. "He's all yours."

"Ta-what?" Sam frowned, trying to make sense of things, a task made more difficult with Polly standing so near beaming up at him. "He's all…mine?"

"Not to keep. To bathe. Or help bathe. Max said you'd be happy to help." She had to squeeze to one side to get herself fully into the small, tiled room. "Said you knew all about this kind of thing."

"*What* kind of thing?"

She turned and cocked her head at him as if he was silly to have to ask. "Flea baths."

"Well, I…" How could he claim otherwise? He'd grown up on a farm, after all. He did know about tending to animals of all sorts. "Look, I just came over to drop off those things. Whatever Max promised, he did it without my knowledge or—"

"Please help me," she said softly. "I've never had a dog and I'm scared I'll get soap in his eyes or the special shampoo will burn and he'll think I'm being mean to him and not trust me anymore."

"—approval," he concluded, because he was the kind of man who followed through on what he started, even if it was concluding that he wasn't going to start anything.

"Please, Sam." Her voice caught in her throat.

She paused to compose herself and he couldn't help noticing the tremble of her lower lip, the white-knuckled grip on the shampoo bottle and the threat of tears in those big eyes. He warned himself to resist the urge to rush to Polly's rescue. What good could come of it after all?

"He's kinda my only pal in town right now." Polly glanced over her shoulder at the dog, then turned and tipped her face up to settle her gaze directly in his. "Other than, well, *you*. I really don't want him to turn on me."

He looked into Polly's eyes. She and her puppy needed him. Sam simply could not say no. He pushed up his shirtsleeves and headed into the small space, chiding himself under his breath as he did, "So much for no complications."

* * *

Polly shut the door behind her in the tiny white-and-yellow bathroom and became instantly aware of how much of the small space was suddenly taken up by broad, masculine shoulders, long legs and cowboy boots.

Sam didn't seem to notice. He simply squatted down by the tub and ran his hand down the wriggling puppy's back. "You didn't use hot water for the little guy, did you?"

"No, of course not. I just had an idea. Would you excuse me a second?"

Polly slipped out the door, and when it closed, she hurried off to the kitchen where she snatched up the hat she had run over and still hoped to make right. As she turned, her plastic makeshift apron crinkled and she thought to grab another trash bag for Sam, to protect him from any splashes or shaking by the dog. Her bare feet pounded down the hallway. Just outside the room she took a deep breath, then eased open the door, pausing when she heard Sam speaking in a quietly compelling tone.

"Look, it's nothing personal, little guy. If it were just me I'd offer to have you live on our farm, but I have these three girls, you see, and they already are crazy about another dog, a dog you could never be, a dog their mom told them about."

Polly sank her teeth into her lower lip to hold back a tiny gasp of surprise at that news. Her gaze dropped down to the hat and she stroked it once, feeling all the worse at this glimpse into how staunchly Sam protected the things that still connected his family to his late wife.

"It's just that my girls need to move forward. It's not good to have someone like you around...to fall in love with...to remind me that there are some things you can't hold on to... I mean to remind them." He cleared his throat.

So now Polly knew. It wasn't his girls he was protecting but his own heart with those hard-and-fast rules. She drew in a deep breath and rapped her knuckles on the door. "Hey, back with your hat and a little something to help you keep...dry."

"Too late!" He looked up at her from where he sat, cross-legged on the shaggy pink bathroom throw rug, with the little dog in a sopping-wet towel in his lap. The animal lifted his head to nuzzle against the man's soaked shoulder.

The sight didn't just melt her heart; it made her knees weak and her chin quiver. She slipped inside the room, shut the door and sank to the floor beside the pair. "Aw. I missed it."

"Just round one." Sam held up one finger and the puppy licked it. Sam laughed. He twisted around and pulled the plug from the drain and the water began to swirl away. "The mixture has to set on him for two minutes, then a really thorough rinse."

Two minutes to sit here and watch Sam coddle her sweet canine charge. Two minutes so close to the man she could see his chest rise and fall slowly with each intake of moist, steamy air. Two minutes before they finished up, he walked away and Polly would have to honor his rules and honor her own commitment to do what was right for the girls, find her lost friend a home.

"So, what's his name?" Polly's plastic covering crinkled as she settled on the floor on her knees and stroked the dog's head.

"You're the one calling him—"

"The dog your late wife told the triplets about," she said softly. "I only ask because, well, I heard you talking to him about it and I thought, well, because I have this dog for now and Caroline will be in my class..."

"Donut."

The dog looked up when Sam spoke.

Polly understood the response as the man's quiet intensity made her unable to look away as well.

"Marie came up with these stories, see, after she got the news that her illness was terminal." Despite the warm, damp air around them, Sam's coloring grew pale. He kept his gaze cast downward. "This mixed-breed dog, called Donut, causes havoc for three little girls on a ranch and their dad, who was a cowboy."

"Ah." She reached for the hat she'd brought with her, but he began talking again before she could produce it.

"In the first story, they learn a lesson about the power of love and God's forgiveness. She didn't have time to write a second one." His jaw went tight. "It was Marie's way of leaving a little bit of herself behind for the girls. They have every word memorized."

"She must have been an incredible mom," Polly said in hushed awe.

Sam jerked his head up and at last their eyes met. He studied her, his mouth set in a grim line for a moment before the tension in his face eased and he nodded. "Yeah, she was. Thank you for saying so."

One last gurgle from the tub, a glug, then all went silent.

"Anyway, the triplets all agree this—" he pointed to

the dog, who had almost fallen asleep in his lap "—is what the dog looks like."

If two minutes was all God granted her, then she would be grateful. Wasn't that the very lesson she had come to Baconburg to learn? That life was about enjoying what you had while you had it, not always chasing after something better, something more?

"A cowboy, huh?" She shifted her weight and became aware of the hat on the floor beside her. "That reminds me. Let's wash the tub out with really hot water, get some really good steam going and…voilà!"

She produced the hat.

"Voilà?" He squinted at the object in her hands with the hint of a smile playing over his lips. "Pretty fancy word for a doggy chew toy, don't you think?"

"It's not that bad." She brushed her thumbs along a rough patch in the felt. "It just needs a little TLC. Like someone else I know."

"You talking about me?" He pointed to his chest, his tone teasing.

The tension in the small space eased and she gave Sam a sidelong glance, a you-know-better tsk and a shake of her head before she leaned toward the dog she had been calling Homer. "I'm talking about him."

Homer lurched forward.

Polly took a cold, wet nose to the cheek and squealed in a mix of surprise and delight.

Sam burst out laughing. "Looks like he thinks *you're* the one who needs the tender loving care."

"Smart doggy." Polly laughed and swiped a wrist over her nose. When she looked up, she found two pairs of soft brown eyes studying her.

Warmth rose in her cheeks. She'd have blamed the hot water from cleaning the tub, but she hadn't started it yet. She scrambled to reach the faucets and turned the hot water on full blast. "I say we stuff the crown of the hat with a small towel and shape the brim a little like so, apply a little heat…" She held it over the cloud of steam and it went limp as a noodle.

She glanced back over her shoulder at Sam, wondering how to apologize for actually making things worse.

Only, Sam didn't look as if he expected an apology. In fact, he seemed to have completely moved on from the whole hat debacle and was getting the dog ready for that final rinse.

Something about his reaction didn't sit right with Polly, but she honestly couldn't say if it was because she distrusted the ease with which he dismissed the keepsake or because he didn't seem to notice how helpful she was trying to be. Was it so wrong that she wanted Sam to notice her in this one slice of time they would probably have together?

For all her big talk about not rushing or pushing or competing, Polly just couldn't let that slide. "You know, you look good in this hat. I'd be glad to replace it if you—"

"Not necessary." He ran his hand along the dog's back and peered into his fur. "The boots I need because I do pitch in around the farm, but the hat?"

"Maybe something else? Something that suits you? Let's see…" She pretended to analyze him, savoring every last moment of their time together. "A gray fedora?"

He frowned and shook his head.

"No. How about a white ship captain's hat?"

"If she tries to order me one of those, you have my permission to drag her keyboard into the yard and bury it," he instructed the yawning dog.

Polly giggled, then gave him one last look and confessed, honestly, "I think you'd look great in a brown trilby. You know, kind of like those dads on old black-and-white TV shows who came home from work to the house with the white picket fence?"

As soon as she'd said it, she wished she'd kept her thoughts, and her visions of Sam as the kind of man she hoped to one day have in her own life, to herself. "I'm sorry, that sounded silly, I know."

"Naw. I...I kinda like that image. All-American small-town dad. There are worse things people could see me as, I'm sure." He grinned, just a fleeting one, then ruffled the dog's fur and cleared his throat. "There is supposed to be a fine-tooth comb to get the fleas out of his coat. Would you go see if it's in the bag I brought?"

"Um, oh, sure." She jumped at the chance to put some space between them. It was time to get her priorities in order. She and Sam were a no-go. And if she hoped to make a home here in Baconburg, the sooner she accepted that and, as Sam had put it, "moved on"—

The chime of the doorbell cut through her thoughts and startled her. She glanced toward the bathroom, then the kitchen where she'd been headed, and decided to get the door, explain the situation if needed and then get back to her mission.

"Hey there, neighbor!" A perky woman with chestnut-colored hair in a long bob stood on Polly's doorstep holding a plate of brownies, which she thrust over the threshold about two beats before she surged into the house herself. The woman didn't even seem to take a breath as she launched into her one-sided conversation, looking around the place and edging farther inside all the while. "I'm Deb Martin. I live across the way. Hope you like sweets. I bake a lot. Sorry to just drop in like this. Hope it's not a bad…time?"

Sam strode out from the darkened hallway, tugging at the huge wet spot on his blue shirt.

"Well, well, well, Sam Goodacre." The woman crossed her arms and gave him a sly smile. "I thought I saw your minivan out on the street."

"He was just helping me give a flea bath to a little dog I found." Polly's words rushed out so fast that they all but tumbled over each other. "I don't want you to get the wrong idea."

"Wrong idea?" She pinched the plastic trash bag over Polly's grubby clothes and gave it a waggle that all but said it was clear they weren't up to anything too wild. "That Sam is finally associating with a girl besides his sister and children again? Nothing wrong with that in my book."

"It's not like that," Polly hurried to say. "We're just…"

"Friends," Sam supplied. "I'm just here helping out a friend, Deb."

"Yeah, I heard. Washing a dog." She made a show of tapping her chin with one finger as though thinking it over. "You know, you and I have been friends since high school, Sam, and I don't think you ever…"

"It'll never happen again." Polly rushed forward so fast that she nearly spilled brownies everywhere. From the cheerful teasing of Deb's tone, Polly truly believed she was just having fun…and maybe indulging in a little of the already-deemed-pointless matchmaking Sam abhorred.

But Polly couldn't get the quiet intensity of Sam's words to the little dog out of her mind. She understood what was beneath the rules. A man with a broken heart who feared if he ever stopped moving forward, his loss would be his undoing. Polly got that. She had long suspected her own family's drive had been more about working through the pain of their broken home than about money or accomplishment.

"Look, I haven't had to think about the rewards and drawbacks of Baconburg's small-town life since... well, never, really, because I was really young when we moved away from here, but I get it." Polly went to the front door and held it open. "I have to be above even the suggestion of impropriety. Sam, I appreciate your help, but I can take it from here. Deb, thank you for the brownies. I have a dog to rinse off and some flyers to make."

"That—" she told the little dog as she toweled him off in the closed bathroom after Deb and Sam had gone on their way "—is that. Why be in a hurry to find a guy? I have my hands full with you. Sam Goodacre? Well, he has his rules and his reasons and I have plenty of time to follow my dreams, right?"

The dog sneezed.

"Yeah, I know. I didn't completely buy it, either." Polly sank against the side of the tub and tried not to think of Sam coming through the front door of her little house wearing that brown trilby and a grin as he announced to her and the girls, "Honey, I'm home!"

Chapter 6

"He's just so sweet and happy. Looking at him just lifts my heart." The very next day Polly juggled her cell phone and adjusted the stack of papers clutched under her arm to walk down the sidewalk of the historic section of Baconburg, hoping to find more places that would post the lost-dog flyers. She glanced down at the golden-brown dog trotting along on a leash at her side and smiled. "I honestly don't know how I am going to deal with not seeing him every day but that's probably what needs to happen. It's a small town, so I'm told it will be nearly impossible, but I'm going to have to find a way to avoid him."

"I can't believe it. One day in good ol' Baconburg and you meet a great guy with all this baggage attached."

Polly certainly did not think of Sam's family or the

issues they had with the dog as "baggage," but before she could set her sister straight on that, she needed to make one thing clear. "I was talking about Barkley, the little dog I found."

"I know you were and *I* was talking about the great big man you found." Essie's voice was soft and teasing. She absolutely knew how to push all of her twin's buttons. "Oh, and I thought you were calling him Homer."

"Now that he's all cleaned up, he doesn't look like a Homer anymore. I'm trying out some new names." Polly paused to study the little fellow, who also stopped, circled around and then plunked his behind down on the sidewalk washed with late-summer afternoon sun. "Not that I have any say over it or that I can let myself get too attached."

"To the dog or to the—"

"To the dog," Polly over-enunciated each word before Essie could even suggest that Polly would allow herself to get too attached to a certain single-father pharmacist and former hat owner. Feeling quite pleased with herself for getting everything under control so neatly, she squared her shoulders, took a good breath and opened her mouth to continue.

Bam. Bam. Bam.

Polly gasped at the three quick raps on the glass behind her. She whipped her head around.

"What was *that?* What's going on?" Essie asked. "Are you okay?"

Polly's tensed shoulders eased and she couldn't help but smile at the familiar face looking out at her from the huge window of Downtown Drug.

"I'm fine. I'm just…" She paused to give Sam Goodacre a wave, then raised the flyers as if to ask if she could post one in his store. She might be able to avoid the puppy and its new owner in the future, but she was just going to have to get used to seeing Sam around. "I like to think of myself as embracing the realities of small-town life."

"What does that mean?" Essie asked.

Sam gave her a nod, pointed toward the front door of the store and started that way.

Polly gave the dog's leash a tug, not unlike what Sam's smile had done to her heart, she thought as she told her sister, "It means I have to call you back later."

"But I thought we were going to talk about my coming for a visit," Essie barged on, never one to be dismissed.

"Give me a chance to get settled." Polly reveled in the chance to be the bossier sister for a chance. Her heels clicked over the sidewalk at a happy, brisk pace. "We'll talk later."

"Later when?" Essie sounded snappish, but Polly heard the concern in her twin's voice. "I need to know so I can make plans, Polly. You know how busy I am. How long will it be before I can come see you?"

"How long? Why, as long as it takes. And not a minute more, I promise." Polly clicked off the phone and slid it into her pocket. When Sam didn't meet her at the door, she stretched her neck to peer back into the window again only to find an elderly couple had sidetracked him. The older man kept gesturing with a bottle of some kind of pills while the woman, her reading glasses perched on the end of her nose, kept trying to read the label.

"I think Sam might be a while," she told the dog. "So do we wait?"

A kid whizzed past on a bicycle so close and so fast that it set the papers under her arm flapping. Polly *could* hang around under the guise that she needed to ask Sam if he would post her flyer in his window.

"Or I could move on. I still have lots of flyers to distribute," she told the dog.

Barkley, or Homer, or whatever name he'd end up with, gave his head a shake that sent his ears slapping against his head. The leash jangled where it attached to his collar. He sneezed, then looked up at Polly, his tail wagging.

She started to lean down to murmur, "Bless you," when the front door came swinging open.

"Hi, Miss Bennett. How are you?" A small redhead in a pink top with a ruffled collar came bounding out into the entryway of the store. "Dad says you have posters for your lost dog. If you want, I can take them *all* and hand them out for you."

The way she stretched out the word *all* put the teacher on high alert. Polly had dealt with small children with their own big agendas before, so she wasn't ready to oblige that quickly. "That's a sweet offer, Juliette, but the dog and finding his owners is my responsibility."

"I'm not Juliette. I'm Caroline." The girl rose up on the ball of one foot and did a spin.

"That might work on other people, but you and your sisters are not going to be able to fool me that easily." Polly smiled. "Now, if you want to take one poster to put up in your dad's—"

"Deal!" Juliette snagged the page that Polly offered,

turned around and ran back to the front door. As she swung it open she looked back and said, "Thanks, Miss Bennett. I'll send Hayley and Caroline out to get posters, too."

Before Polly could call out to tell the child that the goal was to get as many flyers out to different people who might actually help find the owners as possible, Juliette disappeared inside the store. Polly sighed, stole a look in the big window to spot Sam moving his finger as if emphasizing the small print on the large pill bottle to the couple, who were crowded in close to him. For all his talk about moving on, he sure knew how to take his time and take care of others, didn't he?

"Miss Bennett!" A child in a green-and-white T-shirt came rocketing out the door so fast that she set the dog next to Polly woofing in surprise. "Hi, Donut!"

"Actually, I'm calling him…" Polly caught herself before she said anything that might lead the child to think Polly had even considered keeping the animal. "I'm sure whoever his real owners are have given him a perfectly good name. Let's not create any confusion by calling him Donut, okay, Hayley?"

That was not a phony excuse. Allowing the triplets to name the little dog that everyone agreed resembled the character in their mother's stories might well lead to emotional attachments and confusion, not to mention greater hurt when the little guy went back to the home where he truly belonged.

"But he *looks* like Donut," Hayley insisted. "Oh, and I'm not Hayley. I'm Caroline. You know, the one who is going to be in your class this year?"

"Oh, I *know* the Caroline who is going to be in my

class this year. And you're not her." She handed the girl one of the flyers as if it were a lovely parting gift for having played the game, then gave her a pat on the back. "Nice try, though."

This time the child returned to the store with a bit of an obstinate stomp in her step. Just before she went over the threshold she gave Polly a narrowed-eyed glare. "Are you sure I'm not Caroline or are you just guessing to make us think you can tell us apart?"

"I can *really* tell you apart," Polly assured her.

"Hmm." And Hayley was gone.

Polly stood there for a moment not sure if she should go inside and tell Sam what the girls were up to or just move on with the task at hand. On one hand he might appreciate knowing, but on the other they were just testing boundaries and it wasn't anything she and Essie hadn't tried at that age.

The drugstore door swung open a third time. For one second, two, three, nobody came out. Then slowly, with two other sets of hands pushing her shoulders and hips, a redheaded girl in a strikingly familiar pink shirt with a ruffle at the neck, reluctantly appeared.

"Hello…Miss Bennett. Caroline asked me, Juliette, to come out and get a flyer for her like the one you gave me, Juliette, the ballerina." The girl lifted her arm in an arc, halting but in pretty fair ballet form.

"Okay, but I don't want to waste any of these. Promise you'll try to share this with someone who can help get this poor lost doggy home again, okay…*Juliette?*"

She nodded without making eye contact, snatched the paper away, then moved back to the still-open door.

'Fess up. Polly willed Caroline to come clean and admit who she was and what she had been put up to.

For a moment Polly felt herself in Caroline's place. Always the sister in the shadow. She knew that struggle between wanting so badly to be like her more outgoing sister and wanting to just be herself.

Caroline hesitated outside the doorway. Her head bowed slightly, she stole a backward glance. Her gaze fell to the dog.

Honesty is the best policy. I know that's who you are, Polly wanted to urge the child. But she wasn't going to push or make a scene. If she just waited, Polly felt certain the girl would do the right thing on her own, in her own time.

The child sighed and then raised her gaze to Polly, her expression open and vulnerable. "Oh, Miss Bennett, I'm not Juliette. I'm Caroline."

Polly's heart soared at the child's decision to confess. "I know. I knew all along."

"She knew. She knew all along," Caroline said into the open door.

Suddenly two sets of hands yanked the girl back inside.

Polly rolled her eyes, laughed, then tugged on the leash to get her companion up and moving again. "I think maybe it'll be better if we walk back down to the corner, cross over and see if we can put up flyers in the stores across the street."

They had hardly taken two steps when the door to Downtown Drug swung open again.

"Whatever you've cooked up, you'd better understand right now I am not falling for..." Polly's shoulders went back in her best full-on teacher-about-to-lay-down-the-rules mode. Her shoes squeaked quietly as she turned slowly to confront…Sam Goodacre. "You."

"I'll take that under advisement," he said softly.

She had just told Sam she wasn't falling for him. She hadn't meant it as a proclamation, but now that it was out there, Polly sort of wanted to take it back. "I was just… Your girls were trying to…"

He held his hand up. "I know. Or rather, the minute I saw Juliette and Hayley making Caroline trade shirts with Juliette I knew what they were up to. Sorry they pulled a fast one on you."

"They didn't pull anything on me." She smiled and wriggled her fingers at him to wave goodbye before she pivoted and began walking again. "I knew which one was which from the start."

"You did?"

"Yep." She heard his footsteps hurrying behind her but she didn't look back. She just kept walking with a spring in her step, not unhappy to have him following along. "And don't be too hard on them. Juliette wasn't really trying very hard to fool me and when I told Hayley I could tell them apart, I think she took that as a challenge."

"Sounds like her." And just like that, he was walking alongside her.

Following was one thing, even calling out to her, but walking through town with her? "Aren't you supposed to be working?"

"I think it will be okay." He grinned at her and side-stepped the dog's meandering gait. "I know the boss."

She had to hurry to keep up with his long, determined strides, and the dog, seeming to pick up on Sam's energy, rushed ahead, yanking Polly's arm out in front of her. How had her leisurely stroll through the old part of town become a mad dash? At least she had already made stops at the stores they passed along the way.

"Look, I don't want to pressure you or anything." A car passed by and the driver tooted a quick honk. Sam waved.

"Pressure?" Polly waved, too, even though she had no way of knowing who it was. It just seemed the neighborly thing to do even as she rushed along trying to figure out what pressure Sam was about to put on her.

They reached the corner and Sam turned to look down at her. "I just wanted to ask you how the search for the dog's owners is coming."

"Oh." The light turned red. Polly hoped her face was not as bright a shade. "Yeah, um, Barkley."

"What?"

"I started calling him Barkley."

"You're keeping him, then?" Sam's mouth had a serious set that had not been there moments ago.

"No, I'm not. I'd like to...*like* to? I'd love to." She looked down at the dog, who gazed up at her with those sweet brown eyes.

The light turned green. The dog jerked on the leash. For a split second Polly didn't know whether to go or stay. Finally she took a deep breath and stepped off the curb. "But I can't. It's not right."

"Because he doesn't belong to you?"

"Because it wouldn't be fair to you," she shot back over her shoulder.

"Me?" He hurried into the street after her, caught

her arm and spun her around to face him. "What are you talking about?"

"You're the one who told me about the realities of small-town life, how paths cross and you see each other everywhere. And you're the one who doesn't think the girls are ready to deal with a dog so similar to Donut. So it just seems like I need to respect that and not keep the dog, especially because I'll be teaching Caroline and seeing her every day, probably telling the class about what the dog and I are doing…"

"You're giving up the dog for the sake of my girls?"

She nodded.

"Polly…I…" He stared into her eyes.

A car honked.

Polly jumped and started to scurry across toward the other side of the road.

Sam, his hand still cradling her elbow, headed back the way they came. They ended up doing a spin right there in the intersection. At least it gave the driver the opportunity to swerve around them.

"Just kiss her and stop holding up traffic," the man called as he whisked by. "What are you waiting for?"

"Kiss her? I hardly know…" Sam's gaze swung from the moving vehicle to the face of Polly Bennett and in that instant all the intensity of his denial evaporated. Another place, another time, another intersection, even, and he might have just thrown away all his reservations and swept this pretty little schoolteacher up in an impulsive kiss. "I didn't mean that as a slight. It's just that…"

"I know. You have your rules," she murmured softly.

Her words confirmed that she understood, but her eyes told a different story.

Or maybe that was Sam just wishing he had seen disappointment where there was actually relief that he didn't let the moment get the better of him. It would have made quite a story to live down, after all. New teacher steals smooch with local single dad!

He and Polly might as well have taken a billboard out proclaiming their mutual attraction. As it was, Sam still had time to save this mess. He backed away from Polly, stepping carefully over the leash to do so. With his smile fixed, he jogged back to the corner of the street while Polly tugged the puppy along, letting it stop and sniff around along the way. Finally they all hopped up onto the curb on the opposite sides of the street. Now, there was the perfect metaphor for the two of them, he thought. Two people heading toward their own goals, moving at their own pace, too much between them to really ever move forward together.

He looked at her, fussing to untangle herself from the dog's leash. The more she chased after it, the more the dog wound himself around her. Polly Bennett. She was enough to make a guy rethink his whole reasons for his unbreakable set of rules.

She jerked her head up and looked right at him, then lifted her shoulders and laughed at her predicament.

Sam raised his hand to say thanks and…

"Hey, Dad! Uncle Max says to invite Miss Bennett to dinner tonight," three little voices all hollered in unison as they ran full blast down the sidewalk toward him. But when they reached the corner, they all turned and put every last ounce of their considerable energy into making Polly hear the message. "Uncle Max says you have to come out to our house tonight. He's gonna *cook!*"

Sam held up both hands, thinking to tell his girls to take it down a notch, and realized too late it looked as if he might just be surrendering to them. He turned to Polly and shouted, "I understand if you don't—"

"I'd love to say yes, but—" Polly called out at the same time.

She'd love to say yes. To come to his home. Sam glanced over his shoulder at his girls.

"I wouldn't feel right leaving the dog home alone." Polly gave the leash a waggle and the puppy did an excited dance at seeing the girls.

"Bring him with you," the trio squealed in delight at Polly. Followed by three bright, expectant faces focusing on Sam and asking, "Why not?"

Polly in his home. With his girls. And that dog. It was everything that he had been trying to keep from happening. But when all those sets of eyes fixed on him that bright summer day, what could he do?

He was the guy who always moved forward, after all. And having Polly get to know the girls so she could help him guide Caroline wasn't exactly a detriment. Sam sighed and threw his hands up, this time in actual surrender.

"Why not?" He turned toward Polly and shook his head. "We close the store at five-thirty, and dinner is served about an hour after that. We'd love to have you."

Chapter 7

Polly rang the doorbell of the large white-frame farm-house shortly after six. Then, feeling anxious about the dog and the girls and the man she thought might answer the door any second now, she glanced around. Muffled footsteps thundered toward her from behind the door. Since it was too late to run, she bent, scooped up the dog and clutched him close and whispered, "It's you and me, pal. Us against Sam's rules."

The dog squirmed but didn't try to get down.

Hayley swung the door open wide. "Hey, Miss B!"

Juliette extended her arm toward the entryway and made a bow. "Please come in."

Caroline peeked around the door, ending up nose to cold nose with a certain brown-eyed mutt. "Hi, Donut!"

Polly managed a nervous smile and crossed the threshold. A savory aroma drifted into the foyer from the direction of a well-lit doorway to a room clearly filled with laughter and the clatter of dishes. She surveyed the distressed wooden floors, the walls painted in historic hues of sunny-yellow and French-cottage-blue, like something from a magazine. Or a storybook. Or a dream.

The Goodacre girls pressed in close to pet the pup and vie for Polly's attention. They made Polly's heart light.

"Hey, girls, at least let Miss Bennett get inside the house before you swarm all over her." Sam came striding down the hall in jeans, a plaid shirt, untucked, his hair damp as if he'd just cleaned up, wearing socks and with his boots in hand.

Kids. Dog. Laughter. Kitchen. Family. Home. Sam. This wasn't just any dream. This was Polly's dream, come true.

If for only the next few hours.

"Hi." Sam reached her side and settled his empty boots on the floor just inside the doorway.

"Hi." It wasn't exactly sizzling conversation.

The girls giggled.

Polly felt self-conscious. Then she remembered the hostess gift she'd tucked in her bag. "Oh, I brought something for you all. Actual tupelo honey brought with me from the South."

She shifted the dog in her arms to try to get to the heavy mason jar of the rich, sweet honey. The girls all stuck their hands up to try to help her.

Sam stepped in. "If it were winter, I guess I'd offer to take your coat, but seeing as it's not…may I take your dog?"

Polly laughed and handed off the little guy into Sam's strong, welcoming arms. The dog promptly slurped Sam's face.

The girls exploded in another round of giggles.

Polly pressed her lips together to keep from joining them, uncertain if Sam would be irritated, what with his whole no-dog rule and all.

Sam burst out laughing.

The very air around them seemed to ease. Sam set the dog down in the kitchen and directed the girls to set up a bowl of water. Each one wanted to be the one to do it. Max called out a hello to Polly and splashed some olive oil into a pan of vegetables with such style that for a second Polly wondered if she should offer to introduce Sam's younger brother to her twin sister, the chef.

But before she could do that, Gina came up, wiping her hands on a tea towel and, stealing a peek down at the dog lapping at the water, asked, "So, no response yet?"

Yeah, my first response is that I want to move in here and stay for, oh, just the rest of my life, Polly thought. What she said, though, was, "Huh?"

"To your lost-dog flyers? No responses?"

"Oh, the dog!" Polly laughed under her breath at her own scattered thought process, and shook her head. She reached into her purse and produced the jar of honey and offered it to Gina. "Nope, not a single call."

Gina took the jar, said a soft thank-you and then showed it to Max.

"Deb Martin, who lives across the street from me, says she's never seen him around the neighborhood." Polly looked around the room to find Sam pulling out a chair at the table for her. She moved over and allowed him to scoot the seat in. His hand touched her shoulder as she did. A sweet shiver shimmied down her spine as she forced herself to stay relaxed and finish her thought. "No one seems to know where he came from or where he might belong."

All three little girls drew in a breath like a choir about to launch into a robust refrain.

Sam gave them a look.

Max slid the lid onto a pot bubbling on the stove and announced dinner would be served soon.

"I can't wait," Polly said. "I didn't realize you were both a carpenter and a chef."

"Max? He's a jack-of-all-trades, all right. And a first-class cook," Sam muttered, going to the sink to wash up after handling the dog and directing the girls to do the same as he singled out Polly's gaze in the bright, bustling setting. "If by first-class you mean he cooks like he's had only one lesson."

"Play nice." Gina gave Sam's shoulder a shove before joining Polly at the table. She rolled her eyes and shook her head. "Brothers! Do you have any?"

"One." Polly held up one finger, then started to hold up a second to add that she also had one sister but before she could get it out, the girls scrambled, each trying to get a seat beside her.

"Oh, now! All three of you can't sit next to Miss Bennett." Gina jumped up to try to separate the triplets from trying to crawl all over each other and into one of the chairs on either side of Polly.

"There's only room for two," Sam warned, pulling back the chair to Polly's left.

"And one of those two is me!" Max slipped deftly into the seat Sam had slid away from the table.

Sam glared at him, then glanced at Polly.

"I guess that means the other one has to be me." And just like that, Sam took the seat on the other side of Polly. "To keep her safe from you."

"Brothers!" Gina shook her head and everyone shared a laugh.

Dinner was a charming mix of chaos and calm. Pasta made from locally milled flour, eggs from their own chickens and a sauce brimming with Goodacre-grown tomatoes, zucchini, carrots and scallions in the mix. Gina pushed back from the table first, complimenting Max on the meal and accepting accolades for her contribution, a dessert of peach cobbler with homemade ice cream on top.

"It's still light out. Can we show Miss Bennett around the farm now, Daddy?" Hayley tossed her napkin onto the table, practically spilling out of her chair.

"Maybe your dad should do those honors. We have dishes to clean up." Gina stood, raising her own plate as an example of the work awaiting them.

"The farm is your baby, Gina. You've done so much with it in the last few years. You deserve to show it off." Sam leaned back and patted his flat stomach, stretched, then gathered his silverware onto his place. "We guys will take care of the dishes tonight."

"What guys? I cooked. Family rules for meals are 'He who cooks it, books it.'" Max jerked his thumb over his shoulder. He stood, too, empty-handed, and offered his arm to Polly. "My work is done here. I'd be happy to escort you around the old farmstead, Miss Bennett."

"First, that's not a family rule. That's a Max rule," Gina picked up Polly's plate and headed toward the sink. "And we all know…"

"Max doesn't follow the rules," Sam said in a low, rumbling voice, his gaze aimed at his brother.

"Why don't we all pitch in?" Polly pushed her chair back and stood, avoiding Max's still-offered arm as she reached over to pick up the nearly empty pasta platter on the table. "That way it will get done faster and we can all go take the tour of the farm."

"You don't have to do that." Sam reached for the platter. Their hands brushed and their gazes met in the warmth of the kitchen lit by the fading sun of late summer. "You're the guest."

"Yes, I'm the guest." On one hand she didn't like being reminded, but on the other, it was probably a good idea. "I believe one of the *real* family rules around here is that guests get to choose what we do. I choose to help out."

Faster than Polly could cross the kitchen floor, the girls hopped up and began carrying their own plates and silverware to the sink.

Gina turned on the water.

Sam helped the girls clear the table.

Max directed Polly to where she could find foil and plastic wrap and whatever they needed to pack up the leftovers. They worked with each other like a family.

And it struck her how unlike her own family they were. No racing to see who could finish first or who did the best.

Polly paused for a moment to watch them all and it warmed her heart. This was the kind of family she had always longed for, one that worked as a team, not in competition.

The girls did display a bit of one-upmanship when they started off on the short version of the grand tour a few minutes later.

Max had conceded that because he had already seen the farm, had work to do and didn't believe he'd get a minute of Polly's undivided attention, he would stay behind. And Gina decided she should hang around the house to keep the dog company, because they didn't want to risk a bad interaction with any farm animals. Also she wanted to finish up some laundry so that when they returned, the girls could then get their baths and get to bed on schedule.

Of course, Polly saw right through their excuses and half expected Sam to protest the obvious attempt at setting them up. That he didn't made Polly cherish this one special night all the more. She drank in the fresh country air and the quaint setting, enjoying it almost as much as the company. She could get used to this sense of peace and quiet.

She shouldn't. But she could.

That quiet was broken when Hayley wanted the group to go see the chicken she had raised from a hatched egg for 4-H. Juliette wanted to use the open space to show off what she had just learned in ballet class, something called an arabesque. Caroline quietly murmured to Polly that she had named each animal they owned.

"Isn't there a caution about not naming farm animals that might become meals?" Polly asked Sam out of earshot of the girls as they strolled through a wooden gate with the girls in the lead.

"We don't eat any of our livestock. We use them for eggs, milk and cheese," Sam explained. "No judgment on anyone who does. We all like a good burger here, after all."

Sam moved ahead of the group and swung open a door in the side of a red barn with white trim that looked like a painting from a child's picture book. "When we were kids, our folks used to raise hogs that ended up as ham and bacon. It's just not part of what Gina is doing now. Things change. Change is good. I think it's healthy, don't you?"

Polly moved ahead of him through the open door.

"Watch me! Watch me! Watch me!" Juliette bounded into the wide pathway between large stalls on either side of the barn.

Polly tried to follow the action but just as she did, another triplet started up.

"My chicken has its own special nest. Over here, Miss Bennett." Hayley leaped up and down, waving her hand. "Over here."

Caroline looked around, seeming even more lost and uncertain of her place in the large space with her sisters vying for the spotlight.

"Well, yes, change can be good." Polly's chest tightened. How did she get this father to see what she saw? To consider that what worked for him was right for his girls? Who was Polly to talk to him about that, anyway? She glanced over at Caroline gazing off into the rafters while the other girls hurried here and there. She was that sister who didn't quite fit in, that sometimes felt invisible to her parents, that's who. "And I'd never tell you that moving on with things is a bad idea—"

"Great, I'm glad you feel the way I do about it." Sam put his hand on Polly's back and propelled her forward. "That's going to make getting things going so much easier."

"Getting…what…" Polly tried to look back at him even as her feet obeyed his urging her onward.

Straight ahead, Juliette extended one leg out straight. Her knee locked, she raised it high behind her and bent forward. "See, Miss Bennett? My teacher says my arabesque is the best in my class."

Hayley ran for a large wire cage housing a fat black-and-white hen and started clucking at the bird. "This is my chicken. Also be careful where you walk because the barn cat is gonna have babies and she's around here somewhere."

"Daddy says we can't name the kittens, though, because those have to find new homes." Caroline seemed buffeted about in the shuffle of it all.

Polly knew just how that felt. She wanted to throw her hands up and ask everyone to just be still for a moment so she could think. Her head was virtually spinning.

Or maybe it wasn't virtual.

Juliette did a turn.

Hayley moved in a circle around her chicken's cage.

Sam snagged Polly by the elbow and turned her around to face him. "I need your help with Caroline."

In that moment, his humble request, the caring in his voice and the sincerity in his eyes quieted the chaos around them. If she had taken the time to let her heart say a prayer about the situation earlier, it would have been for this, for Sam to invite her into his life and the lives of his girls in just this way.

"We have got to get Caroline involved in some things apart from her sisters. That's where you come in."

Where she came in and where she wanted to get off the merry-go-round. She took a deep breath and reminded herself that if she had prayed for anything it should have been for how best to do God's will.

In the distance Gina's voice called out that it was time for the girls to come in and take their baths.

Sam motioned for the girls to do as their aunt asked.

"Walk us up to the house, Miss Bennett." Juliette and Hayley rushed up to Polly, each taking her hand and tugging her off to the door again.

Sam swept Caroline up easily in his strong arms and tagged along behind them.

"What were you and Miss Bennett talking about, Daddy?" Caroline asked loudly enough for Polly to hear although the other girls did not seem to notice.

"I was just letting her know that we have big plans for you this school year, sweetie. Right, Miss Bennett? You with me on that?"

With him? Polly's heart pounded. All she wanted to do was run away right now. She needed some perspective, which she couldn't get surrounded by these girls or that man carrying his daughter on the pathway of their sweet farm home.

She put up her hand. "This is something we should talk about later, don't you think?"

"I'll look forward to it," Sam said quietly but with a new energy in his step. Clearly the man thought he had formed an ally in pushing his child to fit the ideal he had formed for his family.

Polly's heart sank and when she saw her little lost dog bouncing down the porch steps at the sight of her, she couldn't help but wonder if he truly was her best and maybe only true friend in Baconburg.

Sam watched the girls make their way up the porch steps, each of them taking a moment to pet and coo over the animal Polly Bennett had brought with her for the evening. The dog lapped at their little hands, making them squeal with delight. Juliette tried to hug the dog around the neck. Hayley tried to pick him up around the middle. The excited pup whipped around and whapped Caroline in the legs with his tail. More squeals and laughter.

"Don't… He's too big for… Put the dog down…" Gina couldn't finish a thought, and she couldn't get her hands on any kids or the dog's collar. It was as if his sister didn't even know where to begin.

Polly did not have that problem. She dived in without hesitation and scooped up the dog in both arms, lifting him out of the girls' grasping fingers but still holding him so that they could stroke his paws and ears. It was the perfect solution.

Sam leaned back against the porch rail to savor the image for a moment. He'd had his reservations about Polly coming to his home, but when he couldn't avoid it, he didn't dwell on the problems it presented. He pressed on and made the best of the situation. Now he had Polly on his side.

He looked at her and their eyes met. Polly on his side?

The implications of having this dark-haired woman with the enormous heart anywhere near him made him pause. It went against everything he had worked so hard to create for his girls—a safe situation where they could continue to grow without having to suffer more loss and disappointment.

Polly felt anything but safe to him.

"I guess this is my cue to thank you for a lovely meal and say it's time for me to head home." Polly stepped away from the girls.

The girls all groaned and followed after her.

"You don't have to go yet." Hayley thundered down the steps to put herself directly on the path in front of Polly.

"We'll take our bath really fast if you promise to read to us before bed." Juliette's feet barely hit the ground as she rushed up to Sam and spun around in front of him as if she expected him to back her up. "That's okay, right, Daddy?"

"It's okay with me…" Sam cringed at playing the big softy. Was he trying to pretend to himself that it was only the girls who wanted Polly to stay a little longer? "But Miss Bennett just said she needed to go."

"She didn't say *need*," Hayley corrected.

Sam drew a breath to launch into a lecture about not badgering their guest when Caroline moved around from behind Polly, looked up, and as she stroked the dog's muzzle, said quietly, "Oh, please, Miss Bennett, please stay long enough to read us a Donut story after our bath."

It was like a double sucker punch to the gut for Sam, hearing Caroline's earnest plea and yet not sure how he felt about Polly reading his late wife's story to his matchmaking daughters. "I don't think that's such a—"

"I printed out a few copies. Let me get you one," Gina, who had been waiting at the open door, volunteered.

"Girls, really?" Sam put his hands on Juliette's and Hayley's shoulders and urged them up the steps alongside him. "We invited Miss Bennett out for dinner, then let her help clean up, dragged her all over the farm and now we're trying to make her do bedtime-story-reading duty?"

"I hardly think of it as a duty," Polly said softly.

"But you're our guest." Sam reached her side.

"That's right, and company gets to pick." Hayley made a break and headed for the front door, swinging it open.

"You want to pick to read to us, right, Miss Bennett?" Caroline asked so softly that Sam wasn't quite sure he heard it or just imagined she'd expressed it with her eyes, so like her mother's, fixed in fascination on her new teacher's face.

Polly looked at him, silently asking for his approval or for him to make an excuse so she could back out without being the bad guy.

Sam smiled and shook his head. Never in his wildest dreams could he see Polly as the bad guy. The wrong girl, here at the wrong time, yes. But bad guy? "I think Marie would have liked knowing Caroline's teacher would one day read the story she wrote to the girls."

Polly smiled a smile that Sam could not get out of his mind the whole twenty-five minutes it took for the

girls to get quick baths, get into their pajamas and climb
into bed.

Gina had done bath duty, then stayed to clean up the
bathroom and get damp towels in the laundry.

Max stopped in to tell the girls good-night, then
grumpily excused himself to his own room saying
his "boss" expected him to be at work on the lunch-
counter project bright and early.

Polly had taken that time to take the dog for a walk
and read over the text of the book once, saying she
wanted to do it justice.

Sam appreciated that on many levels. Still, when the
time came for the big "performance," he just could not
stand by and watch Polly with the girls reading aloud
Marie's words. Words written so those girls would not
forget their mom and the love she and God shared for
them.

"'Three precious girls with blue eyes and red
curls…'" Polly began to read from the pages that Gina
had typed up and printed from the story Marie had written by hand a year before her death.

Sam turned away at the girls' room door.

"That's about us." The hushed excitement in Caroline's voice carried all the way into the hall.

Suddenly instead of hitting the stairs, heading for the
front door, getting as far away as good manners would
allow, Sam's footsteps slowed.

"I know it's about you three." Polly's tone was kind
and warm. "In fact, looking at you all here now, it's
like having your mom's book spring to life right in
front of my eyes."

Sam had often felt that very thing, but hearing Polly

discuss Marie so openly in front of the girls hit him hard. Then when he heard the familiar old creak of the rocking chair that Marie used to sit in to sing to the girls or comfort them in when they had a bad dream, the sound practically knocked the air right out of his lungs.

He spun around to rush back into the room, wanting to put a stop to it all, to spare his daughters the same angst that had his chest tight and his jaw clenched. "Maybe this isn't such a good—"

"We think about our mom whenever we say our prayers," Juliette said softly.

Sam froze just outside the door, looking in at the precious faces of his girls gazing adoringly up at Polly in the nearby rocking chair.

"Do you say prayers, Miss Bennett?" Hayley asked outright.

"Yes, I do. And I know that God hears them. Prayer is a powerful thing."

"Do you pray for something special, Miss Bennett?" Again it was fearless Hayley who forged ahead.

"Not *for* something, as in to *get* something, but…" Polly's expression grew slightly somber. "I pray for my students and the school and my family."

"And Donut," Caroline prodded.

Sam peered in to find three little girls sitting on one bed with a funny-looking, long-bodied dog stretched out across them all, managing to get some part of himself petted by each one of them. The contented animal struggled to keep his eyes open.

Polly reached out and stroked the dog's head. "And Donut."

"Don't you miss your family, Miss Bennett?" Hayley asked.

"Well, I haven't actually been away from them for very long, and I can talk to them whenever I want." Polly leaned back in the rocking chair.

"We miss our mom." Caroline's voice was strong but still.

"I am sure you do, but isn't it like a little visit from her whenever you hear the story she wrote for you?"

"It is, but we don't get to hear it very often," Juliette said.

"But you can hear it now," Polly assured them.

The papers rattled. The rocker creaked. Polly took a deep breath, then launched into the story about Donut, the dog who couldn't do anything right and only wanted to be loved. She did not miss a beat or stumble over a single syllable. She used her voice to convey every emotion and sentiment.

For the first time since he had heard the tale from Marie's lips, Sam found himself reminded of the message behind the story—that God meets us where we are and loves us even though we are not perfect.

Sam leaned back against the wall of the hallway outside the bedroom and waited as the story concluded and Polly said good-night to each of the girls.

He leaned into the doorway just as she finished up and promised the girls he'd be back to check in as soon as he saw Donut and Miss Bennett to her car. Donut—yes, even he couldn't fight the urge to call the little guy that—reluctantly but obediently clambered down from the bed and padded softly to the hallway.

One by one Juliette, then Hayley slid from Caroline's

bed and got into their own. Polly rose from the rocker and wriggled her fingers to the girls as she told them good-night and thanked them for inviting her out, telling them it was the very best time she'd had since arriving in town. She slipped by Sam and into the hallway where she told Donut to go on downstairs because it was time for them to go.

Sam stretched his upper body, his hand braced against the doorframe, but he kept both feet outside the threshold. "Good night, girls. Thank you for being such good hostesses to Miss Bennett. Now say your prayers and go to sleep."

"But—" Hayley sat up on her bed with her legs crossed.

"Prayers, then sleep," he reiterated, cutting off any last-ditch efforts at matchmaking, at pleading for them to keep the dog. Well, at least for them to make those pitches to him. What they would pray about, he could just imagine, and thought it best not to hover with Polly so near to listen in on their requests. "I love you guys."

"We're not *guys*," Juliette called back before all three sweet young voices joined to call out, "We love you, too, Daddy."

Sam started to pull the door shut but not before Caroline could add, "And Donut, too!"

Sam shut his eyes and pulled the door closed until it clicked. He took a deep breath, then turned around, took a step and almost tripped over his guest. He had to put his hands on her upper arms to keep from bumping into her.

"I hope I didn't overstep my bounds talking to the girls about their mom. I tried to be careful, but I also had to be honest." Polly did not flinch but held her ground, looking up at him with the most sincere eyes Sam had ever seen. "I wondered when they started asking questions if I should have followed your example and moved on without looking back right after dinner."

"I like having you here." He did not take his hands from her arms. Even though they stood in the open hallway, it felt as if the two of them were tucked away from everyone else in the world.

"It was a lovely dinner. I'm glad I came out to your family farm, too."

"I didn't mean the farm. I meant—" he searched her face, then leaned down, his face just above hers "—here."

"Oh." The single syllable made her lips so kissable.

And so he kissed her. Not a long or lingering kiss, but a sweet, stolen one, brief but still able to convey that he had wanted to kiss her from the first time he had come across her in the driveway.

She raised her hands and he half expected her to push him away, but instead she wound her fingers into the fabric of his shirtsleeves and that's where they remained even after the kiss ended and Sam stood there losing himself in her eyes.

"I guess I'm the one who should apologize for overstepping bounds now," he murmured.

Polly shook her head, her black hair swaying softly. "That would only apply if I had set up a boundary and you crossed it against my wishes."

"Well, a good host always tries to do as his guest wishes." He leaned in again and for an instant their gazes met. He looked deep into those kind, innocent eyes. He should pull back, turn and walk away. No good could come from this. There was no future here, regardless of what they wished.

Sam had learned the hard way in life that wishing was a waste of time. The only thing that helped was to keep moving in the right direction. Kissing Caroline's teacher was definitely the wrong direction.

And yet, he shut his eyes, leaned in and pressed his lips to hers again. For a second time there was nothing but the two of them, no past, no future, no rush.

Then the quietest gasp broke through to his conscious mind.

They jumped apart.

"Who was that?" Polly's head whipped around from the direction of the stairway to the dimly lit hallway lined by the family members' bedrooms.

Rustling came from behind the girls' door.

Down the hall, the door to Max's room rattled, then clicked shut.

From the stairway came Gina's way-too-obviously-loud "conversation" with Polly's canine houseguest. "Hey, little fella, where's the rest of the crew? They didn't send you down here all by yourself, did they?"

"It doesn't matter who it was—somebody saw what happened between us." Sam stepped back, his head bowed as he gathered his resolve.

"I know." Polly touched his arm, his cheek, then she, too, took a step back. "We have to make sure no one sees us doing that again."

"It's not that I wouldn't, under other circumstances, like to—"

"You don't have to explain. I'm Caroline's teacher.

You have your rules. This is how it has to be." Polly held up her hand and retreated a step, still facing him. "School starts Monday. I won't have any reason to see you or the girls until…well, until Caroline gets to class then."

"Polly, if it were just me—"

"But it's not. It's the girls and your late wife and me and Donut, and…I get it, Sam. I don't like it, or maybe even agree with it, but I get it." She shook her head, then turned and hurried downstairs where Gina and the dog were waiting in the foyer.

And Sam let her go. As she has said, she was following the example he had touted time and again. No looking back. Keep moving forward.

He heard the front door shut. Then the car doors open and shut again. The engine started. The quiet little hybrid car chugged off. Not until the front door opened and shut again and he heard Gina moving around the first floor did Sam finally plod slowly down the steps. Knowing he would not see anything in the fading light but the empty drive leading to the country road, he stood at the door and gazed out the window that overlooked the porch. What he was looking for, he couldn't say. He only knew that he would never look around this place, the place where he had grown up and where he had retreated into the depths of his deepest pain, in the same way. After this evening, whenever he helped clean up the dishes or tucked his girls in he'd remember Polly there. And Donut, too.

And Sam wasn't sure he didn't kind of like the idea.

Chapter 8

On the first day of school Polly woke up a full half hour before her alarm went off.

"Finally," she huffed, pushing off the covers and swinging her feet to the soft, braided throw rug by her bed. Glancing back over her shoulder at the sunrise just beginning to peek through a space between her closed drapes, she yawned and scrubbed her fingertips through her hair. "That was one of the longest weekends of my entire life!"

A soft snort from a certain golden-brown, adorable mutt seemed to challenge her.

"I guess that's one thing I didn't take into account when I moved to such a small town. Not a lot for a stranger to do besides work and go to church, especially if that stranger is an unmarried young lady trying to avoid that town's favorite single dad." She tried to keep it all light and cheerful, knowing she was only trying to convince herself of what she was pretending to tell her still-sleepy-eyed friend nestled in his doggy bed. "But I did get a lot more posters made to try to find you a home."

She made herself smile when she said that even though the very thought weighed heavy on her heart. After the visit from Deb Martin and still no calls about the lost pet, Polly had switched from looking for owners to looking for a forever home for the little guy.

She stretched and purposefully avoided looking at the new photo of the sweet dog's face above the caption I Could Be Yours.

"Did I say longest weekend of my life? I should have said the loneliest weekend of my life." She shut her eyes and willed herself not to go all misty-eyed over the thought of saying goodbye to what seemed to be her only connection in Baconburg. But after days of people telling her the Goodacre triplets were asking about the dog, Polly knew she couldn't keep the animal and keep her peace of mind. "I'm probably just missing my family, right?"

The truth was, she was missing a family that was not her own and never could be.

More than once on Saturday she had wondered what the Goodacre girls…and their dad…were up to. On Sunday morning she had tried to not get too distracted while looking around to see if they attended the small community church she had gone to at the invitation of a fellow teacher.

But today the week started all over and the new school year would be under way. Polly couldn't wait to get into her classroom. She dressed and walked the dog and filled his water bowl and gathered her things and… dressed again. The outfit she'd planned out a week earlier suddenly seemed too young and fun. A week ago that might have seemed like a good idea, to project the image of an energetic teacher brimming with new ideas. But now?

"You never get a second chance to make a first impression." Polly muttered her mother's warning as she slipped into her navy blue pants and lavender shirt. But that's what she wanted to do, to make a new first impression on Sam Goodacre, and on his daughters, when they came in this morning escorting Caroline into her new classroom.

"Yes, I look like a no-nonsense professional educator," she told herself with one last glance in the rearview mirror as she parked. "Not like a lost cause."

Thoughts of Sam, the triplets and the dog she was trying to place in a home of his own only added to Polly's already-churned-up emotional state. So when Brianna Bradley, one of the other two second-grade teachers, rapped on Polly's car window, Polly nearly jumped out of her skin.

"Hurry up!" Brianna motioned to Polly to get out of the car. "You're on parking-lot duty!"

"Parking…what?" Polly popped open the door and climbed out.

"I know, it's a rotten thing to do to the new teacher, but we're stuck until we get some parents to volunteer tonight." She pushed Polly toward the front of the school. "All you have to do is stand here and remind parents to keep moving thataway."

Brianna pointed toward the drive with Exit painted on it.

"But—"

"Go drop your things off in your room and flip the light on. You can come inside five minutes before the bell rings. The hallway teachers will keep things in order until then." More pushing. "Say, do you still have that dog? I thought you'd have found a home for him before now."

"Um, yes, I…" She started to ask how Brianna knew about Donut, then glanced back to see the other teacher swiping dog hair off her sleeve where it had brushed against Polly's clothes. Polly looked down at the dark slacks in glaring daylight to see golden-brown hair clinging here and there. She sighed. So much for that first impression.

On the bright side, as parking-lot teacher she'd be so busy that if Sam brought the girls into their classrooms, as many parents of young children did, she wouldn't have to interact with him. Confident in that, she began to try to brush away the worst of Donut's hair off her slacks.

Three quick honks startled her. She jerked her head up and jabbed her finger in the direction that Brianna had pointed earlier only to find Sam Goodacre smiling at her from behind the wheel of the family minivan.

"Miss Bennett! Miss Bennett! Will you be at Sign Up for Your School tonight?" Hayley Goodacre hadn't even gotten fully out onto the sidewalk before she started calling out.

Juliette and Caroline were not far behind.

"Hurry on into your classes, girls. You know the

drill," Sam ordered through the lowered passenger-side window.

"You're not coming inside with them?" Polly shaded her eyes and leaned forward to peer in at him.

"Are you kidding? Treat them like 'baby' first graders? They'd never forgive me. They know what to do."

"Move forward." She nodded.

"It's not a bad thing, you know." He sounded defensive, as if what she thought of his parenting approach mattered to him.

She smiled at that idea, but couldn't allow herself to linger over the notion. "No, I mean, you're holding up the other parents dropping off kids." She waved him on. "Move forward."

"Oh, right!" He laughed and waved, rolled forward but slowed again long enough to say, "I'd like to see you tonight at the sign-up."

"Really?" Maybe it was the loneliness of the past weekend or nerves for the first day of school, but hearing Sam say he wanted to see her made her pulse quicken. Maybe the days since their kiss had him rethinking all his—

"We've got a lot to talk about to get Caroline started on the right track this year."

"Right. Caroline," she murmured under her breath. She pushed back her shoulders, raised her hand and gave another wave. "Move on, please."

This time she was sending a message to herself.

Sam had a plan. In his situation he couldn't afford not to. Although the past ten days—ever since he veered from his course to see if a certain young lady needed his help—Sam's plans hadn't seemed to mean a whole lot. But tonight, the first time the girls would be able to learn about and join school-sponsored clubs and learn about opportunities for after-school activities, Sam had come up with something that couldn't fail. Divide and conquer. Three girls, three adults, one mission—to help Caroline plunge into at least one new adventure while keeping Hayley and Juliette from going off the deep end and signing up for a dozen each.

Sam had laid out the strategy carefully. Gina would guide Hayley through the crowd of colorful booths set up in the school gymnasium. Max would shepherd Juliette. And Sam would prod Caroline along as best he could. If any of them reached an impasse, they had agreed to go to the girl's teachers for advice.

Well, Max and Gina agreed. Sam felt confident *he* wasn't going to need any backup. Caroline was his daughter, after all. He'd just point out the advantages of the groups that he thought might help bring her out of her shell and that would be that.

"Caroline wants to join the book club." Sam poked his head into the open door of Polly Bennett's second-grade classroom barely five minutes after he had made that bold proclamation to himself.

"Good for her." Polly twisted around to look at him from her perch, standing halfway up a short stepladder, hanging scalloped trim along the top of a long bulletin board bearing the sign I CAN.

"Actually I was hoping you'd help her choose something else," Sam confessed, sheepishly. "I'd like her to be a Go-Getter."

"Joining the book club can be a way of being a—"

Polly went up on her toes on the ladder rung, and stretched her whole body all the way to her fingertips to try to push in the last tack. The ladder wobbled.

In an instant Sam rushed to her side. Using his own weight as ballast, he planted his boot on the bottom rung. While he grabbed the side of the ladder with one hand, the other cupped Polly's elbow to keep her steady. He leaned in to further protect her from falling, but at the last second she righted herself.

Looking down over her shoulder at him, a little breathless from the near spill, she finished her thought in a whisper. "A go-getter."

He should have pulled away immediately, especially after what had happened between them in the upstairs hallway at the farm. But standing there so close he could see the way her black bangs caught on the tips of her long eyelashes, the last thing on his mind was moving on.

"The Go-Getters is an after-school program to get kids involved in the community and keep them active." Reluctantly he took a step backward. "They go on supervised hikes, learn square dancing, do physical fitness challenges."

"Hiking and dancing? Sounds more like Juliette and Hayley's style." She stepped down a rung. The ladder rocked from side to side slightly.

"I know, but it's not like it's a bad thing for me to want that for Caroline, too, is it?" Sam held out his hand to help her down.

"Bad?" She slid her hand in his.

It felt good to be there with her, to stand so close to her, to be asking her advice about Caroline and trusting that what she said would bring with it the best of intentions.

Polly paused a moment gazing down at him. She shook her head just enough to make her hair sweep free of her eyes as she pressed her lips together as if maybe she was trying to keep herself from saying too much. She took a breath, then stepped down to the floor and tipped her head back to meet his gaze. "Not for one moment do I think you want anything that would be bad for Caroline."

"Thanks. I thought for a minute—"

"But…" She withdrew her hand from his.

He closed his suddenly empty fingers into a loose fist and smiled, reminding himself of his conviction that Polly had what was best for Caroline in mind. "But what, Polly?"

"Sam, I just think you need to keep in mind that your triplets might be identical, but they are still individuals. What works for one, or even two, might not be right for the third sister."

"I've thought about that, Polly. I really have, but in the car on the way here, we talked about doing things that make us happy and Caroline told me she really wanted to do that this year."

"Good, then I assume you've thought that maybe she was saying that what she wanted to do this year was make *you* happy."

Not since Marie had anyone spoken to him so directly and honestly about his handling of the girls. Sam tightened his jaw. On one hand he liked finally hearing somebody give him some real advice that might actually help him. On the other hand… "I think I know my girls, Polly."

She nodded and moved to her desk.

Watching Polly sitting all proper in her teacher's chair going over her day planner, he kept getting flashes of her in his drugstore, her at his table. He could see Polly needing his help with her dog, Polly reading to his daughters. After this short time she was already that much a part of his life.

However, that didn't change the reality that she was a new girl in town who had told the triplets that she missed her family. What if she decided not to stay after the end of the school year? He couldn't risk what that might do…to his girls. No, better to stick with his plan, not because it was the best choice, but because for him, it was the only one.

He wanted to go over, put his hands on her shoulders and tell her that, but the sound of multiple little tennis shoe–clad feet came thumping and bumping down the school hallway outside the door.

"Daddy! Daddy! We all got signed up for clubs and stuff!" Hayley flapped a paper as she and Juliette practically tumbled over each other to get inside Polly's classroom.

"Hayley! Juliette! No running!" Gina's voice echoed after them followed by Caroline winding around into the threshold with a piece of paper of her own tucked tightly to her chest by her crossed arms.

"Hey, sweetie, did you join the book club?" Sam tried to sound enthusiastic. He really tried.

Caroline shook her head.

"The current-affairs club?" He went for the second

choice on the child's list, more than a little surprised to find himself rooting for a positive answer.

Another shake "no."

"Then what did you join?" he asked, stealing a sideways glance at Polly.

"The Go-Getters!" Hayley and Juliette shouted in unison.

Caroline ventured forward, extending her hand to show him the paper he had to sign to allow her to join the club Sam had decided she should join.

He smiled, but deep down he couldn't help feeling a lump in the pit of his stomach. He looked down and shifted his feet, telling himself this was a good thing. Caroline needed this.

But when he raised his gaze to Polly's again, he couldn't help wondering if he had been fooling himself all along. Polly might just be right about the girls and it made his chest ache. How could he cope with knowing that the only person who could make him a better parent was the one person he believed also had the power to break his daughters' hearts?

Chapter 9

"Friday at last!" Katie Williams, one of the other second-grade teachers, who was only a couple of years older than Polly, stuck her head in the open door Friday afternoon as the rest of the staff was heading home. "Big plans for the long weekend?"

"You mean they get *longer?*" Polly blinked at her teaching colleague.

"It's Labor Day, silly." Katie came in and leaned back against the wall, crossing her arms over her yellow-, red- and black-plaid apron bib dress. "We have three whole days off."

"Oh, that's right. I…uh…" Three whole days. It sounded like an eternity. It had her wondering if she was really cut out for small-town life. As soon as she thought that, memories washed over her to contradict it. From the first day when Sam lay on the drive to help her rescue the lost dog to the day his family invited her out to eat, she had loved every minute of that. Of course, that probably wasn't just small-town homeyness.

"I don't know. I've been so busy planning so that the school week stays on track I haven't put much thought into the weekends." Polly pulled out the large drawer of her desk where she kept her purse. Her gaze fell on her car keys and a sense of possibility seized her...or maybe it was panic. "I guess I could always go home to Atlanta to visit."

It was an impulsive idea, but once she'd said it, it didn't seem so far-fetched.

"Really? Atlanta?" Katie turned around to gaze at the map of the United States unrolled over the chalkboard from the last lesson of the day. She tipped her head and peered closer. "Isn't that, like, almost a twelve-hour drive?"

"Ten hours and about fourteen minutes, door to door," Polly murmured, thinking of how long it had taken to drive from her mother's home to her rented house in Baconburg. Then she drew in a deep breath and shook her head, losing enthusiasm for a weekend spent bouncing between her parents' respective houses and her sister's restaurant. The whole thing would be a blur. And she'd probably end up being reminded how much more her family expected of her. Could her self-esteem take it right now with her big, bold move for independence still so shaky? "Of course, that could be give or take fifteen minutes depending on *whose* door I chose to go to."

"So you'd spend most of tomorrow and then Monday in the car." Katie tapped her finger to her cheek and narrowed her eyes. "Not much time to visit. Then there's the issue of the dog… I guess you could take him with you."

And turn the way-too-happy-for-comfort puppy loose in her mom's perfectly appointed home or the home her dad now shared with the big, hissy cat given to him by his wife-to-be? Her sister's restaurant was obviously out and her brother was allergic. And really, deep down, Polly didn't want to go. "Maybe I'll just hang around Baconburg."

Katie perked up a little too much for such a non-committal remark. "So you're staying at home, then?"

At home. Polly liked that. She tugged her purse out of the drawer, grabbed her keys and tossed them up to catch them again. "Looks like that is exactly where I'll be."

"And you don't have plans?" Katie raised her voice.

"Nope, just to stay at home and—"

"Great!" Brianna Bradley popped into the room from the hallway where she'd clearly been hovering, waiting for this very news from Polly before she appeared. "That means you're available!"

"Available?" She pushed her chair back and stood up. "For what?"

"The Go-Getters are having an event tomorrow to raise money to go to the Museum Center in Cincinnati. It's a dog wash at the fire station."

Dog wash with the Go-Getters? Red flags went up all over the place in Polly's mind, but she couldn't quite figure out how to explain her reservations to the other teachers without confessing her attraction to Sam Goodacre.

"They need extra sponsors and a little bird…three of

them, actually, told us you'd be the perfect one to ask to pitch in," Brianna summed up.

"You do have a dog, after all," Katie rushed to add. "And unless you just gave him a bath last night…"

"No, I haven't bathed him since…" The image of Sam sitting on the bathroom floor rubbing a towel over the dog's back while the little guy tried to lick his face filled Polly with the sweetest warmth tinged with sadness. "Um, no, he hasn't had a bath lately."

"Perfect. You can set the example for everyone, you know, to get them started." Brianna came to Polly's desk and wrote down the time, underlined, then circled it.

Polly chewed her lower lip. This was it. Her invitation to be a part of the community.

"What do you say?" Katie asked.

What could she say? The weekend stretched out before her and for the first time she realized she couldn't go "home," not now, or she'd never really *be* home in Baconburg. And the truth was, she *was* the perfect one for this particular job. She had the time. She had a special interest in watching over Caroline's progress or lack of it. And she had a dog that needed washing…again.

"What do I say? I say—" she picked up the piece of paper, folded it and tucked it into her purse "—I'll be there."

Out in the hallway giggles rose, then faded with the sounds of small feet hurrying away.

Polly clutched her purse to her chest and sighed. She had moved to a small town because she craved the slower pace, but Polly couldn't help thinking those triplets had just pulled a fast one on her.

* * *

"This is Caroline's day, girls." Sam waved to Juliette and Hayley from the drive while they waited on the porch pouting. This was his plan, the new-and-improved version. He wouldn't just push Caroline to find things to help her forge ahead; he'd use this as an opportunity to give her some special attention. So much for Polly's concerns about his not allowing Caroline to explore her individuality. "It's Caroline's club. Her fundraiser."

"Her plan," Gina muttered as she tucked Caroline into the passenger seat and double-checked that her seat belt fit properly.

"What?" Sam glared at his sister over the top of the minivan's hood.

"You don't think she's all excited to spend her Saturday morning washing just *any* old dog, do you?" Gina laughed and shook her head. "No wonder it was so easy to get you to volunteer to be a parent sponsor."

"Nobody 'got' me to volunteer. I'm doing this to support Caroline and…" And that's when Gina's point hit him. He thought about swapping kid duties with his sister, to have her attend the event and let him take charge at home. He glanced inside the car at Caroline. "Miss Bennett is going to be at this deal, I take it."

"Just give in and make the most of it, old man. Invite Polly and Donut out to the house for our barbecue Monday," Gina called out as she walked toward the house, not even looking back as if his agreement was a foregone conclusion.

"*Your* barbecue," he corrected, realizing that if he didn't take Caroline to the Go-Getters dog wash Gina would just make sure Polly and the pup made it out here for the holiday get-together. "*I'm* just going to hang around for the food and if you need any heavy lifting. Besides, I thought that barbecue was for the people helping you run the Pumpkin Jump. Polly's not in that group. Doesn't make sense to invite her."

"Makes perfect sense to me," Gina shouted at him from the porch.

"Us, too," Juliette and Hayley mimicked her.

"Let's go, Daddy!" Caroline kicked her feet and beamed at him. He hadn't gotten a smile that big out of her or heard her that excited to do anything in a long time.

"I have to go," he concluded. *Have* to, not *want* to. As he'd pointed out to Polly, you can't really hide in a small town. The sooner he crossed paths with the pretty teacher again, the better. From then on, it would be smooth sailing, right?

"Let's do this, kiddo," he said as he slid behind the wheel and started the van. "Full speed ahead."

Minutes later they parked behind the drugstore and headed through the drugstore as a shortcut to the firehouse, just down the block.

"I can go in your place and you can stay here to mind the store and try to figure out how to install this countertop if you—"

"No, thanks." Sam didn't allow his brother's offer to break his momentum as they passed through the store toward their destination. "We have a job to do."

That's how Sam decided to play it. Giving Caroline the best start was his job and that included sometimes interacting with Polly.

The fire chief directed everyone where to drop off kids, where to park and where the children should gather for instructions. Sam searched the scene, just to scope things out. One long table piled with poster board, paint, dog shampoo and a metal cashbox. Two bright blue plastic kiddie pools set up alongside the firehouse. Two firemen and the town's one firewoman filling those pools with water.

Caroline tugged at his arm. "Do you see them, Daddy?"

"See who?" He swept his gaze along the crowd, still trying to find a certain energetic young woman. It wasn't an emotional thing. Polly was just a teacher, just another partner in his plan to do the right thing for his girls. Nothing about this was personal.

His gaze landed on a knot of kids. A flash of black hair at the center, then a soft woof and Sam smiled. In a few steps, with Caroline keeping up pace for pace, he reached the cluster of children oohing, giggling and petting a golden-brown dog held in the arms of the prettiest teacher with no personal connection to him that he'd ever seen.

"Hi," she said to him softly as he stopped a few feet away from her.

"Hey." He gave her a nod. "You might have made more money for the cause charging tickets to pet that little guy, not to have the Go-Getters wash *other* people's dogs."

Polly shook her head. "He's not really mine."

The dog squirmed and licked her nose.

She made a face and laughed.

The children squealed, then the fire chief called

them over for instructions on how to conduct themselves around the firehouse. They straggled off, although Caroline lingered longer than the others.

Polly looked sheepishly up at Sam, her face flushed.
"I really have tried to find him a home."

"Looks to me like he found his *own* home." Sam
crouched, putting his eyes level with Polly's. He stroked
the dog's head just as the animal lifted it, trapping Sam's
hand against Polly's cheek.

Their eyes met. His chest tightened. *Nothing personal,* he reminded himself.

The dog moved again and Sam slid his hand free.

Polly shut her eyes, then looked down. "I don't want
you to think I haven't tried to keep my promise. But it
just doesn't seem like anyone wants him."

"*I* want him," Caroline protested, throwing her arms
around the dog's neck. "And I know Juliette and Hayley want him, too!"

Sam winced.

"Well, actually, Caroline, I'm thinking that maybe
I might want him, after all." Polly came to his rescue.

"That's okay," Caroline shot back instantly. "If you
take Donut we can still see him all the time, right?"

Polly fixed her big eyes on his face. The blush of
color that had flooded her cheeks drained.

Sam wanted to rush to her rescue in return, but he
hesitated. What could he say that wouldn't threaten his
rules, wouldn't interfere with his plans? Was giving in
to this going to stall any progress he might have made
with Caroline, keep her too connected to the past?

"Okay, Caroline, enough for now." Sam played it
safe. It was the right thing to do for his daughter, and to

stick to his no-matchmaking rule. He could not promise to see Polly whenever his girls wanted a Donut fix.
Things just didn't work that way. He gave her a smile
and started to stand.

Polly stood up at the same time, faltering slightly
when the dog in her arms wriggled.

Sam reached out to steady her, his heart thundering
so hard it actually muffled the world surrounding the
two of them for a moment.

"Hey, Grover! Hey there, boy!" A smiling brunette woman in blue work pants and a T-shirt with the
Baconburg Fire Department insignia on it pointed toward Polly and the dog.

Polly shot Sam a look that he could only call pure
panic.

He put his hand on his daughter's shoulder and gave
her a nudge. "Go on, Caroline, you need to go listen to
what the fire chief is saying."

"But I don't really want to." Caroline dragged her
feet.

"Some things aren't about what we want," Sam told
his daughter, although he kept his eyes on Polly, letting
her know her messages to him hadn't gone unheeded. "I
know you don't really want to be a Go-Getter, but the
fact is, you signed up for it and for this event, and you
need to honor your commitment." As Caroline reluctantly headed off to hear the instructions, Polly turned
to face the firewoman who had called out to her, and
squared her shoulders.

At that moment Sam realized he couldn't keep telling himself that things between him and Polly weren't
personal. He may have known her only a short time,

but that was more than long enough to sense the pain in her past. He'd have given just about anything to spare her any more.

He put his arm around her to lend whatever comfort and support he could. He raised his hand and called out to the woman who kept glancing their way as she finished filling the kiddie pool. "Hey, Angela! You, uh, you talking to Polly's dog?"

"I don't know Polly, but I do know Grover. It's so cool you brought him to the dog wash." She finished up her work and jogged toward them with her hand extended. "You must be Polly. You Ted's neighbor? Oh, or maybe…you're not…*the* girl?"

"*The* girl? No, I don't think so," she said with a quiet bravery that the slight tremble in her shoulders belied. "I don't see how I could be *the* girl because I don't know any Ted."

"You're not the girl Ted wanted to impress by getting a dog?" Angela stopped and put her hand over her mouth. "Oops. Maybe I wasn't supposed to say that. I'm a cat person myself, but I still don't get it. Ted's a great guy, really, but I don't see getting a dog for any other reason than love, do you?"

"No," Sam said in a firm, calm voice when Polly couldn't seem to find hers. He kept his arm lightly around her. "I can't see any reason at all, except love."

Polly tipped her head back to look up from beside him.

Sam did not meet her gaze. He just couldn't. He *could* forge ahead, though, get some answers, maybe clear up any questions so Polly wouldn't dwell on the worst. "So what makes you think this is Ted's dog? Is he missing?"

"I don't know. Ted's out of town until next Thursday for some specialized training." The brunette came toward them again with an assured spring in her steps. When she got close enough, she reached out and scratched behind the dog's ear. "I assumed he had put the dog in a kennel or had a friend watch it. This is absolutely his dog!"

Chapter 10

"*G*rover! *Gro-o*-over. Grover?" Each time Polly called a variation on the name, the dog wagged his tail.

With the dog wash in full swing and Polly's emotions clearly on a roller coaster, Sam had suggested the two of them head to the drugstore to pick up cold soft drinks as a reward for the Go-Getters.

It only made sense to bring the dog, especially when they hung a sign on his back that read A Clean Dog Is a Happy Dog with info on the dog wash under that.

Polly eased the sign off the dog, then slumped on the floor, leaning back against the refrigerated drink unit. She gazed into the dog's eyes, patted his head and sighed. "I can't deny it. He does seem to like that name."

"Don't read too much into it." Sam let the drink-case door fall shut. He came to her side and offered her an ice-cold bottled water and some consolation. "I think he likes the person saying his name."

She managed an unconvincing smile as she reached up to take the drink.

He braced himself for the little emotional jolt he always felt whenever their hands touched. And for the wave of regret that would follow when Polly would almost instantly withdraw shyly.

Only this time she didn't pull away.

Sam didn't exactly know what to feel or do about that. So he stood there looking down at her, his fingers practically entwined with hers. She had taken the news of potentially finding the dog's original owner in stride. Tried to pretend it was a good thing, even. Sam wanted to play along with that.

Why wouldn't he? It was what he'd have done. Looked at the new development as something to be accepted and moved past. It didn't hurt that it occurred to him that with the dog safely back in his first home that he and Polly could start to cultivate a workable relationship, meaning maybe they could be friends. Maybe even more, one day, when the girls were older.

"At least he's a firefighter. That generally means he's a good guy, right?" Her hand still on the drink he hadn't turned loose, she looked up at him with tears shimmering in her eyes above her wavering smile.

Who was he kidding? They were already past starting a workable friendship. Polly Bennett mattered to him. And if that meant taking her dog and all…

"I'd like to think so, but let's look at this a minute." Sam crouched down, surprising himself with the line of reasoning he was about to launch. "Angela Bodine couldn't tell us for sure that Ted's dog had even gone missing."

"She was fairly certain it was Ted's dog, though."

"Yeah, but you won't know until we talk to the neighbor and find out if that dog is missing, right?" Sam smiled knowing that while Angela had given Polly the name of the neighbor she thought was supposed to be minding the dog Ted called Grover, Sam had taken a minute to get Ted's cell-phone number from one of the other firemen. Yes, Sam had a plan, and this time it wasn't about propelling his own agenda, but about protecting Polly.

She shrugged, her finger flexing against the plastic bottle. The fact that she had not taken the drink told Sam that despite her seeming indifference, she was still listening.

"So, why are you, of all people, rushing to a conclusion?" He lowered his head, seeking to keep her eyes on his. "Angela said this Ted guy got the dog to impress a girl and had only had the animal a week before he volunteered to go to specialty training school."

"Yes, so?" Polly nodded and tugged the bottle toward her at last.

Sam tugged back to keep his hold. "So technically by the time he gets back, you will both have had the dog roughly the same amount of time. Plus he left the dog with an unreliable caregiver."

Another nod. Another tug.

Sam took a deep breath and let go of the bottle as he looked into her eyes and grinned. "So don't get in such an all-fired hurry to give up, Miss Bennett. You should know that. Give it time to see how it works out. You may be pleasantly surprised."

Her smile trembled, then grew. She looked down, laughed and shook her head. The dog in her lap licked her chin. "Did you hear that, Donut or Grover or whatever your name ends up being? Mr. Just Keep Moving Forward thinks time might be on our side."

Sam had to laugh, too. If he hadn't said it himself, he'd have never believed it. He stood and offered his hand to her. "But for now, we've got to get these drinks over to the kids."

She got up without his help, brushed off her jeans, then pulled on the leash to get the dog to cooperate. A deep breath. A swig of water. She squared her shoulders and headed for the door, but just before she opened it for Sam, who had a box filled with bottled drinks, she looked back. "I just don't know how I'm going to fill the time between now and when I find out what happens next."

"I have a suggestion!" Max's voice came practically bouncing off the walls from the back of the store.

"Didn't anyone ever tell you it's rude to listen in on other people's conversations?" Sam hoisted the heavy box high against his chest.

"Yeah, you'd have thought my older brother would have taught me stuff like that but he's pretty rude, too—not inviting the pretty new teacher to—"

"I was getting to it," Sam hollered back before looking down at Polly as he brushed past her. "I really was."

Yeah, he'd told Gina it wasn't a good idea, but that was before Polly had looked so vulnerable, so much as if she needed a friend. He wouldn't let himself be more for now, but he could be that much, couldn't he? "Why don't you come out to the house for the Pumpkin Jump planning-committee appreciation barbecue Monday? If you can stand more of Max's cooking."

"Pumpkin Jump?" Polly stepped out into the sunshine and shaded her eyes, but under the shade she created she wore a playful smile. "Are you just making that up to take my mind off Ted Perry?"

"Much as I'd love to take credit for anything that takes your mind off another man..." He could have worded that a little more, uh, *friend*ish. He cleared his throat. "Off the situation with Donut, or Grover or—"

"I get it," she said softly, her smile soft and sweet.

"Please come out to the house Monday." He clutched the box and held his ground until he got an answer, ready to stay put until he got the answer he wanted. "Bring Donut. Around three?"

She walked past him to check traffic, and motioned him to follow her into the street. "I'll think about it."

Like so many things where Polly was concerned, Sam's plan did not work out as he'd expected and she left him no way to just push through to get his way. He shook his head and followed along, laughing at himself softly as he added, "I guess that's all a guy can ask for."

The rest of the event went by quickly. She and Sam agreed not to tell Caroline and the other girls about the new development until they had more solid information. Polly tried to wheedle more about this Ted Perry from Angela—and the allegedly negligent neighbor he had left his pet with—without seeming as if she was trying to find out about him. She stayed upbeat. She cheered on the Go-Getters. She waved signs to draw in customers. In other words, she was pretty much just herself, even though it took a lot of effort to do so and to keep Sam from knowing how anxious this all made her.

She had begun to like coming home to the little dog after work and certainly didn't mind having another living thing in the house at night. She had come to Baconburg to create a life she thought would make her happy, make her finally feel she belonged. Donut had helped her begin to do that. Now she imagined taking a photo of the little golden-brown dog and sitting it up on the mantel with all the other loved ones absent from her life.

Polly glanced across the firehouse drive to see Sam prodding Caroline step by step to keep helping the others clean up after themselves. The day she had found the man in front of her new house she had felt so confident that she stood on the very verge of her small-town dreams of friends, family and home coming true.

No dogs. No matchmaking. The man's rules echoed through her thoughts.

Polly's stomach knotted at how quickly her big dream of a new life grew smaller and smaller every day. She had come all this way and it seemed she hadn't really found or gained a thing.

"C'mon, Donut. Let's go home and wait for Ted Perry or his neighbor's phone call." She turned away from the firehouse.

"Hey, Polly, um, that is, Miss Bennett!" Pounding footsteps accompanied Sam's voice. "You can't run away now."

Polly tensed at the phrase that echoed Essie's assessment of Polly's behavior. But she couldn't deny it; Sam was right. She needed to stay and see this through as an example to the kids and to honor her commitment, no matter how disenchanted she had become with life in Baconburg so far.

She tugged on the leash and turned around saying, "Sorry, Donut, we still have to—"

"Hop on!" Sam motioned to her from the second row of seats inside a shiny yellow fire truck.

"What? What's this?" Polly blinked.

"For a job well-done." Angela, the lady firefighter, leaned over the driver and motioned to Polly to get on board.

"And a last grab for donations," Sam added as he leaned down with his hand extended to her. "The Go-Getters and their sponsors get a ride down Main Street on the fire truck."

Polly hesitated. "But Donut…"

"Hey, dogs and fire trucks are a natural," the fireman behind the wheel shouted. "Bring the little guy along. He'll be a great nudge for people to fill our boots with cash."

"You can help, too!" Angela hoisted up a big, black rubber boot with yellow reflective-tape trim.

"People will feel especially happy to help make our favorite new Baconburg-ite and schoolteacher feel at home."

Polly laughed, the weight on her shoulders and in her heart lifting at least a little. Here was her invitation to be a part of this place, to stop running and be at home. That it came from Sam's lips didn't hurt.

She scooped up the dog and handed him up to Sam and Caroline, then climbed on herself. With the sun on her face, and Sam and Caroline and Donut at her side, all her cares and concerns melted away. She shut her eyes and in her heart made a prayer of gratitude.

"Not in my time, but in Yours," she whispered. She didn't control how fast or slow things went by dragging her feet or moving to a new place any more than Sam did by pressing relentlessly onward.

She opened her eyes and looked at him holding Caroline in his lap, and her with Donut in hers. The man was so full of surprises. If only he could see how happy his daughter looked right now, just being herself, being with him, maybe he'd back off trying to make the child conform to his expectations. Polly grabbed her cell phone and captured the moment.

"Now you take one of Miss Bennett, Daddy," Caroline urged.

"My hands are full. Besides, there'll be time for pictures on Monday," he said before he dropped a kiss on his daughter's head, endured a lick from the dog in her arms, then met Polly's gaze and smiled. "Miss Bennett is coming out for the barbecue with us, right, Miss Bennett?"

It was totally unfair means for him to get his way. And it worked.

Polly took a breath, pressed the button to save the photo in her phone and laughed. "Right. Okay, I'll be there."

Maybe he'd listened in or maybe he was just entertaining the kids, but just then the fireman driving let the siren go.

Polly's gaze met Sam's, and she knew deep down that the sudden blaring sound was not the only reason her heart rate had begun to race.

Chapter 11

Polly and Donut made the drive out to Goodacre Organic Farm without incident. If you didn't count reconsidering the wisdom of spending the day with Sam and his family...all right, mostly Sam...so much that she almost turned around twice a non-incident. The second time she thought about not going ahead, her cell phone rang. That gave her the perfect excuse to pull over to the side of the road.

"Hello?" Maybe the barbecue had been called off. She squelched the silly thought as soon as it popped into her head.

Actually, it turned out she would have liked that turn of events better than the news she got.

"Of course, of course," she found herself saying to conclude the short, slightly panicky conversation with Ted Perry's neighbor because she didn't know how to say what she really wanted to say. "Of course I can bring him over. Tomorrow? After school?"

She clicked the button to end the call, then stole a peek over her shoulder at Donut. "She says she checked the dog pound daily and didn't see any of the flyers. I think she saw them and thought I'd make a convenient dogsitter until somebody Ted works with saw you."

The dog's thick tail beat against the side of the carrier.

The sound echoed the heavy pounding of Polly's heart. She thought of calling the Goodacres and canceling, but she'd told the neighbor she couldn't bring Donut over because she was on her way to a party. So if she didn't go, she'd need to give the dog back sooner. A lump rose in Polly's throat. She didn't know when she had ever felt so alone.

She grabbed the keys to start the car again, but reached for the phone instead and called her sister, Essie.

"I should have known I'd get your voice mail." Polly *had* known, if she were honest with herself. She had probably wanted to get it, in fact. Just hearing her sister's voice eased her jangled nerves. And if her sister had actually answered, Polly probably would never have had the gumption to speak her heart as she did. "I miss you. I miss the whole family, but you especially. And not just because of your cooking because Sam, you remember Sam? The widower whose hat I ran over? Well, he has a brother who is cooking today. So I am covered in the getting-fed-without-eating-my-own-cooking department."

Polly clenched her teeth and paused to keep her voice from breaking. "Listen to me, stalling, when what I really want to do is pour my whole heart out to you. Essie,

I really thought I was making a good move coming here. That I'd finally find my way, but I am so afraid I'm not fitting in here, and if I don't fit here and I don't fit in Atlanta, then…"

An electronic beep on the line told her she'd run out of time. She gazed at her phone and contemplated calling again to finish her thought. Or recant it. She didn't want her family to worry.

After a moment, she decided to leave it as it was. Essie would understand and in a way only a sister could. Polly started the car again, then checked the clock in the dashboard.

"Oh, great. On top of everything else, the new girl is going to be late!" She hit the gas and took off down the vacant road. The rural countryside that had reminded her on her first trip out to the farm of quaint paintings and photos from calendars whizzed past. She didn't waste a minute admiring those kinds of scenes.

"What?" she asked the dog, who was safely tucked into a borrowed carrier in the backseat. "Peace? Acceptance? Happiness? I've chased it so long without a real definition of what I've wanted out of life that I'm not sure I'd even recognize it if I ran into it."

Sam's poor hat. Her thoughts raced faster than her quiet little hybrid car, jumping from her concerns to her desire to make a good impression to the still-crumpled hat sitting in her kitchen. She really had to get that taken care of. Not that he seemed to miss it. "That's the thing, though, isn't it? The fact that he acts like he doesn't care about it, this whole get-over-it, keep-moving-forward attitude of his? I don't buy it."

A quick, sharp woof seemed to ring out in agreement.

Before she could compliment her canine companion on his obvious people skills, Polly heard the voices of the triplets behind her. How was she going to tell them about the neighbor wanting Donut back?

"Wait! The *triplets?*" She hit the brakes. She had completely missed the driveway where they were standing waving their arms.

She'd come out here today as a comforting distraction, but in doing so, had she just employed Sam's just-keep-pushing-onward strategy? Was she becoming more like her own family and Sam's ideal of a family than becoming her own woman? The notion gave her a shiver.

She backed up slowly, careful of the three girls jumping up and down and calling, "Miss Bennett! Miss Bennett!"

Polly motioned for the girls to stay clear as she parked at the end of a row of vehicles. Suddenly she wondered how many people would be there, and what they would think of the new teacher being invited out by the local most-eligible single dad? She just managed to get out but not to get into the backseat to let Donut out of his carrier when the girls surrounded her.

"We've been waiting for you, Miss Bennett!" Juliette clapped her hands and jumped up and down.

"Hurry up and come with us." Hayley pointed to the band of wide gravel intended for farm visitors' vehicles. "We have a lot to get done!"

"What is it with you Goodacres? In the South we at least take a minute to welcome our guests before we put them to work." She meant it to sound teasing, not scolding, but as Juliette and Hayley hurried off, Polly began thinking of a way to make sure they knew she wasn't mad.

She shut her eyes and drew in a deep breath and then heard a small, sweet voice.

"Did you bring Donut?" Caroline rose up on tiptoes as if she might catch a glimpse in the car. "Daddy told us that the lady firefighter thinks she knows his other owner. Do you still have him?"

"He's right here." Polly put her hand on the girl's back reassuringly as she reached for the car door handle.

Caroline looked up at Polly, her brown eyes somber but filled with hope. "Can I help take care of him today while everyone does stuff?"

One last time. The little girl didn't say it but it was in her tone. That, on the heels of the call Polly had made to Essie, cut right through to Polly's heart. In that moment she felt not much older than the triplets herself.

The memory of being the sister who always lagged behind welled up within her. Deep down, Polly was still the one whose dreams seemed small and unambitious, her skills and accomplishments never measuring up to her twin's, the one whose simple plans never quite came true. If there was any way she could help Caroline grow up without that legacy, Polly determined she would do it.

She could start by giving Caroline something to take pride in, being the one Polly trusted with this important task. "It's okay with me if it's okay with your dad."

They got the dog out and while Polly did hold the leash, Caroline kept her hand on it, too, and marched along at Donut's side. They followed Hayley and Juliette's path to the back part of the farmhouse and straight into a scene of chaos already in progress.

Gina, standing beside a large paper flip chart with all sorts of frantic-looking scribbles on it, waved a large black marker in her direction. "We're divvying up assignments. This is everyone who's going to run games, booths, parking or sell food, for the Pumpkin Jump. Everyone, this is Polly Bennett."

The half dozen or so people seated at the long picnic table in front of her all turned their heads to peer at the late arrival.

"Hi." Polly tried to wave and ended up slapping herself in the knee with the dog leash.

The group didn't seem to notice. They waved, and some called out, "Hi, Polly."

"Miss Bennett, Miss Bennett!" Juliette and Hayley all but did acrobatics to draw her attention. "Everyone has stuff to do! You can do something with us, too, if you want."

Max stepped away from the large brick barbecue and gave a salute with long silver tongs. "Juliette, Hayley and I could use some help here. We've got platters of burgers and hotdogs to grill. Or you can help my grumpy old brother collect some pumpkins for the committee photo. I have to warn you, though, *that's* not the glam job it sounds like."

"Yep, it's just me, a field and a little red wagon." Sam came wheeling out a child's wagon with slatted sides. He let the handle drop and bounce off the sidewalk.

The group groaned.

Gina shook her head.

"No fair playing the pity card, old man." Max brandished the tongs with a flourish. "Although of the two of us, you probably do need the most help, lifting those heavy pumpkins and getting them back to the house."

"Yeah, yeah. Walking and lifting and working in the fields isn't nearly as hard as flipping burgers." Sam gave his brother a snort, then rolled his sleeves up over his forearms and elbows, exposing the bulge of his tanned biceps. "But you're welcome to tag along if you like, Polly."

All eyes fixed on her just in time to catch her stealing an admiring glance at Sam's strong arms.

"Oh, I don't know about that." She quickly looked away and cleared her throat, trying to match her tone to the light banter between the brothers. "It might not seem proper, the new schoolmarm going off into the pumpkin patch with a man and his little red wagon."

As soon as the words left her lips it struck her that they might sound more flirtatious than funny, more so when she scanned the amused expressions of the people around her. One of whom—Max, Gina, one or all of the triplets—might have seen her and Sam kissing in the upstairs hallway not all that long ago! Polly started to explain, couldn't find the words and so sank down to sit on the edge of one of the picnic benches on the patio, hoping it looked as if she meant to do so.

"Smart girl." Max started to head toward her with his hand out to guide her to the barbecue area. "Better to stay where there are plenty of chaperones."

"Or take your own along," Gina called out. "Take Donut."

The dog's whole body wriggled at the sound of the name. In a heartbeat he slipped away from Polly's grasp and ran right up to Sam, who dropped down on one knee to stop him.

Caroline rushed up and tugged at Polly's hand to get the teacher on her feet again. "You said I could take care of Donut today, so can I go, too?"

Polly staggered a step with Caroline pulling her, then paused and gathered enough composure to walk over to Sam. "What do you think?"

Sam hesitated.

Polly gazed down at him on bended knee before her for a moment longer than she probably should have before she realized everyone was watching. She leaned down then to grab up the dog's leash again, using that movement to whisper to Sam, "I just got off the phone with Ted Perry's neighbor. She wants me to return the dog tomorrow."

Sam pulled back and met her gaze.

Polly didn't want to look him in the eyes. She wasn't ready, and she knew his gaze would reveal how disappointed this turn of events made her feel.

He stood up and gave her hand a squeeze before turning to take up the wagon handle again and starting off. After only a couple of steps, he looked back at Polly and Caroline. "Well? What are you waiting for?" He motioned for them to follow him. "Let's go."

Polly went along, promising the other triplets she'd make time for them later. She launched into a conversation with Sam that began loudly enough for everyone to hear it was purely platonic. "So, I have yet to hear a serious explanation of this 'Pumpkin Jump' deal. What is it exactly? Do you have a contest to see who can jump over the most pumpkins in a row? Or one by one like leapfrog? Or is it more like pole-vaulting to see who can clear the largest pumpkin?"

Caroline giggled at the empty chatter and ran ahead down the path away from the house.

"No, no and no." Sam laughed and shook his head.

Gradually the farmhouse grew smaller behind them and the long rows of vines and pumpkins surrounded by long, low stone walls came into view.

Polly stopped to take in the sight for a moment, her thoughts filled with the words of Ecclesiastes. *To everything there is a season...*

For a split second it all seemed right again. Just for now she had friends and Donut and the beauty of a day with them when the sun was low and the shadows long and she didn't have to rush anywhere or compete for anything. "This is just like I imagined it would be."

"You *imagined* our farm?" Sam stopped to turn back to face Polly.

Caroline took advantage of that to load Donut into the wagon and hop in beside him herself.

"I imagined my life," she corrected, her heart halfway between nostalgia over her naïveté and shyness at revealing something so personal. "When my parents split up and I never seemed to be able to keep up with all their activities and expectations, I imagined there was a place where seeds were planted and nurtured and simply allowed to grow into what they were meant to be."

"Are you talking about people or pumpkins?" Caroline asked, clearly not sure what Polly was driving at.

"Both. That is, I'm taking about how in the years after my family moved away from Baconburg, I couldn't help remembering it as a place where people moved at their own pace." She raised her head slightly to find Sam and Caroline, and even Donut, staring at her. Heat rose in her cheeks. She hooked her thumbs in her belt loops and gave a one-sided shrug. "And when the time came those people weren't afraid to jump over a few pumpkins!"

"Leaves!" Caroline shouted even as she laughed at Polly turning her heartfelt vision into an act to keep from feeling she'd revealed too much.

"What?" Polly cocked her head. "You want me to leave?"

"Leaves. You know, that change color and fall from the trees every autumn?" The golden rays of sun highlighted the crinkles around Sam's smiling eyes as he held open the wooden gate in the wall for her. "We rake up all the leaves around here and haul them into huge piles in the yard. That's what we jump into."

"We?" she asked as she moved past Sam through the opening, so close that the sleeve of her lightweight summer sweater brushed the pearl buttons of his cotton shirt. "*You* jump in piles of leaves? I'd like to see that."

"Me, too," Caroline announced. Obviously impatient with not going anywhere, the pint-size redhead jumped out, grabbed the leash and pushed her way between the two of them with Donut in tow. "Only Daddy hasn't done it since back when Mommy got sick. Us girls don't even remember it."

Sam's whole body tensed.

Polly sank her teeth into her lower lip to keep from impulsively blurting out an observation about the ruined hat, the ridiculous rules or what price he might be paying for pushing his kids to move on before they were ready. Just before she joined Caroline and Donut on the quest for the best-looking pumpkins, she said, "To everything there is a season, Sam. You can't make Caroline bloom on your schedule any more than you can make these pumpkin vines produce on cue."

Chapter 12

"Actually you *can* force a flower to bloom *and* affect the growth of crops. That's how they get those monster pumpkins." Sam winced at how childish he sounded. He had known what Polly meant. The fact that he fully understood it was probably the very reason he reacted as he did.

To his relief Polly had already hurried along after Caroline and Donut. She didn't seem to have heard his argumentative tone as she tipped her head to one side to listen intently to his daughter, who had stopped to admire a lopsided, squatty pumpkin. They made a nice scene standing there in the fields of this farm that he loved. Polly looked good here, looked right.

The little dog leaped about and barked, and suddenly Sam couldn't help thinking how the girls would react to the news of Donut going away. He gripped the cold metal handle of the wagon. Maybe if things were different. But Sam knew that unlike Polly he did not have the luxury of imagining a world the way he wished it could be and then running off to try to re-create it. He had to deal with the realities of three little girls who had already lost too much and could not afford to lose anything else.

"Let's get this over with. Just point out the ones you want and I'll load 'em in the wagon." Sam reached them in a few long strides and parked the wagon. The handle fell into the dirt with a clatter and a clank. "Gina said we need at least three, but I think six this size will fit."

"Uh-uh." Caroline waved her hand through the air and took off running down the row. Donut bounded along behind her with his ears flapping and his leash flying.

"Uh-uh?" He looked to Polly for a translation.

"She says it's too…" Polly crinkled up her adorable nose, pursed her lips, then puffed out her cheeks.

"Too…" Sam tried his best to imitate the face Polly had just made.

Polly burst out laughing at his attempt, then shook her head. "She says she'll know what she wants when she sees it."

Sam tipped his head back and groaned. "We may be out here until dusk."

"Are we in a time crunch?"

I am, he wanted to say. *I can't spend any longer here with you than is necessary because you and Donut are not a part of our future.*

Polly shaded her eyes, her face turned his way. "Well?"

"I guess not," Sam admitted grudgingly. "They still have a lot to accomplish with the committee and the grill wasn't even ready when we left."

"Do you think Max needs our help?" She folded her arms in what a kid might have seen as a teacherly way, challenging him to thoroughly examine the situation and come to the best conclusion.

Sam couldn't help himself—future or not, he just saw her trying to guide him around to her line of thinking as charming.

There were worse things, he decided, than spending a few extra minutes of his day with Polly. And with Caroline, he was quick to remind himself. They were here to see what they could do to help Caroline have the most successful school year possible. Letting the child take the lead here might even finally show Polly what he was up against in getting the girl to make decisions and put them into action. That was what he needed to focus on. He cleared his throat and squinted across the field back toward the house, then looked at Polly again.

She had not budged. He probably should have seen that as a sign that she would not be easily swayed. But all he saw was how the breeze ruffled her perpetually ruffled-looking hair. How the sunlight warmed the healthy glow in her cheeks. How her lips, even pressed tightly together as if warning him to think carefully about how he proceeded, seemed so kissable.

"Max will clang the dinner bell when the burgers are done, so until then…" He bent slightly and held his hand out as if offering her the breadth and width of the Goodacre pumpkin patch.

"Until then…" She did a little sashay of a step past him and started after Caroline.

Sam tried to throw himself into the spirit of the outing. He really did. Time after time he bent to gather up what seemed like a perfectly acceptable pumpkin only to have Caroline reject it before Sam could settle it into the wagon. Each was deemed too bumpy or too lumpy or not pumpkiny enough.

"Now, this—" Sam said as he pointed to a tall, oblong and flawlessly orange specimen "—*this* is the model pumpkin. In fact, one might call it the supermodel of pumpkins."

Caroline frowned. "It's kinda skinny."

"Don't make up your mind until you see it on the runway." Sam abandoned the still-empty wagon, grabbed up the pumpkin he'd picked out and hoisted it up on his shoulder. He walked away, then did a turn to the delight of his little girl, and the obvious amusement of her pretty teacher, and walked back toward them. "And remember, the camera adds ten pounds."

"So that would make it look like twice its size?" Polly said with a smile.

"Hey, we're talking supermodel, not super math genius here." He grinned back at Polly, then lowered the pumpkin just above the wagon. "What do you say, kiddo, do we finally have a keeper?"

Caroline squinted hard. Her mouth scrunched up on one side.

Sam waited as patiently as he could possibly manage for five, ten, fifteen seconds, then exhaled. "Caroline, honey, it's just a snapshot on the farm's webpage. People will never notice a few imperfections."

Caroline lowered her gaze, then curled her hands into fists and looked across the way. "I think I see a better one a couple rows over."

And off she went, just a blur of red hair and golden dog, barking behind her.

Sam shut his eyes and clenched his jaw. "Do you see now why I feel I have to give her a nudge now and then to get her moving in the right—no, scratch that—in *any* direction?"

"Maybe she's the kind who needs a little longer to find her *own* direction?" Polly tried to tuck a strand of hair behind her ear, but the wind whipped it right back across her face.

Sam studied her for a moment. A day ago he had wondered how Polly's input on raising the girls might compare to Marie's. Now he wondered if Polly really understood his girls and him at all.

"Hayley and Juliette aren't like that. I can't hold them back." Even if chasing after them from one extracurricular activity to the next wore him thin, Sam refused to see that as a bad thing. "I'm afraid if I don't lay down the law with Caroline she'll just drift along, or keep waiting until everything is perfect to make her move. If I don't push her to push herself to meet a few basic expectations *now* she'll never do anything."

Polly ignored the hair pressed by the sweep of the wind to her cheek, shaded her eyes and watched the girl walking slowly around a plump, round pumpkin.

"Did you ever think that maybe she *is* doing something, Sam?" Polly took a few steps toward the girl, paused, then turned to him, her voice strained as spoke fast and heated. "Just because it's not what you'd do or what Juliette or Hayley would do does not mean it's nothing."

"Whoa!" He held up his hands in a sign of surrender. Only he wasn't surrendering. Not where his girls were concerned. "This is *my* family we're talking about here, Polly. Not some family you quilted together out of your memories."

"That was kind of harsh." Polly pulled her shoulders back. She blinked her big eyes at him, but she didn't shed a tear or sniffle. Her face went pale but she did not deny his observation. "I only wanted to help you see things from Caroline's point of view."

"You don't know Caroline's point of view, Polly." He kept his tone calm, almost comforting. He did not mean to hurt or humiliate her, just to hold his ground where his daughter was concerned. "You don't know what it means to have lost your mom so young, to know you'll grow up as a motherless girl. Or what it's like to have two sisters who could easily outshine you at every turn if you don't step up and grab a little of the spotlight yourself."

"I may not know Caroline's exact point of view, Sam, but don't presume you know enough about *me* to make those remarks." She lashed her hand through the air. "I actually have some pretty good insight into how it feels to have your family in pieces from a young age. I know what it is to always be in the shadow. I have some insight into at least some part of what Caroline is going through."

"Hey, you guys! I found one!" Caroline leaped in the air, her arms waving wildly. Above a barrage of excited barking, she put her hand to the side of her mouth and yelled, "I found a perfect pumpkin!"

"She's my daughter, Polly." Sam bent to take up the handle to the wagon and started toward the post Caroline had staked out. He was simply stating the facts as he saw them. "I think I know what's best for her."

Sam gathered up the pumpkin Caroline had singled out. Even he had to admit it looked far better than any of the previous choices and probably would make the best display of the farm's bounty on the webpage. From that point on she seemed on a hot streak, selecting another, then another until they had a wagon full of produce so round and orange that Polly observed, "If you hired an artist to make a painting to convey 'pumpkin' to people who had never seen a single one, the result wouldn't look any more pumpkin-rific than these. Just like professional book illustrators."

"Did you hear that, Donut? Professional book ill-o-stators!" Caroline beamed.

The dog wagged his tail as if impressed by this bit of news.

In the near distance a clanging from the back of the house sounded and Max called out, "Come and get it!"

"Cool!" Caroline surged ahead.

Donut started after her, then whipped his head around to look at Polly. She smiled at the small animal.

Sam half expected the bighearted educator to grab Donut and hug him as hard as she could. He held his breath, not sure what he would do if she reacted that way.

Polly only nodded and said quietly, "Go on, boy. It's okay."

The animal ran off, staying right at Caroline's heels.

Polly called out some instruction for Caroline not to let the dog bother anyone and to get him some water and so on. When the pair got out of hearing range, she sighed and looked at him. "Still friends?"

"I think we're mature enough to get past a difference of opinion now and then." Sam had to use both hands to tug the wagon over the rutted dip where the gate stood open.

"As long as I concede that you're right?" she added with a grin.

He didn't answer that. Instead he moved on to a topic he had wanted to broach all day. "So you going to be okay if it turns out you have to hand over the dog?"

"Me? You're worried about *me?*" She shook her head, then turned and, seeing him bogged down with his load, helped him wrangle the wheels up and over onto flat land. When they started to roll again, she said, "I was genuinely surprised you let Caroline spend so much time with him today."

Sam shifted his shoulders. A day's physical labor had them tight and aching, he decided, refusing to consider any other reason he'd be feeling tension during a simple, civil discussion with Polly. "Now that it's a very real possibility that he belongs to someone else, the dog is less of a…"

"Threat?" she supplied helpfully.

He didn't grin but he didn't frown, either. Instead he fixed his attention on not losing any off the pile of roly-poly pumpkins. "I was going to say 'distraction.'"

Polly stood her ground, arms folded, and pushed the limit of their fledgling friendship yet again. "Ah, you mean seeing Donut, or Grover as Ted Perry calls him, going back to his happy new home will provide a living, breathing, face-licking lesson in moving on without any of the mess of letting go or saying goodbye forever. Score a point for Sam's way."

He turned abruptly to face her, not sure what he would say because she was, essentially, right. He did think of the whole finding-the-dog's-owner situation, however it worked out, as a valuable lesson in just the kind of thing he'd tried so hard to instill in his girls. If the dog went with Ted, then Polly would move on and they'd see that. If the dog stayed with Polly, then…

"Miss Bennett! Miss Bennett!" Juliette, Hayley and Caroline came practically tumbling over each other down the hill straight for them. "Will you sit by me at dinner?" Hayley asked.

"No, me!" Juliette pleaded.

"Sit by me!" Caroline called.

"You got to spend the last hour with her," Hayley protested.

Sam squared his shoulders, set his jaw and began to pull the loaded wagon up the hill without another word.

"Is Daddy mad?" Caroline asked softly.

"No, I'm not mad," Sam shot back even as he forged ahead. "I just want to get this wagon unloaded."

"C'mon, girls, let's see what we can do to help your dad get that done." Polly came jogging up the hill to scoop one of the pumpkins up off the top of the heap. To Sam's surprise even one less made it easier going.

Next, Hayley and Juliette each came up and Polly used the toe of her shoe to point out the smallest of the bunch and the girls each took one.

"What can I do?" Caroline asked, peering at the remaining large pumpkins.

"Push," Polly told her.

So Caroline pushed and the wagon rolled along with much less effort from Sam.

"Things sure do get a lot easier when you work together instead of trying to stubbornly stick to your own way." Polly twirled around to walk backward for a moment as she added, "That sounds familiar. Where have I heard that?"

"Corinthians." Sam kept moving as he recited the familiar verse. "'Love is patient and kind. Love is not jealous or boastful or proud or rude. It does not demand its own way. It is not irritable, and it keeps no record of being wronged. It does not rejoice about injustice but rejoices whenever the truth wins out. Love never gives up, never loses faith, is always hopeful and endures through every circumstance.'"

Polly stood there with the group in the background and listened to him, her mouth slightly open as if she'd just watched him lift the wagon over his head and carry it one-handed up the hill.

"Impressed?" He grinned at her. "I memorized it to read when my parents renewed their vows a few years ago."

Her whole face had gone bright red. She looked away. "Boy, I sure am hungry."

"Really?" He only gave her a sideways look as he passed her on his way to join the group. "I'd have thought you'd be full already, after the bite you took out of me."

Caroline stopped in her tracks, her eyes big. "Miss Bennett! You *bit* my dad?"

Sam started to laugh, but Max beat him to it. The rest of the group joined in and Sam couldn't help thinking that it was going to be a long time before he was able to move on from a remark like that.

Chapter 13

Sam looked surprised by Caroline's loud proclamation for maybe a millisecond. He made an expression that seemed to say, *What just happened?*

Polly held her breath.

Sam cocked his head and narrowed his eyes at his child. Everyone looked at him, then at Polly, then at him again. Sam shrugged. Then he laughed.

The whole group joined in. Within a minute he had begun to pass pumpkins off to eager helpers as if nothing had happened.

It was the perfect way to handle it and Polly knew it the instant he did it. If it had been left up to her, she would probably have rushed headlong into some lengthy explanation of her having given him a piece of her mind and why she had done that and what she had meant by it all. Minutes would pass and maybe the group would have forgotten the "teacher bites dad" image in their heads, but only because her actions replaced that image with a "teacher puts foot in mouth, newcomer bites off more than she can chew" one.

With the wagon unloaded and the whole group on their feet, Gina asked Sam to say the blessing for their meal. Every head bowed.

"Dear Lord, I was just reminded of Ecclesiastes and Your design, that to everything there is a season. As we enter into this season of harvesting and celebration, of planting and planning for the future, the time for our children to learn and to grow, we ask Your blessing on those who have a hand in these things. For the farmers, the parents, the teachers, those who help in all aspects to support each other and love You. And as it says in Ecclesiastes, 'People should eat and drink and enjoy the fruits of their labor, for these are gifts from God.' Amen."

"Amen," the whole group said in unison.

"Amen," Polly whispered one beat behind.

Sam's way worked. Polly took a seat at the end of the picnic table and considered that as they enjoyed their meal.

The afternoon faded slowly into evening with the group sharing stories of Pumpkin Jumps past. It did not escape Polly's attention that each person there made a point of telling her a tale about Sam. The year Sam was thirteen and Max was nine and Sam wanted to keep Max busy, so he came up with a maze made of hay bales and when Max got lost and scared how Sam plowed straight through the walls of hay to Max's rescue. Then there was the story from a couple of years

ago when the local weatherman had predicted an early
snow for the day of the Jump, much to the girls' delight.
When it didn't come, Sam spent half the night scour-
ing the patch to collect the right-size pumpkins to stack
up like three small "snowmen" to greet the girls in the
morning. Time and again she heard the phrase "Nothing stops Sam."

Nothing stopped him, Polly thought, except his own
rules, or his own reasons for sticking to those rules.

Sam reacted to the praise and teasing with humil-
ity and good humor until someone said, "You know,
my favorite Sam story was the year he dressed up as
'Pumpkin Pete the Cowboy.' Marie laughed so much
at the getup—"

Others laughed and nodded in agreement. "I think
that's enough storytelling." Sam stood and clapped his
hands together before anyone tried to elaborate. "The
girls have school tomorrow and they have to get their
baths, so if you'll all excuse us…"

Despite their groans and complaints Sam prodded the
girls to go tell everyone goodbye and go into the house.

Polly watched in awe. She glanced from person to
person, wondering why no one else seemed to notice.
How could they have just been sharing those stories one
minute and now getting up and going home the next?
Didn't anyone see what had just happened?

They probably all assumed that was just Sam. He'd
made up his mind and that was that. But didn't anyone
else see that the time he decided to up and move on was
the moment when he and the girls might have shared a
moment remembering Marie Goodacre?

He called to Juliette not to try to tumble up the hill

to the house and directed Hayley not to forget to clear away her dessert plate. Then he held his hand out to Caroline to bring her along.

A knot twisted in the pit of her stomach. She wished she had known this when she had confronted him earlier. It all seemed so clear now. Sam wasn't pushing his girls to move forward to the future so they wouldn't experience more loss. He was running away from having to deal with the pain of his own past.

If Polly understood anything it was running away. She glued her gaze to the man's back, took a deep breath and hopped up. "The girls aren't the only ones who have school tomorrow. I better go collect Donut and be on my way."

More protests from the girls even as they followed their father around to the front of the house. "Please, Miss Bennett, please, stay and read the Donut story to us."

Polly shook her head. She didn't think she could read Marie Goodacre's story tonight, written for those adorable girls about a dog who only wanted to be loved. Not after her words with Sam and the realization that he had not fully dealt with his wife's death. Not knowing she might have to give up both her dog and now her ideas about helping Caroline because she couldn't wait to blurt out her opinion. "I really shouldn't, girls. I can walk with you up to the house, though."

The whole way Juliette and Hayley vied for Polly's attention, which she happily lavished on them.

The handful of committee members who hadn't already gone home trailed along, calling out their goodbyes and thank-yous and began to leave as Polly got to the house.

"Donut is in the kitchen," Gina said as she pointed in the direction of the brightly lit room while herding the girls upstairs.

Polly thanked Gina for having her, and hurried to collect Donut and get back to the door. Before she left, she looked up the stairs and called out, "Good night, girls. I'll see you all tomorrow at…"

A torrent of water rushing through old pipes resonated from upstairs through the house.

"School." Polly looked around the dimly lit foyer. The hallway was dark, the living room silent. Light shone from the kitchen like a beacon. Sam's kitchen.

The last time she had been alone with him in this house, he'd kissed her. Of course, the last time she was alone with him outside the house she had scolded him. She put her fingertips to her lips, unsure what any of that meant. Unsure if she could face the man alone again…or if he was even in that kitchen.

She held her breath. She could do this. Whatever "this" became she could—

Essie's special ringtone cut off that thought, filling the foyer and seeming to ricochet all around the quiet, cozy home.

"Hello? Someone in the house? Polly?" Sam's voice came from the kitchen.

Polly fumbled with the phone.

Before she could answer it, three exuberant voices called out from upstairs, "Miss Bennett! Miss Bennett! If you're still here, don't go. We still want you to read *No, No, Donut* to us."

Sam and Essie, the girls and the dog who had come to represent so much. Polly felt pressed in on all sides and so she did the very thing she had tried too hard to convince herself she wouldn't do. She gave Donut's leash a yank and hurried out the door.

Even as she dashed down the porch steps, she hit the answer button on her phone and whispered to her sister, "Can't talk now. I'm running away."

"Polly?" Sam stepped out from the kitchen where he'd been cleaning up the water dish and food they had set out for the dog. He thought he heard footsteps on the front porch, but with the sound of Gina coming down from upstairs he couldn't be sure.

"Did she leave already?" Gina paused on the bottom step, her head tilted so she could hear the girls getting into their pajamas in their room above.

"I guess so." He willed himself not to chase after her, not to go to the door and call out into the evening for her. What would be the point? He took a step into the hallway, his eyes fixed on the door. "She didn't even say goodbye."

"You'll see her tomorrow when you take the kids to school." Gina gave a wave of her hand. "Don't *you* run off. After the girls are in bed, I want to hear this story about Polly biting you."

"She didn't bite me." He rubbed the back of his neck, choosing not to admit to his sister that while he didn't feel Polly had metaphorically chewed him out, her words had stung. He wanted to tell himself that was because they were so unfounded, but he was old enough to know that if there were no truth behind her observations, he'd have forgotten them already. "She made the mistake of saying she'd taken a bite out of me in front of Caroline and the kid took it wrong."

"Good for Polly." Gina laughed.

"You don't even know what she got onto me about," he protested.

"Did she have a point in what she said?"

Sam started to turn away, then stopped and leaned against the doorframe. "Maybe."

"I thought so." Gina laughed. "I like her, Sam. In case I haven't told you that yet. I like her a lot and anyone with eyes can see you do, too."

"Yeah, well, we all liked that little dog, too, but that isn't going to keep its real owner from coming along and taking him away." His gaze went to the bowls he'd just washed, deciding he'd take them out into the garage so they wouldn't be in the kitchen as a reminder of the times the real-life Donut—and Miss Polly Bennett—had been a part of their lives. "I don't know how I'm going to comfort the girls if that happens."

"If I know you, you'll do it the way you always do things." She turned and headed back upstairs.

"Probably." Sam rubbed his face and wished he felt better about that realization. "I guess we'll find out when the time comes."

Chapter 14

Polly remained closed up in her classroom long after school had let out that next day. She used the quiet time alone, even with the rest of the school still bustling with after-school programs, to put together a montage of drawings and photos the children in her class had chosen as their best using the green-screen technology she had been working on the first day she brought Donut to school. She had brought him again today, having run home after the kids had gone to get him and bring him here to wait to hear from Ted Perry's neighbor. She raised her head to watch him sleeping in the corner of the room and a tightness gripped her throat.

He raised his head and she smiled at him but decided not to coo over him as she might have done a day ago. The letting go had to begin sometime and if she didn't make too big a fuss, it would all go smoother, right?

She focused on the task at hand, matching children's photos with the artwork they had given to her today for the class theme, "I Can." She stopped at Caroline's. "I can illustrate the book *No, No, Donut.*"

Polly swept her fingertips over a drawing of a short-legged golden-brown dog with big brown eyes and long, floppy ears that appeared on her screen. It was not the only picture Caroline had done but it was her best. Polly contemplated not using it, though, what with Donut, that is, Grover, going away and Sam's feelings about the whole dog thing.

Her finger hovered over the button to click through to the next image when a small tapping on her class-room door made her jump. "Oh! Um, yes?"

Sam stuck his head in the door. "Hey! Where'd you disappear to yesterday?"

"You came all the way to the school at..." She glanced at the clock and realized it was after five. Ted Perry's neighbor would be here any minute. She clicked to reduce the image on her computer and bring up the screen saver. "...after work, to ask me that?"

Sam stepped fully into the room, chuckling.

Donut hopped up and ran over to him, tail wagging.

Polly tried to be more reserved, even though inside she was so happy he had showed up in the nick of time to be with her when she had to turn over the animal she had come to care about.

"Not exactly." Sam squatted down to scratch behind the dog's ears as he looked up at Polly and grinned. "The Go-Getters are having a rehearsal in the gym for the square-dance routine they're doing for Parents' Night next week."

Polly pushed back her chair and stood. Her knees wobbled slightly. Was that nerves over turning over Donut or a reaction to having Sam show up when she needed him and looking so handsome and happy doing it? She smoothed down her skirt and adjusted her collar. "How's that going? Caroline and the square dancing?"

"She sort of has the square part. The dancing?" He stood and gave an exaggerated wince. "I'm not ready to call what she's doing that but she'll get it. She just needs to…"

"Push herself?"

"I was going to say learn her left foot from her right." He put his hands on his hips and cocked his head. "But your way works, too."

"Actually, that's *your* way, Sam." Her low heels clacked softly on the tiled floor as she crossed the room to him. "I hesitate to ask you this, but—"

"But you're going to ask it, anyway."

She couldn't help giving him the slightest smile at calling her out on that. "Is that your way of telling me to mind my own beeswax?"

"No. No, not at all." He laughed out loud. "It might surprise you—it sure surprises me—I kind of like having someone around to meddle in my 'beeswax' about the girls. It's been a long time since I've had an objective opinion about them."

Objective. Polly knew exactly what he meant by that—outsider. Having met Max and Gina, seen him at work and heard the way people talked about him, Polly knew he had plenty of opinions handy about how he raised his daughters. Everyone had had plenty of time to form those opinions. Hers differed because she wasn't one of them. "So, about yesterday, what I said to you about... We're okay?"

"We're okay." He nodded.

She expected him to say something more, to admit her thoughts on Caroline had some validity or even dismiss it outright as having been completely forgotten.

He just kept petting Donut.

"Okay, well, maybe we could go down to the gym and take a look at how Caroline is doing?" Suddenly her own classroom felt closed in. She shifted her weight, looked down at Donut, who watched them contently, and her heart ached. "Objectively, of course."

She directed the dog to go back to his bed, jotted down a note for Ted Perry's neighbor and taped it on the window of her room before she opened the door. She and Sam stepped out into the hallway only to find Hayley and Juliette sitting on the floor with schoolbooks in their laps.

Polly's gait slowed. She could hardly swallow. She hadn't imagined that the Goodacre girls might be there to witness her surrendering Donut for good. She turned to him and in a voice hushed and constricted she said, "You didn't tell me the other girls were here."

"Homework," he said as they walked up to where the girls were waiting. "It's not just for home anymore."

"Homework? I didn't think we were assigning a whole lot of that in second grade."

"Oh, it's not a whole lot. Not unless you don't do it and let it build up." He gave Juliette and Hayley a stern look. "Neither of them have done their Parents' Night projects."

"I'm supposed to do a collage of what we hope to

learn this year," Juliette said. She flipped through a magazine in her lap and tore out a page, flopping over with her hand on Hayley's shoulder as if the minimal effort had worn her to a frazzle. "It's so hard. All that sitting still for cutting and pasting. It's too much."

Especially when your time is taken up with activities from dance and gymnastics classes to Pumpkin Jumps, Polly thought, though she kept her outsider opinion to herself.

"We're doing a mobile from what Miss Bradley calls 'found objects' that show our interests." Hayley scrunched her face up. "But I can't find anything."

"Oh, I'm sure you can. It should be interesting," Polly said when what she meant was *That should be easy.* Hayley had so many interests. She could gather leaves and flowers from the farm, toy farm animals—Polly could think of a dozen things right off the bat, but she held her opinion, not comfortable interjecting herself into the situation at the moment.

Sam didn't give her a chance to speak up, anyway. He had already started toward the big double doors of the gymnasium. With a single gesture he encouraged Juliette and Hayley to come along.

Polly held her breath. She had expected having a moment as they walked along to tell Sam about the neighbor. She hurried up to him and reached out to grab him by the wrist, hoping to get him to stay back.

The girls hit the doors to the gym with a whomp. Those doors went swinging open.

Polly couldn't help but stand there, mouth open at the scene of total chaos inside.

"Caroline, please, the other way. No, the *other* other

way." The school's music teacher, Allison Benson, churned her arm in a small, frantic circle trying to illustrate the way she wanted the small redhead at the center of the group to spin and move. Allison did so in perfect rhythm, never missing a beat as she continued calling the dancers' moves. "Form a circle hand in hand. Turn to your partner, right and left grand."

Caroline staggered, went the wrong way, then pivoted and fell in step. Literally, fell in her steps.

"Find your partner do-si-do." Mrs. Benson valiantly pressed on.

Caroline's partner grabbed her by the elbow to help her up and ended up sitting on the floor beside her instead.

Polly cringed and bit her lower lip to keep herself from rushing in to Caroline's rescue.

"Do-si-do?" Sam gave a nod toward Caroline and the young boy sitting beside her. "Looks more like a do-si-don't to me."

"Sam!" Polly's scowl went unnoticed as Sam continued.

"Get up, Caroline. That's the key. It's okay to fall, just keep getting up again." He clapped his hands the way she had seen her father do when her brother played soccer or when her sister, Essie, had participated in a bake-off.

Without meaning to, Polly clenched her back teeth. Tension wound across her rigid shoulders like a mantle. It took every ounce of composure she had not to grab Sam by the shirtsleeve and haul him out into the hallway like a rowdy kid.

Look at yourself! She tried to get her point across

in a glare. *You have two daughters who are flailing with simple school projects and another who is literally stumbling around looking for a way to please you.* Maybe Sam's way did work for him, but he needed to take a good long look at—

"Is there a Polly Bennett in here?" A sour-faced man stood in the open door of the gym reading her name from a note in his hand. He shifted his weight from one heavy work-booted foot to the other.

Polly's mouth went dry. She had spoken with the man on the phone but had hoped his gruffness was more an outgrowth of age than of attitude. She gave Sam a fleeting glance, then stepped away from the children, not wanting to include them in this exchange. "I'm Polly."

The man raised one beefy hand with a chain leash and choke collar dangling from it. "I came for the dog."

Despite having readied herself all day, Polly froze.

"No!" Hayley rushed to Polly's side.

"Miss Bennett?" Juliette was on Hayley's heels, her eyes huge, her face tipped up at the exact angle, in a mirror image of her sister's.

Caroline scrambled to her feet and darted from the cluster of square dancers to grab her father by the hand. "You're not going to let someone we don't know take Donut, are you, Daddy? Not Donut!"

Polly swallowed hard to push down her own emotional reaction and allow herself to speak calmly and evenly about how they all knew the dog's time with them would probably be brief.

"No. No, Caroline, I'm not." Sam gave his daughter a pat that deftly guided her to the side. In two strides he was at the door with his hand extended. "I'm Sam Goodacre."

"Calvin Cooper." The man seized Sam's hand and gave it a hard shake. "I came for the dog."

"You said that, but I think you came for nothing. We're not handing the dog over to you, Mr. Cooper."

Polly covered her mouth with her hand to keep from cheering out loud. For all her criticism and concerns about the way Sam handled things, Polly felt a surge of gratitude for it. Her way, giving up and retreating, certainly would never have had the same impact.

"Ain't your dog to keep." The neighbor's jowly cheeks shook slightly with the sharpness of his words.

Sam did not back down an inch. "Nor is he yours."

"Neighbor left him with me." He gave the chain and collar in his hand a shake.

Sam crossed his arms. "And you lost him and didn't really seem to make much effort to find him."

The man gave a huff that was clearly not a denial or an admission.

"Then I think we can agree that as long as you know where the dog is and know that he's safe, your neighbor won't mind." Sam put his arm around the man and turned him away from the watchful anxious gazes of Polly and the children.

"Have to take it up with him," the neighbor grumbled.

"I've already called." He gave the man's slumped back a pat that was part camaraderie, part urging him down the hallway. "Got his number from Angela Bodine, the lady who identified him as Ted's puppy."

"Did ya?" He studied Sam.

Polly's stomach felt as if it was taking more tumbles than Caroline in the square-dance routine.

"I did what I thought was right, Mr. Cooper."

No matter how this all turned out, Polly would always remember the way Sam Goodacre took charge today. Maybe one day, if she lived in Baconburg long enough, that would be the Sam story she'd tell.

Ted Perry's neighbor heaved a weary sigh. "Don't make no never mind to me but wish you'd told me before I come all the way down here for nothing."

"I'm sorry for your trouble." Another pat from Sam that was also a little bit of a push.

The man stood there for a moment sizing up Sam through squinty eyes.

Sam made a gesture with his hand as if showing the man the way to the outside door.

It felt as if no one in the whole gymnasium so much as took a breath.

"Well, all right, then. Guess it's okay. She seems a nice enough one." He gave Polly a nod. "Told that fella he didn't have no business with a dog, anyways, him being a bachelor who stays at the station for long shifts, but he said it was a chick magnet."

"Oh, really?" Sam shot Polly a look that said he thought they had an angle they could work with, with that bit of inside information. "Did he happen to say which chick he wanted to magnetize with this dog?"

"No, but how many can there be in this town that you could meet being a fireman?" The stout older man shook his head and turned to leave, muttering as he did, "I don't get the attraction, though. Walked that dog up and down the street a dozen times the two days before he runned off and I didn't get so much as a 'howdy' from the ladies."

He shambled out.

Sam stood at the door waving and thanking him until the older man disappeared, then he turned to the group.

The whole room broke out into a cheer.

Mrs. Benson threw up her hands and declared they didn't stand much chance of getting more done today and dismissed the group.

The girls ran to Sam, throwing their arms up to hug him.

Polly wanted to do the same, but she managed to control the urge long enough to walk to his side and tell the girls to go to her room to tell Donut the good news, then turn to him and smile. "Why did you do that? And when did you talk to Ted Perry?"

Sam didn't look directly at her. "Didn't say I talked to him. Said I called him."

Polly gasped. "You lied?"

"Nope, I did call." He turned to her and grinned. "I had to leave a message, but I called. The man knows his dog is in good hands."

"Nothing does get in your way, does it?"

"Is that a good thing or a bad one?"

"Yes." She answered looking him straight in the eye as she moved past him, heading back to her classroom.

"What does that mean? Polly? Polly, what does that…" He took a few steps after her and there they were, in the hallway, alone together. He reached out to snag her by the arm. "If you have something to say to me, Polly, just say it."

"Just say it? Really? That's what you want? And you'll listen this time?"

He opened his mouth to say…something…but he didn't have a chance to form a thought much less a word before she grabbed his sleeve right back and gave a jerk. In three quick steps they were outside a door marked Supplies.

Polly paused to look up and down the empty hallway.

Sam followed suit, but before he could turn his head a second time, the door creaked open and she slipped inside the eight-by-five-foot walk-in closet.

Naturally, Sam didn't see any reason not to do the same.

The door shut with a bang.

She turned toward him, her lips pressed closed and her eyes flashing.

Emotions that he couldn't quite nail down played through her expressions and posture. Aggravation? Agitation? Appreciation? Maybe a little attraction, even? It didn't matter—just standing here so close to Polly with not another soul around made Sam content. And a little bit crazy. But mostly content.

"First, thank you. Thank you very much for stepping in and taking charge with Mr. Cooper. I am making myself accept that Donut will probably have to go back to his original owner, but I hated the idea of leaving him with the person who had let the little guy run away, then concluded it was for the best to leave him lost."

Yes. *Content.* In the years since Marie's death he had been resigned, accepting, motivated and even happy, but this was a feeling that he didn't think he would ever feel again. And here it was wrapped up in the guise of a dark-haired schoolteacher with a big heart and no small habit of butting into his "beeswax," as she'd put it, where his daughters were concerned. He looked deep into her eyes and smiled what he had to assume was the biggest, goofiest smile he'd smiled in a very long while.

"You're welcome," he said.

"Well, don't be too quick to think that settles everything because, you know, you *did* ask what I thought." She tipped her chin up and folded her arms, which meant she had to brush against him in the contained space.

"And I gather you think I'm just a shade shy of perfection, right, Miss Bennett?" He folded his arms, too, which had the effect of ever so slightly pushing her back and at the same time pressing their forearms against each other.

She looked down where the fabric of his rolled-back shirtsleeves met the lightly tanned skin of her bare arms. For a moment she seemed to lose her train of thought.

Sam smiled at the idea that just by being close to her he could derail her, if only for a few fleeting seconds. Somehow that seemed to make things a little more balanced out because she had completely knocked him for a loop ever since…well, since he first laid eyes on her, if he was perfectly honest with himself.

"Well, I…" She inched backward until she bumped against a shelf piled with cleaning supplies.

A bottle wobbled.

"And you wonder if I realize that this almost-imperceptible imperfection on my part keeps me from seeing that all three of my girls are struggling just a wee bit with their Parents' Night projects."

"I don't know that I'd have said—"

"Imperfection? It's all right, I'm a grown-up who can handle the criticism." Mostly by beating her to the punch with humor, he added in his mind. It was a technique he had practiced many times in the years since Marie had first gotten sick—redirect if you must, but remain in control. "Look, all kidding side, Polly, it's a new school year. There are bound to be bumps. You've probably had a few yourself already."

"I pulled you in here to talk about the girls, Sam, not about me."

"I understand your concerns. Don't worry, I've got this." He opened the door and stood back, allowing her to go out first.

He followed and let the door shut with such a wham that three other doors in the hallway swung open—and two teachers and three little girls all peeked out into the hall at them.

Don't get any big ideas. The rule still applies. No matchmaking. If the teachers hadn't been in the mix, Sam would have been tempted to shout out that warning. Instead he managed a smile and the truth, acknowledging that it sounded really weak. "Parent-teacher conference. No big deal."

"Are we in trouble?" Hayley wanted to know as Sam and Polly came toward the open door of Polly's classroom.

"No, but Miss Bennett has some very, um, legitimate worries that not one of you three is on top of your Parents' Night projects. We need to do—"

His cell phone ringing cut him off. He reached for it,

explaining, "Got to take this. I'm pretty much always on call because of the pharmacy."

Polly nodded and herded the kids inside, calling out to Donut in a sweet, upbeat tone that churned up that unexpected contented feeling in Sam all over again. "Who's my good boy? Who's my pal?"

"The guy who just saved the day and let you keep your dog a little longer." Sam murmured the answer he secretly hoped was running through her head as he withdrew his phone and pressed the answer button. "Goodacre, how can I help you?"

"Yeah, Sam Goodacre? The one who left me a message?"

Sam tensed. "Could be. What was the message about?"

"My dog. I'm Ted Perry and I think you've got him."

Sam held back as the rest went inside the classroom. "Yeah, that's me. What can I do for you?"

Sam tried his best. He explained the situation about Polly being new in town, all she had done to care for the animal and even played the "owning a dog when you work long hours just for a chick magnet isn't really a great idea" card. That was one play too many.

At the mention of the potential for the dog to impress a girl, Ted turned to stone. Totally unhearing, unsympathetic, immovable stone. Sam couldn't really argue his way around a guy willing to try anything to score points with a girl. Getting a dog and leaving it with a negligent neighbor hardly made for the fuzzy-wuzzy feelings in women. The best the guy would agree to was to let Polly visit when she wanted. Other than that, the guy wanted his dog back and he wanted him back in two days.

So much for near perfection. Sam rubbed his hand over his face and groaned. He should never have gotten mixed up in all this. He should have stuck with his plan from the very beginning. He should have done things the way he always did.

His girls were floundering because he hadn't pushed them enough. Time to fix that. The only way to do that was to take control. Sam knew just how to do that, but he might have to break one of his rules to get it done. Hey, as long as he was the one doing the rule-breaking, right?

Sam didn't allow himself a chance to rethink the question. He grabbed the door handle and came strolling into Polly's classroom with his head high. "I've been thinking. Because Grover already has an owner and everyone here really seems to have caught a bad case of puppy love…"

The girls giggled at the phrase.

Polly's back went stiff, her eyes guarded.

Sam slapped his hands together in a thunderous clap and even as everyone jumped he announced his new plan louder still. "So, how about this? If you girls buckle down and get everything done to show well at Parents' Night on Friday, I will be willing to reconsider *one* of my rules."

"You're going to date Miss Bennett?" Juliette leaped up.

"No!" Sam held up his hands. Pressing on without daring to look Polly's way after the definitiveness of his response, he kept his focus strictly on the girls and said, "I'm going to look into us getting our own dog."

Chapter 15

"A dog? He promised those children a dog if they came through with their Parents' Night projects?" Essie's disbelief about Sam's rash decision came out clearly through the phone, then was softened by a laugh. "Did he not think about the implications of breaking his own rules?"

"Well, that's the deal with him, I think." Polly had started off the very conversation with her twin with the incredible news of Sam's announcement. He had been so proud of his solution, but now, three days and one returned dog later, Polly still couldn't quite believe it. "It was so obvious that he wanted to make everyone feel better about the situation. Wanted it badly enough to do this. He *makes* the rules, so he's just making a new one. That's okay with him as long as he sees it as progress."

"I can see that."

"I thought you would. Go, go, go. Win, win, win," Polly said like a cheer, knowing her sister would revel in it, not take it as criticism.

With Parents' Night at Van Buren Elementary only an hour away, Polly used the call to try to calm her nerves as she dressed for the event. She put the phone on speaker so she could contort herself to try to zip up the yellow dress she'd chosen because it looked so cheerful and also because it wouldn't show any leftover dog hair.

In the background of the call Polly heard an electronic ding and a car door slam. She gave up with the zipper still halfway open. "Speaking of going, tell me you are not going to drive and talk on the phone at the same time. I know you're busy, but—"

"I have Bluetooth, but rest assured I am not driving and talking on the phone anymore."

The doorbell rang.

Polly jumped. Her mind filled with images of Ted Perry returning her dog or Sam showing up with a puppy, even as she told herself that would never happen.

"Hold on, someone's at the door." She hurried through the living room and peered out the small window to see who was on her front porch. "Essie!"

In a second she'd clicked off the phone, swung open the door and had her arms around her twin. The two laughed and hugged and chattered so quickly that no one else would have been able to keep up.

"Why? How?" Polly asked, guiding Essie inside, overnight case in tow. "Don't you have to work?"

"I deserve a weekend off now and then." Essie spun Polly away, zipped up the dress, then spun her back.

"Now and then? Meaning once in a blue moon?"

Polly double-checked to make sure the top of the zipper got buttoned down. "You never take time off."

"I do when my sister needs me. After that phone call saying you were running away and the email saying how happy you were that Donut had been reunited with his very, very, very nice owner, what else could I do?"

"Was it that obvious I'm miserable?" Polly started to search for her shoes.

Essie didn't even ask what Polly was looking for, just bent to peer under the couch, nabbed them and handed them to Polly. "The last 'very' did it."

She slid her feet into the practical but pretty flats, then headed off for the kitchen to grab her purse. "Ted Perry is a nice guy."

"I'm sure he is but he's not the guy I want to know about." Essie followed along and had hardly gotten through the kitchen door when she plucked up Sam's hat. When she brandished it, she didn't need words to warn Polly that she had her all figured out.

"I keep meaning to find a way to have that fixed." Polly sighed. "Though I'm almost convinced he doesn't really want it back. It's all about this moving-forward idea of his. He thinks it is progress. I think it's a way not to deal with the pain of his loss."

"Some things you can't fix, Polly. This hat is only one of them. A grown man who has made up his mind about how he wants to live his life and raise his kids is another."

"But those girls need some balance in their lives." Polly reached out and took the hat from Essie's hand. "And Sam? Sam looked good in this hat. Though I have thought he'd look better in this smoky-brown trilby with a black band that I found online."

Essie laughed and stood up. Smack off a ten-plus-hour drive, she looked fresh and ready to go without doing anything more than whisking her hand down her navy blue skirt and then over her slicked-back black hair. "In other words, it's too soon for you to give up on them."

Polly had never thought of it that way. For all her big ideas about slowing down the pace of life and taking things as they came, did Polly have her own drive to succeed, to try to make things turn out "her" way?

It was with that question in her mind and a jumble of emotions—sadness over Donut, anxiety about the girls' big night tonight, joy at seeing Essie and conflict over whether to tell her twin there was dog hair on her blue skirt, mingled in with her tender feelings about Sam—pinging around inside her, Polly and Essie headed for school and Parents' Night.

"Mrs. Williams says my collage is super-creative, Daddy."

"It's not all pictures of dogs, is it?" Sam teased Juliette as he stood by the open side door as the girls climbed out.

"Not *all* of it," she shot back with a sly smile. "Just one, I think."

"You *think*?" He watched her lead the parade of redheads into the school building. "Girls, wait!"

"We can't wait, Daddy, we have to go-o-o," Juliette called as they hurried along the hallway.

The threesome reached the little girls' room and Hayley turned around and waved him away. "Go get us a seat in the bleachers. A *good* seat."

Caroline added, "Don't wait for us, Dad. We're not babies."

"I guess they told you." Polly came out of the restroom brushing dog hair from her dark skirt, wearing a smug smile and her usually untamable hair in a tight ponytail at the back of her head.

He started to say something, but nothing came readily to his lips. He knew she was still smarting from having to hand over the little lost dog, but it was not in him to dredge up pain or loss that belonged in the past.

It didn't matter because Polly didn't linger long enough to chat. She gave a wave and headed off to her classroom.

That made sense, of course, because parents were already arriving, although he couldn't contain a subtle grin when he spotted her peering in at the doorway a little bit later during the Go-Getters square dancing routine.

Mrs. Benson took her position and called to the children to get their "sets in order" and they all took their places. Sam stole a peek at Polly only to find she had whipped out a cell phone, clearly to record the event.

The song began and he could hear Juliette and Hayley cheer her on, but he admittedly missed some of Caroline's performance. Partly because he wasn't sure he wanted to see it, missteps and all. But also partly because he kept glancing Polly's way hoping to catch her delighting at Caroline's willingness to stick with it no matter what.

Juliette gasped.

Hayley giggled.

Sam whipped his head around to see Caroline falter, overcorrect and start out doing an allemande left in the wrong direction, then give a twirl and correct herself.

"That a girl." Sam beamed with pride in Polly's direction only to find she had left.

When the music stopped, Sam was the first on his feet applauding, which seemed to embarrass Caroline and then Juliette and Hayley rather than impress them. For all his talk of pushing them ahead, in that moment it dawned on him that they were growing up so fast.

He leaned down to Hayley, who had been sitting next to him, and asked above the shuffling of children as the Go-Getters left and the next group of performers came onto the floor. "I don't suppose you girls want to take me to your classrooms to see your projects now, do you?"

The two exchanged looks, then searched to find Caroline in the crowd. Hayley put her hand on his leg and gave him a nudge away from them. "You go on, Daddy. We'll stay and watch the next group."

He didn't wait around to be told twice. Of course, he started with Caroline's teacher first. "Hey, saw you got the big square-dance number on your phone."

"I, uh, yes." Polly's ponytail bounced as she looked around the large metal cart where she'd been adjusting the feeds hooked to a big television set. A slide show of smiling faces and school projects faded in and out accompanied by a hit-or-miss audio track. "Look, I think you should know—"

"You don't have to apologize." He held up his hand. "It worked out well for the girls and that's what matters."

"Apologize?" She stood straight and narrowed her eyes at him in a way he'd never seen her do before. She shook her head and pointed her finger at him in a way that felt like if he'd been closer, she'd have jabbed him in the shoulder as she spoke. "Oh, I get it. You're talking about that entirely ill-conceived 'win a pet for your performance' deal you made with your daughters, aren't you?"

"Ill-conceived? Win a pet? Polly, that doesn't sound like you."

"Because it's not me." Black hair barely contained by a headband, Polly stood up from behind the oversize TV cart.

"There's—" Sam looked from one to the other "—there's two of you?"

Polly came and stood beside her carbon copy. "Sam Goodacre, meet my sister, Esther Bennett. Essie, meet Sam."

"You're..."

"Identical," they both said at the same time.

"But only one of us has a reason to ask you what on earth you think I would have to apologize to you for." Polly crossed her arms and met his gaze in that spitfire-with-a-cause way of hers.

Immediately he knew he'd never consider them identical again. Amusement met the sense of contentment Polly seemed to always awaken in him. How could he have ever thought this stiff-backed, slick-haired, neatly contained woman was his Polly? *His* Polly! The thought threw him off-balance for a second.

That was long enough for Polly to swoop across the room and have him by the shirtsleeve. She was all fire and feistiness as she opened her mouth and said, "Now, listen to me, Sam Goodacre, I—"

"I like it when you grab my shirtsleeve," he murmured.

"W-well, you're not going to like what I—" she glanced down at the place where her hand held the soft blue fabric of his shirt "—have to say."

"Never mind me." Polly's twin all but disappeared behind the TV as she called out, "I'll keep on working to get this sound synced up and running."

"Maybe I won't like it, but I'm so glad you're talking to me that right now I'm happy to hear you out."

She blinked her big eyes as if she couldn't quite remember what she intended to say. Then she shook her head, pressed her lips together and gave his sleeve a shake. "That's a sweet thing to say, but I'm not talking to you as a friend right now. Well, not as *just* a friend. I have to tell you this."

He shifted his feet as if bracing himself for some big news when really he just wanted to move a little closer to her. "Yeah, I know. You don't think much more of my promising the girls a dog than your sister does."

"Actually, I don't really know what to think about getting the girls a dog, but I do have something to tell you about what they have done to live up to your demands."

"Demands?" He stepped back at that.

She stepped forward after him. "Sam, I think the girls have been running the oldest game in the identicals' playbook. The old switcheroo."

"The old… Polly, are you saying Caroline, Juliette and Hayley have been trading places?"

"Trading places is just one part of it. Sam, I haven't confirmed it with Mrs. Williams and Mrs. Bradley yet because I wanted to talk to you about it first, but I think Caroline may have done some of Hayley's and Juliette's work while Juliette did the square dance in Caroline's place."

He pulled his arm away, freeing his sleeve, trying to laugh off the notion. "How could you say that? Polly, you weren't even there."

"That's one reason I can say it." She went over and shut the door, the accepted signal that a parent and teacher were talking and to wait until they were done to come inside. "When I watched the replay of it on Essie's phone—"

"You sent your sister to spy on my kids?"

"No! No, Sam, she went down while I was setting up here. I asked her to record it because I wanted to see the performance. Because—"

He tried to make sense of it all and in doing so could only come to two conclusions. Either he was all wrong about the way he'd handled the girls or—

An image flashed on the screen behind Polly.

"You think you know better than me what's right for my kids," he said, his jaw tight.

"No, Sam, I never said that."

"You don't have to say it. I'm looking at the proof of it right now." He pointed to the image of Caroline in front of a drawing of a dog that Sam recognized instantly as Donut. "Why would you let her draw a picture of a dog she could never have, then choose it to show at Parents' Night?"

"I don't tell the kids what to draw or write about, Sam. The project was to write a poem, story or do a piece of art with the topic 'I Can,' and that's what Caroline drew."

"Donut, Polly? 'I can have Donut as my dog'?" His gut twisted, not from anger but a kind of helpless emptiness that he hadn't felt in a long time. He had worked every day since Marie had gotten sick to keep the girls from dwelling on how fragile relationships could be, how quickly someone we love could be lost and now— "Why would you do that to a little girl who had already had so much sadness in life, Polly?"

"No, you have to hear the audio that goes with it."

"I think I've heard enough." He turned to leave, his head so clouded with a whirlwind of thoughts that he didn't trust what he might say if he stayed. "I have to get going."

"So that's how you're going to handle this?" Polly hurried to place herself between Sam and the door. "Like you do everything. Sam's way. Just charge straight ahead, no looking back, no time to stop and consider if you're headed in the right direction?"

"Step aside, Polly." He did not meet her gaze this time. "The girls are in the gym. I need to get them and meet with their other teachers."

"I know loss is painful. Even for people of faith it's hard to understand how a loving God would take away someone we love, especially when we still need them so much. But plunging blindly forward isn't the way to get past that. Some things take time."

"Don't lecture me. Don't you lecture me, Polly Bennett." She wouldn't let him go, wouldn't let him do what he thought was best—keep moving. Sam felt hurt and embarrassed at that hurting. He was angry, but not sure why he was angry. His head throbbed and his heart ached, and when Polly wouldn't get out of his way physically, he did the only thing he knew how to do. Plowed right over her, verbally. "You've come running home to a place mostly made up in your imagination to keep from dealing with the fact that life never measured up to your expectations. You accuse me of running from the past. Well, you've run *to* the past and what has that gotten you?"

His harsh words worked, too. Polly stepped back and let him go.

He couldn't just let it go at that, though. "I do not think my girls would do that, and even if they did, don't you think I'd know it?"

"Yes, I do think you would if you weren't so fixated on them being the best and always having to come out on top of whatever they tackle." Polly's words rushed out and her voice went a notch higher with the power of her emotional connection to what she wanted to express. "A family should support each other, not compete, not try to have to win approval of their parent with every endeavor."

"Whoa, I never said they had to be the best at anything." He held up his hand to stop her right there. "I know you think Caroline is doing all this to make me happy, Polly, but the rest of this… I don't think that's about me at all."

Esther Bennett popped up from behind the cart, her

eyes wide and her mouth open. After she got Polly's attention, she folded her arms and tipped her head to one side.

Sam didn't have to be the father of multiples to recognize the silent communication between the two. And suddenly a few other things became clear to him.

"Polly, this is *my* family. I know yours had problems and you wish things had been different but you can't fix your past here." He spread his arms wide to indicate the classroom and, in a larger sense, all of the town she had come to in search of a new life. "You have to come to terms with it and move on, find something better, make it better. That's how you heal."

"Have you done that, Sam? Come to terms with losing Marie?" Polly never took her eyes from his despite her sister's looming presence and the muffled voices from the hallway outside. "You've moved on, you've tried and tried and tried to find something better, but has any of that made your life better?"

Sam honestly could not answer that, so instead he crossed to the door and opened it, saying quietly, "I told you my rules, Polly. I never lied to you or pretended to be anything or anyone but who I am. I wish you had honored that."

"I did honor it, Sam," she called after him. "I honored it by being your friend and telling the truth when nobody else would. You can't keep running forever. At some point you need to slow down and take a good hard look at what's going on around you. Maybe then you'd see that I am on your side."

Polly's words stayed with Sam the rest of the evening. So much so that he found himself arguing against them when he should have been paying attention to the tour of Juliette's and Hayley's classrooms. Neither of those teachers even hinted at anything amiss with the girls' work, though. That proved Sam was in the right here, right?

Sam was still wrestling with all of it when he and the girls got home. Max leaned back in his chair at the kitchen table and hollered out as the girls ran upstairs. "So do we need to build a doghouse or not?"

"Yeah." Gina, who had met them on the porch and, true to the small-town grapevine, had already heard that Polly and Sam had had words, prodded Sam through the doorway. She pushed past him to tell their younger sibling, "By all means, build a dog house—then we can send Sam to it."

"Me? *Why me?*" Sam knew why. At the very least his behavior on this night meant to let the children show off was in bad form. "Polly's the one who accused the girls of pulling the old switcheroo. I was just defending my daughters."

Gina glared at him. "I think what you were defending was your own wounded ego."

Sam clenched his jaw. "She was trying to—"

"She was trying to be a good teacher, Sam, *and* a good friend."

"Whoa, switcheroo? Defending what?" Max stood and gestured broadly as he spoke. "Clue a guy in, will ya?"

"There's nothing to clue you in on." Sam pivoted on his boot heel and headed for the hallway. He didn't have to take this in his own home. He was Sam Goodacre. He had a plan. He had a way of doing things that always worked for him. No stopping, no looking back.

Except…he twisted his head to glance over his shoulder at the door just as headlights slashed across the front of the old farmhouse.

"Who's that?" Gina rushed into the hall. "Do you think something's wrong?"

Sam ignored his sister's question as he headed for the door, flung it open and stepped out into the September night air to greet the woman he knew he'd find coming up the walk.

Chapter 16

"I saw Caroline mess up in the routine." Sam came out of the house on the defense but not sounding like a man fully convinced of what he was saying. "If Juliette had been doing it, she would have gotten through it without a hitch."

"Not if she didn't have a chance to rehearse it," Polly called out as she climbed from her car.

Sam slowed his pace.

Polly's already-rapid heartbeat kicked up into at least double-time. She leaned in to look at Essie in the passenger seat and said, "Are you sure this is a good idea?"

"Hey, you know me, I'd never suggest anything half-baked." Essie waved to her to go ahead to talk to Sam. Then she put her hand on the door handle. "If you need me, I'll be here for you."

"Will you?" Polly asked sincerely. "Because it seems

to me you've been mostly somewhere else, Essie. Always ahead of me. Always putting in a few more hours of work to stay ahead of everyone."

"If you felt that way…" Essie caught herself. "Why am I saying 'if'?"

Essie's eyes met Polly's. "I know I've bought into the whole 'do more, be more' attitude of Mom and Dad. And I know what it did to you, Polly."

"If it helps, in watching Sam and his girls, I'm beginning to see what it did to *you*, too, Essie."

"I guess we both need to deal with the pressures of our past, huh? That's what you were doing by becoming a teacher and moving here. I can't tell you how much I admire you for it."

"Really?" Tears welled in Polly's eyes. "For once, maybe you could follow my lead."

"I'll take that under consideration."

On the drive out here they had had a long-overdue heart-to-heart where Polly unloaded her feelings of never measuring up. Essie had laughed at that, not to be dismissive but because she had always felt that Polly was the one who had everything figured out, not bowing to their parents' need to push the family so hard as evidence the divorce hadn't left lasting scars.

Their parents had meant well; they wanted to make the best out of a lousy situation, the twins had concluded. Just as Sam was trying to do with his girls.

In seeing her own folks as loving and wanting so badly to do the right thing for their children as Sam, even if they didn't go about it in the best way, Polly began to view things differently. That led her straight out to the Goodacre family farmhouse.

"You saw a redheaded girl with her hair in a pony-tail like Juliette's instead of Caroline's pigtails make a mistake and recover from it without causing so much as a stumble." Polly shut the car door and turned to Sam. She kept her tone even, reasoned and, some might say, loving. "Isn't that just what someone might do if they had a handful of gymnastics programs and dance recitals under their belt?"

Sam stopped. He was halfway between the house and Polly's car. "Polly, you're saying you honestly want me to believe my girls...my Sunday school–going, raised-to-know-right-from-wrong girls pulled off this elaborate switch? That they'd lie, in essence, to fool their teachers and cheat me into giving them a dog of their own?"

"I don't think they thought they were lying, Sam." She came to him. There in the quiet of the darkening September sky she moved in until she stood so close that she only had to tip her head back slightly to look up into his kind, searching-for-understanding eyes. "I think...I *know* in my heart...they thought they were *helping* each other and helping *you*."

His brow furrowed. He did not look directly into her gaze. "Helping *me?*"

"Making you happy, Sam." She took a deep breath and held it a second, thought of all the years of keeping her true feelings to herself and what that had cost her, then reached out and slipped her hand in his. "They got a clear message that doing all these things and doing them well—following your rules—was what it would take to make you happy."

"But I made the rules to try to make them happy,"

he said softly. He raised his head and looked into her eyes. "Honest, Polly, that's all I ever wanted."

"That's all you *think* you wanted, Sam. But happy wasn't really your primary concern after Marie died, was it?"

He looked toward the front door, then up at the light shining from the second-story bedroom of the three little girls. At last he looked at Polly, then bowed his head slightly and gave it a slow shake. "No, I wanted to protect them from all the pain I was going through."

"You accused me of running away to a dream that never existed, Sam."

"Polly, I—"

"No, you were right. My own family said pretty much the same thing." Polly held her free hand up, then brought it down to join her other hand on top of his. "They were right and they were wrong. Maybe I did run to an overly romanticized, even imaginary, past, but I arrived in Baconburg, met you and came home."

He looked at her hands around his, then at her.

Her heart rate slowed. Her breathing, which she just realized had been quick and shallow, eased. Looking into Sam's eyes now she knew he hadn't just heard what she'd said, he had listened. She really did feel now that the things she had dreamed of were possible—family, home, even love someday.

Sam's shoulders rose and fell, then he took both her hands in his, turning them over as if studying them to see how she had done this trick of getting right to the heart of the matter. "I don't see how this changes any-thing, Polly. I still want to protect my girls. I still want to teach them the skills I think they need to cope with all that can go wrong in life."

She heard his words, but she had to ask, to clarify his meaning. "And I am something that can go wrong?"

He looked at her and said nothing.

The night seemed to close in around them. The light of the Goodacre home over Sam's shoulders now made it seem distant and unreachable.

"I see." She tried not to burst into tears right there on the spot.

Sam stood there talking about teaching his children his way to deal with the pain of loss. Wasn't that just what she had done coming here? Full speed ahead without looking back? She thought about warning him, once again, that his way did not work for everyone.

It sure hadn't worked for her. So she relied on what worked for her. She turned to leave. "I hope I *am* wrong, Sam, about the girls and the switcheroo."

"Polly, I didn't mean for things to turn out like this," he called after her."

"Neither did I." She reached her car.

"I'm sure I'll see you around," he said, as if a neighborly shout-out would somehow move them quickly and smoothly into the next phase of their relationship. "It's a small town, after all."

She turned and looked at him standing there framed by his home, his life still every bit intact as it was the day they met. She made a mental photo, one more moment frozen in time of someone who would no longer be in her life. "It could be a whole city of strangers, Sam, the way I feel right now."

He stepped toward her.

She shook her head to tell him not to bother. He didn't want her to interfere in his life or the lives of his children unless she did things his way. Trying to make the man happy was a waste of time. He didn't want to be happy. He wanted to be in control.

There were some things she couldn't fix, couldn't teach and now, couldn't run away from. If that was the only lesson she learned from all of this, Polly decided that would be enough for a long time to come.

Three little girls with red hair in curls.

Sam peeked in to see the triplets all sitting on the same bed, talking with their heads pressed together.

He tapped on the doorframe before he stepped across the threshold of the open door. "Prayer time, girls?"

They scrambled to their own beds and knelt beside them.

Sam's stomach knotted. He didn't want to think his children could have played this trick on him and the teachers, but even more than that, that they could kneel and say their prayers in front of him knowing they'd done it. It didn't sit right with him. He straightened up. "You know, girls, before we start prayers, maybe we should take a minute to talk."

The three exchanged glances.

"About what?" Hayley, the bold, asked without exactly meeting her dad's eyes.

"Well, for starters, I don't want there ever to be secrets between us." As soon as he said it, Sam wished he hadn't. He thought of Polly, the kiss they had shared. Then of his attempts to get Ted Perry to hand over Donut while still adhering to his no-dogs rule for the girls. "That doesn't count for the things that are just for adults. Things that I'm not ready to share with you."

They definitely looked confused.

Last he thought of the argument he'd had with Polly tonight at the school and her saying she suspected they'd pulled "the old switcheroo." Sam had to know that news of him and Polly clashing was probably already making the rounds. He could just imagine someone in his girls' Sunday school overhearing the story even now.

"But then there are things that happen out in the open, things other people in town might be talking about." He fumbled to find the right way to tell just the part they needed to hear.

All three faces tipped up in unison and at the same angle. In the dim light even their expressions seemed exactly the same. Sam had to concede that under the right circumstances even he could have been duped into believing Juliette was Caroline in the gymnasium this evening.

He crossed to the three desks where the girls usually did their homework, trying to give them time to unburden themselves if they had gotten up to any funny business to cash in on his Parents' Night promise. He leaned in to peer more closely at stacks of paper and extra clippings left over from the collage still hanging in Juliette's classroom. On one hand it did not seem likely that Juliette sat still and cut neatly around each picture pasted onto white foam board. He surveyed the desk with pink pens and stickers and even a small bottle of pink glitter on the corner. On the other hand, he had no proof she didn't.

He turned and some chicken feathers dangling by

bright green yarn tied to a small tree limb smacked him along the side of the face. He turned and blew a wayward feather from in front of his nose. He thought the girls would giggle at him tangled up in Hayley's mobile, but instead they grew strangely quiet.

He thought of the day at the drugstore when the threesome had tried unsuccessfully to fool Polly and how Caroline had cracked and confessed everything so quickly. He'd certainly had the impulse to lay everything out in the open about his words with Polly when he'd seen their faces.

The fact that they didn't say a thing made him think maybe he was right about the girls. They just sat there listening to him, seemingly in no hurry to talk to him about anything, anything at—

"Wait a minute. What's up here?" Sam spun around and once again the chicken feathers went dancing on their green yarn tethers. "I have been in this room three whole minutes and not a one of you has asked when we're getting that dog I promised."

Three worried looks.

"We don't want any dog but Donut, Daddy," Caroline finally said softly. The other girls nodded almost simultaneously.

Sam's heart sank. All this. He had broken his rule, asked his girls to give the proverbial one-hundred-and-ten-percent, gone to Parents' Night and not even taken the time to properly appreciate or even look at their handiwork. And for what?

They didn't want any dog but Donut.

Polly didn't want anything but what was best for his girls.

Sam didn't want anything but for his life to go back to the way it was when he was in charge of it all and nothing held him back.

He groaned and rubbed his eyes, then motioned for the girls to get to their own beds and say their prayers. As they knelt down to begin, Sam slipped into the hallway, not sure he could stand by and hear those three sweet kids ask for God to bless the dog they couldn't have and the woman who thought they would resort to cheating just to please him.

Sam shut his eyes to keep from allowing himself to overthink that. Polly was a good person, a *really* good person. But she did admit she'd re-created the Baconburg of her childhood into something straight out of *The Andy Griffith Show,* starring him as the kindly single dad who needed the loving guidance of the local schoolteacher. She suspected the girls of pulling this prank because it fit with her idea of how things would work out. She'd point out the problem. He'd see the error of his ways and then—

"And if our mommy is near You, tell her it's okay. We have Miss Bennett to help us down here now."

Sam jerked his head around to peer into the darkened room but not soon enough to identify which girl had said that.

Then nothing. Sam had formulated his plan with careful forethought. He had a job to do where the girls were concerned and allowing them to form attachments to a dog and now Polly were big mistakes. But mistakes that could be undone.

He just had to get the girls to really kick things up a notch. Tomorrow he'd call the mom in charge of the

Go-Getters and offer to have the group hold another fundraiser at the Pumpkin Jump and maybe he'd just suggest they'd be welcome to do their square-dance routine, as well.

That's exactly what he'd do—full speed ahead.

Chapter 17

The next two weeks flew by for Polly. Her pupils had settled into the school routine nicely and the other teachers informed her that fall was a crazy-busy time for the small Ohio town that relied heavily on agriculture and tourism to pay the bills through the winter. This left very little time for Polly to sit and pine for Donut or her family. But somehow she still had plenty of time to think about Sam Goodacre.

"It's that hat," Polly told Essie on a late-night phone call while Polly graded test papers over what her students had learned in the first six weeks. "I need to get it back to him."

"Or throw it away," Essie countered. "He doesn't want it."

"Then *he* can throw it away. *I* can't. Not a hat his late

wife gave him." Polly set down her pen and rubbed her eyes. "Maybe I can mail it to him."

Essie laughed.

"Better yet, come up to the Pumpkin Jump on Saturday, pretend to be me and give it to him yourself."

"That sounds more like wanting to *be* right than to do right," Essie used another of their mother's sayings to call out Polly. "It's time to stop hiding in the past, Polly. There are some things you can't fix, but you're living proof that you can start again."

"That's a nice idea, but how can you start again with someone who won't slow down long enough to notice the things around them that they *can* fix?" Polly sighed and said her goodbyes. She started to put the phone down, but as she stretched to put it far enough away that it wouldn't further distract her, the photos on the mantel came into her line of vision.

She picked up the phone again and touched the button to look through her contact list. After only a couple clicks she pulled up the pic she'd taken of Sam, Caroline and Donut on the fire truck. She tried to smile but couldn't quite pull it off.

"I was not wrong about the triplets," she told the man smiling out at her from a moment frozen in time. She pointed at his face, then gave it a poke for emphasis. "I am not hiding in the past. And I am definitely not going to the…"

"Hello? Polly? Are you okay?"

"…Pumpkin Jump," she murmured, realizing she had tapped Sam's name, placing a call to him, when she meant to tap the photo. Her heart stopped.

"You calling about the Pumpkin Jump? At this hour? Polly?"

"Hi, Sam, actually I didn't mean to call at all. Sorry." She moved her thumb to the end-call button.

"It's good to hear your voice."

She curled her hand closed and said softly, "You, too."

"I… What was that about the Pumpkin Jump?"

"I tried to get Essie to come to it, but…"

"She should. You should bring her."

"I wasn't planning to come if she doesn't, Sam, but it was good to hear your voice." She did hang up this time.

Polly thought that was that until the morning of the big event when her doorbell rang.

Even after all this time, Polly still hoped, just a little bit, that she'd find Sam holding Donut on the other side. Instead—

"Essie! You said you couldn't come for the Pumpkin Jump!" Polly threw her arms around her sister.

"I wasn't going to, but I went online to find this…" She thrust out the smoky-brown trilby Polly had admired as perfect for Sam.

Polly gasped and took it in her hands as the two of them came inside.

"And then I had to check out this Pumpkin Jump and lookie what's going on there." She held up a printout that included not just a photo of the pumpkins she and Sam and Caroline had picked out, but also a schedule of events that included a dog-wash fundraiser and a square-dance routine by the Van Buren Elementary Go-Getters.

* * *

Chaos and fun, work and worry, it all came together the morning of the Goodacre Organic Farm's Annual Pumpkin Jump. Sam actually had very little to do with the event, which meant he was the one everyone expected to be available to help them with their part. He didn't mind. He liked being able to move around the edges of the activities; it gave him a chance to see who was there.

"Nobody has seen her," Max muttered as he pushed past Sam carrying a tray piled high with hamburger buns.

Sam opened his mouth to deny he'd been looking for anyone in particular then caught a glimpse of the girls trailing along behind their uncle, each carting her own giant jar of mustard, mayo or ketchup. He grinned at them, so proud to see them pitching in like that. In fact, for the past two weeks, they had pretty much been giving every effort their all and everyone seemed very happy.

The operative word being *seemed.* A dull heaviness lay on his chest. Sam just couldn't believe that after having Polly and Donut in their lives, things could go back to normal so easily. He tried to tell himself that kids were resilient, they bounced back quickly, but if he had ever really trusted in that he would never have had to come up with even his simple set of rules.

"If we see her, we'll tell her you're looking for her," Max called back as he led the girls toward the place where he was about to fire up a huge portable grill.

"Her, who?" Hayley asked, never even looking Sam's way.

"We aren't looking for a 'her.' We're looking for a 'him,'" Juliette announced as she passed.

"Him?" News to Sam. "Him, who?"

"Donut, Daddy." Caroline paused long enough to get a better grip on the plastic jug of mustard in her arms. "The Go-Getters are having another dog wash and the firemen are helping. That means Donut is coming, right?"

Sam felt as if he'd just taken a punch in the gut. "Dog wash? I didn't plan for—"

"There are some things in life you can't plan for, Sam."

"Polly!" Without thinking over the implications, he grabbed her by the shoulders, leaned in and kissed her cheek. "Am I ever glad to see you."

The minute she was in his arms, everything felt right with the world. Or at least as if she could help him make it right.

Polly gave a nervous laugh and pushed at his chest, probably to give herself some breathing room—a stark reminder that no matter how good it felt to see her again, there was still a lot standing between them.

"Did you know about this dog-wash deal?" he asked before she could even get a word out.

She shook her head. "Not until this morning when—"

"And you just came? You weren't going to come, but you did." He grabbed her by the hand and began to walk. "We can still get this under control, but we need to go, and go fast."

"Sam?" She stumbled forward a few steps before she caught up with his pace. "Have you ever stopped to think that just because *you* aren't in control it doesn't mean things are *out of* control?"

"I've missed you, Polly." He glanced back at her and chuckled. "But we don't have time for philosophy. If the girls have Donut taken away again, I don't know what it will do to them."

"You mean what it will do to you." She twisted her arm to free her hand from his, then turned toward the stand where Max and the girls were busy setting up. "Sam, the girls look fine."

"Of course they do. They probably have some wild idea that they will be able to get Donut as the dog I promised them. It's the only dog they wanted." He scanned the field where people were arriving, then the path leading toward the barn where the doors were flung open and a local band was warming up for the performances to come. "Let's see if we can find Gina and find out where this dog wash is going to be set up."

"Or you could just go over to the big yellow fire truck." Polly pointed to an area in the open field where the truck sat surrounded by kids.

"Great." Without hesitation, Sam grabbed her arm and started out again.

"Sam!" More foot-dragging. "Did you listen to yourself? I said the kids are fine. You're trying to fix something that hasn't even happened yet."

"That's my job." He cupped her elbow and kept walking.

This time she dug in her heels and they stayed dug in enough that Sam's hand slipped and she jerked to a stop. He pivoted to face her.

Even standing in the middle of a small crush of people, amid booths being set up, hay bales and pumpkins stacked to direct people to various venues, when Sam looked Polly's way, she was all he could see. And despite all the things whirling around them, she made him smile.

"Your job? Really? I thought Sam's way was to teach the girls that no matter what happened you could just push your way through and get on with life." She folded her arms. "I thought *that* was your job."

"You got me." He held his hands out to his side. "Where Hayley, Juliette and Caroline are concerned, I… Look, Polly, I made this impulsive promise to the girls that they could have a dog if they came through for Parents' Night and the only dog they want is Donut. So if Ted Perry shows up with that dog and leaves with him, it will be like I am the one taking him away from them. I don't think I could stand that."

"Oh, Sam." She put her hand to his cheek. "That is the first time you ever actually said it."

He leaned into her hand. "Said what?"

"The real reason why you have pushed the girls to do things your way. Because you can't stand the idea of their being hurt," she said quietly. "Sam, did you ever consider that this is about your grief, not the girls'?"

Before he'd met Polly, he'd have shot that down in a heartbeat. Now he actually stood there with her hand on his and could hear his own heart pounding in his chest, steady and strong. "I have no idea what to say to that, Polly."

"That's probably the best answer you could have given, Sam." She dropped her hand and laughed.

He opened his mouth to say more, but the sound of

the fire engine's siren reverberated through the air, cutting him off.

Polly jumped forward.

He caught and steadied her by putting both hands on her arms. Their eyes met and they both broke out laughing at being taken by surprise.

"Hey, I…" Max came thundering up on them, stopped hard and leaned back, a stunned expression on his face.

Sam stepped away from Polly. Open as he was to exploring that he hadn't properly grieved for Marie and the life he and the girls had lost, he didn't want his family to get any ideas that he and Polly were suddenly fair matchmaking game.

"Look, Max, I…"

"You…" Max pointed at Polly. "You're…"

"Look, don't read anything into this." Sam waved his hand, and put his back to the fire truck and his plans to head off any potential issues with Donut and Ted Perry. "I just met Polly out here and—"

"And I just met her back there." Max jerked his thumb over his shoulder.

"Your sister?" Sam looked at Polly.

She nodded.

"And you and the girls thought you've been talking to Polly?" he asked Max.

"Well, we haven't talked to her—she was on her cell phone the whole time—but she looks like Polly and sounds like Polly and she…" Max made an overly played wince, then a slow look of realization came over his face. He started to chuckle. "The girls don't know?"

"I didn't tell them." Sam looked at Polly. "I sort of

stopped their talking about you except as Caroline's teacher after…"

"This should be interesting," Max said as he turned and headed back to his booth, motioning for them to follow. "C'mon, I need your help, old man."

Max grabbed Sam by the arm and shoved him into the forefront of the three of them. Sam tried to look back to say something to Polly about how they should tell the girls about her twin but before he could, the triplets came rushing up to him, Juliette in pink, Hayley in green and Caroline…also in pink?

"Dad! Dad! Dad!" they called all together. "Miss Bennett is here, Miss Bennett…"

Hayley pulled up short. Juliette bumped into her back and Caroline into hers.

"Hi, girls!" Polly wriggled her fingers in a wave.

They looked from the real Polly to her twin.

Sam braced himself for them to break out laughing with delight to have learned that their new friend had something more in common with them. But nobody laughed.

Hayley looked at Juliette. Juliette looked at Caroline. Caroline looked at Hayley.

Sam shut his eyes as everything Polly had said to him on the night she suggested the girls had pulled "the old switcheroo" came flooding back to him. He took a deep breath. "You girls don't want to tell me something, do you?"

"We only wanted to make you happy, Daddy." Caroline broke first, running to hug him around the waist.

"You wanted us to do good for Parents' Night so bad that you even said you'd break your rule." Hayley charged in to take up the rest of the story and to join her sister in the death grip of a hug.

"I did the square dance for Caroline and she did the mobile and the collage for Hayley and me." Juliette came flying, arms wide to complete the circle.

Only, for the first time since Marie had died, the circle did not seem complete to Sam.

Sam looked down on those three little redheads and realized there was something—someone—missing.

"How did you know, Daddy?" Hayley tipped her head back to look up and ask.

"I didn't know. Miss Bennett did and I guess you can figure out now how she knew." Sam turned his head to look Polly's way. "I just now put the pieces together when I saw two out of three girls dressed in pink. Makes it easier to trade places last-minute, huh?"

Caroline and Juliette bowed their heads, their way of 'fessing up to the plan.

"I think I had a clue when I saw that Juliette had managed to make a collage and still have a full bottle of pink glitter and that Hayley had a complete mobile hanging in her classroom and a half-finished one hanging above her desk at home."

He looked down at his daughters and his chest ached. What had he done? He had pushed his girls so hard to learn his way of coping that he'd forgotten to share with them things like waiting on the Lord, accepting God's will and trusting that there is a time for every purpose under heaven.

That had to change. He had to slow things down and…

He lifted his eyes to meet Polly's. "I don't suppose you want in on this, do you?"

"Sam, I'm a twin and a teacher, but that hardly qualifies me to talk to your kids about the moral implications of trading places to fool people."

Sam shook his head slowly and extended his hand, making a space within the circle of his arms. "I meant do you want in on this group hug?"

Polly hesitated for a moment. She looked to her sister, who actually lowered her cell phone—she'd been on nonstop talking to her staff in Atlanta—for a moment. Esther nodded to urge Polly to hurry up.

Polly did just that, running with her own arms wide to embrace the man and the family she had waited so long to find.

Sam pressed his cheek to her soft but wild hair and drew her close. The girls entwined them both in a tangle of small arms, red hair and a million joyous giggles. In that moment Sam knew that his time for grieving had come to an end.

He laughed softly, then tipped his head back and looked at the sky. He groaned. "I suppose I looked like a real fool to you, Polly. Barreling through life like that, not even taking the time to see what the girls had gotten up to."

"No." She stepped back and took a minute to look at Hayley, then Juliette, then Caroline. "You look like a father who wants what's best for his daughters, but couldn't quite figure out what that was on his own."

"Maybe the problem is that I shouldn't be on my own?" He took her hand and guided her free of the cluster of kids, grinning.

"Don't you have a rule about that?" She smiled back at him.

"Hey, I make the rules." He got her far enough away that he could give her a spin and put them face-to-face again. "So if I finally get smart enough to change the rules, then wouldn't you say—"

"Sam?" She pressed two fingers to his lips.

"What?" he asked when she lowered her hand from his mouth.

"Stop while you're ahead and just kiss me," she murmured.

"I can do that." And he did. He pulled her deep into his embrace and kissed her.

The girls squealed with delight.

The crowd cheered.

The fire-engine siren wailed.

And out of nowhere a little golden-brown dog with floppy ears, short legs and a long, low body came bounding toward them.

"Donut!" The triplets ran for him.

The dog began to jump and bark and wag his tail and loll his tongue as if he wasn't sure which kid to start licking hello first.

Polly didn't know where to look. The dog. The girls. Essie. Sam.

Sam won out simply because she wanted to take her cue from him. She was so happy about having shared this moment with him, but she understood more than anyone Sam's fear of how much losing Donut again would hurt the girls. It was killing her not to run and hug the little guy.

"Hey, Donut."

"Oh, Donut."

"We love you, too, Donut."

"Grover! Grover! Come back here!" Ted Perry came pounding through the crowd, his face red and the chain leash in his fist banging against his legs. When he saw the girls hanging all over the wriggling pup, he stopped in his tracks.

"See?" Angela Bodine, the lady firefighter, came up behind him. "I told you! *That* is a kids' dog."

"He's *these* kids' dog!" Caroline announced, looking up at the pair who were now walking toward the opening in the crowd where the redheaded triplets and little golden-brown dog were all over each other.

"I know. He cries all the time and tries to push his way out the door whenever I open it." Ted sighed and shook his head. "Maybe I shoulda got a cat."

Angela's eyes brightened. "I love cats."

Ted jerked his head up. He looked at Sam, then Polly.

"I think I know where you could have your pick of a litter," Sam told him. "Don't suppose you'd want to make a trade?"

Ted opened his mouth as if he was going to say no, then he caught Angela practically bouncing out of her boots.

Ted grinned, swung his gaze around to meet Sam's and stuck his hand out to give Sam the leash and shake his hand. "You got a deal, man."

"That's *old* man, if you don't mind." Max slapped Sam hard on the back.

"He didn't look so old when he was kissing the schoolteacher a minute ago," Angela observed, then added, "You said something about kittens?"

"In the barn," Max directed her absently, then looked

up, saw her and offered her his arm. "I'd be happy to show you."

Ted stepped in between the charmer in sandals and a barbecue apron, and the lady firefighter. "I think we can find it on our own."

Max threw up his hands. "Is every single lady in this town already attached to someone else?"

"Not *every* one." Polly dipped her head toward Essie coming across the open space. She could see by the box in her sister's hand that Esther had gone to the car to retrieve the hat Polly had picked out online long before she ever really believed she'd be standing here with Sam's arm around her.

"Well, well, well." Max rubbed his palms together. "Hello, pretty lady. Can I help you with that?"

"I don't need help with this. Just hand it to my sister." She pushed the box into his chest. "Then follow me back over to that grill area. Because you are in need of some serious help if you plan to cook actual food, mister."

"I like her," Max said as he handed Polly the box. "Can I keep her?"

Sam and Polly laughed and watched Max trying to corral Essie, who had already taken charge of the situation.

"Can we take Donut into the house and show him his new home, Daddy?" Caroline asked before she turned to Polly and added, "That is, if you aren't going to take him home with you, Miss Bennett."

Polly went all gooey at Caroline's thoughtfulness. "Angela was right, sweetie. Donut will be happiest with kids around. I'd love for him to stay with you, as long as I can visit sometimes."

"Anytime!" Hayley yelled to speak for the triplets and her whole family.

The other girls leaped up. They all called for Donut and began to run through the crowd toward the house.

"I really am glad Donut is going to have a home with you and the girls." Polly hugged the hatbox close, not exactly sure what to do next.

He'd said he was ready to change his rules and did just that by letting the girls have Donut. But what did that mean for her?

The fire-engine siren sounded again. This time followed by a blare of microphone feedback, a fumble broadcast over a loudspeaker and then Gina's voice. "I'd like to welcome you all to the Goodacre Organic Farm's Annual Pumpkin Jump."

She listed all the events, booths and performances as people gathered in a semicircle around her, listening. "And at last the time has come to open the main event of the day, the thing that this fest is named for—the big pumpkin jump on the main lawn!"

A cheer went up from the group. The girls, after leaving Donut safely in the house, rejoined Polly and Sam standing to the side. Max and Essie had wandered over from his burger fry booth, leaving a volunteer in charge.

"Are you going to jump this year, Daddy?" Hayley prodded.

"I, um, don't you girls think that's kind of embarrassing behavior for the local pharmacist?" Sam bent down to ask them eye to eye.

"You're asking me?" Caroline stuck her thumb in her chest. "I'm going to have to do that square dance!"

Sam gave the three of them a stern look. "Yes, you

are. And we'll talk about the punishment for pulling the old switcheroo later."

"Yes, Daddy." They looked properly chastised for maybe three whole seconds before their faces brightened and they asked again, "Are you going to jump, Daddy?"

He turned to Polly. "Actually, I'd love to jump…if Polly is willing to take the leap with me."

Polly's heart raced. "You mean, into the leaves, right?"

"I was thinking more of…into the future." He took her free hand in his, then reached for the hatbox. "Can I set this aside?"

"Actually, you can set it on your head, if you want. That's not being flip, it's just…well, look inside the box." She bit her lower lip.

The girls gathered around.

He lifted off the lid, looked inside and grinned. He pulled out the vintage-style hat and put it on his head. The perfect fit.

"You look handsome, Daddy," Caroline said.

Polly couldn't have agreed more. There with the autumn leaves tumbling around them, the sights and sounds of Sam's family's home in full-on local celebration, he looked perfect.

"I like it!" Hayley cried.

"I like it a whole lot better than that awful cowboy hat." Juliette crinkled up her nose.

"Me, too." Sam laughed as he tugged the hat to put it at an angle over one eye. "I never did like that cowboy hat. How's that?"

"It's you! I got it for you to replace the… Wait!"

What Sam had said just sank in. All these weeks she had worried and mulled over the meaning of what she had done to that hat and how Sam had reacted to it. "You never liked that cowboy hat?"

"You did me a favor by not stopping Donut from grabbing it. It was the start of all this." He tossed the hatbox aside and opened his arms wide. "Marie gave it to me as a gentle reminder to not become like the rancher dad in her *No, No, Donut* story."

"You mean the man who chased the little dog away and thought the dog could never learn?" Polly laughed.

"The man who had forgotten the power of God's grace and the healing power of faith and forgiveness." He came toward her, his arms still open.

"I don't think that sounds like you at all, Sam." She came into his arms again. "Maybe at one time. But now?"

"Now is what matters." He closed his arms around her. "The past is out of our control and the future is in God's hands. So what do you say, Polly Bennett? You going to take the leap? Are you going to marry me?"

"Yes," she murmured as he pulled her close and kissed her in the way she had longed to be kissed ever since she saw him.

Polly wrapped her arms around him and kissed him right back. Kissed him with all the joy and confidence she had been missing for so long.

For the first time since this whole adventure began, Polly believed she had found everything she had been searching for since her own family began to unravel all those years ago. She had found the insight to forgive her parents their shortcomings. To reevaluate her relationship with her twin sister and to follow her own dreams to make herself feel productive and fulfilled. And she had found Sam.

"Marry?" Essie's voice drew Polly back to the present. "After only knowing each other a couple of months? Isn't that rushing things?"

Polly pulled away and looked up at Sam sheepishly. "Small towns, huh? People who are always there for you are also always there whether you want them to be or not."

"Do you mind?" he asked.

"I love it," she whispered. "And I love you, Sam Goodacre."

"I love you, too, Polly. Now, hold on to your hat... or rather, *my* hat." He thrust it out in the direction of Essie and Max.

They both reached for it and their hands touched. Suddenly neither of them seemed to have anything more to say.

Sam took Polly by the hand. "Let's do this!"

They made the run without reservations and leaped without fear. Seconds after they hit the leaf pile and came up in a shower of red and yellow and orange and pale green leaves, three little red-haired girls joined them. Polly's heart was fuller than she'd ever thought a human heart could be, and as she threw her arms around her future husband and daughters, she sent up a prayer of thanks.

* * * * *

Margaret Daley, an award-winning author of ninety books (five million sold worldwide), has been married for over forty years and is a firm believer in romance and love. When she isn't traveling, she's writing love stories, often with a suspense thread, and corralling her three cats, who think they rule her household. To find out more about Margaret, visit her website at margaretdaley.com.

Books by Margaret Daley

Love Inspired Suspense

Lone Star Justice

High-Risk Reunion
Lone Star Christmas Rescue
Texas Ranger Showdown
Texas Baby Pursuit
Lone Star Christmas Witness
Lone Star Standoff

Alaskan Search and Rescue

The Yuletide Rescue
To Save Her Child
The Protector's Mission
Standoff at Christmas

Visit the Author Profile page
at Harlequin.com for more titles.

THE NANNY'S NEW FAMILY

Margaret Daley

To all people who work with service dogs

For if you forgive men their trespasses,
your heavenly Father will also forgive you.
—*Matthew* 6:14

Chapter 1

Dr. Ian McGregor sank into a chair at his kitchen table, exhausted after wrestling with Joshua to take a much-needed nap. With his elbows on the oak surface still cluttered with the lunch dishes, Ian closed his eyes and buried his face in his hands, massaging his fingertips into his pounding temples. How did Aunt Louise handle Joshua when his youngest was dead tired yet fighting to stay awake?

With a lot of practice, no doubt. Something he lacked. Ian glanced at the clock on the wall and shot to his feet. The next candidate for nanny, one who had come highly recommended, would be here in ten minutes. He had high hopes she would work out because no one else had since Aunt Louise had passed away six months ago. Ian missed his aunt's bright, cheerful smile and all the love she'd had for his family.

Locking away his sorrow, Ian looked at the chaos around him and noted he now had nine minutes. He snatched up all the dirty dishes and crammed them into the dishwasher, leftover food and all. Then after wiping down the counters, he stuffed all of his four-year-old son's toys and the clothes he'd dragged out into the utility room off the kitchen and slammed the door closed.

Two minutes to spare. He wanted to be outside before Annie Knight rang the doorbell. He didn't want Joshua scaring her away if he woke up from his nap, especially without the rest he needed.

Lord, please let this one work out. On paper she looks great. We need her.

He'd turned to God so many times in the two years since his wife had passed away. There had to be an answer to his most recent problem somewhere.

As Ian made his way toward the foyer, the doorbell chimes pealed through the house. He sighed, realizing that he should have foreseen, after the day he'd had so far, that Annie Knight would arrive early. He rushed across the foyer and swung the door open before she rang it again.

The woman greeted Ian with a bright, wide smile, and he looked at it for a few seconds before he lifted his eyes to take in the rest of her... His mouth began to drop open. He quickly snapped it closed and stared at the *young* lady, probably no more than eighteen, standing on his porch. She couldn't be Annie Knight. That nanny had worked for six years, the past three years for a doctor he knew. She had graduated from college with a double major in psychology and child development.

Ian craned his neck, peering around the woman

with thick shoulder-length blond hair and the biggest brown eyes he'd ever seen. Maybe she'd come with Annie Knight. But no one else was there. "Yes, may I help you?"

"Are you Dr. Ian McGregor?"

He nodded, surprised by her deep voice.

"I'm Annie Knight. Am I too early for the interview?"

"No, right on time," Ian finally answered as he frantically thought back to reading her résumé. She'd graduated from high school ten years ago, which should make her around twenty-eight, twenty-nine. "Come in." He stepped to the side to allow her to enter his house.

As Annie passed him in the entrance, he caught a whiff of…vanilla, and he thought immediately of the sugar cookies Aunt Louise used to bake. The young woman paused in the foyer and slowly rotated toward him, waiting.

Ian waved his arm toward the right. "Let's go in there."

He followed her into the formal living room that he rarely used. As she took a seat in a navy blue wingback, Ian sat on the beige couch across from her. The large chair seemed to swallow her petite frame. She couldn't be any taller than five-one. His eldest son would surpass her in height in another year or so.

Ian cleared his throat. "I'm glad you could meet me here. My youngest son, Joshua, didn't go to school today. He's been sick the past two days but is fever-free as of this morning."

"How old is he?"

"Four. He's in the preschool program at Will Rogers Elementary."

"Dr. Hansen told me you had four children. How old are they?"

"Jade and Jasmine are eight-year-old twins and Jeremy is nine, soon to be ten, as he has informed the whole world. I'm sure Tom told you that I need a nanny as soon as possible. My aunt who helped me with the children passed away six months ago and since then, I haven't found anyone who fits my family."

Annie Knight tilted her head to the side. "What has been the problem?"

All the good nannies have jobs. My family can be difficult. My children—and I—are shell-shocked after losing two important people we've loved in the past two years. Ian could have said all of that, but instead he replied, "The first nanny stole from me, and the second woman was too old to keep up with my children—her words, not mine, but she was right. Then the third one decided to up and quit without notice and left my kids here alone while I was in surgery. That was last week." And the seven days since then had not been ones he would like to repeat. Ian had had to rearrange several operations he'd scheduled and change appointments.

Annie frowned. "That's so unprofessional."

"Tom is moving at the end of this week. I know he wanted you to go with the family to New York. May I ask why you didn't?"

"My family is here in Cimarron City, and a big city like New York doesn't appeal to me. Besides, his two eldest are teenagers and don't need a nanny. His youngest will be twelve soon. Dr. Hansen will be able to hire a good housekeeper."

Ian watched her as she talked and gestured. Warmth radiated from the woman across from him. Her face was full of expression, and when she smiled, dimples appeared on her cheeks. She had nice, high cheekbones. Her hair curled under and covered part of her face, which wasn't unpleasant but not what most people would consider beautiful. As a plastic surgeon he was always drawn to how a person looked, but from experience he knew the importance of what lay beneath.

"Tom told me he hated losing you." Why didn't she use her college degree? Why did she choose to be a nanny? Ian decided to tell her everything so she would know what she would be up against. He heaved a composing breath. "Four children can be a handful."

"I loved working with Dr. Hansen's three children. We fell into a good routine. One more child shouldn't be a problem. I grew up in a large family—four brothers and two sisters. I'm used to a full house."

"I want to be blunt with you because I don't want you to decide to leave after a few days. My children need stability. There have been too many changes in their lives lately. Their mother died two years ago, then my aunt. Joshua is—" he searched for the right word to describe his youngest "—adventurous. He'll try anything once. He's fearless."

"Which could get him in trouble. My younger brother was like that. Actually, still is. He certainly tested my mother's patience."

"Jade and Jasmine desperately need a woman's touch. They can be adorable, but if they don't like you they will pull pranks on you. I suspect the reason the last nanny left was because of them, but I couldn't get the truth out of any of my kids."

"Are the twins tomboys?"

"Jade is, but Jasmine is totally the opposite. That's the way you can tell them apart, because they do look exactly alike." Ian stared at a place over her left shoulder while trying to decide how to explain his eldest son. "And Jeremy is angry. That his mother died. That Aunt Louise did, too. That I have to work to make a living. That the sky is blue. It's sunny. It's rainy."

There—he'd laid it all out for Annie. If she stayed he would be surprised, but he didn't want another nanny starting then leaving right away.

"I've worked with kids like that. They haven't moved through the anger stage of grief. When my mother died, I got stuck in that stage."

Ian studied Annie's calm features, and for a few seconds he felt wrapped in that serenity. She seemed to know how to put people at ease. "He went to a children's counselor, but little was accomplished. Frankly, I don't know what to do next." The second he said that he wanted to snatch it back. He was Jeremy's dad. He should know what to do, shouldn't he? "I've reduced my hours at the clinic to be around more, but all Jeremy and I do is butt heads."

A light danced in the young woman's eyes. She leaned forward, clasping her hands and resting her elbows on the arms of the chair. "There will be a period of adjustment with any new nanny, but I don't run from problems. I like challenges. They make me dig in. They make life interesting."

Ian would be trusting Annie with his children, so he needed to trust her with all the background on his eldest child. "I should warn you, Jeremy is also having trouble at school. He never talks about his mom like Jade and Jasmine do. They are always asking me to tell them stories about Zoe and me. Whenever they start talking about her, Jeremy leaves the room—or rather, stomps away. I'm at my wits' end." For three months he'd been thinking that, but now he'd spoken it out loud to another person. The very act made some of his stress dissolve.

"Counseling is good, but sometimes you need to be with a child outside an office to understand what's really going on. I'll do my best to help Jeremy."

When Annie said those words, Ian felt hope for the first time in a while.

"I've checked your references, and they are excellent. I know how picky Tom is, and he never would have recommended you if you weren't good. Do you have any questions about the job?"

Annie sat back again, scanning the living room. "What are my duties?"

"I have a cleaning lady who comes in three times a week, but in between there may be light cleaning. I love to cook, but there will be times when I'm held up at the clinic. Tom told me you are a good cook."

"I like to when I get a chance."

"The kids will be out of school for the summer in six weeks. The older ones have some activities you'll need to drive them back and forth to, but Joshua doesn't yet."

"In other words, he'll need to be watched closely," she said with a chuckle.

"Yes. One time he managed to climb to the top of the bookcase then couldn't get down."

"Where will I be living?"

"I have an apartment over the garage you can use. We have a breezeway that connects the garage to the house. You'll have your own place but be close if needed quickly. Will that be all right?"

"That will work perfectly. I'll need Sundays off unless you have a medical emergency, and I'll take off the other time according to the children's schedules."

"That's fine with me. I'll supply health insurance and a place to live. Your starting salary will be five hundred a week on top of your benefits. After three months we can discuss a raise. Is that all right with you?"

"Yes."

"When can you start?"

"Monday. I'll move in on Sunday. I'll have my family help me."

Only four days away. "Great. Will you share Sunday-night dinner with us so I can introduce you to the children? I'm cooking."

"I think that will be a good way for me to meet them. A school day is always hectic with everyone trying to get where they need to be."

"I have a Ford Explorer you'll use to drive the children. It'll be at your disposal at all times." Ian rose. "Let me give you a tour of my house, then the apartment, before you leave. I'm afraid it was a mess from the last nanny. The guy remodeling it will be through in a couple of days. We'll only be able to peek inside because he's refinishing the wooden floors today."

"Will I get to meet Joshua before I leave?"

"Probably. When he takes a nap, it's usually only an hour or so."

Annie pushed to her feet, looking around. "I imagine you don't use this room much, or your children are neater than most."

"They don't come in here often. The cleaning lady comes every Monday, Wednesday and Friday morning. She has her own key, so she'll let herself in."

"That's good. If I have to do any shopping that'll be the time to do it. Do you want me to go to the grocery store for you?"

"Yes. I understand you did that for Tom and his wife."

Annie nodded as she followed Ian into the dining room. "If you plan some meals, you can add what you need to my list. With such a large family, I'll probably have to go twice a week."

When Ian walked into the kitchen, he swept his arm wide. "Right before you came, this place was a disaster." He crossed to the dishwasher and opened it. "I'll have to empty this and refill it properly after you leave."

She laughed, a light musical sound that filled the room.

Ian went to the utility room and swung open the door. "This is where I stuck all the mess I couldn't take care of. I didn't want to scare you away."

"Then, why are you showing me now?"

He smiled. "Because I believed you when you said you like a challenge."

"I don't scare easily." Annie chuckled.

"Good. The nanny who stole from me used to hide the mess rather than pick up. Sadly, I copied that method." Ian gestured toward a door at the other end of the utility room. "That leads to the short breezeway and garage."

The next place Ian showed her was the huge den. "This is where the family hangs out the most." He indicated the room full of comfortable navy-blue-and-tan couches, a game table, a big-screen TV and several plush chairs with ottomans.

"I can see kids relaxing and enjoying themselves in here."

"The only other room downstairs is my home office." Ian pointed to the closed door across from the den then headed for the staircase. "On the second floor I have six bedrooms. I had the first nanny staying in Aunt Louise's room, but my kids got upset. I quickly renovated the area over the garage, but she was fired before she had a chance to move into the apartment."

"Those women give the nannies of this world a bad name. The ones I've gotten to know love children and go above and beyond."

At the last room at the end of the hallway, Ian stopped and gestured. "This is Joshua's bedroom. I'm surprised he isn't up, but he's been getting over a virus or—" He eased open the door to find his son drawing on the wall.

After church on Sunday, Annie joined her large family at her twin sister Amanda's house for the noon meal. When not working, Annie spent a lot of time with her twin. Annie had been thrilled when Amanda had married Ben last year. Amanda would be a great mother, and Annie knew her sister wanted children.

The day was gorgeous with the temperature around

seventy degrees and not a cloud in the sky. Annie made her way around back where her father stood talking with Ben at the grills, flipping hamburgers. With his thinning blond hair and the deep laugh lines crinkling at the corners of his brown eyes, Dad was no doubt telling her brother-in-law another Amanda and Annie escapade from childhood.

The scent of ground beef saturated the air and Annie's stomach rumbled. She scanned the yard, enjoying the sound of merriment from the children playing on the elaborate swing set. Her twin might not have children yet, but she spoiled her nieces and nephews.

"Ah, it's about time you arrived," Amanda said as she put a Band-Aid on the youngest child's knee. "We're almost ready to eat. What took you so long?" She rose as her nephew ran back to play with the others.

"I went back to the house to say goodbye to the Hansen family. The moving van will come tomorrow. They were heading to the airport when I left."

"Aren't we supposed to help you move later today?" Her dad laid the spatula on the plate for the burgers and turned toward her. "Is everything boxed up?"

Annie nodded. "Ben and Charlie's trucks should be enough for the small pieces of furniture I have. After we empty my suite of rooms at the Hansen house, I'll lock up and we'll go to Dr. McGregor's. Then the hard work starts. There are stairs on the side of the garage that we'll have to climb with all the boxes."

Her youngest brother, twenty-year-old Charlie, came out of the house and clapped her on the back. "Remember, you promised me my favorite pie for helping. I've been thinking about that for days." He rubbed his stomach in a circular motion.

"I'll bake you an apple pie this week."

Charlie's dark eyebrows shot straight up. "Apple? Bah! Double-chocolate fudge is the only one I'll accept." Then he said to Ben, "I've been sent to find out when we're going to eat."

Ben pressed the spatula down on each patty. "One minute, so get the kids to wash up inside."

As Charlie corralled the children and headed for the house with them, her dad chuckled. "Get ready for the onslaught."

Annie stood back with Amanda as ten children from the ages of three to fourteen invaded the deck, all talking at the same time. The other day Dr. McGregor had wondered if she could handle looking out for four children, but Annie was usually the one assigned to keep her nieces and nephews in line or make sure the older ones kept an eye on the younger ones because Annie enjoyed helping with them.

Her gaze drifted to Amanda, an exact replica of Annie, although her twin usually wore her long blond hair pulled up in a ponytail. She doubted there was anything Jade and Jasmine could pull that she and Amanda hadn't tried years ago. They had never fooled her parents, but they had confused a couple of their teachers when they exchanged places in each other's classes. Now they went out of their way to be different.

Annie herded the kids into a line so they could fill their plates with hamburgers, coleslaw and fruit salad while Amanda and Samantha, who was married to her eldest brother, Ken, helped the two youngest children with their food.

As Annie's nieces and nephews sat at their table, she arranged older ones to be near younger ones. "Let's pray. Carey, do you want to say the prayer?"

"Yes," her ten-year-old niece said, then bowed her head. "Bless this food and, Lord, please don't let it rain tomorrow on my soccer game."

When the children dug into their meal, Annie went to make a plate for herself. As she dished up an extra helping of coleslaw, she glanced at the lettuce for the burger. The green reminded her of the color of Dr. McGregor's eyes, except his had a sparkle in their depths, especially toward the end of their conversation about his kids. She'd felt his relief that he'd told her everything about them and she hadn't declined the job. He didn't understand—instead of frightening her off, he'd intrigued her. Annie had decided years ago to help children in need, and Jeremy needed her whether he knew it or not. The Hansens' middle daughter had, too, at one time, but now she was fourteen and growing up to be a mature young lady.

"You haven't told me much about your new position," Amanda said when she joined Annie at the end of the food line. "What's your boss like?"

"He seems a little overwhelmed at the moment."

"Four children will do that."

"More than that. He lost his wife and then his aunt, who was assisting him with the kids. All in two years' time."

Amanda gave her a long, assessing look. "Sounds as though you want to do more than help the children."

"Any kind of loss can be hard to get over. I don't think Dr. McGregor's even had time to think about either his wife or aunt. He's had his hands full."

"You got all of that from an hour interview?"

Annie started for the adult table. "Well, not exactly. I asked Tom and his wife about him. I have a nurse friend at the hospital where he does surgery. She told me some things, too."

One perfectly arched eyebrow rose. "It sounds as though you also checked his references."

"I could be working for him for quite a while—his youngest is four years old. I discovered that his colleagues respect him as a surgeon, but what I particularly like about him is that he spends some of his time at a free clinic for children, fixing things like cleft palates. Tom told me Dr. McGregor has had to reduce his regular work time because of his trouble with the nannies, but he didn't decrease his hours at the free clinic."

Seated at the table, Amanda leaned close to Annie. "So he's a plastic surgeon. Maybe you should talk to him about your situation."

Annie gripped her fork and whispered, "No. I was told there's nothing else that can be done."

"That was fourteen years ago. Methods are bound to be better now."

"I don't have the money. The last operation nearly cost Dad his house. I can't do that again. I'll live with the scars. I have for over fourteen years. Besides, the fire wouldn't have happened if I hadn't left the candle burning when I went to sleep."

Tears filled Annie's eyes. She'd forgotten about the

candle that day at the cabin because she'd been too busy moping and missing her boyfriend.

The memory of that day when she had been fifteen and the family had been staying at their grandparents' cabin on Grand Lake inundated her with feelings of regret. The fire that had destroyed the vacation home had also nearly killed her when a burning beam had pinned her down. Part of her body was burned. The pain swallowed her into a huge dark hole that had taken a year to crawl out of. But the worst part was her mother had never made it out of the cabin. Her dad had managed to get to Annie, but when he'd tried to go back in, the building had been engulfed in flames.

"You have four brothers and two sisters who can help you with the money. We all have jobs. Even Charlie works, and he's still in college."

"He has to pay for his classes. And each of you has a family to support and your own expenses. Amanda, let this go before I get up and leave."

Amanda harrumphed. "You're stubborn."

"So are you. Remember, I know you better than anyone, probably even Ben."

Amanda narrowed her brown eyes. "And the same goes for me. Annie, it was an accident. The family doesn't blame you for Mom's death. You need to forgive yourself and let the past go or you'll never have the life the Lord wants for you. When are you going to figure that out?" Her twin raised her voice above a whisper.

"Annie, what do you need to figure out?" her father asked from the other side of the table.

"Nothing, Dad. Amanda and I are just arguing."

"What's new?" Ken, her older brother who sat across

from Annie, picked up his hamburger to take a bite. "Ouch! Which one of you kicked me?"

The twins pointed at each other.

Emotions clashed inside Annie when she turned into the McGregors' driveway and drove to the large white stone house set back from the road on the outskirts of Cimarron City, Oklahoma. She was excited for a new opportunity to help children in need, but it had been several years since she'd been challenged with a grieving child. The Hansen kids' drama had been normal teenager or preteen stuff for quite some time. What if she'd lost her touch?

Annie glanced in her rearview mirror and saw her brothers' vehicles at the entrance of the driveway. Parking in front of a three-car garage, she inhaled a deep breath, then climbed from her red Honda, hefted a large box with her pots and pans from the backseat and headed toward the stairs on the side. Dr. McGregor had told her yesterday he would leave the apartment unlocked.

She carefully started her climb up the steps, her view partially blocked by the carton. A giggle from above drifted to her. She lowered the box and gasped.

Grinning at her, Joshua stood on top of the upstairs railing wearing a red cape that flapped in the breeze.

"I have special powers. I can fly." The four-year-old spread his arms wide as though he was going to demonstrate.

"Don't!" Annie shouted as Joshua wobbled.

Chapter 2

I shouldn't have shouted. Annie sucked in a breath.

Joshua regained his balance.

Heart thumping, Annie dropped the box on the stairs, jumped over the cardboard box and scrambled up the steps. "Joshua, it's great to see you again," she said in the calmest voice she could muster. "I sure could use a big, strong superhero like you to help me bring my stuff upstairs. How about it?"

By the time she reached the landing, the four-year-old had turned his body so he could see her better, but the motion caused him to wobble again on the six-inch-wide railing. He flapped his arms to catch his balance. This time, Annie lunged toward him as an ear-piercing scream from below split the air.

She grasped his ankle as the little boy fell backward and held his leg with both hands. Annie leaned over the railing as she heard footsteps behind her and the wailing sound still coming from the bottom of the stairs. While Joshua dangled two stories above the ground, someone pounded up the steps.

Muscular arms came around her and gripped Joshua. "I've got him. Let him go, and I'll bring him up."

Relief washed over her as she released her fingers. Annie dropped down between Dr. McGregor's arms and moved to the side so he could hoist his son up to the landing. While she watched, she took deep, fortifying breaths to calm her racing heartbeat.

Giggling, Joshua hugged his dad. "That was fun. Can I do it again?"

"No." Thunder descended over Dr. McGregor's features as he put down his son and glanced at Annie. "Thanks. One second he was playing in the den and the next he was gone. I figured he'd come out here since I told him to give you and your family time to unload your possessions." He picked up Joshua and held him tight as though afraid the child would somehow wiggle free and try again to fly from the railing. "Young man, you and I are going to have a talk in the house about following directions."

"But, Dad, I wanna help Annie. That's why I'm here wearing my cape."

The first time Joshua had seen her when he had awakened from his nap a few days ago, he'd called her Annie, which was fine with her, but Dr. Hansen and his wife had insisted on "Miss Annie" when she'd worked for them. She was quickly sensing the McGregors' household was much more laid back.

Her employer started down the stairs. "I'll return in a while, Annie. And by the way, you can call me Ian."

As her brothers mounted the steps with boxes, including the one she'd dropped, and furniture, she watched Ian and Joshua exchange a few words with Ken and Charlie, then disappear around the corner followed by a little girl, who had to have been the one who'd screamed.

"That one is going to be a handful." Ken waited for her to open the door. "Reminds me of someone I know." Her eldest brother looked pointedly at Charlie, who was bigger and more muscular than Ken.

"I grew out of wanting to be a daredevil." Her youngest sibling poked Ken in the back with two cartons he held.

"Boys, let's try to be good role models for the McGregor children." Annie trailed them into her new apartment. "And, Charlie, the only reason you quit, no doubt temporarily, was because you broke an arm and leg performing that death-defying skateboard trick."

The bantering between her brothers continued as they brought up all the boxes and furniture from the three vehicles while Annie tried to decide which boxes to open first and where to put the ones she wouldn't have time to empty today. Annie paused to look at her first real apartment. When she'd gone to college, she'd lived at home to save money, then she'd moved into the homes of her employers after that.

Excitement bubbled to the surface as she walked to a door and discovered her bedroom with a double bed, a chest of drawers and one nightstand. Her grandmother's cushioned chair would look good in here. She checked the closet and smiled when she found it was a walk-in with plenty of storage space.

Then Annie moved on to the only other door and went into the bathroom, a pale-green-and-ivory color scheme. It had a tub with a showerhead, so she had a choice. She liked that because sometimes a hot bath worked the kinks out of her body on a particularly active day, and with Joshua she'd probably have a lot of them. She wouldn't have to exercise much with him around if that stunt was any indication.

When she went back into the main room with a living area at one end and a dining table with four chairs and a small kitchenette taking up the other half, her brothers stood in the middle of the stack of boxes, arguing.

Annie put two fingers in her mouth and gave a loud whistle. They stopped and stared at her. "Are you all through bringing up my belongings?"

"Yes. We were just waiting to see if you want us to do anything else. We were discussing the merits of our favorite basketball teams and as usual our little brother has it wrong. The Thunder *will* win the NBA championship. If you're from Oklahoma, you have to root for them." Ken shot Charlie a piercing look.

Annie needed a few minutes of peace before she was introduced to the rest of Ian's children, especially after that incident with Joshua. "I think I can handle this. Thank you for your help." She grinned. "Try not to hurt each other on the way down the stairs."

When they left, Annie sat on the tan couch and laid her head against the cushion. Quiet. Tranquil. She'd better cherish this moment because tomorrow she officially started her new job. The memory of Joshua standing on the railing revved her heartbeat again. Then she remembered Ian leaning over her and clasping his son. Remembering the brush of his arms against her gave her goose bumps.

Ian was strong. Capable. Caring.

Annie quickly shook the image from her thoughts. They were employer/employee, and that was the way it would stay. She remembered the scars on her body, a constant reminder of the tragedy that had taken her mother away.

If only I could relive...

But there were no do-overs. She had to live with what was left. She was damaged goods.

A knock at the door roused her from her thoughts. Annie pushed off the couch and weaved her way through the stacked boxes to the entrance. Maybe having quiet time wasn't the answer right now. When she let Ian inside, she spied a very contrite child trudging behind his father. Head down, Joshua chewed on his thumbnail.

She wanted to scoop the adorable little boy into her arms and tell him everything was okay, but she wouldn't. Ian's stern expression spoke volumes about a serious talk with his son, and rightly so. But he was so cute with blond curly hair, big dimples in his cheeks, the beautiful brown eyes and long, dark eyelashes that any girl would want.

"Joshua, don't you have something to say?"

The child mumbled something, but Annie couldn't make out what it was. She knelt in front of the boy. "What did you say? I didn't hear you."

Joshua lifted his head enough that she had a peek

at those beautiful eyes that told the world what he was thinking. "I'm sorry. I promise I won't do it again."

She hoped not, but she knew Joshua still had to be watched carefully until he developed a healthy respect for dangerous activities. "I'm glad to hear that. I noticed some cushions on the ground. Did you put them there?"

He nodded. "They're soft."

"But not soft enough to break your fall."

"I know. Daddy told me. I have to put the cushions back—by myself."

Annie rose. "That makes sense." She glanced at Ian and saw that, like his son's, his eyelashes were extralong, framing crystalline green depths. She took in his disheveled dark brown hair that looked as though he'd raked his fingers through it when he'd talked with his child. She could just imagine how he'd felt when he'd seen her gripping Joshua's leg, his only safety line. Her heart went out to him. In the past two years Ian had buried two loved ones, and she suspected he was still dealing with his grief like Jeremy.

"Joshua, I'll watch you from the landing," Dr. McGregor said. "You need to put the cushions back exactly like you found them."

"Yes, sir." With slumped shoulders, the little boy made his way out of the apartment. The sound of his footsteps on the stairs resonated in the air.

Annie went out onto the landing with the doctor. Looking at the ground twenty feet below reminded her all over again about how tragic today could have been. She saw a flower garden with stones around it that Joshua could have hit his head on.

"Thanks, Annie, for grabbing Joshua. I went into the

kitchen to make sure I had all the ingredients for dinner tonight. When I returned to the den five minutes later, he was gone. At first I'd thought he'd gone to his room, then I remembered all his questions about when you were going to show up. Something told me he went to see you. I was coming to bring him back inside so you could get settled without stumbling over him. He can get underfoot."

While Joshua wrestled with a two-seat cushion from the lawn furniture, finally deciding to drag it, Annie took in the beautifully landscaped yard with spring flowers bursting forward in their multicolored glory. The air smelled of honeysuckle. She leaned over and saw a row of bushes below the staircase. "I like your yard. Is gardening a hobby of yours?"

"More like a means to keep my sanity. When I'm troubled, I go outside and tinker in the yard. My wife got me hooked on it. She started this, and I'm just keeping it going. How about you?"

"Can't stand to garden, but I love to look at a beautiful one. I'm a great spectator—not such a good participant."

Ian turned toward her, not a foot away, and smiled.

"How about your children?" she asked. "Do they help outside?"

Watching Joshua finish with the last cushion, Ian pressed his lips together as though weighing what he said. "Joshua loves to, but his assistance isn't quite what I need. Jasmine helps often. She takes after her mother, but Jade and Jeremy will do anything to get out of work—whether outside or inside." He frowned.

"In fact, if Jeremy joins the family at all it's an accomplishment."

"Will he be at dinner?"

"Yes, for as long as it takes for him to eat. I used to make him sit there until we were all ready to get up. Finally, I decided the hostile atmosphere he created wasn't fair to the other children."

"How was Jeremy with the other nannies?"

"He had as little to do with them as possible. The only one who seemed to get through to him was Aunt Louise. When she died, he took her death doubly hard."

"He's old enough to understand the losses he's had," Annie said over the stomping of Joshua's feet as he came up the stairs. "Can I help you with dinner?"

"Nope. You aren't officially on the clock until tomorrow."

"What time do you want me to come to eat tonight?"

"Six-thirty, and I hope to have the food on the table shortly thereafter." Dr. McGregor clasped his son's shoulder to keep him from going into her apartment. "No guarantees, though. Joshua, we're leaving. You have a room to clean."

"Do I hafta? I told Annie I'm sorry."

"Yes, but it has nothing to do with your room. It's Sunday, and it's supposed to be done before you go to bed."

Joshua huffed and raced down the stairs, jumping to the ground from the third step.

"If he doesn't give me a heart attack, I'll be surprised," Ian said with a chuckle.

But Annie had spied the tense set to his shoulders and the clamp of his jaw as his son had made the leap.

"I imagine my parents felt the same way about some of my brothers."

"But not you?"

"Well…probably so." Some of Annie and Amanda's antics could rival her siblings'. "But nothing like my younger brother."

Ian grinned. "What is it about the youngest in the family?"

Annie smiled and shrugged, then watched Ian descend the steps. He moved with an ease and confidence.

Her new employer was easy to talk to. He was nothing like what she had expected. Tom had told her yesterday Dr. McGregor could work anywhere he wanted and make a ton of money. His reputation as a plastic surgeon was known throughout the United States. He chose to stay in Cimarron City, his wife's hometown, and to donate part of his time to the free clinic. Annie couldn't deny that the man intrigued her.

As she entered her apartment, she remembered an article she'd found on the internet when she'd applied for the nanny position. Recently, a world-renowned model had gone to Dr. McGregor to erase the effects of a car accident. Even with the scars from the wreck she'd been beautiful, but once the surgery had been performed and she'd recovered, there wasn't a trace of what had happened to her.

Annie had an hour until dinner and decided to take a long, hot bath. As she stood in front of the counter in the bathroom, she pulled her turtleneck off. She usually didn't look at herself in the mirror, but her gaze lit upon her reflection—zeroing in on her pink-and-white scars. She'd learned to accept them, but she recalled once when one of her nieces had glimpsed them, wide eyes glued on the scarred tissue, she'd clapped her hand over her mouth in shock. Annie wouldn't forget that look—ever.

The door in the kitchen from the utility room opened, and Ian glanced at Annie entering the house. Dressed in jeans and a black turtleneck, she looked more relaxed since the scare with Joshua earlier. Her shoulder-length blond hair framed her face and emphasized her expressive dark brown eyes. She wasn't classically beautiful, but she was cute and pert. And those eyes were so appealing and mesmerizing.

Suddenly he realized he was staring at her. He dropped his attention to the pot on the stove and stirred the sauce. "I hope you're hungry. I think I went overboard."

Annie inhaled and smiled. "It smells delicious. Italian?" She bridged the distance between them. "Spaghetti. I love it. From scratch?"

"Yes, that's the only way. It's one meal all of my kids will eat. That's not the case with a lot of food. Their palate hasn't expanded much beyond pizza, macaroni and cheese and hamburgers."

"I saw some hope the last few years with the Hansen children."

"Oh, good. I have something to look forward to. There are a lot of recipes I'd like to try, but I know they won't go over with my kids." Ian continued to stir the sauce.

"I have a niece who is five and loves snow crabs. She will crack the shells and eat them until you think there couldn't possibly be any more room in her stomach. I'm usually right there with her, but the last time she kept going when I couldn't eat another bite."

Ian laughed. Annie was easy to talk to, nothing like the other nannies. Earlier, when she'd caught Joshua, she'd been calm and efficient. He remembered when the second nanny had freaked out when Jeremy was cutting up an apple and sliced his finger. Thank goodness he'd been home to take care of the wound because the woman had frozen when she'd seen the blood then yelled for him. He imagined Annie would have handled it and had the bleeding stopped before he came into the kitchen.

Ian put the spaghetti noodles on to cook then glanced around to make sure everything else was ready.

Those beautiful eyes connected with his. "Can I help you? Set the table?"

"It's already set in the dining room." Ian swung back to the stove, stirring the sauce when he didn't need to. He had to do something. Looking at her was distracting.

"Do you usually eat in the dining room?"

"No—" he waved toward the table that sat six in the alcove "—usually in here, but this is a special occasion. We're welcoming you to our home. I want this evening to be a nice calm one. Now, if only my children cooperate, it might be."

"The least I can do is help you carry the food to the table."

Ian made sure he had eye contact with Annie then said, smiling, "What part of 'you are our guest' do you not understand? Guests are supposed to relax and enjoy themselves. Nothing more than that."

A grin twitched at the corners of her mouth. "Aye, aye, sir. I've got that. It's awfully quiet. Where are the children?"

Ian frowned. "Come to think of it, Jade was the last one in here. That was fifteen minutes ago. I haven't heard a peep out of them since." He walked to the intercom and pressed a button. "Time for dinner, everyone. Don't forget to wash your hands."

"I like that. Does it work?"

"Yes. Saves me yelling or going in search of them, if you meant the intercom. Otherwise, not always about washing their hands."

A few minutes later, the first to appear in the kitchen was Jade quickly followed by Jasmine, exact replicas of each other down to the clothes they wore. "You two can help put the food on the table. Where's Joshua? He was with you in the den doing his homework."

Jasmine put her hand on her waist. "He was coloring. He doesn't have any homework."

"You and I know that, but since you, Jade and Jeremy do, he thinks he should. Did you leave him in there alone with the crayons?"

"No, he left to go to the bathroom."

"How long ago?"

Jade looked at the ceiling and tapped her chin. "I guess a while ago."

"Jade, Jasmine, this is Annie, your new nanny." Ian turned off the oven then headed for the hallway. "Annie, would you remove the pasta when it's done? I'll be back after I find Joshua. He marches to his own music."

"Don't worry. I'll help your girls get everything on the table."

Ian paused at the doorway, started to tell her she didn't have to and then decided instead that he'd give her an extra day of pay. He was afraid she would earn every bit of the money and more by the end of the evening. For starters, his daughters dressing alike didn't bode well.

Ian went to the downstairs bathroom and checked for Joshua. It was too clean and neat for Joshua to have been there. He mounted the stairs two at a time. He knew Joshua was still in the house because he'd set the alarm to beep twice when someone opened an outside door. The last time it had gone off was when Annie had come in.

The children's bathroom on the second floor was empty, so Ian made his way to the one connected to his bedroom. No Joshua. He returned to the hall and looked into his youngest son's room. Empty.

Maybe he got outside somehow. Giggles wafted to him. He marched down the hallway to where Aunt Louise used to stay and turned the knob. More laughter pealed. Quickly Ian crossed to the bathroom and found Joshua in the big tub, washing himself.

Sitting in a foot of water, Joshua beamed up at him. "I'm washing my hands."

"I see. Why did you come in here?"

"I miss Aunt Louise. Jeremy was asleep, so I came in here. Is Annie here?"

Joshua's sometimes-disconnected thoughts could be hard to follow. "Yes, she is and hungry." Ian held a towel open for his son. "Time to get out, get dressed and come downstairs." At least this time Joshua had taken off his clothes before getting into the bath.

Joshua jumped up, splashing the water, and stepped out onto the tile floor. "Okie dokie."

Ian waited at the doorway for his youngest to dress himself. When Joshua ran past him and toward the stairs, Ian made a detour to Jeremy's room and knocked on the door. No answer. He decided to make sure Jeremy was there, so he pushed the door open and found his eldest curled on the bed, his eyes closed.

Ian sat next to Jeremy and shook his shoulder to wake him up.

His son's arms lashed out at Ian. "Get away." Blinking rapidly, Jeremy pushed away as if he was coming out of a nightmare and didn't know where he was.

"What's wrong? A bad dream?"

Jeremy looked around him, then lowered his head.

"Dinner is ready." Ian spied Joshua in the doorway and waved him away.

His eldest son clenched the bedcovers. When he didn't say anything, Ian rose, not sure what was going on. "I expect you downstairs to meet the... Annie."

Jeremy flung himself across the bed and hurried out of the room—leaving Ian even more perplexed by his behavior. Not sure his son would even go to the dining room, Ian hastened after him.

Chapter 3

Annie took the seat at the end where the twins indicated she should sit. All the food was on the formal dining room table, and Jade and Jasmine sat on one side, constantly looking over their shoulders toward the foyer or staring at Annie.

She checked her watch. "Maybe I should go see if your dad needs help."

"Knowing Joshua, he's probably hiding. He does that sometimes," the girl closest to Annie said.

Jasmine? They were both wearing jeans and matching shirts and ponytails. According to Ian, they didn't dress alike anymore. Obviously, tonight they had other plans.

The other sister grinned. "We should go ahead and eat."

Annie shoved her chair back. "Wait until the others

come. I think I'll go see what's keeping them." Something didn't feel right. She started for the hallway and found Joshua coming down the staircase, his lower lip sticking out. She hurried to him. "Is something wrong, Joshua?"

"Daddy is in Jeremy's room. He made me go away."

She escorted Joshua to his seat across from one of the twins. "Well, sometimes parents need private time with a child without any interruptions."

"Jeremy was telling Daddy to leave. I saw his angry face."

"Jeremy is in one of his moods," one of the twins chimed in.

"Jade, I think—"

"I'm Jasmine."

"Okay, Jasmine. I think we should go ahead and eat before the food gets cold."

"But you said we should wait," the real Jade said, her pout matching Joshua's.

A sinus headache, common for her in the spring, hammered against Annie's forehead behind her eyes. Remaining calm was the best way to deal with children. She took a moment to compose herself then bowed her head.

"What are ya doin'?" Joshua grabbed a roll from the basket near him.

Annie glanced at him. "Blessing the food."

"What's wrong with it?"

"Nothing, Joshua. I pray over my meal before I eat."

All evidence of a pout vanished, and he grinned. "I pray at night before bed."

"We used to with Aunt Louise, but those other nannies didn't," Jasmine said, grabbing the bowl of spaghetti and scooping pasta onto her plate.

"We do when Daddy eats with us." Jade folded her arms over her chest. "I'm waiting."

"I'm not. I'm staaarving," Joshua said.

While Jasmine joined him and piled sauce all over her spaghetti, Jade glared at her sister, then her little brother. When her two siblings started eating, she slapped her hand down on the table. "We should wait."

Out of the corner of her eye, Annie spied Ian entering the dining room with a scowling Jeremy trailing slowly behind him.

"Good. You have started. Spaghetti is best when it's hot." Ian winked at Annie then took his chair at the head of the table. "Jeremy, this is Annie."

"Hi, Jeremy," Annie said.

"I don't need a nanny. I'm gonna be ten at the end of next month." Jeremy's mouth firmed in a hard, thin line.

"Neither do we." Jade mimicked her older brother's expression. "We're eight. Nannies are for babies." She sent Joshua a narrow-eyed look as if he were the only reason Annie was there.

"I'm not a baby." Joshua thumped his chest. "I'm four. I'm gonna be five soon."

"How soon?" Annie asked him, hoping to change the subject.

Joshua peered at his father.

"Two weeks. The twenty-seventh."

"You act like a baby. Look at what you did today. You could have *died* today." Jade shoved back her chair, whirled around and ran from the room.

Annie's first impulse was to go after the girl, but

she didn't know her yet. Jade must have been the one who'd screamed at the bottom of the steps earlier when Joshua was on the railing.

Instead, Ian stood. "Keep eating." Then he left the room.

Wide-eyed, Joshua looked at Jeremy, then Jasmine and finally Annie. "I won't die."

The pounding in her head increased. "Jade was just worried about what you did today. Standing on the railing is dangerous."

"Yeah, dork. You have a death wish." Jeremy snatched a roll and began tearing it apart.

"Death wish?" Confusion clouded Joshua's eyes. Tears filled them. "I don't wanna die."

"Then, stop doing dumb things." Jeremy tossed a piece of bread at his younger brother.

Joshua threw his half-eaten roll at Jeremy. It plunked into the milk glass, and the white liquid splashed everywhere.

Grabbing for a roll in the basket, Jeremy twisted toward Joshua.

"Stop it right now." Annie shot to her feet. "The dinner table is no place for a food fight. If you don't want to eat peacefully, then go to your rooms."

Jeremy glared. "I don't need a nanny telling me what to do."

Annie counted to ten, breathed deeply and replied, "Apparently you do, because civilized people don't act like this at the table. It's your choice. Stay and eat politely or leave." She returned his intense look with a serene one while inside she quaked. She might be fired after tonight.

Jeremy took the roll and stomped away from the dining room while Joshua hung his head and murmured, "Sorry."

"Apology accepted." Although her stomach was knotted, Annie picked up her fork and took a bite. "Delicious. Your dad is a good cook." If only she hadn't walked around the yard enjoying the beautiful flowers before coming inside, she wouldn't be contending with a headache. In spring she limited her time outside because she had trouble with her allergies.

"One day I'm gonna be a good cook, too." Jasmine continued eating.

"Jasmine, I can teach you a few things. I especially enjoy baking."

"I'm Jade." The girl lowered her gaze. "Sorry about that. We were just playing with you."

"I understand. I have a twin sister."

"You do? I have a girlfriend who has a twin brother. They don't look alike, though."

"They're fraternal twins. You and Jasmine are identical, like I am with my sister, Amanda."

"I'd like to meet your twin." Jade—at least Annie hoped that was who she was—took a gulp of her milk.

Ian reentered the dining room with Jasmine. "I'd like to meet your twin, too." He scanned the table. "Where's Jeremy?"

"He chose not to eat." Annie took another bite of her spaghetti as the knots in her stomach began to unravel.

Joshua huffed. "He threw food at me."

Ian's eyebrows rose. "Why?"

"He's mean."

Ian swung his attention to Annie, a question in his eyes.

"Jeremy chose to leave rather than calmly eat his dinner," she answered while her head throbbed.

Ian nodded then said to the children, "Tell Annie about what you're doing this week in school."

Later, contrary to what Ian had asked, Annie finished putting the dishes into the dishwasher. She had to do something while she waited for Ian to return from upstairs.

He came into the kitchen after putting Joshua to bed. "He fell right to sleep. Thankfully he usually does, while Jade and Jasmine rarely do. Often I'll find one of them in the other's bed in the morning. They shared a room until a year ago when they decided they should have their own rooms like their brothers."

"I shared one with Amanda until I went to college." Annie hung up the washrag and faced him.

His gaze skimmed over the clean counters and stove. "I should have known you would do the dishes."

"I figured it was part of my job."

"Let's go into the den and talk where it's more comfortable. I'm sure after the evening we had, you have a ton of questions."

Annie went ahead of him from the kitchen. "A few."

In the den she sat at one end of the tan couch while Ian took the other. A fine-honed tension electrified the air. As she turned to face him, he did the same. Exhaustion blanketed his features, his green eyes dull. The urge to comfort him swamped Annie, but she balled her hands and waited for him to speak first.

He cleared his throat. "What happened tonight has been the norm ever since Aunt Louise died. Life wasn't perfect before, but she established a routine and gave my children boundaries." He combed his fingers through his brown hair then rubbed his palm across his nape. "I'm finding it hard to make a living and be here for my children. I've tried to do what Aunt Louise did, but my efforts seem to fall flat."

A dilemma a lot of parents had. "We live in a society that seems to be constantly on the go. If we're not busy, we're bored," Annie said. "A lot has happened to your children in the past two years. This especially affects Jeremy because he's the eldest and knows what's going on. Even to a certain extent your girls do, especially about your aunt's death."

"I've talked to each of my kids about Aunt Louise unexpectedly dying."

"Have you ever sat down and talked with them all together? I think the best thing my parents did was have a family meeting once a week, or more if needed."

"Sometimes because of our busy schedules it's hard to do that. Tonight was the first time in a while we've even eaten together."

"Decide on what you feel has to be done, what you can do away with and what would be nice if there's enough time."

"I love my children and have rules that they need to follow, but I can't seem to get a handle on it. Maybe when you've been with the kids awhile, we can talk again."

Annie thought of the day planner she'd used to track the children's activities and school functions at her other employers'. She wished her mother was still alive to talk to, but she could go see her eldest sister, Rachel, who'd taken over and helped raise them when their mother died. "I'd like to get a weekly calendar and put it up in the kitchen to help us and the kids keep up with everything. That's where family time can be scheduled."

"I'm interested in hearing more about your family meetings. What did you talk about?"

Thinking back to a few she'd had with her siblings, Annie chuckled. "Some could get quite heated, but a rule my parents had was that no one left the room until a solution to a conflict was reached. Once we were two hours late going to bed."

"So there are rules?"

"Yes, a few my parents insisted on and some we got to add. It's a time for everyone in the family to have a voice."

Ian smiled, and for a moment the tired lines vanished from his face. "I like the concept. After you've been working for a week or so, I'd like to see if we could try that."

"Have your children talked with a grief counselor?" *Have you? Have you let life get in the way of grieving?*

"As I told you, I had Jeremy go to a counselor, but he refused to cooperate. Our pastor came over after Aunt Louise's funeral and talked with the whole family. The same when my wife died."

"How long has Jeremy been so angry?"

"He was some before Aunt Louise died, but mostly since then. It's getting worse. There are times he almost seems frightened. Before all this began, he was the sweetest child, but in the past nine months... I don't know what's going on."

"Is he being bullied at school?"

"I've talked with the teacher. She's noticed he keeps to himself more. In fact, a few months ago he bullied another classmate. That's when he started counseling. So far there hasn't been another incident. I won't tolerate bullying, and he knows it."

The feeling that the child was screaming for help kept nagging her. Was it grief? Something else? A stage he was going through? "What does he say?"

"Nothing. He used to tell me everything. Now I can't get anything out of him. I feel like I'm losing my son."

Not if she could do anything about it. This was why Annie had chosen to be a nanny and why she had been led to this family. "No, you aren't losing your son. If it's a phase he's going through, he'll grow out of it. If it's something else, we'll find out what it is and deal..." Her words faded into silence.

Surprise flashed across Ian's face.

Did the word *we'll* sound presumptuous? Ian was her employer. Yes, she would help with Jeremy, but he was the parent. Not her. "What I mean is as his nanny I'll try to help you and him as much as possible. But you're his father, and whatever you say is what I'll do."

A gleam sparkled in Ian's eyes. "I want your input. I need it. So I think you're right—we're a team. I'm determined, at the very least, to get my family back to the way it was when Aunt Louise was here."

Annie heard the sincerity in his voice. *A team.* It might be the closest she'd come to raising children as if she were their mother. The Hansens had been great to work for and had valued her input, but she'd always felt like an employee. As of late, she realized she wanted more, and yet she hadn't dated much. She was always so busy with her own family or the children she was taking care of.

"I won't be going into work tomorrow until after we take the kids to school," Ian said.

"I thought that was something you wanted me to do."

"You're right, but I want to go with you so I can introduce you to the teachers. If there's a problem with one of them at school, sometimes I can go take care of it. But if I'm in surgery, that will be hard. I don't anticipate trouble with the girls, but there might be with Joshua or Jeremy. I've already had to go to school for Jeremy four times this year and once for Joshua when he fell on the playground and hit his head." He shook his head. "Probably one of many times he'll have to have stitches."

"I like the idea of meeting their teachers. I want to find out what kind of homework to expect from them. That way we can get it done before you come home on the days I'm not taking them to lessons. I find if they tackle it after getting a snack when they come home from school they'll finish quickly so they can play. It cuts down on whining later when they're more tired."

"The other nannies didn't want to help with their homework, which left me doing it late and yes, they usually complained and made the process longer."

Annie tried to stifle a yawn, but she couldn't. "I think it's time I go to bed. Six will be here in—" she glanced at her watch "—nine hours, and I still need to find some of the items I'll need tomorrow." She stood and stretched out her hand toward him.

Ian rose, clasping hers and shaking it. "Thank you, Annie."

"For what?" She slipped her hand from his warm grasp.

"Taking this job. I'm not sure what I would have done. I know you had several offers. What made you accept mine?"

"I prayed about it, and like I said, I love a good challenge."

"You may regret those words."

Would she? If she became too invested in the family and Ian remarried, no longer needing her services, she might. She wanted to care but not so much she would get hurt.

"Dad! Dad!" one of the girls shouted.

He hurried into the foyer with Annie right behind him. "Why aren't you in bed?"

"Something is wrong with Jeremy. Come quick."

Chapter 4

Annie followed right behind Ian as he took the stairs two at a time and rushed down the hallway. He pushed his way between his twin daughters into Jeremy's bedroom. With a glimpse at the bed, Annie knew what was happening. His head was thrown back, his stiff body shaking: Jeremy was having a seizure.

One of the twins grabbed the other's hand, tears running down both girls' faces. "What's wrong with Jeremy?"

Annie herded them away from the door and closed it behind her. Jeremy was in good hands with his father being a doctor, but right now the twins were scared and upset. Trying to decide what to tell them, Annie drew them away from the room a few yards before the one dressed in a nightgown jerked away.

"What's wrong?" the child shouted at Annie.

The other girl threw herself at Annie, wrapping her arms around her and clinging to her. "Is he going to die?"

"No, Jeremy will be fine. Your dad is helping him." Annie forced calmness into her voice to counter the twins' raising panic. Since Ian had never told her about the seizures, this must be the first one. She'd gone to school with a friend who'd had epilepsy, and Annie had learned to deal with the episodes when they happened. Some of her classmates had steered clear of Becca because of that, but she hadn't. Becca had needed friends more than ever.

The twin who wore the nightgown pointed toward her brother's bedroom, her arm quavering as much as Jeremy had been. "No, he's not. His eyes rolled back."

The door opened and Ian stood in the entrance, his attention switching back and forth between the girls and Annie. "Your brother will be all right. He had a seizure, which makes him act differently for a short time, but he's falling asleep now, and you all need to go to bed, too. You have school tomorrow."

"But, Dad—" the twin wearing the nightgown said.

"Jasmine, this is not the time to argue."

Annie clasped both girls' shoulders. "Would it be okay if they peek in and see for themselves that Jeremy is fine now?"

Ian glanced at her, and he nodded. "Quietly. Then to bed."

Annie walked with them and peered into the bedroom. Jeremy's eyes were closed and his body was still, relaxed. "See? After a seizure a lot of people are really tired and will sleep."

Jade slanted a look at Annie. "Will he have another one?"

"I'll be here if he does," Ian answered then leaned over and kissed the tops of his daughters' heads. "Good night. Love you two."

After the twins hugged their dad, Annie gently guided them toward their end of the hall. When both entered Jade's room, Annie didn't say anything to them. Given what they witnessed, they'd probably start the night together.

"Have you two brushed your teeth?"

"Yes," they said together.

"Do you have your clothes laid out for school tomorrow?"

They looked at each other then at Annie as if she'd grown another head. Jasmine said, "No, why would we do that? I never know what I feel like wearing until I get up."

Jade glanced at her closet. "Well, actually I do know. The same thing I always do, jeans and a shirt. So I guess I could."

Jasmine jerked her thumb toward her sister. "She wears boring clothes. I don't, and my mood makes a difference."

Jade charged to her closet and yanked down a shirt and tossed it on a chair where a pair of jeans lay. "And that's why we're always late."

Before war was declared, Annie stepped between the twins. "We won't be late tomorrow. Jasmine, do I need to wake you up fifteen minutes early so you can pick out your clothes?"

"No! I need my beauty sleep." A serious look descended on Jasmine's face.

Annie nearly laughed but bit the inside of her mouth to keep from doing it. These twins were polar opposites. Even if they dressed alike, their behavior would give them away eventually. At least Amanda and she were similar in personalities, especially when they were young, which made it easier to change identities.

"Fine. We'll be leaving on time so you'll need to be ready. I won't make the others late because you are."

Jasmine's eyes grew round. "Dad won't like that."

Annie smiled. "Be on time and there won't be a problem."

"What about Jeremy? What if that happens on the way to school?" Jade asked, drawing Annie's attention away from her sister.

"Again, don't worry. We'll deal with what happens at the time. My mom used to say we shouldn't borrow stress by worrying. What we fear might never happen." Annie paused a few seconds to let that bit of wisdom sink in then added, "Time for bed. Have you said your prayers?"

Jade shook her head. "But we will. Jeremy needs our help."

"Yes, he can always use your prayers." Annie stood back while the twins walked to the double bed.

The two girls knelt and went through a list of people to bless. At the end Jasmine said, "God, please fix my brother. Amen."

When they hopped up, Jade crawled across the bed to the other side while Jasmine settled on the right.

Annie moved to the doorway and switched off the overhead light.

"Good night, girls."

Jasmine turned on the bedside lamp then pulled the covers up over her shoulders, saying, "I need a light on to go to sleep," while Jade murmured, "Good night."

"Door open or closed?" Annie clutched the knob.

"Open," Jade replied while Jasmine said, "Closed."

"I'll leave it partially open."

Surprisingly, the two girls remained quiet, and Annie hurried toward Jeremy's room to see how the boy was doing. She rapped lightly on the door and waited for Ian to answer. A few seconds later, he appeared with a weary expression on his face.

He stepped into the hallway but glanced at Jeremy asleep on the bed. "I need to call a doctor I know who deals with seizures in children. I hope to get Jeremy in to see him tomorrow before his office opens. He'll need to run some tests and possibly prescribe medication for Jeremy. Will you watch him while I make that call?"

"Of course. I'll stay as long as you need me."

"Thanks. How are the girls?"

"They are in bed in Jade's room. They prayed and asked God to help Jeremy."

"Then, He's been bombarded with prayers this evening. I'll be back in a few minutes." Ian gave her a tired smile and headed for the staircase.

Annie checked to make sure Jeremy was still sleeping then took the chair Ian had been sitting in. She needed to come up with what she'd do when Jasmine was late to go to school. If not tomorrow, she would be probably soon, and the child needed to know the consequences. Annie could remember some of her own battles with her mother over boundaries and how neither parent ever backed down. No meant no. She realized she needed to talk with Ian to see how he'd want her to handle it.

Ian returned ten minutes later and motioned for her to join him in the hallway. Some of the tension in his expression relaxed as she came toward him.

"You couldn't have come at a better time. I don't know what I would have done if you weren't here. More and more I realize a person can't be in two places at once." One corner of his mouth hitched up. "Although I've been trying to these past months."

"Take it from me, it's scientifically impossible. I've tried myself, though. Did everything work out with the doctor?"

"Yes, Brandon will see him first thing tomorrow morning, but I'll need to postpone introducing you to the teachers until Tuesday. I've let the school know that you'll be bringing them and picking them up, so it'll be okay. The one thing that's working for us is they all go to the same school."

"So you want me to take Joshua, Jade and Jasmine in the morning?"

Ian nodded. "And be prepared for a hundred questions from Joshua the whole way. He'll want to know exactly what happened to Jeremy and what the doctor will say even before we know it."

"What do you think is happening?"

Sighing, Ian glanced toward his son in his room. "It could be epilepsy, but it takes more than one seizure to determine that." He rubbed his chin. "Now I'm wondering if some of Jeremy's behavior these past months might have indicated petit mal seizures. I haven't had a lot of experience with epilepsy, so I might be wrong."

"I'm glad I'm here for you and your family."

Ian grinned. "Just in the nick of time. Do you have any questions about tomorrow?"

"I may be wrong, but I have a feeling Jasmine will test me about getting ready for school on time."

"No, you aren't wrong. She even did with Aunt Louise. She has always been my prima donna, even as young as two. I think she was trying to be as different from Jade as she could."

"I've told her I won't allow her to make her siblings late for school, so I have a plan to stress my point." Annie looked into Ian's green eyes and for a second lost her train of thought.

"What?"

Okay, he had great eyes. She had to ignore them. Annie peered down the hall toward the girls' bedrooms. "She will ride with me to school dressed or not. I'll drop the others off, come home and let her finish getting ready, then take her back to school."

"But that's—"

"The consequence of having me drive twice to the school is that the next morning I will be waking her up thirty minutes earlier. That means she'll go to bed thirty minutes earlier, so she'll get the required amount of *beauty rest* she insists she needs."

Ian chuckled. "My daughter is an eight-year-old going on eighteen. I wish I had thought of that diabolical plan."

"So you're okay with it?"

"Yes. I like your creative way of dealing with it."

"I try to look for ways to have natural consequences for a child's actions. It tends to work better."

Ian checked his watch. "You'd better catch some sleep yourself."

"I'll peek in on the girls and Joshua, then leave."

She started to turn when Ian clasped her upper arm and stopped her. "Thanks again. Just taking the girls to their room and putting them in bed was a huge help."

Ian's touch on her skin riveted her attention to his hand for a few seconds before he released his hold. Her heartbeat kicked up a notch. In her previous nanny positions she usually dealt with the mothers, but since Ian was a single parent she would be working with just him. She'd never thought that would be a problem—until now.

"It's part of my job," she murmured then continued toward Joshua's room next to Jeremy's.

When Annie climbed the stairs to her apartment, she stopped on the landing and rotated toward the yard. She saw a few lights off in the distance. The cool spring air with a hint of honeysuckle from the bushes below caressed her skin. The sky twinkled with stars—thousands scattered everywhere.

Her first unofficial evening had gone okay. It reinforced she'd made the right decision to work for Ian McGregor, instead of one of the other five offers she'd received. The family needed her, even more so because Ian was a single parent. Her only concern was the man she worked for: he was attractive, intelligent and caring, all traits she at one time had dreamed of in her future husband. Now, though, she thought of herself as a modern-day Mary Poppins, going where needed then moving on before her heart became too engaged. No sense getting attached.

Annie kept an eye on the kitchen clock while she scrambled the eggs, expecting the kids and Ian any second. When she glanced at the doorway, she spied Joshua dressed in the clothes they'd picked out together this morning. Other than his tennis shoes on the wrong feet, he appeared ready to go to school.

"Good morning, Joshua. Are you hungry?"

He nodded and plodded to the table, evidently not a morning person. He usually talked a lot, but earlier when she'd gotten him up, he'd said only a handful of words by the time she'd left him to dress.

As she turned off the burner, Ian and Jeremy entered the room. Neither looked happy. "Good morning, Jeremy, Ian." She set a platter of toast in the center of the table, then milk and orange juice. "Did you see Jade and Jasmine?"

Ian poured some coffee and settled into the chair at one end. "They were both supposed to be coming right away."

"I'm here," Jade announced from the entrance. She looked ready for school. "But Jasmine is still in the bathroom. She's decided to put her hair in a ponytail."

"I'll go help her." Annie placed the eggs next to the toast then started for the hallway.

"I tried. As usual, she didn't want my help." Jade plopped into the chair across from Jeremy.

Annie hurried up the stairs and poked her head into the doorway of the girls' bathroom.

Jasmine yanked the rubber band from her hair. "Ouch!" She stomped her foot and glared at herself in the mirror. "I can't do this."

"I can." Annie moved toward the child.

Jasmine whirled around, her lips pinched together. "No one can pull it as tight as I want."

"Okay. Breakfast is ready. We leave for school in half an hour."

"I can't be ready by then."

"That's your choice. You know what happens when you aren't ready." She'd informed Jasmine when the girls woke up. Annie left, preparing herself for the next hour and the battle to come.

When she returned to the kitchen, everyone watched her as she made her way to the table.

"Where's Jasmine?" Ian asked, finishing up his last bite of eggs.

"She doesn't need my help, so I reminded her of the time we're leaving for school." Annie sat at the other end of the table. "Which, Joshua and Jade, is in thirty minutes. Seven forty-five."

"I can't tell time," Joshua said as he stuffed a fourth of his toast into his mouth.

"I'll tell you. And you're ready except for brushing your teeth and changing your shoes."

"Why?"

"Dork, your shoes are on the wrong feet."

"Jeremy, that word is unacceptable." Ian carried his dishes to the sink.

"Well, he is one." Ian's eldest took his nearly full plate over to the counter then stormed from the kitchen.

"I'm not a dork. I like my shoes like this."

"It's not good for your feet. Here, I'll help you." Annie slid from her chair and knelt next to Joshua.

Once she fixed the problem, Joshua jumped up and raced toward the hallway. "I'm gonna be first ready."

"No, you're not." Jade quickly followed.

The sound of their pounding feet going up the stairs filled the house.

Ian came up behind Annie to help clear the dishes. "Ah, quiet. I've learned to cherish these moments. Is Jasmine going to be ready?"

"I don't know. She had her dress on but no shoes, not to mention she hasn't eaten breakfast."

"I'll be leaving right after you. I don't know how long we'll be at the doctor. He'll probably run some tests."

"How was Jeremy when he woke up this morning?" Annie hated seeing the concern and weariness on Ian's face. She hated seeing what Jeremy was going through.

"Grumpy, which isn't unusual, but when we talked about the seizure, I saw fear in his eyes. He rarely shows that. I tried to explain about what a seizure was, and he wouldn't listen."

"Denial. That's understandable. When Becca, my friend at school, had seizures she fought it. Finally she learned to accept the situation. Being less stressed helped Becca lessen the symptoms." Although she didn't have epilepsy, Annie had been in her share of denial while recovering from her third-degree burns. And she'd been angry at the world, too.

"Do you think Jeremy knew something was going on?" she asked. "My friend had petit mal seizures for a while before she had her first grand mal. I'd find her staring off into space, but she just said she was thinking."

Ian frowned. "It's possible. He's spent a lot of time in his room lately. I'd try talking with him, but he would just say his brother and sisters bothered him. I can remember going through a stage like that when I was a kid, so I thought it was that."

"It might be."

"It could explain some of what's been going on."

Annie caught sight of the clock. It wouldn't do for the nanny to be late with the kids the first day on her job. Jasmine would never let her forget it if she didn't leave on time. "I've got to go. I might have to get up earlier tomorrow instead of Jasmine."

"I don't know if I'll be taking Jeremy to school today or not. It'll depend on what happens at the doctor. I'll keep you informed of what happens."

"Don't worry about the others. I'll take care of them." Annie went to the intercom and announced, "Time to go to school, everyone."

She heard a shriek from upstairs, then a few seconds later, Joshua and Jade hurrying down the steps, each trying to be the first out the kitchen door to the garage. If only she could get Jasmine to buy in to racing her siblings to the car.

With a deep sigh, Annie mounted the stairs. Jasmine came out into the hall carrying her shoes, her hair a wild mess as though she'd teased it. She'd changed her outfit.

"I need more time. I can't go to school wearing this. There's a stain on the blouse. I just saw it." The girl's voice rose to a shrill level.

"You have two minutes to make it down to the car in the garage."

Jasmine stomped her foot. "I have to look my best."

"Your choice. I can bring you back if you want to change, but I'm leaving in ninety seconds to take the other two. They have a right to be at school on time."

Jasmine charged into her room then returned with a blouse clutched in her other hand with her brush. "I hate you. You just don't understand." Tears filled her eyes as she marched past Annie, grumbling the whole way down the stairs, through the kitchen door and to the navy blue Ford Explorer. After Jasmine flounced into the backseat, she glared at Jade sitting in front.

Ian stood near the door from the breezeway, trying to suppress his grin. "I think I needed that. You know she won't get out of the car."

"I figured. Even if she changes her blouse and puts her shoes on, she would never go inside the school with her hair like that. I'll bring her home and let her get ready then take her back. She'll have to explain to the office why she was late."

"We'll need to compare our day this evening. I'm not sure whose day will be more challenging. Thank you again."

For a few seconds Annie felt as though they were in this together—but not just as employer and employee. With Ian's casual manner, it was easy to forget their relationship was strictly professional. "Nothing I haven't encountered before." Annie walked toward the vehicle, feeling Ian's gaze on her. It sent a shiver up her spine.

Later that night, after putting Joshua down, Annie went in search of Jasmine. Her door was closed while her twin's was wide-open with Jade sitting on the bed, listening to music. Annie rapped on Jasmine's door.

Silence greeted her. She tried turning the knob, but it was locked.

She went to the entrance of Jade's bedroom. "Why is Jasmine's door locked?"

Jade waved toward her twin's room. "She told me she would go to sleep when *she* wanted."

Annie felt an urge to march down to Ian's home office and get a key from him to unlock the door right that minute. She curbed that reaction and instead said to Jade, "Thanks. She might go to bed when she wants, but she will be up earlier tomorrow."

"This is gonna be so much fun." Jade giggled and returned to listening to her music.

Annie neared Jasmine's room and said, "If you want your beauty sleep, you should go to bed soon. Good night."

Annie made her way downstairs to retrieve a key from Ian to have tomorrow morning. She knocked on his office door and he immediately said, "Come in."

Annie stuck her head into the room, expecting Ian to be at his desk trying to catch up on his work. But the chair was empty. She stepped farther in and spied him at the French doors to the patio, staring out at the night.

"I need a key to Jasmine's room. She's locked the door."

Ian turned, shaking his head. "How bad was it this morning?"

"She was an hour late because for forty-five minutes she refused to let me help her get the tangles out. When I took her to school, she said nothing the whole way. Tomorrow morning I'll wake her up early. If I have to, I have a bullhorn I can use."

Ian chuckled. "Thanks for the warning." He went to his desk and opened the top drawer. "I have a key that opens all their doors." When he pressed it into her palm, he added, "Keep it. It's a copy. This isn't the first time she's locked her door. It also comes in handy with Jeremy."

"How did it go with the doctor? Jeremy wouldn't talk about it. He just stalked off and slammed his bedroom door."

"He's not happy with what the doctor told him."

"Epilepsy?"

"There are a couple of more tests, but it looks like it, especially when Jeremy mentioned he's blanked out for a few seconds several times."

"Like what you told me when he got so angry at you in his room?"

Ian nodded, his forehead furrowing. "The doctor started him on antiseizure medicine today. I tried talking to him before bringing him home, but I got the silent treatment, too. I'm not sure what to do." He leaned back against his desk, gripping its edge.

"The only experience I have is with my friend, but there was a time Becca went through an angry stage. She was so scared she would have seizures at school. She didn't sleep at night, which wasn't good for a person with epilepsy." When Annie was eleven and this had happened to Becca, she'd been scared, too. She hadn't known what to do at Becca's first seizure. She'd hated feeling helpless.

"Yeah, I've been reading up on it. Stress and lack of sleep can lead to seizures. Did she get better?"

"Yes. When she did have a seizure at school, our

teacher was great. Because she handled it matter-of-factly, the rest of us didn't flip out. She sent me to get the teacher next door and asked the class to step out in the hall. I got to stay because she knew we were friends."

Ian rubbed his chin. "I'm going to school tomorrow with you all, and I'll suggest that to Jeremy's teacher. If he knows there's a plan in place, it might help him feel better. They need to know what is going on, what's causing the seizures."

"My twin's husband, Ben, has a service dog. Ben came back from the war with post-traumatic stress disorder, although now he's doing much better. Ben's sister, Emma, trains service dogs. Emma's first husband had epilepsy, and she regretted that he didn't have the use of one."

"A service dog for epilepsy?"

"Yes, I wish my friend had had one in school. Emma is part owner of Caring Canines right outside Cimarron City. If you're interested, I could set up a meeting with her. That might be something that'll help Jeremy adjust better."

"We used to have a dog, but Aunt Louise was allergic to him so we had to give him away. A neighbor down the street took him. My children visit him from time to time and have asked me for another pet."

"A service dog is devoted to one person, although everyone will interact with him."

"So I should look into one for Jeremy and another dog for the rest of us?" Ian pushed himself away from the desk.

"It's a thought. But first you need to convince Jeremy this will help him. We'll meet with Emma Tanner, the trainer, and she'll explain what the dog can do for him. Otherwise it won't work well if he doesn't agree to the dog."

"There's a lot to consider. There may be certain things my son will have to know and take into consideration, depending on how severe his epilepsy is, but I also want him to live as normal a life as possible. Jeremy was the most upset when we gave the dog away. In fact, for a long time he was angry at Aunt Louise, but she won him over."

"Then she died. That's a lot of loss to deal with, even for an adult."

A flash of pain darkened Ian's eyes. He frowned, plowing his hand through his hair. "I know. I think the only one not affected much was Joshua."

As Annie suspected, it was evident that Ian had his own battles with grief to fight. "Speaking of Joshua, has he always been adventurous?"

"From the second he could move around."

"On the way home from school today, he told me all about his day. I also got a little out of Jade but nothing from Jasmine. I know they can be difficult, but you have precious children."

Ian's eyes widened. "Where have you been all my life? I needed you six months ago. Of course, Tom would never have let me persuade you to come work for me instead."

The heat of a blush singed her cheeks. "There are other good nannies."

"Not from my perspective. So if you're planning to leave, please let me know. I'll offer you a deal you can't refuse. I never had this kind of conversation with the other nannies. Yes, with Aunt Louise, but not them."

Annie turned away, uncomfortable with compliments. The Hansens certainly had told her how important she was to the family, but for some reason it was different when Ian said it. She felt special and appreciated. "I'm going to check on the kids, then I need to get my own sleep. I'm getting up extra early so I can get Jasmine moving." Annie started for the hallway.

"Tomorrow, if Jasmine isn't ready, I could always carry her to the car then into the building."

At the entrance Annie turned around, not realizing Ian was only a few feet behind her. His nearness sent her heart beating faster. He was so close she caught a whiff of lime, most likely from his aftershave lotion.

Ian smiled, his eyes gleaming. "I'll check on Jeremy. I don't want him to run you off with the mood he's been in."

Out of all the children, Annie most identified with Jeremy because after the fire she'd felt what Ian's son was experiencing: angry at the world. "He won't run me off. It takes more than an angry kid to do that."

"Like what?"

Not feeling needed. But Annie wasn't going to tell Ian that. She shrugged. "Back to what you said about Jasmine—I considered that myself, but I'd rather the children decide to get in and out of the car. Taking a child kicking and screaming into a place will do more harm in the long run. At an earlier age, it might be the answer, but Jasmine is eight. Not only would it set her up for her classmates to make fun of her, it doesn't get to the root of the problem."

"That makes sense. Jasmine has always taken longer to get dressed than the others, but lately it has been worse. She won't even accept help. I remember she used to let Aunt Louise brush her hair. Now no one can touch it."

"Interesting. I wonder what made her change her mind."

"I'm not sure. Nothing she'll tell us."

"Maybe Jade knows. They may be very different in personality, but they're close."

"Yeah, they've always had a special bond. I should have thought about that." On the top step Ian angled toward her. "Why didn't I?"

"It's tough being a single parent with one or two, let alone four kids. Don't beat yourself up. Good night, Ian." Annie parted from Ian and made her way toward Jasmine's room.

Using the key, she unlocked the door and peeked in to see if she was in bed. She was, and Annie backed out. After checking on Jade, who was asleep, too, she walked to Joshua's room and slipped inside. She found him lying on the floor. Gently she scooped him up in her arms and placed him on his bed. When she began to straighten away from him, his eyes slid open halfway.

She brushed his hair away from his face and smiled at him. "You were on the floor with no covers." Then she kissed him on his forehead. "Good night."

"Annie, are you gonna leave us?"

"I don't have any plans to leave."

Joshua sighed and rolled over onto his side. "Good. All the others did."

As she backed out of the room, Annie's heart constricted at the need and longing in his voice. The best thing Ian could do to help his family was to find a wife. The kids needed a mother. As much as she could see that as a solution for him, she couldn't visualize him with a wife. The thought bothered her.

Chapter 5

The next morning, as Annie took the breakfast casserole out of the oven and placed it in the center of the table, Jade and Joshua came into the kitchen.

"It smells great. What is it?" Jade asked as she sat down.

"It's a recipe along the idea of French toast minus the syrup."

"Can I put syrup on it?" Joshua took his chair, staring at the dish.

"Try it first without. If you need syrup, then it's fine with me." When Joshua reached for the serving spoon, Annie added, "Wait until everyone shows up."

"Jasmine probably won't be down for a while. She's having trouble with her hair. I told her we need to shave it off, then she won't have any problem." Jade poured milk into her glass and Joshua's.

Joshua giggled. "That would be funny."

"No, it wouldn't be." Annie headed back to the counter. "Jade, could you help me put the rest on the table?" When she handed the girl the pitcher of orange juice, she said, "Jasmine used to let Aunt Louise help her with her hair. Do you know why she doesn't want help anymore?"

Jade nodded and took the drink. "The first nanny we had kept pulling her hair. When Jasmine screamed, she didn't care."

"Why didn't Jasmine say anything to your dad?"

"We just started pranking her. She didn't stay long."

"If you have a problem, you should tell your dad. I may have something to deal with the tangles." Annie followed Jade to the table and set down a tray of cut fruit.

When Ian came into the kitchen with Jeremy, Annie retrieved from a counter a spray bottle and brush she'd brought from her apartment and walked toward the door. "Start without me. I'm going to check on Jasmine."

"Jasmine's not ready. I told her we would be leaving in twenty minutes," Ian said.

"I know."

Annie found Jasmine in the bathroom, struggling again with her hair. "I got something for your hair. It was great for my sister. She had the same problem."

When Annie put the bottle on the counter, Jasmine scrunched up her face as if she wasn't sure about it.

"Try it and see. It works best when your hair is wet, but it still helps in dry hair to get the tangles out without a lot of pulling."

Jasmine tried brushing the back. She winced and cautiously reached for the bottle.

"Do you want me to spray the back and make sure it's all covered?"

The girl studied Annie in the mirror. "I guess, but I don't want you touching my hair."

"I won't unless you ask me, but it might make it better if I lift the hair and spray underneath, too. Okay?"

Jasmine clutched the brush but nodded warily, keeping her stare on Annie in the mirror. "It didn't used to be this bad."

"The longer it gets, the more tangles."

Jasmine's eyes grew round. "I love my long hair. No one is going to cut it."

With the patience she'd learned to cultivate as an aunt, Annie said, "I love your long hair, too."

"You do? Jade told me I should shave it off."

"She was kidding. Each person has to find what works for her. Shorter hair can be easier to manage, but as you see, my hair is long." She captured Jasmine's look in the mirror. "So here I go."

She sprayed the liquid on Jasmine's hair then took the detangling brush out of her pocket. "I got this, too, for you. Between the two you should be able to manage."

Jasmine looked stunned. "When did you get this?"

"This morning at the twenty-four-hour drugstore."

"For me?"

Annie smiled. "No sense pulling your hair out. If you need any help, I'll be downstairs eating breakfast. We leave in fifteen minutes."

The child stood still as Annie left. She hoped this

helped Jasmine because she would have more important battles to fight with her.

When she reentered the kitchen, the kids and Ian
were halfway through their breakfast. Ian saw her first.
"How did it go?"

"We'll see." Annie sat, dished up part of the casserole
then scanned the nearly empty plates at the table. "Do
you want me to make this again sometime?"

All of them, even Jeremy, said yes.

"Great. It's easy because I make most of it the night
before."

Jade finished first and hopped up.

"Jade, don't forget to take your plate to the sink."
Annie ate a bite of the casserole.

"But I never—"

Ian scooted back his chair and picked up his dishes.
"That's a good idea. Isn't it, kids?"

A few mumbles followed his question. Each one took
his or her plate to the counter next to the sink and shuffled out of the room while Ian poured some more coffee.

"It was almost civil this morning except for a couple
of outbursts from Jeremy."

"Is he concerned about going to school?"

"Hopefully when I talk to his teacher, he'll feel better."

"I hope so." Annie noticed Jasmine standing in the
doorway, dressed, her hair pulled back in a ponytail.
"You have a little time for something to eat." She remembered the child complaining all the way to school
the second time yesterday that she was starving. "Five
minutes."

Jasmine hurried to the table and looked at the casserole. "It's cold."

"There's fruit if you don't want to eat it cold. You should have been here on time, when the casserole was hot," Ian said.

While his daughter stared at the slices of fruit, Ian went to the intercom and announced they were leaving in four minutes. Suddenly she stuck a fork into a slice of pineapple and scooped up some grapes, then began stuffing them into her mouth. She never sat but started toward the hallway.

"Jasmine, please take your plate to the sink." Ian took a sip of his coffee.

"It's practically clean. All I put on it were some grapes."

"It will still need to be washed."

Jasmine snatched it up and rushed to the counter, then into the hallway to get her backpack and jacket.

"I haven't seen her move that fast in a long time. Did she let you do her hair?"

"No, but I gave her a couple of things to help with the tangles, and they obviously worked."

"Why didn't I think of that? Aunt Louise used to sit patiently and work her way through the tangles, but once, when she drove the kids to school, she got a ticket for speeding."

Annie chuckled. "They're girlie products—a detangler spray and brush. Most guys don't have hair long enough to tangle like hers."

"Jade's hair never tangles as bad as Jasmine's, but then Jasmine is a restless sleeper. I should take her to get it cut. Jade's been talking about cutting hers."

Typical of a man to think of the practical solution. "I wouldn't advise you to do that. Jasmine loves her long hair. All she needs to do is learn to handle it."

"That's why it's good to have a woman around. My solution would have been taking her in for a cut."

"Kicking and screaming all the way." Annie chuckled.

Ian finished his coffee and set the mug on the counter. "Why can't she be more like Jade? Jade isn't nearly as dramatic as Jasmine. My biggest concern for her is getting a sports injury."

"I notice Jade's going to softball practice this afternoon." She pointed to the schedule she had put up on the kitchen wall. "You might take a look at that and make sure I've included all the activities."

As the four children poured into the kitchen, Ian said, "I'll take a look at it tonight and add anything of mine I need on it."

"Everyone ready?" Annie led the siblings to the garage.

Except for Joshua, everyone was silent on the trip to Will Rogers Elementary School. Ian took his own car.

After parking, Annie felt Ian's youngest clasp her hand and tug her toward the building. "I wanna show you my room."

Annie glanced back at Ian and the other three walking behind her. What Joshua had said to her last night still touched her. And yet there would come a time when she would have to leave. She felt a heaviness in her chest.

After Annie met Joshua's teacher and saw where he sat in his room, the next stop was Jade's class then Jasmine's across the hall.

Jasmine's teacher smiled and said to her, "So glad you're here early today, Jasmine. But you don't have to come to the classroom until the last bell rings. I know some of your friends are in the hallway by the back door."

Jasmine put her backpack at her desk and hurried out of the room, passing Ian, Annie and Jeremy in the corridor making their way to his class.

Suddenly the boy stopped, looked away and said, "Dad, I don't want anyone to know about what happened. I'm taking the medicine. I won't have another one."

"Mrs. Haskell needs to know. We won't know about the medication's effectiveness until you've been on it awhile."

Jeremy's mouth dropped open. "You mean I could have a seizure at school?"

Ian nodded. "Not all your tests are back yet, and even then seizures can be unpredictable."

"Then, I don't want to go to school. Not until we know what's going on."

"You only have six more weeks, Jeremy. Nothing may happen during that time."

Fear washed over Jeremy's face. He backed away from Ian and Annie then whirled and raced down the hallway and out the door.

When Ian started forward, Annie touched his arm. "Let me see if I can find him. You need to talk to his teacher without Jeremy. He's scared." She knew that feeling well. Pain from her burns and fear of the unknown had flooded Annie when she woke up in the hospital after the fire. "I need to get some rapport with Jeremy. Let me try. We'll find you in a few minutes."

Later Annie found Jeremy in the parking lot by Ian's car. With his hands crossed over his chest, he slouched back against the Explorer. He saw her and turned away, but he didn't run.

Annie took that as a good sign. "I told your dad I would find you because he needs to talk with your teacher."

"Why? It's none of her business."

"Yes, it is. You're scared, but—"

He folded his arms over his chest. "No, I'm not. I just don't want other people knowing my business."

"I know how that feels."

"No, you don't. I saw a kid at school have a seizure once, and there were a couple of boys laughing."

"Did you laugh?"

Jeremy shoved off the car, his arms ramrod straight at his sides, his hands fisted. "I'd never do that. You don't know me."

"You're right. I don't, but I'd like to, Jeremy. I'm here to help you and your family."

"Yeah, until you find something better. Then you'll be gone just like that." Jeremy snapped his fingers in her face.

"I'm not leaving. I had five other job offers and chose to be with you all."

"Maybe you shouldn't have. I'd rather you leave now than later." Jeremy charged past her and hurried toward the building.

Annie followed, hoping he'd at least go to class. She was a little disappointed at how the conversation had turned out because she knew it wouldn't be easy for her to establish a connection with Jeremy. But she would keep trying. If Amanda hadn't with her after the fire, no telling where she would be today.

At the door into the school, Ian stopped Jeremy and talked quietly to him. Annie stood back, praying Jeremy would go into the building. She could remember how she had built up in her mind all kinds of scenarios if someone saw her scars. She could take a lot of different reactions, but pity was the worst.

When Jeremy stomped toward the entrance, angry but going in the right direction, Ian signaled for her to join him. At Jeremy's classroom door, Ian paused for a few seconds, nodded his head then went inside.

"Mrs. Haskell, I wanted you to meet Annie Knight. She'll usually be dropping off and picking up my kids. I've given you her number in case you can't get hold of me."

Annie shook the middle-aged woman's hand. "I'm so happy to meet you. I want you to know I can be here in twenty minutes if there's a problem."

"I'm glad to meet you, too, Annie. I'll talk with Jeremy and reassure him," the woman whispered. "I've had other students with seizures, and I know what to do. We have a nurse who will be summoned. He'll be fine."

As Annie walked with Ian to the car, he said, "I guess all we can do is wait and see. I would like you to check into Caring Canines, if you don't mind, since you know one of the trainers." He paused at the trunk of the Explorer. "My family needs help."

"You've got it. I can set up a meeting with Emma Tanner."

"Let's keep it quiet. Until I know if this is going to be the best thing for Jeremy, I don't want to say anything to him. I'll have my receptionist call you with times I have available. I do know that noon to one is usually free because my staff goes to lunch."

"I should know something tonight."

After Ian drove away from the school, Annie decided to pay Amanda a visit. She had met Emma at only a couple of combined family gatherings. Besides, she needed to talk to her sister.

A few days later, Ian shook Emma's hand. "I'm so glad you could meet with us."

Annie stepped forward. "It's nice seeing you again."

"Please have a seat." Emma indicated two chairs across from her in the training room. "Amanda told me you'd like to look into getting a seizure dog for your son."

"Since I asked Annie to contact you—" Ian glanced at Annie and smiled "—I've done some research on it. I want to give Jeremy everything that can help him. He isn't dealing well with the idea of having epilepsy."

"So he's been diagnosed?" Emma asked.

Besides Annie, whom he told on the way to Caring Canines, no one else knew, not even Jeremy, that the doctor had confirmed it this morning. "Yes. It appears he'd been experiencing a series of petit mals before he had his grand mal."

"What do you want from a seizure dog?"

To cure his son, but that wasn't a possibility. Seeing Jeremy even more vulnerable the other night when he'd had his seizure heightened Ian's own feelings of helplessness. "One that can alert people if Jeremy has a seizure, stay with him, help him adjust and be a companion, because right now Jeremy needs that. His life, especially in the past six months, has been disrupted again and again. He needs a dog to calm him down. Stress may have been a factor in what triggered his grand mal."

"I have a dog I'm training, but he needs a couple more weeks with me. I could use Jeremy helping me if you think he would like to do that. After school? What do you think?"

Ian grinned, excited at the prospect. "That would be great. Annie, will you be able to bring him here?"

"Sure. Emma, do you think the other three children could play with the other dogs? They're a four-year-old boy and twin girls who are eight."

"Sure. It would be nice if the dogs could interact with different people, especially children." Emma gestured around the large training room. "Our clients have doubled in the past few years. Abbey, my partner, and I are thrilled at all the interest."

"Then I'll be here with the kids, supervising," Annie offered.

"Madi, Abbey's sister-in-law, is often here with the dogs, as well. I'm teaching her to train. She's a natural."

Ian sat forward. "Do you ever have dogs you start to train but they don't work out?"

"Yes, but we also train therapy dogs and a lot of them can do that. A therapy dog is often used to help people through difficult or stressful times. Are you looking for another dog besides the service one?"

When Emma mentioned therapy dogs, Ian wondered if his family would benefit from an animal like that. "I've been thinking about getting a dog for my other three children. They've gone through two deaths in the family in the past two years. Would that interfere with Jeremy's seizure dog?" Ian hadn't thought about the two dogs clashing until now.

"Not necessarily, but if it's all right with you, I'd like to find a dog that's compatible with Rex, the black Lab I think might be a match for Jeremy."

"That's fine as long as it's good with children." Ian rose. "When do you want Jeremy to start?"

"Tomorrow is Saturday. Why don't you all come out here and let Jeremy meet Rex, take a look around?" Emma got to her feet.

"I can come in the afternoon. I have several patients I need to see in the hospital in the morning."

"That's fine with me." Emma shifted toward Annie. "Every time I see you I think you're Amanda. I'm so glad you two wear your hair different or I might never tell you apart. Thanks for coming." Emma gave Annie a hug.

As Annie and Ian left Caring Canines, he glanced at her. "I need to meet this twin of yours. Does she work with children, too?"

Annie chuckled. "No, not yet. She wants to have children, but right now she works as an accountant. I'm glad someone in the family has a good sense of numbers. I struggled through algebra."

"Whereas my forte was math and science." Ian opened her car door for her.

"Well, I hope so since you went into medicine."

Ian rounded the hood and got in. Soon they pulled out onto the highway, heading into Cimarron City. "Since we live on the opposite side of town, you'll be driving a lot after school, especially when Jade goes to softball and Jasmine to ballet."

"I met Jasmine's teacher this week. A remarkable lady."

"Jasmine loves Miss Kit and ballet. They started rehearsing for their big end-of-the-year recital. That's all Jasmine talks about."

At a stop sign Ian peered at Annie. Being around the new nanny made him want to know all about her. He knew how she was with children, but she held part of herself back when they talked. Why? "What did you do as a child?"

"I was like Jade. Sports and camping. I was on the high school softball team until..." Her words faded into silence, and she averted her face.

"Did something happen?" Ian wanted to know what made Annie love children so much. She had a gift with them. In five days she had won over Jade and Joshua and was making progress with Jasmine. He hoped Jeremy would follow suit.

"I lost interest. That's all." Annie looked at him. "How about you?"

Ian glimpsed a flicker of sadness in her eyes, but it quickly disappeared. For some reason, he sensed it was more than losing interest that made her quit softball in high school. What? "After softball did you do something else?"

"No." Her tone was abrupt, tense. As if she was slamming a door in his face.

A car behind him honked. Forcing a chuckle to lighten the mood, Ian drove across the intersection. "I guess I should be paying more attention. I didn't know someone pulled up behind us. To answer your earlier question, I was a science geek and two years ahead of others my age. I went to college at sixteen, which I wouldn't recommend to others. I felt lost and socially behind, so I buried my head in my books."

"When did that change?"

"Who said it has changed?" Ian grinned.

"Ian, I've been around you for the past five days, and I haven't seen a lost and socially behind guy."

"Thank you. At least I think it was a compliment. Zoe, my wife, changed everything. She forced me to adapt because she loved the social life." He remembered their first meeting his senior year in high school. For the first year after her death, he couldn't even think about her without being swallowed in grief. Ian was thankful now he could think and talk about her without getting depressed.

"The kids don't say too much about their mom."

For months after Zoe died, Ian had spent much of his time in his home office working as if it would take his pain away. Aunt Louise finally had demanded he join the family more. "That's probably because of me. I couldn't talk about her much at first. When they stopped asking questions, I was relieved."

"But those questions don't go away. They fester inside, waiting to be answered."

Ian clutched the steering wheel tighter. His defenses rose. "I haven't stopped them from asking." *Not in words anyway.*

"But have you encouraged them to talk about their mother?"

When Ian thought back over the past two years, he

realized all he had done was survive from one day to the next. "No, but you think I should."

"My mother died when I was fifteen. For the longest time no one would say anything about her, especially me."

Had Annie's mother's death been what had stopped her from playing softball? Ian could sympathize with her about losing someone special and being thrown into a downward spiral. "I'm sorry about your mother."

Annie sighed. "Finally as a family we came together and talked about all the good memories we had of Mom. That helped me tremendously, but I didn't realize it until afterward. I went reluctantly to that family meeting."

Maybe I should start with a family meeting. "Annie, I need to eat lunch before going back to work. Do you want to join me, then I'll take you back to the house?"

"Sounds good."

"Good, because up ahead is one of my favorite restaurants." A few minutes later Ian pulled into the parking lot next to Doug's Steakhouse. "Give me a good juicy steak anytime."

"I'm not a big meat eater, but I'm sure they have a salad."

Inside, a waitress showed Ian and Annie to a table in the corner, not far from the stone fireplace.

After they ordered and received their iced teas, Ian said, "Tell me more about having a family meeting."

"It became a necessity for our family with seven children. We were often going in different directions, and besides breakfast in the morning, we didn't sit down together much."

"You got together for breakfast, not dinner?"

"We all started the day pretty much at the same time, but in the evening, some would be at practice or some other school activity, except Sunday-night dinner. Then we would eat together and have our family meeting. Nothing else could be planned during that time."

Would this help his children? Ian's focus had to be on healing his family. "What was your agenda?"

"Whatever we needed to cover, which varied, but there was a schedule of sorts. My dad would open with a prayer and my...mom would close with one." Annie dropped her gaze and cleared her throat. "After she... died, the eldest sibling took her place."

Ian could see her sadness, her struggle to continue, and he knew what she was going through. The pain of losing a loved one could surge to the foreground even after years. He reached across and covered Annie's hand, wishing he could do more to comfort her. "If you don't want to talk about—"

"No, I don't mind. I think a family meeting would be good for yours." Annie slipped her hands into her lap.

But she did mind—at least a part of her. It was written in her tension-filled expression. "What was the first order of business?"

"We each started out giving someone a compliment about something he or she did during the week. Usually it wasn't hard, except when my youngest brother went through his rebellious years. After that we dealt with the problems we were having. And not just those between the kids, but any we had with our parents, too. If something had to be decided, we came up with a solution as a group, but our parents could always veto it."

"Did they?"

"At the beginning when we made ridiculous decisions, but they always told us why. It didn't take us long to see the way we should go. We couldn't stay up till all hours of the night or skip our homework."

"How long did these meetings last with seven children?"

"Usually not too long—maybe an hour or two—unless one of us was straying and needed to be put on the right path. Those 'interventions' could last awhile." Annie picked up her tea and took a long swallow, her gaze on a spot to his left.

There was more to that, but Ian didn't feel he could ask about it. They were just getting to know each other, and Annie was good at putting up a wall. Had her family done an intervention with her? If so, why? In five days he felt she knew all about him and his family while he knew little about her, other than that she was excellent with children, caring and reliable. "After discussing the problems, what did you do?"

"We each told the group something good that happened to us during the week and what we were thankful for. Then the closing prayer."

The waitress brought their food. She set the steak in front of Ian and a Greek salad before Annie.

Ian cut his rib eye. "Okay, when you and your twin became the eldest, who said the closing prayer?"

She chuckled. "We traded each week, although technically Amanda was older by four minutes."

"A diplomatic way of handling it. I'm going to have to remember that with Jade and Jasmine."

"When do you think you'll start having the meeting?"

"I've got to do something. I should have months ago.

You've seen us at meals. We don't really talk. Usually Jeremy is upset and angry at someone and everyone feels that tension."

Ian held his knife and fork poised over his steak. "It's been two years. I need to get my act together. I hope with your help."

Annie forked a few pieces of lettuce. "You have it."

A hint of red brushed her high cheekbones. There were times Annie acted shy, but other times she was a take-charge kind of person. She didn't like a lot of meat and usually ate little, but she loved bacon and had fixed it already several times, enjoying three or four pieces. She was a woman full of contradictions. A woman who fascinated him.

Ian drove the Ford Explorer on Saturday afternoon to Caring Canines with all the children packed into it. Annie looked back to see why everyone, even Joshua, was silent. He was nodding off while Jeremy, sitting next to him, was glaring at the back of his father's head. Jasmine was brushing her hair, and Jade's attention was glued to the ranch where the Caring Canines building was. Horses, some foals, frolicked in a pasture to the left while a lone one was on the right. Probably a stallion.

When Annie saw the training facility, she wondered if she'd had a therapy dog after the fire she would have recovered faster. At the beginning she wouldn't even talk to Amanda about her feelings concerning her mother and the guilt she felt. Instead, she'd kept it locked inside as though that would make it go away.

But it didn't.

Ian came to a stop in front. No one moved to get out

of the car. He gripped the steering wheel so tight his knuckles whitened. Right before he'd come, Ian and Jeremy had had a huge shouting match with his son refusing to come. It was Joshua going into his big brother's room and calmly asking why he didn't want a dog that changed Jeremy's mind. Ten minutes later he agreed to go, but it was clear he wasn't sold on the idea of having a service dog.

Annie put a big smile on her face and turned toward the children. "Are you ready? When I was here yesterday they had twenty dogs being trained for various types of service. Do you know they have one for people with diabetes? It's amazing what these dogs can do."

Joshua grinned. "I wanna see. I want a dog, too."

"You can have mine," Jeremy mumbled under his breath.

"Oh, good." Joshua clapped his hands.

Ian finally twisted around and tried to smile. "I hope we can get two dogs. The one for Jeremy and another for the whole family."

"Let's go," Jade said, opening her door and hopping down.

Jasmine followed, although without much enthusiasm. Joshua waited, but when Jeremy wouldn't leave, the four-year-old scooted across the seat and exited with his sisters.

"I said I'd come to get Joshua to stop pestering me. I didn't say I would get out of the car." Jeremy crossed his arms and dropped his head.

Chapter 6

"I'll take the other kids inside," Annie said and shut her car door.

Ian looked pleadingly at Annie, not sure what to do. He remembered what she'd said about forcing a child to go kicking and screaming somewhere—it wouldn't work. *Lord, help me.* Annie smiled at him then hurried after the children.

Ian fortified himself with a deep breath then turned toward Jeremy. "We need to go inside, son. I've read about what a service dog can do for a person with epilepsy. It's there to help you through seizure and comfort you afterward. This could be good for you."

"How do you know it's good for me? You don't have epilepsy," Jeremy shouted as though he'd kept a plug on his feelings too long and they'd begun leaking out.

"True, but—"

"You don't know everything about me. I'm not sick. I don't need fixing. I don't need a babysitter or a dog." Jeremy hugged his arms against his chest as though he were freezing.

"I never said you were sick."

"I have to take medicine like a sick person."

"That's so you won't have a problem. It's for preventive reasons." Ian's stomach churned with frustration. Getting angry wouldn't solve this problem. "Go inside and at least meet Rex. Don't look at him as a service dog but as the one you wanted when we gave Lady away."

"I'm glad we couldn't get one. I don't want one now."

"Why? You love animals."

"I don't love anything."

Ian glimpsed the hurt behind Jeremy's declaration, and his heartbeat slowed to a throb. "You lost a lot in the past few years. We all have, but you can't give up on caring about others." As Ian said those words, he realized part of him didn't believe what he was saying. Wasn't that what he was doing? Shutting down his emotions and protecting himself from getting hurt again?

"You can't control how I feel."

"True. Tell you what. Meet Rex, and if you still don't want him after spending a few sessions with him, then we won't get him." Because no matter how much he wished it, Rex wouldn't work if Jeremy didn't buy in to the concept of a service dog.

"Sessions?"

"Mrs. Tanner wants you to help her with some of Rex's training. He has a couple of weeks before she feels he's ready to have an owner."

The tense set of his son's shoulders relaxed a little. "How many times do I have to see him?"

"Three. Today and two training sessions. Okay?" Ian prayed his son's love of animals—despite his denial—would have him saying yes to Rex.

Jeremy nodded and shoved open his door.

Before Ian could get out of his car, Jeremy charged toward the building entrance as though going into battle. Ian hurried to catch up.

Ian found his children with Annie and Emma in the fenced play yard out behind Caring Canines. Jeremy stood by the gate. "Let's go in."

"You didn't say I had to participate."

"But you do need to be with the dog. Whether you participate with Rex or not is your choice."

Ian opened the gate and let Jeremy go inside first.

"Jeremy, isn't Rex a beauty?" Jade petted the black Lab with golden-brown eyes.

"Yeah, he's so sweet." Jasmine held her hand out for the dog to lick it.

"Dad, I want this dog." Joshua sat on the grass while a puppy that was part terrier climbed all over him.

"We'll see, Joshua." Ian joined Annie and Emma near Rex while his eldest moved only a few feet forward.

When the twins turned their attention to a couple of the other dogs, Annie said, "It didn't go well?"

"I wasn't even sure if I would get him here." With Annie, Ian didn't feel as if he was alone fighting this battle with Jeremy.

"That's a shame. A service dog won't work for a person unless he wants him," Emma said, reinforcing what Ian already knew. She walked over to Rex, rubbed behind his ears and then headed toward Jeremy with the dog.

Ian tensed, not sure what his son would do. Jeremy straightened, his shoulders thrust back while Emma introduced Rex to him.

"If this doesn't work, I'm not sure what to do for Jeremy."

"Did he tell you why he didn't want Rex?" Annie faced him.

His gaze still trained on Jeremy, Ian said, "He told me he wasn't sick, that he doesn't need fixing."

"It can be hard to accept something life changing like epilepsy, but a lot of children do get used to it. With some modification and the right medication, it can be manageable."

Ian glanced toward Annie, her nearness a balm. "Have you been reading up on it?"

"Yes. I like to be informed as much as possible, but I also know from experience with my friend."

Another thing Ian found he liked about Annie: she was proactive. "I realized in the car I couldn't make him take Rex. There are some things I can't resolve for him."

"Isn't that true with all your children?"

Ian faced Annie, her vanilla scent surrounding him. Everything about her, from her expressive face to even her fragrance, calmed him. "Yes. I'm finding that out. He's hurting, and I can't do a lot but be there for him."

"What did Jeremy say in the car?"

"He's lost too many people and a dog that he loved. He doesn't want to care about anything else." They were the same feelings Ian found himself fighting these days, so he knew exactly what his son was going through. "I think that's the biggest hurdle to having Rex. He was really beginning to respond to Aunt Louise when she died. Then we've had one nanny after another. I'm not sure he'll ever accept you, through no fault of yours."

"I'll keep trying. I'm not easily defeated when I set my mind to something."

The expression on Annie's face confirmed her words and reinforced yet again that Ian wasn't alone. For a long time he'd felt that way, even when Aunt Louise had come to help him. "I've seen that. I predict in a week or so that you and Jasmine will be best buddies."

"Well, I don't know about best buddies, but she'll accept help sometimes in order not to be awakened by my whistle. This morning she asked me for an alarm clock so she could get up by herself."

Ian chuckled. "That's not a bad idea for all the kids. We'll stop on the way home and let them pick out what they want."

"I predict Jasmine will want something pink and frilly."

"They make alarm clocks like that?"

With a grin, Annie nodded and turned to watch the children.

"Is she laying out her clothes the night before yet?"

"No, but she'll have to come to that conclusion on her own."

"I'm glad Joshua is, and he's taking your advice on what goes together."

Annie glanced over her shoulder at Ian. "Having his big sister laugh at his choice on Wednesday did the trick, and I didn't even ask Jasmine to do that. He assaulted her fashion sense with the purple-and-lime-green T-shirt and yellow shorts."

"It took all my restraint not to laugh out loud. He's always loved bright colors."

"Yes, I know. He's always coloring with bright crayons—and not necessarily on paper."

"Oh, look." Ian gestured toward Jeremy stepping closer to Rex and petting the top of his head. "I'd be encouraged if he wasn't frowning so much."

"Rex has two more visits to win him over." The pair started walking toward the kids.

When Ian had covered the distance between him and Jeremy, he knelt next to the black Lab and stroked him. "Rex reminds me of a dog I used to play with when I was young. He lived across the street and was so friendly. Does he do any tricks?"

"A few I taught him. Sit. Lie down. Stay. Come. Lose it." Emma turned to Jeremy. "Here, I'll show you some of them."

Good thing Emma didn't ask his son if he wanted to see the tricks. Judging from his sour expression, Ian expected Jeremy would have probably said no.

After Rex demonstrated sit, lie down and come, Emma withdrew from her big apron pocket a treat. "Stay, Rex." Then she went a few feet away and put the bone on the ground. Rex fixed his attention on the treat but didn't move. "Come." He rushed the bone and snatched it up. "Lose it." Rex dropped it.

Jeremy watched with a gleam of interest in his eyes but didn't say anything.

"Now, I'd call that a well-trained dog. What do you

think, Jeremy?" Ian asked, encouraged by the boy's attention to Rex.

His son lifted his shoulders, spun around and headed for the gate.

After Emma gave Rex the treat, she straightened and said quietly, "He hasn't accepted his situation yet."

"No, but he promised me he would come for two training sessions with Rex. I'm hoping that will change his mind."

"I'll do my best to draw Jeremy in."

"Thank you, Emma." Ian pointed to his other kids. "As you can see, the rest would love to have a dog."

Over the sounds of Joshua giggling as the puppy licked his face, Annie joined Ian, looking around. "This may not have been a good idea. Each one has gravitated to a different dog."

Ian said, "Jasmine, Jade and Joshua, it's time to leave. You all will be coming back on Monday."

Jasmine said goodbye to a black poodle while Jade hugged a cocker spaniel. Joshua ignored his dad's announcement.

Annie smiled. "I'll take the girls and find Jeremy. We'll be at the car. Have fun trying to get Joshua to come with you."

"I'll trade jobs," Ian said then walked toward his youngest, the sound of his laughter sweet to hear. For a brief wild moment, he considered getting a dog for each of them but quickly dismissed it. Annie would be stuck with caring for all of them, and he didn't want to lose her.

Ian sat on the grass next to Joshua. "He's cute."

"I wanna take him home. Can I?"

"No, he isn't ours to take. He belongs here, but you're coming back on Monday."

Joshua picked up the squirming puppy and held him against his chest. "I don't wanna leave." His lower lip stuck out. "I wanna stay."

Ian had one son who couldn't get out of the place fast enough, and the other he would have to pry away from the puppy. Ian took the terrier mix and passed him to Emma standing nearby. "We've got to go. If you don't leave now, Joshua, you won't get to come back on Monday." Which meant he would have to find someone to watch him, since Annie would be with the other children. When Joshua jumped up and ran for the gate, relief washed over Ian, and he hurried after his son to make sure he didn't let the dogs out.

As they strolled toward the building, Joshua took Ian's hand. Something as simple as that reminded him how much he loved each of his children.

At the car Joshua climbed into his car seat, and Jade buckled him in. In the far back sat Jasmine, while Annie slid out of the Ford Explorer and motioned to Ian to come near.

When he did, she whispered, "I think Jeremy was having a petit mal seizure when we were getting into the car. For a few seconds, he didn't respond or even know we were here."

"Thanks. I wonder how many he has that we never see."

"It's hard to say. I'm trying to keep an eye on him, but he loves to stay in his room."

Before Annie got back into the front seat, Ian clasped

her hand. "Thanks. With everything that has been happening, I'm feeling a tad bit overwhelmed."

One of her eyebrows arched. "Only a tad?"

"I was trying to be tough and strong and not admit the full extent." Ian smiled and rounded the hood of the SUV, wondering what he would be doing without Annie's help.

On Sunday evening Annie sat on one side of Joshua while Ian was on the other. The rest of the children were seated in chairs in the den so that the family formed a loose circle.

Ian finished the opening prayer, took a deep breath and said, "This is our first family meeting, but we are going to have one every Sunday evening at this time."

"Why? What's a family meeting?" Jasmine asked.

"It's a time we hash out any problems we're having. But not just that. It's also when we can talk about the good things happening to us." Ian shot a look at Annie, as if to tell her to step in at any time.

Annie held up a squishy yellow ball. "Only one person should talk at a time so we can hear what's being said. The person with the ball will have the floor but can't hold it the whole time." She passed it to Ian.

"I thought we would start by telling the person to our right one thing good about them. I'll start." He turned to Joshua, saying, "You were ready for school every day this week." Then he gave his youngest the ball and pointed to Annie.

"I love your pancakes. Can we have them again?" Joshua grinned and passed the ball to Annie.

Looking at Jasmine, Annie tried to decide what to

say. "Jasmine, I think your idea about an alarm clock was great."

By the time it was Jeremy's turn at the end, his frown had evolved into a scowl. "This is a dumb idea." He tossed the ball to his dad.

"I need to go over the few rules we'll have. If you can't tell someone something good, don't say anything. When you're through talking, put the ball on the coffee table. Then the person who wants to talk will grab it. If we are discussing a problem, everyone needs to listen to the others. Every family member has a voice in this meeting."

Joshua snatched the ball from his dad's hand. "Even me?"

Ian laughed. "Yes. During the week if you have a problem you want to talk about, write it down on the chart in the kitchen. Joshua, you can have Annie or me do it for you. Some things have to be dealt with immediately, but there are a lot that we'll be able to decide as a family. Oh, and the last rule is no shouting. Speak in a calm voice." Ian put the ball on the table.

Annie knew that would be the hardest one to keep for some of them.

Jade took the ball and said, "I like this, and I have a problem I want to talk about. We need a dog."

Through the discussion about having a dog everyone gave an opinion except Jeremy. He folded his arms over his chest and lowered his head.

"It looks as though you all want to get a dog. We saw some yesterday. Which one do you think would be best?" Ian looked around the circle while Jasmine, Jade and Joshua gave their suggestions.

Suddenly Jeremy shot to his feet. "I don't want a dog! I don't need Rex!" Then he whirled around and ran from the room.

Annie remembered the time she'd hurried away when her family gathered to talk to her about the fire. No matter how much they reassured her, the guilt still ate at her. If only she'd blown out the candle before going to bed, her mother would be alive today. That fact wasn't going to change. But slowly the anger toward others had abated, and she'd learned to deal with her anguish internally rather than lash out at her family.

Annie stood. "I'll check on Jeremy while you guys talk." She wanted somehow to get through to the hurting child. She knew what deep pain Jeremy was in.

Ian nodded.

Annie headed for the staircase to check Jeremy's room, where he usually hid out. But when she started down the hallway, she noticed the door was open, and he kept it closed when he was there. After checking it and the bathroom the children used, she went through the rest of the house then returned to the den and motioned for Ian.

He came out in the corridor. "What's wrong?"

"Jeremy isn't inside. I wanted you to know before I look outside. Does he have a special place he would go?"

"No. I'll take the back while you search the front." He poked his head into the den. "Jasmine and Jade, watch Joshua. We'll be outside."

While Ian made his way to the kitchen to go out to the backyard, Annie stepped out onto the front porch. About forty-five minutes of daylight were left. She prayed they found him before that.

Descending the stairs to the sidewalk, Annie looked up and down the street and spotted Jeremy three houses away, sitting on the curb.

She started to yell his name but didn't, afraid Jeremy would run. Instead, she went to the gate on the side of the McGregor home and quickly found Ian in the backyard. "He's a few houses away."

Ian joined her, and they started for Jeremy, who was still sitting at the curb. The boy looked up and spied them coming. He bolted to his feet and turned to flee. He took two steps and then collapsed to the ground, his body stiffening and quaking.

Chapter 7

"Keep track of the time," Ian shouted as he hastened to his son. His heart pounded his chest the way his steps pounded the earth as he cut the distance to Jeremy. "Son, I'm here. You'll be all right," he said in as soothing a voice as possible. He didn't know if Jeremy heard him or not, but he wanted him to know he wasn't alone.

Wishing he had something to cushion Jeremy's head, Ian turned him on his side and protected his thrashing body as much as he could without restraining him.

When Annie arrived, he glanced at her. "How long?"

"One minute but he's calming down some." Annie gestured toward Jeremy on the small patch of grass between the street and sidewalk. "Thank God he hit the ground, not the concrete."

Ian closed his eyes for a second and sent up a prayer. Finally—an eternity in Ian's mind—Jeremy's eyelids stopped fluttering, and his rigid body began to relax. Ian checked his son for any injuries caused by the fall.

Behind Annie, a neighbor asked, "Is there anything I can do to help?"

Ian glanced up and noticed several others who lived on the street standing around. "He'll be okay. Thanks for your concern." Then to Annie, Ian added, "I'm going to carry him back to the house."

She nodded and asked the people to move back.

Ian wanted to get Jeremy inside before he became angry, his probable reaction when he came out of the seizure, especially if he saw all the people watching him. Although not unconscious, Jeremy hadn't gotten his bearings yet, his gaze still dazed.

Annie went ahead of Ian and opened the front door, only to find all the children gathered in the foyer.

"Is Jeremy okay?" Jade chewed her bottom lip.

"Did he have a seizure?" Jasmine rubbed her hands up and down her arms.

Joshua's eyes filled with tears.

Ian answered, "He had a seizure, but he'll be fine. Go with Annie and start getting ready for bed."

"But it's too early—"

"Jasmine, go." Ian started for the staircase while Annie tried to calm them.

He'd seen people have seizures before, but when it was his son, he needed to detach himself to handle it in a matter-of-fact way. Otherwise his children would sense all the emotions rampaging through him. With time he prayed he'd do a better job of masking his fear that Jeremy wouldn't pull out, and he'd lose him like Zoe and Aunt Louise.

When Ian placed Jeremy on his bed, he caught his son's look, his forehead knitted.

"What happened?" Jeremy murmured, blinking his eyes several times.

"You had a seizure in front of the Clearys' house."

Red flooded Jeremy's pasty complexion. "Who saw me?"

"A few of our neighbors. All adults."

Jeremy firmed his mouth in a hard line and rolled to his side. "I'm tired."

Ian backed away from the bed. He removed a pile of clothing on a chair then sank down onto it. He didn't feel comfortable leaving Jeremy. What if he had another seizure on top of this one? More than ever he realized Jeremy needed a dog to let Ian or Annie know when he had a seizure. What happened outside earlier could have ended badly, and Ian might not have known about it. He didn't want to restrict his son's activities, but he might have to until his medication controlled his seizures better. Ian didn't look forward to yet another battle with Jeremy, but his safety came first.

A sound behind him drew his attention. Annie started toward him, but he rose, palm out, and made his way to her, moving out into the hallway. He didn't want Jeremy overhearing any discussion about him.

"How is he?" Annie asked, her large brown eyes full of concern. "The kids have a million questions. I told them I'd talk to you. They're worried."

"He's alert now. He told me he's tired, but that may also be his way of avoiding talking to me."

"If you want, I'll sit with him while you talk with the kids."

"Thanks. I need to reassure them." And hope he could put at least their fears to rest. "I want to call his doctor, too. Good thing Brandon's a friend."

"Don't worry. I'll take care of Jeremy while you do that, and if you need me to stay part of the night with him while you sleep, I can."

For one impulsive moment, all Ian wanted to do was hold Annie in his arms and draw comfort from her. When he'd first met her, he'd thought she wasn't ugly but not a beauty, either. But now all he saw was a woman whose beauty shone from deep inside her. Would things have been different with his children if she'd been their first nanny rather than the fourth one? Would Jeremy have come to him about his concerns about blanking out?

"I'm going to sleep again in his room. It worked okay the other night, but I appreciate the offer. You come back here from your day off and end up dealing with all this."

"When children are involved, schedules and plans often get discarded. I'm used to it." She smiled.

He chuckled. "I'll be back in a little while. Kids first, then Brandon."

Ian found the children in Jade's bedroom, his two daughters sitting on the bed with Joshua between them. He'd been crying, his eyes red. The twins were comforting him. Now Ian had to do the same for all three of them.

He lifted his son into his arms. "Your big brother will be okay."

"He isn't gonna die?"

"No, he'll be fine." Jeremy's health wasn't in his

control, but it felt right saying that to his children. Ian sat at the desk and placed Joshua on his lap. "Annie said you all are worried and have questions. I'll try to answer them."

"Is this gonna happen all the time?" Jade scooted back on her bed and crossed her legs.

"I don't know. I hope not. I hope the right medication dosage can be found soon to control the seizures."

"I saw him on the ground. Did he fall?" Jasmine asked.

"Yes, sometimes a person's muscles go slack and he drops. So you were looking out the window?"

Jasmine nodded.

"How much did you see?"

"Not much. You blocked my view. What do we do if one of us is the only person around?"

"Good question, Jasmine. Get help. Place something soft under his head. And if you can, roll him onto his side, but don't hold him down. Sometimes a person who has a seizure flails and thrashes. He could hurt you and himself if you try stopping him. You should move anything dangerous away from him. Above all else, be calm and stay close until help comes. The seizure will run its course." As he said this, his children's eyes grew rounder, and none of them spoke.

"Calm? How?" Jade finally asked.

"I know the first time I saw a seizure, it scared me, but remember Jeremy will get better. Talk to him if you want. Tell him he'll be okay." If they said it, hopefully they would believe it. It had helped Ian to do that.

"I'm scared." Joshua snuggled against Ian.

"I know it can be scary, but don't let Jeremy know that. He already feels as if people think he's strange.

Come to me instead. Everyone has problems. Joshua, you do something without thinking about if it's dangerous or not. Jeremy has seizures. That's his problem right now."

Jasmine glared at Joshua. "Yeah, remember when you were standing on the railing? You could have really hurt yourself. You scared me."

"And me," Ian added.

"It wasn't gonna hurt me. I wasn't scared. I had my cape on."

Jasmine leaped to her feet, her arms straight at her side. "You can't fly with a cape." With a huff she said, "I'm going to lay out my clothes for tomorrow and get ready for bed." She marched from the room.

"Did I hear right? She's choosing what she's gonna wear now?" Jade shook her head in wonderment.

"Yep." Ian stood, holding Joshua in his arms. "And it's time for you to get your pj's on and brush your teeth."

"I don't wanna go to bed."

"Sorry, dude. You have school tomorrow." He carried his youngest from Jade's room, set him down and watched as he scurried to his room.

Ian walked toward his bedroom to call the doctor and passed Jeremy's. He glanced in the doorway and spied Annie. Of late, he'd felt as if he was taking one blow after another. If it hadn't been for Annie this past week, he didn't know if he could have kept it together. But he had—because of her presence.

Tuesday all the children piled out of the Ford Explorer and hurried to Caring Canines. Jeremy remained in the front seat, staring out the windshield.

"You worked well with Rex yesterday." Annie removed the key from the ignition.

He harrumphed.

"You didn't say much when I picked you up from school. Everything go okay today?"

"It was just great," he said in a sarcastic tone.

"What happened?"

"Nothing."

"Sometimes talking about it helps."

Jeremy swiveled around and narrowed his eyes. *"Nothing happened."* He drew those two words out.

"Okay, that's great." Annie heard the doubt in her voice. She was sure Jeremy knew she didn't believe him.

He pressed his lips together, his gaze scissoring through her. "Okay. I was moved to the front of the classroom this morning, close to the teacher's desk like I'm a troublemaker. I haven't done anything wrong."

"Did you talk to your teacher about it?"

"Yeah. She wanted to keep a closer eye on me. Even Joshua, Jasmine and Jade look at me like I'm weird."

"How so?"

"As if they're waiting for me to have a seizure and worrying what they're gonna do."

"The unknown is scary for them and they love you, so they're worried."

He crossed his arms. "I'm not broken."

"I know that. You know it and your dad does. It might take others a little more time."

Jeremy shoved open the door, stepped out and walked toward the building.

As Annie followed, her cell phone rang, and she saw

it was Ian. She greeted him then said, "We just arrived at Caring Canines."

"Good. My last patient canceled, so I'm heading there. Did Jeremy give you any problems?"

"Nope. He's already inside." Annie opened the door and slipped into the building, the sound of dogs barking in the background.

"His teacher called and said Jeremy was angry when he left. He got moved to the front by her desk, and he doesn't want to be there. He doesn't want any special treatment. I'll email her and see if she'll move him back."

"I'm not sure you should. That might draw even more attention to him."

"True. I'll see what happens this week. I'm turning into the ranch. I'll be there in a moment."

Annie said, "See you soon." She disconnected and returned her cell phone to her pocket then continued her trek to the back training room to make sure Jeremy was working with Emma and Rex. She paused at the doorway.

For all his complaining about attending, Jeremy was focusing his attention on what Emma was saying, Rex sitting next to him. Suddenly Rex got up and went behind Jeremy just as the boy crumbled to the floor, keeping his head from hitting the tiles.

Emma rolled him on his side and glanced at her watch while Annie found a small pillow and placed it under his head. Rex positioned himself next to Jeremy.

"I think Rex sensed the seizure coming on." Emma looked up at Annie. "I didn't see anything until he started dropping to the floor, but Rex was behind him before he fell."

"They're connecting." Annie heard the sound of footsteps in the hallway. "Ian is coming."

As Ian entered the room, Jeremy came out of his seizure, confused, scowling. Rex wiggled closer to Jeremy and settled down.

"How long was this one?"

"Ninety seconds," Emma replied and moved so Ian could check his son. "Rex cushioned Jeremy's head, so he didn't hit it on the floor when he went down."

"Is Rex okay?" Ian stroked the dog next to his son.

Emma ran her hands over the black Lab. "He's fine. That's one of the ways a service dog is able to help."

Annie remembered the other children outside and said, "I'm going to check on Jasmine, Jade and Joshua."

As she made her way to the outside play area, she hoped Madi was out there today like yesterday. The twins had listened to every word the teenage girl said. Jade had even declared on the way home that she wanted to volunteer at Caring Canines like the owner's sister-in-law.

Outside, Madi leaned against the chain-link fence talking to Jade while Joshua played with the cocker spaniel Jade had on Saturday. Annie opened the gate and walked into the enclosure as Jasmine turned her attention to the cocker spaniel.

"What's her name?" Jasmine called out to Madi.

"Daisy. She's a sweetheart. I wish I could have another dog, but my brother says I already have a kennel full."

Jade smiled at Annie then turned to Madi. "Is she going to be trained?"

"Maybe as a therapy dog. She was left a few weeks ago out by the gate."

"I can't believe people dump their pets like that." Jade knelt near the cocker spaniel.

"It happens at least once a month. It makes Abbey and Emma mad. I help them find homes for the ones that aren't trained. Have you all decided on a dog to take home yet?"

"We can pick today?" Joshua asked.

Madi looked at Annie who answered, "Yes, if you three can decide on one. Your dad talked with Emma yesterday about it." Then in a lowered voice, Annie continued, "Madi, I need to go inside to see how Jeremy is doing. Will you help the children choose a dog?"

Madi grinned. "I would love to."

At the door into the building, Annie glanced over her shoulder at the three children with Madi sitting on the ground in a circle around Daisy. Knowing they were in good hands, she hurried inside to see what was happening with Jeremy. As she approached the training room, Jeremy ran out, anger stamped on his face.

She started to go after him but stopped to see what Ian wanted her to do. She stepped into the room. His haggard look showed how bad the situation must have gotten. "Do you want me to try talking to him?"

"You can try. He wouldn't listen to Emma or me. I'll go get the other children. We need to leave and let Emma get back to work." Defeat coated each word.

Annie wanted to comfort him, but at the moment Jeremy was her priority. The torment the child was going through tore at her heart. Annie found him on the other side of the Ford Explorer, sitting on the pavement, crying.

Suddenly a memory intruded into her thoughts: the first day she'd glimpsed herself in a mirror after she'd been discharged from the hospital. Stunned and broken, she'd sunk to the floor and sobbed at the sight of the red scars from what remained of her right ear and across her torso to her left hip, where the beam had landed on her.

No one could reach her at that time. She wouldn't listen. But she had to try with Jeremy. She didn't want him to go through the heartache she did.

She sat next to the child, about a foot away, and rested her arms on her raised knees. Staring off at a pasture with a stallion, she remained silent, waiting for Jeremy to say something. He needed to let his emotions out, then she would see if she could help.

Slowly his tears abated and he peered at her, more drained than angry. "Why are you here?"

"To be here for you."

"I don't need…" Tears welled into his eyes again, and he knuckled them away.

"Everyone needs someone, Jeremy. What you're going through isn't easy. I know. I went through something similar when I was fifteen."

"You had seizures?"

"No, something different, but it affected my whole life."

Jeremy's forehead wrinkled. "Then, you don't—"

Annie turned toward him and lifted her hair away from the scarred side of her face. "I was in a fire and burned badly from here—" she ran her hand across her chest to her thigh "—to here and was in the burn unit for weeks. I went through several operations. I missed a semester of school."

Jeremy's eyes widened while she combed her hair back into place.

"It changed my life. My mother died in that fire, and I miss her every day."

His bottom lip trembled.

"I don't tell people about it. I still try to hide it, and I prefer that you don't say anything until I at least tell your father and your siblings myself. My burns could define who I am if I let them. You can let your seizures define you if you want, but they aren't really you."

Jeremy blinked, opened his mouth to say something but snapped it closed.

"I worried about people staring at me, making fun of me or looking at me horrified. The people I loved never did, and I learned over time the others weren't important. The first person outside my family to visit me was my friend Becca, who had epilepsy. She accepted me for who I was and was there to support me. I was so angry I didn't make it easy for her to stick by me."

Jeremy looked at the stallion. "I don't want to die from a seizure."

"Why do you think you will?"

"My mom had one in the hospital right before she died."

"I understand from your father your mother died from a stroke. That can sometimes cause a seizure, but you aren't having a stroke."

"Then, why am I having seizures? What did I do wrong?" A tear ran down his face, and he swiped it away.

"Not a thing, Jeremy. Things happen to us that we have no control over. That's when we have to turn our lives over to the Lord and not worry about the future. It's in His hands. About the only thing worrying does is stress us out, and that's not healthy. Jeremy, have you told your dad about your fears and your mother?"

Jeremy shook his head. "Mom's death makes him sad."

"He'd want to know this. You should talk to him." Annie knew how much Ian loved his children. He made mistakes like all parents, but he was a good father.

"Maybe." He looked again at the stallion.

"May I tell him? I won't if you don't want me to."

A long moment passed before Jeremy finally nodded.

"How about Rex? I saw him cushion your fall. Rex can do some amazing things."

"I know, but I don't want to take him to school. The kids will know something is wrong with me."

"Why don't you tell them? Most kids would be interested, especially your friends. And dogs are a great way to start a conversation."

"Maybe."

"Your dad is rounding up the other children to leave. If you think you might take Rex, you need to let him and Emma know."

"Rex was right next to me. He even licked my face."

"You'll never be alone when you have a seizure with Rex."

"He'll sleep with me?"

"Yes. He'll become your buddy. I understand you used to have a dog and loved her."

"Yeah. She died. I don't want to lose another pet."

Annie heard Joshua's voice, which meant the family was almost at the cars. "Death is hard, but it's part of life. If you never have a pet, you can't enjoy years of companionship with one." She rose and held out her hand to help Jeremy to his feet.

He stared at it a few seconds then clasped it. "I won't say anything to the others about your scars." His words, spoken in a serious tone, forged a bond between them.

"Thank you."

When Jeremy stood, his siblings climbed in the other side of the Ford Explorer while Ian talked with Emma at the entrance into the building. He held a leash with the cocker spaniel on it.

"It looks as though your brother and sisters picked Daisy as their pet."

Jeremy skirted the front of the Ford Explorer and walked toward his father.

Annie trailed Jeremy to find out what was going on concerning Rex.

Daisy greeted Jeremy with her tail wagging. He patted her, then stood next to his dad.

"Have you decided to continue training with Rex?" Ian asked.

"Yes, but I don't know about taking him to school."

Ian clasped his son's shoulder. "We'll take it one day at a time."

"You won't make me?"

"No. I think you'll find Rex is good for you and want to take him." Ian turned to Emma. "I guess they'll be back tomorrow. Okay?"

"Yes. Jeremy, Rex is already bonding with you so I'm glad you decided to continue the training."

Ian said, "For the rest of this week, I'll clear my schedule so I can bring Jeremy. I want to be involved." He shook Emma's hand.

As Jeremy, Ian and Annie walked toward the Ford Explorer, the boy said, "You don't have to if you don't want to, Dad. I'll be okay."

"I know that, son, but I saw Rex in action today, and it's fascinating to see what a dog can do to help people."

"In the meantime, your sisters and brother can acclimate Daisy to your home so hopefully they won't complain too much that they aren't coming." Annie opened the back door to the Ford Explorer and the cocker spaniel got in with Jade's assistance.

While Jeremy slid into the front seat, Annie accompanied Ian toward the rear. She paused and lowered her voice, saying, "Jeremy said I could tell you. One of his concerns is that his mom died after a seizure."

Ian closed his eyes for a few seconds. "I forgot he was visiting his mom when she had her last stroke, and she did have a seizure. Everything got so hectic after that. I wish he'd said something to me."

"He thought you were sad when you talked about your wife."

Ian sucked in a large breath and released it slowly. "He's right. I'll have a talk with him. In fact, I will with each of my children. They need to know they can come to me with anything."

"Sounds good. See you at home." Annie turned toward the SUV.

Ian caught her arm. She glanced back at him. The look of appreciation in his eyes made her feel special in that moment, more than she had in a long time.

"Annie, I don't even know where to begin thanking you for your help."

She covered his hand with hers, the physical connection making everything, except the man near her, fade from her consciousness. She smiled. "You just did." Then she continued around the Ford Explorer to the driver's side, missing his touch. Too dangerous for her to get used to that. Annie had let down her defenses in college, risked her heart with David and ended up brokenhearted. She couldn't go through that again.

Annie realized as she started the car that when she'd said, "See you at home," she'd felt as if Ian's house really was her home. More than she had at any place she'd worked as a nanny. The realization stunned her.

Later that night Annie fixed herself a cup of tea to sip while she read a suspense story. After the eventful day, she needed some downtime before trying to sleep. Dinner earlier was the first time that Jeremy hadn't been angry or ready to argue over everything being discussed. He even paid attention to Daisy. The dog chose to sleep with Jade, much to Joshua's disappointment.

As Annie moved toward the living area in her apartment with her drink, a knock sounded at the door. She detoured and opened it to find Ian standing on the landing. "Is Jeremy okay?"

"Yes. They all are, even Jade with Daisy. I won't keep you, but I wanted to thank you again for letting me know what was going on with Jeremy. Tonight he actually participated in the dinner discussion. I wish he'd felt he could tell me, but at least he told you. I intend to talk to him tomorrow on the way home from Caring Canines."

"You're welcome, Ian. Come in. I need to talk to you."

"As long as you don't give your notice." He grinned.

"No, definitely not that, but it's something I should have told you from the beginning."

Confusion clouded his face as he shut the door and moved toward the living area, sitting down on a chair while she took the couch.

"Sorry. That sounds as though it's serious. Well, I guess it is but only to me." Ian's intense look, as though he were trying to figure out what she was going to say, made her nervous.

"Something wrong?"

"No." Annie swallowed hard. "I told Jeremy about a problem I had as a teenager and how hard it had been on me. I was angry at life. I feel I need to tell you, too, and if it's okay, I want the rest of your children to know."

"What are you talking about?"

Annie glanced toward the kitchen, stalling. "Would you like some tea?"

Ian sat forward in his chair kitty-corner from her on the couch and took her hand. "No, but I would like you to tell me before I go crazy wondering what you want to say."

Her breath trapped in her lungs, Annie brushed back her hair and pushed her turtleneck collar down to reveal her scarred ear and neck.

Chapter 8

Deeply scarred tissue, mostly red with a few white streaks, took Ian by surprise. He'd been thinking all kinds of things Annie could tell him, but this wasn't one of them. "What happened?"

"I was in a fire at our family cabin. A beam fell across me, pinning me. My father managed to rescue me, but not—my mother in the other room." Tears filled her eyes.

The urge to comfort her overwhelmed him. Ian had helped burn victims throughout his career, and the pain associated with that kind of injury was intense. He moved to the couch, drawing her against him. If in that moment he could have wiped the memory and effects of the fire from her, he would have. She had done so much for him and his children in a short time. "I'm so sorry. I know how hard that must have been for you."

Annie shuddered as though memories inundated her. "I didn't even get to go to my mother's funeral because I was in the burn unit."

It had been important to Ian to go to Zoe's funeral to say goodbye. If he hadn't been able, there was no telling the emotional state he would be in now. "Did your family have a memorial service for her later so you could attend?"

"Yes…" She pulled back, erecting a wall between them. "But I'm not the issue. Jeremy is. I told him because I wanted him to realize I know what he's going through. His life has been changed suddenly, and he has to find ways to deal with it. Until his seizures are under better control, he'll need to be watched more. He's rebelling. I did, too."

Ian clamped his teeth together to keep all his questions about her situation to himself. His inquiries wouldn't be appreciated, and that saddened him. He wanted Annie to share her life with him as he had with her. "So that's the reason he changed his mind about Rex," he finally said.

"I don't know if it was, but when you're hurting like he is, knowing others have survived difficult situations helps. I told him about losing my mother, too. He needs Rex, and I think he'll figure that out once Rex comes to live with him."

Are you all right? The urge to ask her overwhelmed him, but he couldn't. Ian had the feeling Annie didn't share her experience with many, and he tried to respect her privacy.

Her hair, back in its usual place now, effectively covered her visible scars. The doctor in him wanted to examine them and see what he could do. Did she see her scars as a penance because she'd survived the fire and her mother hadn't? Why hadn't she done more to diminish them? There were creams and makeup that could help. Her ear could be replaced with a prosthetic one. Was it money? Or something else? As the thoughts swirled through his mind, Ian realized he needed more information, but he didn't feel he could ask her. Maybe after she'd worked for him longer, he could get her the help she needed.

"At least tomorrow I can reassure him that his mother didn't have epilepsy and didn't die from a seizure. When are you going to tell the others?"

"When the time is right. I don't want them to think it's a big deal. I've learned to accept my scars."

"There are some procedures that would mask—"

"Don't. They are part of me now."

"But you can get help."

Annie bolted to her feet. "I can't afford the medical procedures. End of conversation."

Ian knew when to back off, but that didn't mean he would forget it. He could help her. He needed to help her. "I shouldn't have overstepped my boundaries. In a short time, you've done so much for my family that…" The anger in her expression stilled the rest of his sentence. "I'd better return to my house."

On the short walk to the back door into the kitchen, Ian couldn't shake the idea there was something he could do for Annie. It was hard for him to turn away from someone in need, especially someone who had been there for him. Someone he cared about. Maybe once they got to know each other better, she would be willing to listen to what he could arrange for her.

"That went well with Rex today." Ian pulled away from Caring Canines the next day, still not sure how to approach his son about his mother.

At a four-way stop sign on the highway into Cimarron City, Ian glanced toward Jeremy. His son had been active in the training with Rex rather than a bystander. That might not have happened without Annie sharing her ordeal. When they'd talked in her apartment last night, Ian had gotten a glimpse of what had made her who she was today. She'd acted as though she'd accepted what happened. Ian wasn't so sure she really had, and if not, she could never live her life fully.

He pulled out into the intersection. "I had a talk with Annie yesterday. She told me about when you saw your mother have a seizure right before she died. Jeremy, I want you to know that a seizure didn't cause her death. Not at all. She died from a second stroke." His voice quavered with the memory.

"I miss her."

"So do I, but I know that your mom would want you to move on. She would want the best for you." *And for me.* Ian needed to listen to his own words. Zoe wouldn't want him mourning her for the rest of his life. "Son, you can talk to me any time you want about anything. In fact, at our next family meeting, we should talk about your mother. I don't want you to think you can't."

"Did… Annie…tell you anything else?"

"Yes. She told me about her scars."

Jeremy blew a long breath out. "Good. I didn't know

how long I could keep that a secret. Why does she hide them?"

"Probably for the same reason you don't want any-one to see you having a seizure."

"She's embarrassed? She thinks someone will make fun of her?"

Ian nodded.

"But she's a grown-up."

"Age doesn't have anything to do with it."

Jeremy was silent for a long moment, then asked, "What do you do when someone makes fun of you?"

"Did they?"

"No, not yet."

"If it happens, ignore them." Had someone made fun of Annie? He hated the thought that she might have been ridiculed because of her scars.

"How?"

"Walk away. Once you engage them you feed into what they want. Most people make fun of a person be-cause they are scared what might happen to them or they're trying to get attention."

"There's a guy at school like that."

"Have you ever told your teacher?"

"I'm not a tattletale."

"There are times you need to speak up." Ian pulled into the garage.

"How am I supposed to know when?"

"If it's hurting someone in any way, you should let your teacher know. Has this guy ever bothered you?"

Jeremy shook his head. "But if I have a seizure, he will."

"Let me know if he does."

His son climbed from the Lexus.

"Jeremy, will you?"

He sighed. "Maybe." Then he hurried toward the door to the breezeway.

At a slower pace Ian made his way into the house, not sure how successful he'd been with talking with his son. Only time would tell.

When he came into the kitchen, Annie was drawing a star over April 27. She looked back at him and smiled. "Joshua told me I forgot to mark his birthday."

"He won't let anyone forget." Ian started across the room but stopped when he spied a vase full of red tulips. "Where did these come from?"

"I think I have a secret admirer. They were in my car seat this morning when I drove the kids to school." She finished the yellow star and faced him. "Any idea who?"

"A secret admirer?"

"Perhaps."

Or...something else. "I'll be right back to help with supper."

Ian entered his office and put his briefcase on his desk then went to the window on the left side of the house. His red tulips were gone. Cut. He laughed and decided not to say anything to Annie.

A week later Annie entered the dining room to find Joshua standing at the window looking out front. Daisy sat next to him. "Are you watching for Jeremy and your dad?"

"Yes. So is Daisy."

"She is?" Smiling, Annie crossed to Joshua and sat

in a chair near him. "Your sisters are upstairs watching from Jade's room."

"Yup, but I'm gonna get outside faster."

"Not without me."

A few days earlier he'd darted across a parking lot at school without looking. A woman had had to slam on her brakes and barely missed him. His teacher had still been shaken when Annie had picked up Joshua from school.

He hung his head. "I know."

Annie peered out the window and saw Ian's car turn in to the long driveway. "They're here."

Joshua started to run for the front door, but Annie caught up with him and stopped his mad dash. She offered her hand to him as Jade and Jasmine stormed down the stairs.

Ian pulled into the garage but left the door up. By the time Jeremy climbed from the car and Rex followed, they were surrounded by everyone wanting to pet the new dog.

Ian joined Annie. He looked tired. He'd left the house early that morning for surgery. "How did it go?"

"Jeremy was actually excited about getting Rex." Ian leaned close and murmured, "Although he tried to hide it."

His whispered words tickled the side of her face, creating goose bumps on her arms. "I've noticed he's been researching black Labs and service dogs. I'm not sure he'll admit it, but I think he's glad he went ahead with getting Rex."

"Did you get everything set up for Joshua's birthday party Saturday?"

"I've invited his classmates and have the All-Star Combo bounce house being delivered that morning. They'll be able to jump, climb and slide."

"And they'll be exhausted when they leave."

Annie backed away as the children left the garage with both dogs. "I think Daisy and Rex will be the hit of the party."

"I think so, too. Has Jeremy changed his mind about taking Rex to school?"

"No, but give him time," she said, "especially when he sees the younger kids wanting to know all about Rex."

"I'm praying he doesn't have an incident at school before that." Ian strolled with Annie toward the front door.

"Do you see how Daisy follows Rex? Emma told me they were buddies at Caring Canines. She's been a good choice for the kids."

Ian held the door open for Annie. "Have you gotten anything else from your secret admirer?" A gleam lit his eyes.

"Yes, how did you know?" It couldn't be Ian. She felt as though one of the kids was behind the gifts she'd been receiving the past week.

He shrugged. *Does he know something?* "A candy bar, my favorite kind. I remember all of us talking at dinner the other night about what we liked, and surprise, I had one on my seat in the Explorer this morning."

"I'm sure this secret admirer will come forward eventually." Ian looked away. "I've got some literature you might be interested in. I meant to give it to you last night, but with the kids going to all their activities and then getting them ready for bed, I forgot."

As the four children ascended the stairs, Annie tried to decide if she should point-blank ask him who her secret admirer was. "Literature? If it's not a suspense story, I won't be reading it."

"This isn't a book. I'll be right back." Ian headed toward his office on the ground floor.

What was he up to? When she saw him carrying a brochure, Annie's stomach tightened. Something told her she didn't want to see it. She straightened, tensing as though preparing for a hit.

"This is about prosthetic ears." Ian handed it to her.

Annie stared at it but wouldn't take it. "I can't afford it, so there's no reason to read it." Anger welled in her, quickly replaced by hurt. Why couldn't he accept her, flaws and all? "I'm going to check on the kids then start dinner. I don't need help this evening." She started for the stairs.

"Wait, Annie. I didn't mean to make you mad."

She rotated toward him. "I'm not angry. Disappointed."

She hurried up the steps, needing to put space between them. She had set out trying to hide her scars with her long hair covering her ear and turtleneck shirts even in summer, but she didn't like being the center of attention or the idea people thought she needed to be fixed.

After checking on the children and dogs, Annie prepared a Mexican chicken casserole that would be easy to serve without her here. Then she called her sister and told her she was coming over. By her own choice she had very few days or nights off, but this evening when the family sat down for dinner, she was leaving to see Amanda.

* * *

Annie paced the back porch at Amanda's. "Nothing is wrong with me. Why does he want to fix me?"

"I'm getting whiplash with your pacing. Sit so we can have a conversation. People have said things to you before. You don't usually get this worked up, so why are you getting upset now?"

Annie stopped in front of her twin. "Ian was supposed to be different."

"He was? Did you let him know that?"

"I told him I couldn't afford it. That should have been the end. It wasn't. He gave me a brochure about a prosthetic ear. Why?"

"Did you ask him?"

"Well, no, not exactly. I told him again I didn't have the money then handed the brochure back." Annie sat across from her sister.

"He's a plastic surgeon. That's the kind of thing he does for a living. I once dated a dentist who kept staring at my teeth. He told me that's the first thing he checks out on a person."

"So since I told him last week, he's been trying to figure out a way to make me better." Annie heard the sarcasm pour from her voice, mingling with hurt.

"I know we've talked about this before, but you usually shut it down. Annie, why won't you look into treatment for your scars? You were burned almost fourteen years ago. There have been so many advances in medicine. I don't see why you don't at least investigate your options and how much each one costs. You know we'd help you as much as possible."

Annie rose and began pacing again, her hands fisted

at her sides. "That isn't the kind of support I came here for. You of all people should understand."

Amanda planted herself in Annie's path. "Understand what?"

Didn't anyone understand what she'd gone through? "It's my reparation for Mom."

"You still believe that?" Amanda's voice had risen several decibels. "That's the last thing Mom would ever want. If that's what you believe, I know the emotional scars will never totally go away. It was an *accident*, Annie. Accept that and forgive yourself."

Each word her sister said struck her like a slap, stinging and hurting. "It's not that easy. Forgive and forget." Annie snapped her fingers. "Just like that. Tell myself and it's done."

"I didn't say it was easy. If God can forgive you, why can't you forgive yourself? I think that's why you won't do anything about your scars."

Annie charged to the sliding glass doors and headed toward the front exit. "I needed sympathy, not accusations. Good night."

She sat in her car, clutching the steering wheel until her hands ached. Annie thought the one person who would understand was her twin. A van passed her, its headlights illuminating the interior of her vehicle. She caught a glimpse of herself in the rearview mirror, the edges of her scars peeking out from behind her hair. The sight taunted her.

Annie looked down and tried to compose herself before returning to the McGregors' house. She released her hold on the steering wheel and flexed her hands. A tiny voice inside her kept insisting she leave Ian before she began to care about him. Who was she kidding? She cared about him now. Hadn't she learned her lesson with David?

For a brief time Annie had thought a man could overlook her scars, but David's disgust had destroyed that dream. She'd finally started dating and begun to let down her guard with David. When she'd showed him the scars, he hadn't been able to get away from her fast enough.

But Annie had promised the children she'd be there for them. They'd lost so many caretakers in two years. She couldn't leave now, especially with Jeremy fighting to accept himself. He was fragile, warming to her and yet still holding himself back. Jasmine, too.

Annie finally started the car and drove back to her apartment. She'd get a good night's sleep and be all right tomorrow. The next few days wouldn't be as hectic as the weekend with the birthday party.

She parked in the three-car garage and rounded the corner to climb the stairs to her apartment. For a few seconds her heartbeat galloped at the sight of a man sitting on the bottom step. She gasped.

"Sorry, I should have said something."

"Where's your truck?"

Her youngest brother pushed to a standing position. "Being towed to the dealer. I had Ken drop me off here so I could borrow your car for the next couple of days."

Annie jammed both fists onto her waist. "Have you ever heard of calling before assuming you could take my car?"

"I texted you. I thought maybe you were putting the

kids down, so I told your boss that I'd wait for you on the stairs."

Annie dug into her purse and found her dead cell phone. "I forgot to charge it last night." She assessed her brother for a long moment. "I guess you can use my car."

"Where have you been? Ian didn't know where you were."

"Out. None of your business or his. And if you persist with the questions, I won't loan you my Honda." She placed the keys into his hand and punched the garage door opener. "Did you have a wreck?" she finally asked.

"No, the brakes failed, and I went over a curb. I finally stopped inches from hitting a big tree trunk."

Ian suddenly came into the garage from the breezeway but hung back. Annie didn't have to look to know he was staring at her. A flutter zipped through her at the brief sight of him.

She peered at Charlie, trying to ignore Ian's presence but failing miserably. "Let me know when you can return it."

"Will do."

After her brother backed her car out of the garage, she hit the button on the door opener to close it. Maybe Ian, still in the garage, would get the point she wasn't ready to talk to him.

But what if something had happened to one of the children? Annie started to punch the button again to open it, but Ian beat her to it.

He strode toward her. Worry lines etched his forehead.

"Ian, is something wrong with Jeremy?"

"No. The kids are fine and asleep and so are the dogs—Rex with Jeremy and Daisy with Joshua."

"So he finally persuaded Daisy to sleep with him."

"I think the girls came to an agreement with their little brother. Daisy is going to rotate where she sleeps."

"That seems reasonable."

"But not what I did earlier. I assumed you'd want to look at that information, never thinking of the cost. I'm sorry."

What tension was left in her body melted away. It was hard to stay mad at Ian because he did have good intentions, and when he looked at her scars, it hadn't been with revulsion but like a doctor examining an injury. But still.

"Ian, I am who I am. It's totally my decision what I do."

But Ian hadn't said anything her family hadn't… Annie had her life mapped out just fine, and she helped people. That was her purpose, not to be a wife and mother.

"I didn't want to go to bed without making amends. You're important to this family."

"I'm glad, Ian." *I want to be needed.*

"Good night," Ian said and walked to the door to the breezeway.

Annie made her way toward the staircase on the side of the garage, trying to focus on all the things she needed to get done before fifteen children descended on the house on Saturday. She didn't get far because her thoughts always returned to Ian. If he ever decided to remarry, he'd make some woman a good husband. That realization didn't sit well with her as she mounted the steps.

Chapter 9

On Friday Annie picked up the phone. "The McGregors' residence."

"This is Mrs. Haskell, Jeremy's teacher. May I speak with Annie Knight?"

"This is she." Her heart began beating double-time. Something was wrong.

"I tried Dr. McGregor's office, and they said he was in surgery. Your name is the other one on the contact sheet."

"Is Jeremy okay?"

"He's with the nurse. He had a seizure on the playground after lunch. Physically he's fine, but he was upset when he saw the other kids around him. He refused to come back to class, and the nurse told me he fell asleep on their cot."

"I'll come pick him up."

"Under these circumstances, I think that would be best."

After Annie retrieved Rex from the backyard, she drove toward Will Rogers Elementary. Her cell phone rang, and she saw it was Ian. "I'm almost at Jeremy's school," he said. "He had a seizure. The teacher called and left a message for me. When I got out of surgery, an aide told me."

"He's at the nurse's office."

"Meet you there."

Annie pulled into the parking lot, took Rex out of the backseat and hooked up his leash. Not half a minute later, Ian pulled in next to her. She waited for him, then they walked to the entrance together.

"Good idea about Rex," Ian said. "I didn't insist on Jeremy's taking Rex to school, but I will now." He opened the door.

While Annie and Ian signed in at the office, she said, "We have the weekend to see if he'll come to the conclusion on his own. I brought Rex to remind Jeremy what the dog can do for him. And I have a feeling Jeremy could use Rex for comfort, although I doubt he'll admit it. It upset him that the kids on the playground saw him. His teacher said he freaked out."

"It's time we encourage him to talk about his epilepsy with the other children. Rex could help with that."

At the nurse's office, Ian asked what happened and how long the seizure had lasted while Annie took Rex to the room where the cots were. When they entered, Jeremy was curled on his side, his eyes closed. Annie sat in the chair between the beds with Rex between her and Jeremy's cot.

Ian went in and sat on the other bed, whispering, "The nurse said he went to sleep right away. He's been here about forty minutes. His seizure lasted around three minutes. That was an estimate from the teacher's assistant on the playground. Jeremy fell down on a soft patch of grass, and she couldn't feel any bumps or see any cuts."

"What do you want to do?"

"Take him home. He'll be wiped. That's the longest seizure he's had that I know of." Ian stood and stooped next to his son. "Jeremy." He gently shook the child's shoulder.

Jeremy's eyes blinked open and he looked right at his dad then closed them.

"Son, I'm taking you home. Can you walk?"

No response.

"Then, I'll carry you." Ian slipped his arms under his child's body and hefted him up against his chest.

"I'll get the doors." Annie scurried around Ian, holding Rex's leash, and walked ahead of them out to the Lexus. "Are you going back to work?"

"No. My surgeries went faster than I thought they would."

"I'm going to run one errand, then it will be time for me to pick up the other children."

"I'll see you back at the house in a while."

Annie opened her driver's door while Ian placed Jeremy in the backseat of his Lexus, and Rex climbed in with his son.

Ian straightened. His gaze held her like an embrace. "Thanks for coming, Annie. It's good to know I have someone to rely on." His voice thickened, and he swallowed hard.

"I'm doing what is needed," Annie murmured, wanting to look away, but the sheen in his eyes riveted her.

Ian loved his children, and to see them hurt and vulnerable had to be hard for him. Annie wasn't their parent, but she struggled with her emotions more than when she worked for the others. She couldn't compartmentalize her feelings as she had before. It would be difficult to leave the children—Ian.

Not a word was spoken for half a minute. Annie couldn't have moved if she'd wanted to.

Then Ian's cell phone rang, breaking the connection. Annie hurried and slid into the Ford Explorer. She still had an errand to run, but the whole way to the store, she couldn't shake the idea that something had happened back there. Something had changed between them.

"I can't believe my youngest is five. It goes by fast, especially when you're running to keep up with him." Ian stood next to Annie on the sidewalk, watching ten four-and five-year-olds jumping, sliding and climbing all over the bounce house that took up a good part of his front yard. "I warned the neighbors it might be a tad noisy today."

"You think? I should have given earplugs to Amanda." Annie laughed and raised her voice over the shouting, with Joshua's ten friends and the twins each having one, as well.

"And us. Did you see Jade and Jasmine looking between you and your twin earlier?"

"We dressed exactly alike on purpose. I thought it would be fun to try to fool your daughters."

Ian turned toward the woman beside him and studied her. "Are you Amanda?"

"What do you think?" A twinkle danced in her eyes.

Ian glanced toward her sister by the door to the bounce house. Joshua ran up to her, grinning from ear to ear, and threw his arms around her. Ian returned his attention to the woman standing with him, catching her running her finger under the collar of her turtleneck shirt. "You are definitely Amanda."

"What gave it away? Annie and I are pretty good at changing places."

"You aren't used to wearing a turtleneck."

"True. We fooled your daughters, though. Annie is going to save telling them until later."

"But not Joshua. That hug was for Annie. She made today special for him." Lately there had been a lot of special moments for Ian's family because of Annie.

Amanda tilted her head and scrutinized him. "You like her. I'm glad because I think she's terrific, too. She has a gift with children, and they gravitate to her. I thought Annie would be a teacher. But she wanted to do something more one-on-one."

"I'm glad she decided that. For the past two weeks, my family has finally started settling into a routine. Before Annie, no matter what I did, I couldn't seem to get it together."

"Four children take a lot of coordinating. Annie had the best example. Our mom was always there for us. We knew what she expected, and we knew our boundaries."

Ian smiled. "Zoe and then Aunt Louise always held the fort. When they passed away, I was left unprepared."

"Sounds as though Annie came in the nick of time."

Ian watched Annie among the children in the bounce house, laughing as loud as they were. She gave him hope again. When he'd opened the door to her that first day, he had been desperate. Ian didn't like chaos any more than his kids did. He wanted to help her, too. "Amanda, why won't Annie do anything about her scars?"

"She's become good at hiding them."

"But I think something could be done to diminish them. At least on her face. And certainly her ear could either be reconstructed, or she could have a prosthetic one."

"The ones on her neck and ear aren't nearly as bad as the one across her chest. But in answer to your question, I can't say. If Annie wants you to know, she'll tell you."

Ian faced Amanda, not surprised by her answer. "I understand. You two are very close, like Jade and Jasmine."

"Annie doesn't trust easily. After the accident she discovered who her real friends were. It's sad how some people view beauty only outwardly. But then you should know that—your business revolves around appearance."

"There's more to being a plastic surgeon than cosmetic procedures," Ian said. "The part I love best is the reconstructive surgery. My little brother had a cleft lip, and he got teased to the point he didn't want to go to school. Surgery changed his life."

"Wouldn't it be nice if people would just accept us for what we are? God does." Amanda checked her watch.

"I'm going to relieve Annie. I need to work off that piece of cake."

Ian scanned the children. Jeremy had never come outside after Joshua opened his presents, and everyone had cake and ice cream. He'd said he would. After making sure everything was running smoothly, Ian went inside and found his eldest son sitting on the staircase with Rex next to him.

"I thought you were coming outside. Joshua will wonder where you are."

"What if I have a seizure like yesterday?"

"We're here to help you. You'll be okay. You can't hide in the house forever."

His service dog moved closer and laid his head in Jeremy's lap.

"You've got Rex. He's there to help. Remember what he did that evening at Caring Canines?"

"But on the playground everyone was staring at me." Jeremy chewed on his lower lip.

Ian sat next to his son. Had Annie gone through this after her accident? "Because they didn't know about your seizures. Maybe you need to share it with them. Rex can help you."

"What if someone laughs at me?"

"Then, he isn't a friend. You need to ignore him. I hope you'll take Rex to school on Monday."

Jeremy stroked his dog's head. "I don't know."

"I know Joshua's friends would love to get to know Rex better. Come on. I'll show you." Ian stood and waited.

When his son rose, Ian filled his lungs with a deep breath. Outside, when Jeremy strolled toward the bounce house, several kids came up to him. Before long three more joined them. Jeremy began demonstrating some of the tricks Rex could do. Relief flowed through Ian.

"I'm glad you could talk him into getting out of the house," Annie said from behind. "I tried earlier, but he didn't know if he should."

Ian rotated toward Annie. "This is a good place for him to practice sharing his service dog with others. The more comfortable he is, the more likely he will take Rex to school willingly."

"Joshua asked me this morning after breakfast if he could take Daisy."

"He said something to me, too, right before the party. Obviously you didn't give him the right answer."

Annie chuckled. "Kids don't think adults compare notes. Amanda and I used to do that all the time with our parents." She looked around. "Where are Jade and Jasmine?"

"I don't know. Their two friends are still here, so they can't be too far away. At least I don't have to worry about them—unlike Joshua when he disappears for any length of time."

"I think those older girls are flirting with Jeremy," Annie observed. "The other kids are going back to play in the bounce house, but the twins' friends are hanging on to every word Jeremy is saying."

"He's blushing. I didn't know Jeremy could do that. Want to walk around and look for the twins?"

"Let's check behind the bounce house."

"Over by Jeremy? Maybe we can eavesdrop." Annie tried, but she couldn't contain her grin.

"I think that's a good suggestion. Jade and Jasmine could be on the other side of that monstrosity in my yard."

Annie started forward. "I told you it would be big. Quit complaining so we can hear what the girls and Jeremy are saying as we walk by."

"Why, Annie Knight, I never thought you were capable of such underhanded behavior." Lately he'd noticed he'd smiled and laughed more than anytime the past year. And he was sure it was because of Annie. She was having an effect on the children—but also on him.

"When it comes to protecting children, you do what you have to," Annie replied.

Ian's laughter caused his son and the two girls to glance their way.

Annie jabbed Ian playfully in the side and whispered, "So much for being subtle." They kept walking.

"Did you hear he was explaining what his service dog does?" Ian asked as they circled the bounce house.

"Dad, Annie, look at me." Joshua went down the slide headfirst.

"Joshua, I'm glad that landing is cushioned. And yes, I heard," she told Ian. Annie came to a halt, staring at the front porch, then she burst out laughing.

Ian swung his attention to what she was looking at. His two daughters were coming toward them, dressed exactly alike and wearing the same hairstyle. "It's rare to see Jade wearing a dress. I'm surprised Jasmine talked her into it."

"When it comes to clothes, Jasmine is adamant about what she puts on. Jade couldn't care less." Annie waved at the two girls. "They won't fool me. The minute they start talking they'll give themselves away. They haven't mastered the art of switching places the way Amanda and I have." Annie nodded toward them. "For instance, they walk differently."

"I never thought about that, but it's true."

As Annie greeted the twins by name, the flush to their cheeks revealed she was right. In a short time, Annie had come to know his family well, Ian reflected. In some ways she knew them better than he did, which was disconcerting. He'd been lost in grief the past two years and had distanced himself from his children. That would change today.

Sunday evening, after they'd held the family meeting and the children had gone to bed, Annie left for the night. But instead of going to her apartment, she sat on a lounge chair on the patio to enjoy the crisp, cool spring air with a sky lit with thousands of stars. This had been a weekend full of surprises. First, Annie had thought for sure she could fool Ian when Amanda and she switched roles, but she hadn't for long. That stunned her. Did Ian know her that well? The thought that he did excited and scared her at the same time.

Annie pushed away thoughts of men and focused on another surprise. Jeremy not only brought Rex outside at the birthday party, but he'd taken him to church, too. Both were good dry runs for tomorrow. Tonight at supper, he'd announced Rex was going to school with him.

But the biggest revelation was today when Annie had spent most of the day with her family and all she could think about was Ian and his children. She'd wanted them there, too. Her dad encouraged her to ask them to

come for Memorial Day at the lake, and she was definitely considering it.

The sound of the sliding glass doors opening startled
her. Annie twisted around to find Ian coming out of the
house toward her. Although she'd relished the quiet, his
presence sent a thrill through her. She needed to put a
stop to that—but at the moment she didn't know how.

"I was checking that the doors were locked and
caught sight of you out here. Mind if I join you?"

"This is your house."

"But this is your downtime."

"Haven't you figured out by now that except for
church and family, I have no life beyond my job?" Annie
smiled. Until she'd come to Ian's house, that had been
true. But when she was with Ian and his family, she
didn't think of herself as an employee. Annie slid her
eyes closed for a few seconds and tried to change the
direction of her thoughts.

"So that's why you come back early on Sunday and
join us for dinner."

"Well, that and I don't have to cook the meal." And
Annie enjoyed the family meetings—each one showed
progress toward a good working model.

"I thought you liked to cook."

"I do, but it's nice to be pampered every once in a
while."

"I'll have to remember that." Ian took the lounge
next to her.

Only inches apart. His proximity revved her heartbeat, and she shivered.

"Cold?"

"No, I'm fine." *As soon as I quit reacting to you*

being this close to me. "Tonight is so lovely I decided to spend some time out here."

"I have a feeling the quiet is what lured you."

"You're probably right, after spending today with my large family. I think every niece and nephew was there today. Usually a couple are missing."

"What are their ages?"

"When everyone is present, their ages are two to fifteen, but in seven months there will be a baby. Amanda told me she's eight weeks pregnant. Her first, and I'm excited! I've had plenty of practice with all the stages children go through, but the baby stage is my favorite."

"What about having your own? You would be such a good mother."

Annie tensed, relieved that in the dark Ian couldn't read her expression. The subject always brought a momentary pang of regret and pain. Because of her forgetfulness that night at the cabin, she'd been denied the one thing she'd always wanted: to be a mother. If she could relive that moment she lit the candle, her life would be totally different today.

"Annie?" Ian clasped her hand.

"I can't have children. When the beam fell across my midsection, it caused some internal injuries." The words slipped out before Annie could take them back. Only her family and her doctor knew that information. Why was she telling Ian? It wasn't his concern, but she found herself sharing more with him than any other outsider.

"I'm sorry. I shouldn't…" For a long moment Ian didn't say anything.

Annie swung her legs over the side of the chaise longue and sat up. "You were making an observation, and I appreciate your thinking I would be a good mother. I accepted the fact I wouldn't be able to years ago." But she could still remember that day when the doctor had told her. Something had died inside her then. God had other plans for her life.

Ian leaned forward. "I shouldn't have asked. It's none of my business, but I don't think of us as employer and employee. I've enjoyed getting to know you. I consider you a friend. You're easy to talk to. And I don't know what I would have done about Jeremy without you. For six months I've felt overwhelmed. I don't now."

Annie knew her other employers had appreciated her services, but their words had never affected her the way Ian's did. A glow from deep within spread to encompass her whole body. "I'm glad I could help" was all she could think to say.

"It was a great day when you came to interview for the job."

Annie rose. "It's time to call it a night."

When Ian stood so close she could smell his scent of lime aftershave, her breathing quickened. She wanted to forget her past and focus only on this man, this moment alone with him.

"I'm taking the kids and Rex to school tomorrow morning," he told her. "I want you to sleep in and enjoy the time off. You deserve it."

"But I don't—"

"You've hardly taken any time off, so no argument."

His nearness made her heartbeat accelerate. "But what about breakfast?" The question came out in a breathless rush.

"A bowl of cereal will be fine. Okay?"

Annie nodded, transfixed by his heart-pounding look.

Ian bent his head toward hers, his hands grasping her upper arms. When his lips hovered over hers, she wanted to melt against him.

Chapter 10

Ian knew he shouldn't kiss her, but he couldn't resist. His lips whispered across hers, giving her time to pull away if she wanted. When she didn't, he slanted his mouth over hers and deepened their connection. When he pulled back slightly and looked at her, he saw a woman who had become so important to him in such a short time. He wanted more. Ian kissed her forehead, eyes, the tip of her nose and then her mouth again. When his hands delved into her thick hair, his fingers touched her scars. He didn't care about them.

Suddenly she tore from his embrace, backing away. As she encountered the lounge chair, the sound of it scooting across the patio filled the air. In the shadows created by the light from the den, panic lined her face. She frantically combed her hair over her scars.

Annie glanced down at the askew chaise longue for

a few seconds before her wide-eyed gaze reconnected with his. "It's been a long week. Thanks for the morning off. Good night."

"Annie, I didn't mean—"

"I know you didn't mean to kiss me. Why would you?"

As she started to leave, Ian caught her hand. "First, I wanted to kiss you, but I didn't mean to scare you or make you mad. I'm sorry."

Annie tugged her hand free then hurried toward the side of the garage. Ian watched her escape. She didn't realize how beautiful she was. She was using her scars as a barrier between herself and others. He wanted to change that.

Lord, how do I get her to see her beauty?

Annie didn't stop running until she was inside her apartment—then she collapsed back against the door. She should never have responded to Ian's kiss. But when his lips touched hers, that was all she could think about.

He wanted to kiss me.

Why?

Gratitude. That's all it could be. If Ian could see my scarred body, he would run the other way. That's why I keep my distance from men.

Annie could leave, find another job, but she wouldn't do that to the children. She just needed to toughen her resolve to keep her relationship with Ian as employer/employee. No more.

But the lingering feel of his lips against hers mocked that decision. Annie wanted Ian to kiss her again.

* * *

The next morning a bang against her door drew Annie out of her bedroom. "Just a minute." She tied the sash to her robe as she padded across her apartment to see who had disturbed her morning to sleep in.

She peered out the peephole, but no one was on the landing. Then another bang sounded as though someone was kicking against the wood. She eased the door open to find Joshua, still wearing his pajamas, his forehead furrowed.

"What's wrong?"

"Daddy is sick."

"Did he tell you to come get me?"

"No, but I heard him coughing and coughing and coughing. He needs you."

A vivid memory of the kiss they'd shared the night before flashed into her mind. Annie quickly dismissed that thought and said, "Come in, Joshua. Let me get dressed."

Joshua shifted from one foot to the other, his gaze zooming in on her neck. "Didja hurt yourself?"

Annie brushed her hair forward as much as possible and threw up the collar on her robe. "Not lately. Be right back."

Annie hurried away from Joshua before he started asking more questions. She still hadn't told him or the girls. The time hadn't been right yet. After throwing on a pair of jeans and a red turtleneck, Annie returned to the living room.

Joshua was gone.

She hastened outside, remembering that time he'd tried to fly off the railing. But the landing was empty.

She rushed down the stairs and rounded the corner to find Joshua picking—or rather uprooting—some lilies.

"Joshua, you were supposed to wait for me."

"You didn't tell me to." He grinned and handed her the flowers, roots and all.

Annie thought back to what she'd said and he was right—technically. She knew better than not to spell out what she expected. "Thanks for the flowers, but you should leave them in the ground next time."

"They're pretty like you." He wiped his dirty hands on his pajamas.

Annie was at a loss for words. Was Joshua behind the red tulips, the candy bar and the other little gifts? No, he couldn't be. Later she would replant them and hope the lilies survived, but for now she needed to see about Ian. "Let's go."

When she and the five-year-old entered the kitchen, Ian was pouring a cup of coffee, his face white and haggard-looking. Suddenly he sneezed then starting coughing.

When he turned his red eyes on her, he said, "Annie, you aren't supposed to be here."

"And you shouldn't be out of bed. Joshua told me you were sick, and he's right."

"No, he isn't. This is just allergies. Spring is the worst time for me. That's what I get for spending time outside at night." He quirked a half grin. "But I'm glad I did. It was worth it."

Annie stamped down the rising warmth in her face and concentrated on the situation at hand. "Are you sure that's all it is—allergies?" She put the lilies next to the sink.

"Positive. I'm a doctor. I should know."

Turning away, Annie rolled her eyes. "Since I'm here, I'll at least fix breakfast and help get the children ready for school."

"Sure. I need to make sure the others are up." Ian shuffled toward the doorway, leaving his full cup of coffee on the counter.

Annie started to say something but decided not to. Coffee wasn't the best thing to drink when a person was coming down with something. She wasn't so sure it was just his allergies. Water was much better.

"Joshua, you should go get dressed. I'll have breakfast ready in fifteen minutes."

Ian paused in the doorway as if he'd finally noticed the lilies on the counter. He gestured toward the flowers. "What happened to them?"

"I gave them to Annie." Joshua zipped past his dad into the hallway.

"Oh." Ian continued out of the kitchen.

Annie quickly prepared French toast and set the table. When she set the pitcher of orange juice on the table, she stepped back, satisfied with what she'd done in a short time. She punched the intercom to announce breakfast, but a movement in the doorway caught her attention.

Jasmine, with a huge pout on her face, stood barefoot, her blouse ripped, her hair a wild mess.

"What happened?"

"I can't go to school today. I have nothing to wear, and my hair is awful."

"I'm sure we can find something for you to wear to school." Annie started for the hallway.

Jasmine blocked the door. "No, I don't want to go to school. I haven't missed much school this year. I don't need to go today."

"Are you sick?"

"I have a headache." Jasmine thought for a few seconds and added, "And a stomachache. I might throw up any second."

Jade came up behind her sister. "She isn't sick. One of the popular girls said she was too fat on Friday."

Jasmine punched her in the arm as Jade passed her. She faked a cough. "I got it from Dad."

As Joshua entered the kitchen wearing the clothes he'd laid out the night before, Annie spied Jeremy and Rex coming down the hall. "Jeremy, please make sure your younger brother and sister eat, then brush their teeth and get ready to leave."

Jeremy looked at her for a moment then grinned. "Sure. You two heard Annie. I'm the boss."

Annie took Jasmine's hand and led her toward the staircase. "If you have a fever, you can stay home. Otherwise you're going."

Jasmine stopped dead in her tracks. "I can't go. You don't know what it's like to have someone say something about how you look to everyone."

The words hit Annie with a truth she'd been avoiding. She paused on the step and knew this was the time. She sat and patted the place next to her. "Jasmine, I could tell you that what someone says about you only hurts you if you let it. When I was young I did that. I let others control my actions. I still do." More than she realized.

"But I'm not fat, am I?"

Annie shook her head and shifted to face the young girl. "Absolutely not."

"I don't know why she said that. I thought we were friends."

"I don't know why, either. Maybe she's hurting inside, and she thinks by saying something hurtful to someone else it will make her feel better. It won't in the long run."

Suddenly Annie felt fifteen again—the day she returned to school after the fire. Nothing had prepared her for that—feeling damaged, freakish. Annie had seen it in some people's eyes, and it had cut through her.

"Are you okay?"

Annie dragged herself away from the past and focused on the child who needed her help. "When I was in high school, I was in a fire and was burned. Most of the scars I can hide under my clothes—" she lifted her hair on the right side to reveal her partial ear and disfigurement "—but not this. My hair was short then because of the fire, but as soon as I could I began using it to hide the scars. I didn't want kids to talk about how ugly I was. I let them control my life and what I did."

Tears swam in Jasmine's eyes. "You aren't ugly. You are…you." She hugged Annie. "You care about us."

Annie put her arms around the child, savoring the moment. "And that's how I feel about you. You aren't fat. And even if you were, you are you. Who am I to judge you? Friends won't. They care about us, flaws and all."

As she said those words to Jasmine, their meaning began to sink in. Yes, Annie had scars, but that wasn't who she was inside. If others couldn't accept them, that was their problem, not hers.

"What am I supposed to do about Kayla?"

"Nothing. Go to school and act as though what she said didn't bother you. Words can hurt but only when we give them power to." Annie cupped the girl's face. "Then after school, we'll all go get an ice cream cone. I know how much you love it. So do I. Now, Jasmine, do I still need to take your temperature?"

Jasmine shook her head, swiped her tears away and hopped up. "I'll get ready."

"Good. I'll fix you something to eat on the go." The sound of coughing drifted to Annie. "I have a feeling I'll be taking you this morning."

She walked with Jasmine to the second floor but headed for Ian's room. She knocked and waited. When he opened the door, he used it for support. He was dressed, but his shirttail hung out of his pants and he was barefoot. Without a word, Annie laid her palm against his forehead and felt heat beneath her fingers.

"You can't go to work. You've got a fever. I don't think your patients would appreciate you like this."

"I came to that realization, but I was trying at least to take the kids to school. Then I can come back home and collapse on the bed."

"I'm taking the children, and you're getting back in bed. When I return, I'll check to see if you need anything."

"But you were supposed to have the morning off."

"Not today. Maybe some other time after you're well." Annie gently nudged Ian back toward his bed.

"I've got everything under control. Make sure you drink plenty of fluids."

"I'm a doctor, and I know what to do."

"This from a man who should have never gotten out of bed in the first place." Annie left his room, glancing back to make sure he was following her directions. He was, his eyes drifting closed.

Ian's head alternated between pounding and pulsating. Even moving it too fast caused the room to spin. And yet here he sat in his SUV waiting for the prescription his family doctor had written for him when all he wanted to do was lie down in a dark room and sleep. At least he wasn't driving.

Annie took the sack of medication from the cashier then pulled away from the drive-through window. "I have enough time to drop you off then go pick up the children." She glanced toward him. "Now, aren't you glad you went with me to see your friend? The antibiotic will take care of your sinus infection."

Ian removed the medicine bottle from the bag, took out one pill then washed it down with water. "I can't afford to be sick. I have patients to see."

"Your office will reschedule the ones today and tomorrow."

"You're indispensable." Annie wasn't here just for the children but for him, too.

"You would have done what you needed, but it does help to have a backup."

"Especially since I don't have any family nearby to depend on."

"That, I have plenty of."

"I'm jealous," Ian grumbled and laid his head back on the cushion. He looked forward to the moment he could retreat to his room, a luxury he hadn't had in a long time.

"Which brings up Memorial Day. Would you and your family like to attend our big get-together at the lake? I'd love for you all to meet my extended family. There will be plenty of kids for yours to play with."

"I'd say it sounds great, but right now nothing does. But yes, I think that would be good for the children." *And me.*

Ian had realized since Zoe died he'd isolated himself from friends and even family who lived in South Carolina. Until Annie, he hadn't thought he'd retreated from life, but he had. He'd focused on getting through one day at a time and his work. With Aunt Louise taking care of his children, he hadn't even been that involved with relatives right after his wife died. Ian had been feeling sorry for himself. Zoe had been his college sweetheart, the only girl he had seriously dated. He'd thought he was set for life. Then Zoe had had a stroke followed by another one, and everything had changed.

Then along had come Annie, and life was changing again from the rut his life had become. Ian wanted to find a way to show her his appreciation for going above and beyond in her job, and he'd come up with a way, if he could work out all the details.

He'd had some setbacks, but so had Annie. He wanted her to put her past behind her—as he was trying to do. Both of them had become too focused on what had been, not on what could be.

* * *

Three weeks later, Annie drove to Will Rogers Elementary the last Tuesday before school was out for Super Sports Day. Every class was having a picnic on the playground, then the students would participate in competitions. Jeremy and Ian were going to do a three-legged race while Jade would be putting a potato between her knees and trying to walk from one end of the basketball court to the other. Jasmine and Kayla, paired by their teacher, were going to hold a balloon between their hips and try to make it to the finish line first, while Joshua and Annie would be dancing, then freezing when the music stopped.

Dressed in a blue T-shirt celebrating Super Sports Day, Annie scanned the sea of blue T-shirts before her. She couldn't come without one because according to the kids, everyone would be wearing them. And they were. Even after talking with Jasmine about appearances a few weeks ago, Annie had been hesitant to go without her usual turtleneck at least under her T-shirt. But in the end, she'd realized children learned by example more than words. Annie needed to show Jasmine that what other people said shouldn't control what she felt about herself or how she acted.

Annie, carrying everyone's sack lunches, stopped at the edge of the playground, where she met Ian.

"The trick is to cover all the children today. I'll start with Joshua's class at this end." She pointed to Jade in the third-grade area. "I'll go there next, then to Jasmine and finish with Jeremy with the fourth graders. You do the opposite, and we should meet between Jade and Jasmine's classes."

"Last year they had different grades compete on different days. Whatever possessed them to do it all in one afternoon?"

"Beats me. We'll get a workout for sure. Whether the kids do is still up in the air." Annie glanced from one end of the playground to the other—at least two football fields long.

"I'll take Jeremy and the twins their lunches. See you in a while." Ian strolled toward the area for the third graders.

Since the time Ian had been sick a few weeks ago, Annie had tried to keep a distance between them, but it had been difficult—and she suspected the twins of plotting to get Ian and her alone together. She was sure they were responsible for all those secret admirer gifts. So far she'd managed to foil their plans, but they hadn't let up.

Maybe she needed to talk with them about the impossibility of their dad and her getting together. There would come a time when Ian would be ready to date and possibly marry again. By that time Annie would move on to other children who needed her help. Annie knew she couldn't stay when Ian became serious about a woman. She cared too much to hang around. His kiss had shown that. She still dreamed about it.

Joshua ran to her, throwing his arms around her. "You came!"

Annie tousled his curly blond hair. "Of course. How could I miss dancing with you?"

"Yeah, but when the music stops, we have to stand *real* still. I want to win. If you move we'll hafta sit down."

"I'll try to stay still." She tried to keep a straight face. Joshua was the one always on the move.

When the dance competition was announced, Joshua put on a serious expression, paying attention to everything his teacher said. Then the music started. Holding Annie's hand—they had to remain connected the whole time—he wiggled and twisted, nearly wrenching her arm out of the socket. When the song stopped, Joshua froze, his gaze fixed on her. By the third stop, his body was contorted into a weird position, and he couldn't keep still longer than a second. The teacher pointed to them to sit down.

Joshua walked off with Annie, his shoulders slumped and his head down, while Annie rotated her shoulder. He plopped down on one of the blankets his class had laid out.

"Joshua, you might not have been the last person left standing, but you got some good exercise." Which was the point of Super Sports Day.

Another boy sat near Joshua and stared at Annie. "What's wrong with your neck?" The child pointed at her scars.

Annie had prepared herself for questions from curious children. "I was in a fire."

His eyes got big. "You were? Did a fireman save you?"

"My dad did." A knot swelled into her throat, and Annie swallowed several times, not wanting to think about that day.

"Do they still hurt?"

She shook her head.

By the time she left Joshua, several other children

had said something to her about her scars, more curious than anything. When she arrived at Jade's class, Annie felt hopeful about her decision. It took her telling Jasmine to see that she'd been letting a few callous people change how she felt and acted.

Jade's friends were fun and pumped about Super Sports Day. Not one of them asked about her scars, although they had seen them. Annie knew she'd made a good decision to let them show. For fourteen years her life had revolved around what had happened at the fire. Not anymore.

As Annie walked toward Jasmine, she waved to Ian, who made a detour to talk to her, greeting her with a smile. "You look as if you've been enjoying yourself."

"I have. How did you do in the three-legged race?" she asked, trying to ignore how he made her feel when he looked at her as though she was the only person around.

"I think Rex and Jeremy would have done better." His eyes sparkled with merriment.

"That bad?"

"We came in dead last because I kept tripping. Jeremy was a sport about it, although I'm not sure he's stopped laughing yet."

Annie chuckled at the picture that formed in her mind of the race.

"You're laughing, too! I thought you at least would give me sympathy."

"Sorry." Annie struggled to suppress her smile. "How's Rex handling the crowd?"

"He's loving it. While I was there, Jeremy showed

him off to tons of people, telling them all about what his dog can do."

Annie glanced in the direction of Jeremy's class and glimpsed the boy and Rex with other children surrounding them. "Rex has been great for him. I heard Jeremy last night before bedtime, telling him his problems."

"What kind of problems?"

"He didn't do well on his math test, and there's a girl bothering him, pestering him about Rex all the time."

Ian sighed. "Those kinds of problems I can handle, whereas Jasmine is still having trouble with Kayla. The race they did together was a disaster. The McGregor clan didn't do very well in competition today."

"Jade came in first."

"That's not surprising. She's my sports fanatic. How about Joshua?"

Annie rubbed her shoulder. "I'll recover, hopefully."

"What happened?"

"As you know, your youngest is very enthusiastic, and that carries over to his dancing."

"I volunteered to be his partner, but he wanted you. You've charmed your way into my children's lives. Mine, too."

Ian's compliment warmed her from the inside out. For a second Annie felt beautiful.

She just smiled. She'd better end this conversation before she kissed him on a playground full of hundreds of people. "See you at the end."

"Most definitely."

As Annie headed toward Jasmine, she felt relaxed. Talking with Ian was always easy, even when she'd told him about the fire. Sometimes she had to make herself

remember he was her employer—like a moment ago—
and that being with his children was a job that would
end someday.

Annie approached Jasmine sitting on a blanket with
a couple of her friends and an adult. Not far from her
was Kayla with her mother and a group of girls. Jasmine had her back to Kayla, which was probably a good
thing since the child was sending glares Jasmine's way.
Annie settled next to her and greeted the others, who
had all visited the house at different times.

"How are you doing, Jasmine?" Annie asked when
she heard a remark from Kayla about how she'd tried
to get a different partner for the race but the teacher
wouldn't let her.

"Now that the race is over, fine. I tried to get Kayla
to lock arms so we could work better together. She
wouldn't, so we spent most of the time going back to
the starting line when we lost our balloon." She spoke
loud enough that Kayla would hear it.

Kayla gathered her girlfriends close and whispered
something that caused them all to giggle and look toward Jasmine.

When Jasmine glared at Kayla, Annie laid a hand
on the girl's shoulder. "Ignore her."

"I was here first, and she came and sat down with
her friends. She did that on purpose to bug me."

"You're letting her control your behavior. Do you
want her to have that kind of power?"

Jasmine clamped her lips together.

"Did you see her neck?" a girl behind Annie whispered loudly.

"Yeah, so gross."

Jasmine started to get up, her hands balled. "That's so rude."

Annie leaned close, keeping her in place. "I'm okay." Then she looked at Jasmine's friends. "What are you all going to do this summer?"

Everyone jumped in to answer. Jasmine settled down and said, "We have a pool Dad will open after Memorial Day, so you all can come and swim." That started the girls making plans for a swim party the first weekend in June.

Finally when Annie thought Jasmine was okay, she rose. "I'm heading for Jeremy's class. See you later."

Giggles erupted from Kayla's group. Annie slowed and glanced back. Suddenly she saw Jasmine launch herself at Kayla and wrestle her to the ground. Annie's stomach clenched.

Chapter 11

Annie rushed forward at the same time Ian arrived and pulled his daughter off Kayla, while the girl's mother cried out, "She's hurting my baby!" The woman grabbed her daughter and smoothed her hair away from her face while Kayla sobbed.

"Dad, she said mean things about Annie." Jasmine's eyes shone with unshed tears, a scratch down her right cheek. "I couldn't let her get away with it."

"What did she say?" Ian asked, turning his attention from Kayla's dramatics.

Jasmine glanced at Annie then whispered something in Ian's ear. His expression darkened.

Annie didn't want the child getting in trouble because of her. "Jasmine, don't let Kayla—"

"She called you a monster. You aren't." Tears slipped down her cheeks.

Annie scanned the growing crowd and quashed the impulse to leave. She had to be here for Jasmine—and Ian. That was more important than how Kayla had insulted her. "I'm sorry she said that, but that doesn't mean you need to go after her. Please tell her you're sorry."

"I won't. She was wrong."

"But so were you." Annie saw Jasmine's teacher approaching. Mrs. Evans stopped and talked with Kayla and her mother first, then came over to Jasmine. "Kayla said you hit her for no reason."

"She said some things about Annie. Kayla's the ugly one."

"We don't tolerate fighting for any reason here, Jasmine. I think it's best if you go home with your dad, and I'll see you tomorrow morning in the principal's office before school. Then you can have your say."

When Mrs. Evans left, Jasmine sniffled and wiped away her tears. "I'm not sorry, Dad. Kayla had no right to make fun of Annie."

"We'll discuss this at home. Annie, will you walk with Jasmine while I get Joshua, Jeremy and Jade?"

"We'll be waiting at the car."

Annie and Jasmine walked in silence through the school hallways and out the front door. At the SUV Annie lounged against the hood, trying to figure out what to say to Jasmine.

"Do you think Dad's gonna ground me?"

"I can't say what your father is going to do, but I hope you'll apologize to Kayla for hitting her. Violence isn't the answer, Jasmine."

"She's a bully. She makes fun of people all the time

and gets away with it. How can her mother sit there and let her do that?"

"Kayla and her mom aren't your concern. You can't control them. All you can control is your actions. If you can rise above what she does, others will see that. Girls like Kayla win when they get you in trouble."

"Aren't you mad about what she said?"

"I didn't hear it, and even if I had, I would have ignored it. She can't hurt me unless I let her." As she said those words, Annie realized she really believed them. "I can't make you say you're sorry, but forgiving Kayla will make you feel better. A person who makes fun of others and bullies them is someone who has problems. They are usually miserable. But God taught us to turn the other cheek."

Annie noticed Ian coming out of the school building with his other children. The sight of him brought forth that brief moment on the playground when they'd been talking.

Jeremy stopped near Jasmine. "Way to go, sis. I wish I could have seen it."

"Jeremy, get in the car, and the rest of you, too." Ian waited until his kids had piled inside the SUV then asked Annie, "Are you all right?"

"I'm more concerned about Jasmine. When I decided to wear the T-shirt, I knew something like that could happen. That's why I used to cover up my scars—explaining got tiresome. But today as I was talking to Joshua's friends about my scars, it didn't bother me like it used to."

"What should I say to Jasmine? I'd probably have

said something to Kayla if I'd heard what she'd said. That girl is wrong, too."

"But you wouldn't have hit her." Annie turned to get into the car.

"You aren't going to tell me what you'd do in my place? I know you have an opinion."

"Ask Jasmine what she thinks should happen to her because of her actions. What should she have to do?"

Ian grinned. "Good idea."

After what happened at the picnic, no one spoke on the drive home. When Ian pulled into the garage, the children piled out and waited at the door to go inside.

"Zoe was always the one who disciplined the children," Ian explained. "I worked and she took care of the home. Then Aunt Louise took up where Zoe left off. Until my aunt died, I didn't have a lot of input into how the children acted. I didn't need to. They behaved, except for an occasional outburst. Jasmine and Jeremy have been so fragile lately. I don't want to make the situation worse."

"You'll do fine. The most important thing they need to know is that you love them and care about their problems. Children need love, consistency and stability."

"Not just children."

"True. Change is scary for anyone."

Ian opened his door and got out. Annie met him at the garage entrance to the breezeway. "I'll check on the others while you talk with Jasmine."

As she walked through the kitchen, she caught her reflection in the microwave door. Even in the vague image she could see the scars along her neck. Strange that what Kayla had said about her didn't hurt her. *There's more to me than my injury*, Annie thought, *and the people who count know it.* The smile Ian had given her when he'd seen her in the blue T-shirt told her that.

Ian made his way up the stairs. Jasmine usually retreated to her bedroom when she got in trouble. The door was closed, and he knocked on it.

"Go away!" she shouted from inside.

"Jasmine, we need to talk." Ian waited to see if she would open the door. When she did, he entered and took a seat on Jasmine's bed. His daughter stood in the middle of the room, hugging her arms to her chest and staring at the floor. "Why don't you sit, too?"

Jasmine remained where she was.

"You know, when I was a child, I got into a fight with a kid who used to call me the teacher's pet because I could answer all her questions. By that time I was one grade ahead of my age group and still pretty small. This boy was large."

Jasmine lifted her head. "Did he hurt you?"

"Yes, but I hurt him, too. All my anger welled up one day and exploded. The fight happened after school on the way home. He'd been teasing me all school year, and I'd had enough. I gave him a black eye and made his nose bleed. That's what stopped the fight. When I saw all that blood, I felt awful. The boy was on the ground, holding his nose and crying. Even at eleven I knew I wanted to help others rather than hurt them. I'd seen how my little brother had been hurt by kids picking on him because of his cleft palate.

"So I took off my shirt and gave it to him to stop the

bleeding. At first he wouldn't take it. I sat with him and told him I was sorry."

Jasmine came to the bed and sat next to Ian. "But he hurt you first."

"Yes, but I hit him."

"Did he apologize?"

"No, but he left me alone after that."

"Did you get in trouble?"

"No, because no one saw the fight. My parents never found out until I told them."

Jasmine's eyes grew round. "You did? Why?"

"Because I felt guilty."

"You didn't start it."

"It takes two to fight. I participated. He made me do something I didn't want to do. I didn't like being controlled like that."

"Like Kayla did to me today?"

"Yes." Ian wound his arm around Jasmine's shoulder and pressed her to his side. "So what do you think I should do about you hitting Kayla?"

"I think I should be grounded until Monday."

"I agree. No friends over, no phone calls and no TV. Anything else?"

Jasmine shrugged. "I don't know."

Ian rose and looked down at his daughter. "Jasmine, if someone is bothering you, come and talk to me before it results in fighting. Keeping it inside doesn't solve anything."

As Ian left Jasmine's room, he wasn't sure he'd gotten his point across, but he felt optimistic. Usually Jasmine was anything but calm. Drama surrounded her life. But a few minutes ago he'd strengthened a bond with her that he hoped would help her think through her actions.

* * *

At the campground at Cimarron Lake on Memorial Day weekend, Ian and Jeremy finished putting up the girls' tent and stepped back to admire their work.

His eldest son grinned and said, "I'm glad we decided to come for Sunday night." He swiveled around and panned the people around them. "Boy, Annie has a big family, and she said not all of them are even here this weekend."

"Hi, I'm Nathan," a child about Jeremy's age said as he approached. "Uncle Ben always brings his dog with him, too."

"He does? What kind?" Jeremy glanced around.

"German shepherd. He's a service dog. At least that's what Uncle Ben told us, but I don't know what Ringo does."

"This is my service dog. His name is Rex. I'm Jeremy."

"Do you want to meet my uncle? He's down at the lake, fishing."

Jeremy turned to Ian. "Can I, Dad?"

"Sure." He watched his son and Rex stroll with Annie's nephew toward the water.

"You've been abandoned already?"

He looked over his shoulder at Annie, her arms full of backpacks and bedding. "Yep, for another dog."

"That must be Ringo."

"Normally I would be concerned about a German shepherd, but I know how well Emma trains her animals."

"Ringo was her first service dog five years ago."

"What kind is Ringo?"

"There's a lot of research on how they help veterans

who are suffering from PTSD. They can help with their panic attacks and anxiety."

Jeremy, Rex and Nathan disappeared down the slope to the lake. As he watched, Ian thought Annie's showing up in their lives had to be God's doing. He might never have thought about a service dog for his son, but Rex was just what his son needed. Jeremy was still moody, but he wasn't as angry. The doctor adjusted his medication, and it was finally working much better. That was progress.

"Where did the girls go? I thought they were helping you with our supplies."

Annie put down her load by the tent. "They put your stuff over there, but Carey came over and introduced herself. She's my ten-year-old niece. The girls hit it off and took Joshua to meet some of my younger nephews at the playground."

"Do you have much left?"

"One more trip should do it, then I'd like to check on Joshua. Usually one of the older nieces is watching the younger children. I want to let her know about Joshua and his tendency to get into trouble. By the way, does he swim? Since you have a pool, I was hoping so."

"You would think he was born in the water. He puts my other kids to shame."

After they carried the last of the gear to the tents, Ian walked with Annie toward the playground next to the area where the Knight family had set up camp.

"With so many children, you all got the best site to camp in," Ian remarked to Annie as he surveyed the ten tents of various sizes pitched for the group. "What's your secret? Memorial Day is usually crowded at spots like this in Oklahoma."

"My eldest brother and his family come a few days early."

"Let me see—that's Ken and his wife, Samantha. I need to carry a notepad around to keep everyone's name straight. I came from a small family. One brother who has a boy a little older than Jeremy. A couple of cousins and my mother. That's it."

"And they all live in South Carolina?"

"Yes. When Zoe died, I thought about moving back to be near them, but this is home for my kids. They didn't need any more disruption, and Aunt Louise came to help me."

Ian was amazed yet again how easy it was to talk to Annie. When he was in high school and met Zoe for the first time, he could barely say two sentences to her. "Would you believe I was once very shy?"

"You aren't now."

"That shy guy is still in me, but if I was going to date Zoe and if I was going to work with patients, I had to overcome it."

"How did you do it?"

"My wife. She wasn't shy. I guess I learned by necessity and her example. Zoe never met a stranger. Joshua takes after her."

Annie chuckled. "I guess we can do anything if properly motivated."

"Motivation is the key to change." Ian looked at the outskirts of the large playground filled with children. "How many belong to the Knight clan?"

"All but the three swinging over there." Annie pointed toward the far side of the area.

"That means minus my three, so there's twenty that I've seen."

"I told you I have a large family."

Ian smiled. "And I can tell how much you love your family, all gazillion of them."

"Well, not quite that many. Maybe minus a couple billion," Annie said with a straight face.

Laughter welled up in Ian. What a good start to the weekend. Especially after the past week of school with Jasmine suspended for two days before being allowed to go back Friday for the last day. "How did you get Jasmine to apologize to Kayla?"

"I talked to her several times about how much better she'd feel if she did. Sometimes the best way to deal with a bully is to be nice. To rise above her tactics."

Interesting that both he and Annie had given Jasmine basically the same message. More and more he felt they looked at life the same way. "How did Kayla respond to Jasmine's apology for hitting her?"

"She got mad and stomped off."

"Odd."

"Not really. Kindness often highlights the other person's part in the incident. I'm hoping Kayla isn't feeling as though what she did is a victory." A gleam sparkled in Annie's eyes.

Ian inched closer and grazed his fingers down the side of her neck, the feel of scarred tissue nothing new to him. "In my work, I see them all the time. I'm used to them. I'm glad you don't feel as though you have to hide the scars from us."

"Why?"

"I want you to feel comfortable with us, like part of the family. And the fact that Jasmine listened to you says a great deal."

"Your children mean a lot to me, Ian."

And Annie meant a lot to him. Ian had one more doctor to contact and then he'd approach Annie with his plan. She'd done so much for him. He wanted to give back to her. In not quite two months, he had his family back. Ian wanted Annie to do what he was trying to do: put her past behind her.

"I'm going to the lake to check on Jeremy. Maybe do some fishing."

"I see Melissa supervising. I'm going to talk to her and then find my twin."

As Ian made his way toward the water, he felt a lightness in his steps. A couple of months ago he'd been dreading the summer months because his children were so unsettled, but now he wasn't. He owed Tom Hansen a gift for telling him about Annie.

The sunlight felt good when he stopped where Jeremy and Nathan were with Ben, who was putting bait on their fishing poles. A big smile on his son's face warmed him more than the sun.

"You must be Ben. I'm Ian. Annie's told me about you and your service dog." Ian shook the man's hand.

"As she has told me about Rex and what great things he's doing for Jeremy. My sister is excited that Rex is working out for you."

"He's the best dog." Jeremy moved toward a flat rock to fish next to Nathan.

"I came to see if you had an extra pole. I haven't gone

fishing in years, but I understand the fish we catch will be tonight's meal."

Ben chuckled. "No pressure, huh?"

"You're kidding, aren't you? I'm sure there's a backup plan for dinner if we don't catch enough fish."

"Nope. We'll only have coleslaw and beans if we don't get some. But others will be joining us here and down the shoreline."

"How come?"

"An incentive, so we will have enough fish to eat."

"Okay. Let me see if I remember what I know from being a child."

"The good thing is this lake is teeming with fish."

For two hours, Ian sat patiently on the bank, keeping his line in the water while everyone around him, even his son, caught fish after fish. Then when he was about to give up, he felt a tug on his line. Ian stood up, jerking the pole and hoping to set the hook in whatever he caught.

Jeremy pulled in his line. "I'll get the net. You can do this, Dad."

After the long wait Ian hoped for a big one, but instead he hauled in a white crappie that, according to Ben, weighed barely a pound. He'd envisioned a monster-size fish to make up for all the ones he didn't bring in. Good thing they weren't depending on him for supper.

Amanda came up behind him, whistling at the fish he passed to Ben. "I love crappie." She looked at the others that had been caught. "We're going to eat well tonight. Ian, I think they can do without you for a while. Can't you, Ben?"

"Sure. I'll keep an eye on Jeremy. He and Nathan are having fun."

"What's up?" Ian asked Amanda while glancing at his son, laughing with his new friend. The sound filled him with hope.

"Annie has a surprise for you. I'll show you. It's at the end of the Boomer Trail. Joshua has taken a shining to Melissa and is following her around with her little brother. Brent is six. We have a child or two around the ages of all of your children."

Ian strolled beside Amanda across the area where the Knight family tents were pitched and into the woods on a trail under a green canopy of trees, a light breeze ruffling their leaves.

"I need to get back," Amanda said. "I'm on the cooking detail tonight. I'm leaving you here. Keep on the trail." She pointed where to go. "It ends near a lake overlook. You'll see."

When Ian came to the end and the trail opened up onto a bluff that had a great view of the lake, he stopped and stared at the blanket spread over the ground with a picnic basket in one corner. He walked to the wicker container and lifted the top. Inside was a bottle of sparkling grape juice and two glasses set between bowls of large strawberries and melted chocolate.

He heard a branch snap and looked up. Annie rounded the last bend in the trail. When she saw him, she looked puzzled. She gazed at the basket and blanket, and her expression went blank.

"What's this?" She paused on the opposite side of the coverlet.

"You tell me."

"I can't."

"Your sister said that you wanted to see me."

Annie's eyes brightened with understanding quickly followed by irritation. "Jasmine told me that you wanted to see *me*. I thought this was a strange place to meet."

"Why?"

"Because the locals call this bluff Lover's Leap." Annie averted her eyes to the lake stretching out below. "You know what's going on here?"

Jasmine? Ah, now he did. "How did my daughter rope your sister into participating in this little…" He waved his arm, at a loss for words.

"Rendezvous." Annie's cheeks flamed.

"Yes."

"Amanda is a romantic. It wouldn't have taken much. Now I know for sure who was leaving those little gifts for me. I suspected one of them, but I think it was both!"

"True—if one does something like this, then the other is involved, too." Ian removed the sparkling grape juice from the basket, then the strawberries and chocolate. He chuckled. "They've been watching too much TV."

"No, my sister is a huge romance reader. This is all her. The girls probably came up with the idea of doing something, and Amanda went to town with it."

Ian sat on the blanket. "We might as well enjoy it. I love strawberries and chocolate, not that I've ever had them together."

"I do, too, which Amanda would know."

"But sparkling grape juice?"

"We have this every year on New Year's Eve. We

like the bubbles." Annie sat down on the other side of the blanket.

"With your large family, you must have a lot of traditions, especially during a holiday like this one." Ian opened the bottle and poured the grape juice into two glasses, then passed one to Annie. He'd have to thank Amanda and Jasmine. This was a good idea.

"Just wait until the Fourth. My brothers revert back to childhood with their fireworks display."

Ian raised his drink. "To the next holiday."

"Father's Day. Just a few weeks away. So what do you do to celebrate?"

"Usually we go to the Oklahoma City Zoo for the day. If it's raining, we spend the day inside at the Omniplex next to the zoo."

"No golfing or sleeping in a hammock?" Annie dipped the first strawberry into the chocolate and took a bite.

"I've never played golf and don't own a hammock, although it wouldn't be a bad idea to get one."

Annie fixed another strawberry and held it out for Ian. "So what are we going to do about my sister and your daughters?"

Ian leaned toward her hand and sank his teeth into the juicy fruit. "How about nothing? I'm enjoying this quiet alone time with good food and drink." He scanned the woods surrounding the bluff and whispered, "I wouldn't be surprised if one or all are watching right now. Want to find out?"

"How?"

"I can't imagine my daughters remaining quiet if I kiss you."

Annie's eyes grew round. "You're probably right."

"Feed me another strawberry, and then I'll thank you with a kiss."

"Do you think we should encourage them by doing that?"

"True. No telling what they would plan." But the idea of kissing Annie again wouldn't leave Ian's mind. In fact, he'd often recalled that kiss on his patio. "But it might be fun finding out what they would do."

Annie laughed and picked up a strawberry, dipped it in some chocolate then presented it to Ian. "If I didn't know better, I'd think you wanted to kiss me anyway."

Ian ignored the offered fruit and bent closer to her. "Actually, I do."

A small gasp escaped her beautiful lips, but she didn't pull back. Instead, she leaned toward him.

Suddenly Jade entered the clearing, shouting, "Dad, come quick!"

Chapter 12

"What's going on?" Ian shot to his feet.

"Is Jeremy having a seizure?" Annie jumped up.

Jade shook her head. "Joshua's missing."

The three started hurrying down the trail back to the campground. "How?" Annie asked. "Melissa is always so conscientious."

"We were playing hide-and-seek, and we can't find him."

"Where?" Ian asked.

"Around the playground." Jade looked panicked.

Annie increased her pace to keep up with Ian. "We'll find him. There are a lot of us." But she kept thinking of Joshua's adventurous behavior. He'd try anything he thought would be fun. There were some caves not too far from where they were camping. What if he got lost in one or encountered a bear? Her own fear skyrocketed as risky scenarios ran through her mind.

Slightly behind Annie on her right, Jade said, "Melissa didn't do anything wrong. Don't blame her."

Annie slowed and glanced back at Jade. "I'm not putting blame on anyone. I just want to find Joshua." As her heartbeat raced she accelerated, nearly catching up with Ian. In the distance she heard Joshua's name being called, which confirmed he was still missing.

A few minutes later, Ian burst out of the woods first and headed straight for a group of adults, including Melissa and Annie's father, gathered near the playground. "Where have you looked?" Ian scanned their faces, his shoulders slumping.

Annie touched his arm as she parked herself next to him. "Dad?"

"Ken and Charlie are checking the caves. Ben and some of the older kids are walking along the shoreline."

"I've looked in all the hiding places the children were using," Melissa said, her face pale and her hands shaking.

Annie crossed to her niece and clasped her hands. "This isn't your fault. Things happen that we would never anticipate. And to Joshua especially. How long has he been missing?"

"Fifteen minutes."

Annie's eldest sister, Rachel, pointed to the left. "We've tried all the tents and cars. That leaves the woods. We need to look there, too."

Annie's dad started organizing the family. "Let's form a line with four or five feet between each of us and comb them."

Ian approached Melissa. "Joshua has gotten away from me before. He usually follows directions, but something might get into his head and he forgets what he should do. Don't feel responsible for this."

Tears welled in the teenager's eyes. "He'd been doing everything I said."

Rachel, Melissa's mother, joined them and hugged her daughter. "The best thing to do is help find him, so come on."

While Amanda stayed back at camp in case Joshua returned on his own, Annie said to Ian, "Let's go toward the trail. Maybe he saw us and decided to follow."

"But we were just there."

"He might have cut through the woods at an angle. Joshua looks at everything as an escapade."

"That's something he would do," Ian agreed. He pushed his way through some thick underbrush at the edge of the forest, shouting his son's name.

Annie did likewise about five feet from Ian. As they neared the bluff, Annie thought she heard a voice say, "I'm here!" Halting, she waved to Ian and put her forefinger to her mouth. He stopped yelling Joshua's name.

"Help. I'm stuck!"

The sound came from the area in front of Annie. She hastened forward with Ian running toward her. "Joshua, where are you?"

"Here. In the log."

Up ahead Annie spied a large log, and it appeared one end was hollow. An animal like a fox could fit in it, but a child?

"We're coming, Joshua," Ian shouted.

"I'm here." When Annie reached the log a few seconds before Ian, she knelt at one end of the downed tree trunk and peeked inside.

"I can't move." Annie saw Joshua's legs wiggle as though trying to back out of the log.

Ian went to the other end and peered in. He grinned. "You've got yourself in a pickle, son."

"A pickle? I wish I had one to eat. I'm hungry."

"It means you're in a tight spot."

"Yeah, Dad. That's what I said."

Annie squatted next to Ian, the sight of Joshua's dirty face wonderful. "We could try to pull him out."

"Where are your arms?"

"At my sides."

Ian stood and walked around the six-foot log, knocking against the wood, checking for soft spots. The raps echoed through the woods.

"It's narrower at the end where his head and torso are. We should try pulling him out by the legs." He returned to the other end of the log. "I'll tug on your legs, but you'll have to let us know if you're caught on anything. Annie will stay here and talk to you." He stooped and whispered in her ear, "The wood is rough so it'll probably scrape his arms. Reassure him while I try to dislodge him."

Annie lay on the ground facing Joshua and reached in to touch his head. "I'm staying here while your dad gets you out. What made you hide in here?"

"Cuz I was being found. I wanna fool everyone."

"It fooled them so well they thought you were lost."

"I'm not lost. I know where I am." He giggled. "That means I won."

Ian pulled on Joshua's legs. The boy moved slightly, wincing.

"Does it hurt?"

He wiggled and managed to bring one arm out from under his body. "I'm tough."

"I know you're tough, buddy." Annie peered over the log at Ian.

He continued to pull. When Joshua suddenly popped loose, Ian's furrowed forehead and set jaw quickly relaxed.

Annie hurried to Ian as Joshua slid out. She wanted to scoop the child into her arms, but Ian did first.

"Don't ever scare me like that again, Joshua. I had visions of having to saw you out of the log." Ian held the boy away from him and checked his arms and body for any wounds. "When we get back to camp, I need to clean these scrapes on your arms, but other than those you seem fine."

Joshua threw his arms around Ian's neck. "Thanks, Dad. You saved me."

Ian grinned from ear to ear as he rose with his son in his arms.

Annie patted Joshua's back. "No more hide-and-seek. In fact, I'm not sure you'll leave my side the rest of the weekend."

"Aw. I was supposed to hide. It was a cool place. I didn't know I'd get stuck."

Ian set Joshua on the ground and tousled his hair. "Annie is right. You have to be within view of one of us the rest of the weekend. Trouble seems to find you."

Joshua lifted his shoulders. "I don't look for trouble. Promise."

"C'mon. We need to get back and let my family know you've been located." Annie started toward camp with the five-year-old between her and Ian.

"Now that the kids have gone to sleep, do you want to share the strawberries and chocolate? The grape juice is flat but that's okay." Ian was carrying the picnic basket and sat in the folding chair next to Annie on one side of the fire circle while her sister and Ben sat across from them.

Annie's first impulse was to say no because of how close she and Ian had come to kissing again. But she'd enjoyed the snacks and with her sister and brother-in-law nearby, there wouldn't be a repeat of what Ian had suggested at the bluff. Annie always thought of herself as being strong willed, but Ian was testing that assumption.

"Sure. I hate my sister having gone to all this trouble to set this up and not at least have the treats." She'd raised her voice so Amanda would hear her reply.

Annie slanted a glance toward Amanda and Ben exchanging whispers. Probably plotting something for her and Ian tomorrow. With all that had happened concerning Joshua and then dinner and cleanup, Annie hadn't had the time to tell her sister to stop interfering. Amanda had tried it once before, and Annie had thought she'd made her wishes very clear: no trying to fix her up.

"I think my sister was behind it all and somehow solicited your daughters to help," Annie whispered to Ian.

"Did you say anything to the girls when you said

good-night?" Ian dipped a strawberry into the chocolate and passed it to Annie, their fingers touching.

Annie tried to concentrate, but all she could think about was their almost kiss on the bluff. She had to admit it: she'd wanted Ian to kiss her.

"Annie?"

She blinked and peered at him. "Yes. Jasmine and Jade looked at each other, struggling to keep straight faces, and said that my sister asked them to help her set it up today, then they burst out giggling."

Annie popped the piece of fruit into her mouth then licked the chocolate off her fingertips, trying not to think of when she'd fed the strawberry to Ian.

"Which means they are guilty."

"I'm not really mad at them, but at my sister, who is encouraging them. She knows better."

"She wants to see you with someone."

Annie huffed and glared at Amanda. "Being with someone isn't in my plan." But even as she said it, it didn't feel right. That bothered her even more. Once it had been her dream to have a husband and children.

"What plan?"

"Working with children who need me is my plan. I'm not looking for anything else." If she said it enough, maybe she would believe it.

"How about a man who needs you?"

Ian's question hung in the air. Annie averted her gaze and watched Amanda and Ben get up and walk toward their tent, Ben's arm resting on her sister's shoulder. A pang zipped through Annie at the sight. She'd wanted that at one time.

She didn't know how to answer Ian. He wasn't aware

of her part in the fire. If he knew the truth, would he still want her? "What man?" she finally asked.

"Me. Do you not see how important you are to me and my family? You have given me hope for the future. Hope that my children will be all right. That I'll be okay."

"I understand. You're grateful for what I'm doing." Annie stood. "I appreciate that. I like being needed." Because it eased the pain of her guilt for a short time. "I'm going to turn in now."

Ian caught her hand. "Annie, don't go yet. Please stay."

Annie studied his face, highlighted by the dying fire. He was such a good man. She cared for him more than she should. But—

"Please, Annie. Our one time of quiet was interrupted today."

She sat again, although now she realized how close they were. Only inches separated them.

"Do you realize how extraordinary you are?"

"What am I supposed to say to that? Yes, I am? No, I'm not?"

"I should have said instead that you're a special person, period. No question about it. I think you sell yourself short."

Annie turned her folding chair so she could face him and put some space between them. "I know I can help children. I'm not afraid of difficult cases."

"That's not what I'm saying. When you first came to us, you kept your scars a secret, hiding them. I'm not sure you would have shared them with us if it hadn't been for Jeremy. I'm glad you did, but it doesn't change how I look at you or how I feel about you."

"They're a reminder of what I did." Annie dropped her gaze to her lap. She was going to tell him. Outside her family and a few firefighters, no one knew. And she didn't talk about it, even with Amanda, the person closest to her. But Ian deserved to know, and if it made a difference, so be it.

"A reminder of what? The fire? Why would you want to do that? That's the past. What's done is done."

Annie took a deep breath and held it for a long moment before slowly exhaling. The knots of tension in her stomach remained. "Ian, I'm responsible for the fire. I didn't…" She couldn't say it.

He leaned forward in his chair, resting his elbows on his thighs. "What happened?"

Annie swallowed several times, but she felt as if a fist was jammed in her throat. Tears sprang to her eyes, and she looked toward her tent. She wanted to escape. She shouldn't have stayed. She shouldn't have started this conversation.

Ian reached out and took her hand. "Please tell me, Annie."

She tugged her hand free. "I lit a candle on the table by the open window in my bedroom at the cabin. I was there with part of my family. Usually Amanda and I share a bedroom, but she didn't come that weekend. I thank God for that at least. I fell asleep on my bed and didn't blow out the candle. The curtains…" A vision of the flames licking up the walls when she woke up coughing still haunted her. "They caught fire, and the dry timber of the walls quickly went up in the blaze.

My father rescued me but couldn't get back in to help my mom. She became trapped like I did. She died because of me." Annie rushed the last sentence.

Ian moved from his chair and knelt in front of her. "Annie, it was an accident." He clasped her arms and waited until she looked at him.

Through tears she saw his dear face so full of concern and compassion. "An accident I caused. If only I hadn't…" She couldn't say what she had agonized over for fourteen years.

"Hadn't lit the candle? I've dealt with many patients who have done things they regretted, things that led to bad consequences. Some did them on purpose and others accidentally. The latter are the people who have the most problems dealing with their guilt."

"Of course I feel guilt. My mother died because of me. How do you get over that?"

"By turning to the Lord. I know He's forgiven you. Now you need to do the same thing for yourself. Let the past go."

Annie shot to her feet, tipping over the folding chair, and yanked away from Ian. "It's not that easy."

He rose. "I didn't say it was. Does your family blame you?"

She shook her head.

"So the only one who does is you?"

"Because *I did it*." The words tore from deep inside her.

"You saw with Jeremy what happens when you keep feelings locked away. They eat at you, grow bigger in your mind. God doesn't want that for you."

Annie stepped back, nearly tripping over the downed chair. "You don't know what God wants for me."

"Do you? Are you doing His will or yours?"

"You don't understand. My scars are my..." Annie couldn't get a decent breath. Her throat burned. Her chest tightened.

Ian closed the space between them. "Punishment? I don't see that being the Lord's plan for you. He gave you a beautiful gift for working with children. You didn't cause that fire with malicious intent. When are you going to feel you've paid enough?"

"Why are you doing this?"

"Because I care for you. I lo—" His eyes widened, and he moved back.

Anger swelled in Annie. Not even Amanda had pushed her this much. "What, loathe? Like? Maybe you pity me."

Ian's gaze drilled into her. "I'm falling in love with you."

"The only feeling you have for me is gratitude for my help. Don't confuse that with anything more." Annie swept around and marched toward her tent.

At the opening she paused, trying to calm her trembling. She squeezed her hands into a ball. She didn't want the girls to know anything had happened. Why couldn't Ian let things alone? Let her work for him and care for his children?

Just for a second her heart had leaped when he'd said the word *love*. Now she didn't know how long she could stay at the McGregors'. By the age of twenty she'd realized love wasn't in her future. Not after David.

Ian wasn't David... But still, Annie couldn't risk being hurt anymore.

* * *

Ian wanted to go after her, but he knew she would reject him. Yes, he was grateful that Annie was in their lives, but it was much more than that. Up until a few minutes ago he hadn't realized how much. There was a lot to love about Annie.

Why doesn't she see the beauty I do?

Her guilt was robbing her of the life she should have had. Ian wasn't going to give up helping her see that, or the medical fact that there were procedures that would make her scars less noticeable, especially her ear. Ian knew that until she accepted that what happened was an accident, she'd never be free of the past. Every day when Annie looked at herself those scars reminded her of her mom's death.

Maybe he could solicit Amanda and her family to help convince her to have surgery, especially if it didn't cost her anything. Ian wanted to give her that chance to heal.

"Thanks for coming to help me," Ian said a few days later to Amanda, whom he'd invited to help chaperone Jeremy's belated-birthday swimming party.

"Someone has to shake some sense into Annie. I've been trying. Dad has. Even my youngest brother. She won't listen. I think she's gotten so used to feeling that guilt she's afraid to let go of it. She and our mother were very close, probably closer than any of us were. But I know Mom would be so upset if she knew what Annie is doing."

Ian greeted Ben, who was coming up the steps to the porch. "I'm glad you've been a lifeguard before." Ian shook Annie's brother-in-law's hand. "I probably let Jeremy invite too many, but I was thrilled he wanted to. I couldn't say no when he kept adding boys to the list."

"Are your other children going to be here?" Ben asked.

"Yes, they invited a couple of friends, too."

Amanda laughed. "Good thing they aren't a little older or there might be problems. Four girls at a party with eight boys."

"Please don't remind me about what I'll be dealing with in a few years," Ian said with a chuckle.

"You hope it takes that long," Amanda said as she headed for the kitchen to help Annie with the food.

"Amanda told me about what you were going to do later." Ben crossed the foyer toward the hallway with Ian.

"It's my version of an intervention. No matter what she feels about me, I want her to do this for herself."

"Have the surgery or forgive herself?"

Ian opened the sliding glass door to the patio. "Let the past go. Ben, I just noticed you don't have your dog with you."

"No, I want to focus totally on the children in the water. Besides, this is Jeremy and Rex's show. I want all the attention on them. Ringo can be an attention hog at times."

"By the way, my children, even Joshua with his scrapes, had a great time last week with all the others."

"I understand Nathan is coming to the party."

"Yes, Jeremy and Nathan hit it off that day fishing. I also had Annie invite her niece Carey because Jasmine and Jade really enjoyed themselves with her."

"Where are your kids?"

"Cleaning up outside. Annie has everyone working, even Joshua." The front doorbell rang. "I've got to get this."

"I'll supervise the preparation for the party."

Ian answered the door and let in a steady stream of children while telling the parents when to pick them up. After everyone arrived, he headed for the kitchen to let Annie and Amanda know the party was starting. As he approached the room, he overheard Annie saying, "I'm not going to say anything until I've found someone."

Ian walked through the doorway. "Found someone for what?"

At the sink Annie whirled around and stared at him, her expression stamped with surprise.

"Excuse me. I'm going to help my husband with the children out back." Amanda hurried from the house.

Silence hung between Annie and Ian. His mouth went dry. Something was wrong.

"Is there a problem I should know about?"

"I'm looking for a replacement for me as your nanny."

Chapter 13

The shock on Ian's face made Annie want to snatch the words back.

Ian opened his mouth to say something, shook his head and pivoted. The sound of the back door slamming reverberated through the kitchen. Her body trembling, Annie collapsed against the counter behind her, her stomach roiling. After coming home from the camping trip with her family last weekend, she'd realized she couldn't work for Ian any longer. He threatened everything she had planned for herself. He wasn't really falling in love with her, and he'd realize that and break her heart. Ian was grateful for her help and only said that because he took pity on her. She'd had enough of that the past fourteen years.

Annie couldn't stay here. Ian would see the wisdom when she found him a good nanny to replace her.

Annie would stay until she did. She cared far too much for him to let a relationship based on false assumptions go anywhere.

Annie began taking the food outside. After setting up all the treats for the party, she scanned the children, glad to see so many attending. Several hung around Jeremy and Rex on one side of the pool while the girls remained across from them, giggling and occasionally pointing at the boys. The only ones in the water were Joshua and Brent, Annie's nephew. Once she'd seen Joshua at the lake swimming, she felt more at ease with him in the water. He was a good swimmer for his age.

Then her gaze fell on Ian at the other end of the pool with Ben. A frown carved deep lines into Ian's face. His stiff stance screamed his anger. At her.

Amanda approached her. "Are you all right?"

"No. That was not the way I was going to tell him. I didn't even want to say anything until I had a good lead on a nanny."

"If you really want to leave, he has a right to know from the beginning."

"I guess." But what if he fired her right after the party? Annie wasn't ready to go yet. She hadn't even talked with the children about it.

Make up your mind. You can't have it both ways.

Amanda turned toward her and lowered her voice. "My problem is why you think you need to leave. He's a great catch and you love all his children. This could be the family you've always wanted."

"Being a nanny has satisfied my need."

"Has it really? When we were kids all you talked about was having a family like the one we had."

"Whose side are you on?"

"Always yours, even when I think you're wrong. But that doesn't mean I won't try to straighten you out."

"What if Ian is interested in me because of his children? In fact, that makes the most sense."

"Why are you selling yourself short?" Amanda asked in a furious whisper.

"I'm being realistic. I see myself in the mirror. And Ian hasn't even seen the worst of my scars."

"He's a plastic surgeon. He knows what burn scars look like."

Joshua swam to the steps and exited the water, then walked quickly to Annie. "See, I'm not running." The child grinned.

"Walk any faster and you are. You love pushing the limits." Annie smiled and brushed his blond curls off his forehead.

"No one but me and Brent are swimming. Come in the water, Annie."

Although she'd grown up loving to swim like Joshua, she hadn't planned to go into the pool. Annie wore a one-piece swimsuit under a long T-shirt just in case she needed to help a child in the water, but she didn't wear her suit other than with her family.

When she didn't say anything, Joshua tugged on her hand. At first she resisted, then when all eyes were on her, she gave up and followed, intending only to sit on the top step. When she did, Joshua did a cannonball right next to her, totally drenching her.

"You're wet now. You might as well come in." Joshua swam toward her.

Annie waited until he was within arm's reach and

grabbed him. After twirling him around, she playfully heaved him away from her.

When he surfaced, his giggles erupted, and he came toward her again. Annie slipped into the water and stood her ground until he was right on her, then darted away. He tried to catch her. "Come and get me," she taunted Joshua, her laughter filling the air.

He swam as fast as he could, and this time she let him get her, launching himself at her and taking them both under the water. When Annie and Joshua popped to the surface, the boys started jumping into the pool, seeing who could make the biggest splash. She glanced toward Ian and Ben, who were now both soaking wet.

As she started to look away, Ian's gaze riveted her. Even from a distance she could see his green eyes darkening to a brewing storm. Annie shivered. When he joined the boys in the water, she swam to the steps and hurried out of the pool, making sure her shirt covered most of her scars. To hide what was left of her right ear, she donned a floppy sunhat, then wrapped herself in a beach towel she'd placed nearby.

As the girls dived into the water, Amanda sidled up next to Annie. "You were having fun. Have you thought about how much you're going to miss that?"

"Thank you for that observation."

"Were you aware a couple of times the damage to your ear was visible, and Joshua didn't react to it? In fact, no one did."

"Why are you pushing me so hard?"

"Because I don't want you to make the biggest mistake of your life."

"I already did that the night I lit that candle."

When Amanda murmured, "You don't have to be that way," Annie began walking away.

Annie wanted to throttle her twin. She'd always counted on Amanda's support and needed it to do what she must. Because deep inside, she didn't know how she was going to deal with leaving this family she loved.

Something was up with Amanda and Ian. They had been talking together for the past ten minutes and from the looks of it, arguing. All the guests had left a half an hour ago except her sister and Ben. The surprise was when her eldest brother, who was Brent's father, had invited Joshua to spend the night when he'd come to pick up her nephew. Annie helped Joshua pack. He was so excited about his first sleepover.

She checked on the twins and Jeremy, camped out in the den with Ben watching a movie. The kitchen, poolside and yard were clean, so she decided to go to her apartment and collapse. When Ian had insisted she take the rest of the night off, she hadn't turned down the offer. Today had been fun, nerve racking and draining. Ian could see her sister and brother-in-law out.

In her apartment, Annie sank onto the couch and lay down, cushioning her head on a pillow. She needed to come up with a nanny for the children. At the moment she couldn't think of anyone—everyone had a job already. And Ian's kids needed someone who was special, patient, loving and...

Her eyelids slid closed, her exhaustion catching up with her.

When a loud knock at the door woke her, Annie

bolted up on the couch. She wanted to pretend she wasn't in her apartment.

Another knock sounded and Amanda said, "I know you're in there. I'm not leaving." When Annie opened the door, Ian stood behind Amanda. Annie took one look at both of them and tried to shut the door.

Amanda blocked it with her body. "I told you I wasn't leaving. I could have invited the rest of the family, but I didn't. They think everything is okay."

Annie backed away. "It is." Then to Ian she added, "Why are you here?"

"Actually, I'm the one who wanted to talk to you. Amanda insisted on coming, too. It's hard to say no to your sister."

"Tell me about it. You two might as well come in and have your say. Then you can leave. It's been a long day." *And will probably be a longer night.*

Annie took a chair set across from the couch where they sat. "Ian, I'm sorry you had to find out about my leaving that way."

"That's not why I'm here. I'd planned on talking to you tonight even before I knew that."

"Then, what do you want to say?"

Ian sat forward on the couch, his hands loosely clasped. "I contacted a good friend I went to medical school with. He lives in Dallas and is a plastic surgeon, too. He's agreed to see you and assess your situation."

"I can't afford it."

"Free of charge. I've made all the arrangements. Everyone will be donating their services, so you won't have to worry about how much it is. He thinks a prosthetic ear will probably be the best way to go. He can see you next week. I'll drive you down."

Annie gripped the arms of the chair. "Do I have a say in this?"

"Yes, but you have no reason to say no now. I've taken care of the financial issue."

"And you still want to do this even though I'll be leaving you when a new nanny is found?"

"Yes." She saw a twitch in his jaw.

Do you think I'm that repulsive? Annie almost asked. She bit the inside of her cheek to keep the words to herself. "What about the children?"

"Dad will take care of them that day. His summer-school teaching job won't start for another two weeks," Amanda said.

"I see. You two worked this out without asking me if I would even go to the appointment."

They both nodded, solemn expressions on their faces.

Annie didn't know what she felt. She guessed she could go and at least hear out Ian's friend. She'd been half-afraid when he'd come into the apartment he was going to ask her to leave immediately—he'd been so angry at her today. He'd spoken to her only when absolutely necessary.

"Okay I'll go—on one condition. Ian, I won't leave until you find someone the children will love. That's the least I can do whether or not I agree to have surgery."

Ian stared right through her as though she wasn't sitting a few feet from him. "You'll have the job as long as you want. And believe me, I'll keep my distance and my feelings to myself," he said icily. He rose. "As you said, it's been a long day. Good night."

The sound of his footsteps resonated through her place as he made his way to the door. The last look of disappointment in his eyes nearly undid Annie. But she wasn't the right person for him. She was damaged, and when she left, he would realize that his feelings weren't based on love but gratitude.

"Do you know anyone who could be their nanny?" Annie asked Amanda, suddenly feeling as though she'd let everyone down. But Ian needed to realize what he thought he was feeling toward her could probably be extended to anyone who did a good job with his children.

"Actually I do. She just graduated from high school last year and went to Oklahoma State her freshman year, but she has decided to attend Cimarron Community College in the fall. Mary is great with children. I think she could work her school schedule around the children's in the fall. She wants to be a teacher, but OSU was too big for her. She wants the feel of a small college."

"Mary Franklin? That tall, redheaded beauty with men lined up at her front door during school holidays?"

"Yes. I could talk to her and let you know if she's interested. When she was in high school, she worked as a nanny for the Grimms across the street when their three children were out for summer break."

"I guess you can check with her." This was the answer to Annie's problem, yet she couldn't put any enthusiasm into the sentence.

"I thought you would be excited that I knew someone. Are you having second thoughts about leaving?"

"Of course not." But Annie sounded weak even to herself.

Amanda hugged Annie. "Good. You're having doubts about what you think you need to do. These past couple of months I've seen you changing. You're more open. You've shared with Ian and his children more of yourself than you have with anyone else. That includes your own family members."

"But he wants me to have surgery as if I'm not good enough this way." Annie swept her arm down her length.

"That's not what he's doing, and I think in your heart you know that. Ian wants you to have options and to make your own decision. He took the money factor away so you could look into your heart and decide what *you* want."

Annie straightened, thrusting back her shoulders. "It's my life. People should accept me as is."

"Yes. And in a perfect world, they would. Sometimes people react before thinking."

Mentally exhausted, Annie tried to stifle a yawn but couldn't.

"There's no use talking about the surgery until you hear what the doctor says. You're tired. Go to bed. I'll let myself out."

Annie switched off the lamp and walked toward the light streaming from her bedroom. But even after she got ready for bed and lay down, she couldn't quiet her thoughts, all centered on Ian. Even if she let herself love, Ian was used to making people as close to perfect as he could. And she would never be that.

"You've been awfully quiet on the ride back. Do you have any questions you didn't ask Neil?" Ian glanced at Annie sitting in the passenger seat of his Lexus.

"Dr. Hawks was quite thorough. I have all the information I need."

"What do you think?"

"I don't know. It's happened so fast, and the fact he can do the surgery next month makes me feel rushed."

Ian gritted his teeth. He'd hoped Annie would be excited once she heard from Neil what could be done to improve her scars and replace her ear. She'd helped his family so much—why couldn't she see that and accept the gift for what it was, a thank-you?

"The choice is yours, of course."

"Then, why did you arrange this?"

Ian gripped the steering wheel tighter. "Because you'd said you couldn't afford it, and I wanted at least to take that barrier out of the decision."

It had been nearly a week since Jeremy's swim party, when Annie's news about leaving had rocked his world, and he still hadn't been able to right it. She wanted to quit. Ian was trying to keep his developing feelings for her to himself, but it was hard when all he wanted to do was hold her and make her life better. To love her as she deserved. He might never have considered a service dog for Jeremy if she hadn't suggested the possibility. Rex was the best thing that had happened to his son.

"My life is fine the way it is."

The defensive tone in her voice made Ian wonder if she was trying to convince herself. "Are you sure you feel that way?"

"I should know how I feel."

"Your words don't match your tone."

Annie folded her arms over her chest and stared out her window.

Fifteen minutes later, Ian exited I-35 onto I-40, not far from Cimarron City. The closer they got to home, the more the tension thickened in the car.

"I don't want you to leave." Ian had to try one more time.

Annie didn't respond.

No one could replace Annie. Disappointment, anger and a deep hurt mingled inside him. "I haven't told the kids. I don't want to until the plans are firm."

"I won't tell them. But I have a lead on a good applicant."

Oh, joy. Ian had been hoping Annie couldn't find anyone. Maybe this applicant wouldn't be acceptable. "Annie, I have feelings for you that have nothing to do with gratitude."

"How do you know that?"

"And how do you know they are? To quote you, I should know how I feel."

"Touché." Annie sat forward. "I see the exit to Cimarron City. We should be at your house shortly. I'll talk with Mary Franklin today and set up a time for you to interview her."

"I won't interview her at the house. If she doesn't work out—" and he was sure she wouldn't "—I don't want the children upset unnecessarily."

"How about I take the kids to Sooner Park? They love going there. According to Jasmine the playground is 'to die for.'"

"Your leaving won't change what I feel for you. I know you feel something for me. We work well together as a team."

"Yes, employee and employer."

"You're scared to really feel. Be honest with yourself and me. Annie, do you care about me beyond being your employer?"

Again she stared out the window. Ian didn't know if she would answer him.

"Yes," she finally said. "But I have my life figured out. I know what I'm supposed to do."

"What?"

"As I told you before, help children in need. My mother was the best there was. I'm continuing her work."

"How?"

"My parents used to take in foster children, and Mom especially would be the kids' support until a home was found for them. Being single, I can't easily take in foster children, so I chose to work with families whose children needed something extra."

"Like mine," Ian murmured.

"Yes."

"They still need you."

"But you're doing great with them, and with the right nanny you all will be fine."

"Can you guarantee that?" Sarcasm edged his voice, frustration churning his gut. After Ian pulled into his driveway and parked in the garage, he turned toward her. "What if everything you've started falls apart? You aren't your mother. You are Annie Knight. God has His own plan for you."

"Don't you get it? I'm the reason my mother isn't alive. I'm filling her void. Then maybe…" She pressed her lips together and unbuckled her seat belt.

"You can't forgive yourself for your mother's death.

But her path isn't yours. The Lord has a unique plan for each person."

Annie shoved open the door and scrambled out of the Lexus, then leaned down, glaring. "Who are you to tell me what's best for me?"

"A guy who wants a great life for you, who loves you." Ian finally said aloud what he'd known in his heart for days. He wasn't just falling in love. He'd loved Annie Knight for a long time now. She'd been a breath of fresh air in a very stale life.

Her eyes grew big. She straightened, closed the passenger door and hurried toward the breezeway into the house.

Ian slammed his palm against the steering wheel. His love hadn't made any difference.

Chapter 14

Annie couldn't get away from Ian fast enough. He was delusional to think he was in love with her. And yet, when he had said it, her heart had soared—until she'd forced reality into the situation.

Annie found her father coming into the McGregors' kitchen as she entered the house.

"The doctor couldn't help you?" he asked, covering the distance between them.

"No, actually, he could."

"Why the sad face, then?" Her dad glanced over her left shoulder.

Although Annie hadn't heard Ian enter, she knew he was behind her. "Lots of decisions to make. Are the children in bed yet?"

"I just said good-night to Joshua. The girls are playing a game, and Jeremy and Rex are watching TV. I think Rex is more into the show than Jeremy."

Annie walked to her father and kissed him on the cheek. "Thanks for helping today. I'm going to say good-night to Joshua and check in with the others before I go to my apartment."

Annie didn't even know how she strung words together to form coherent sentences, but she did. The closer Ian came to her in the kitchen, the faster her heart beat. She had to get out of there before she actually believed he could love her.

Ian had so much to offer the right woman. But Annie wasn't that person.

Upstairs she eased open Joshua's door to see if he was asleep. There was a hump in the middle of his bed with a light shining through the sheet. She tiptoed to his bed and began tickling him. "Boo! A certain little boy hasn't gone to sleep like he was supposed to."

Giggles floated from behind the blue sheet, then Joshua popped up and Daisy shot off the bed and raced out of the room.

"What were you doing?" Annie said in a stern voice while trying not to laugh.

"Trying to sneak Daisy in here." Joshua grinned. "We were hiding, but she doesn't like the dark. I got the flashlight."

"I think the only one around here who doesn't like the dark is you." Annie sat on the edge of his bed. "And you know it's Jade's turn for Daisy to sleep with her."

"Shh. She doesn't know I sneaked into her room and got Daisy."

At that moment Jade stomped into Joshua's room,

carrying Daisy. "I did, too. What goes around comes around." Then she spun about on her heel and left with the dog.

He scrunched up his nose. "What's that mean?"

"One day she's going to take Daisy from you when it's your night to have the dog."

"That's not fair." Joshua plopped back onto his bed.

Annie inched forward and drew the sheet up to the child's shoulder. "Time to go to sleep, and I'll turn on the night-light."

"Your dad forgot to."

"Did you tell him you like it on?"

"I never do with you. You always just do it."

She shook her head and leaned over to kiss Joshua's forehead. "Good night."

Annie started to stand. Joshua clasped her hand, keeping her sitting on the bed. "Will you read me a story before you go?"

"Sure." Annie usually did. She picked up his favorite book and switched on the light on the nightstand.

Within five minutes Joshua's eyes were closed. Annie rose, turned the night-light on and the lamp off then headed for the hallway.

"Annie, I love you," Joshua said in a sleepy voice.

Her heart cracked, a pang stabbing her. Emotions swelled inside. Tears threatened.

Annie hurried to give the girls a brief update on the trip and tell them good-night. She needed to escape to her apartment.

After she poked her head into the den to see how Jeremy was doing, she was going to sneak out the sliding glass doors since she heard her father and Ian talking in the kitchen.

"Jeremy, how did it go today?" Annie asked from the doorway.

"Your dad took us fishing. Everyone liked that except Jasmine."

"Did she behave?"

"For a girl."

"No other problems?"

He shook his head, his hand stroking Rex's back.

"See you tomorrow."

As Annie made her way to the breezeway and heard her dad starting his car, she thought of the last time Jeremy had had a seizure—almost two weeks ago. His medication was working much better. That was a relief and would make it easier for her to leave and a new nanny to take over.

As she neared the staircase to her place, she saw a shadow sitting on a step. Charlie? But then the figure rose, and the security light illuminated Ian's face.

"Just checking to make sure you're all right. You fled the kitchen so fast your dad was concerned, and I told him I would look in on you."

"I'm tired of talking and thinking about my scars. I'll be fine tomorrow." *Yeah, right. What makes you think that?*

"Here is Neil's number. When you decide, call him. This is totally up to you. There's no deadline on the offer." Ian came to her and pressed a small sheet of paper into her palm. "Good night."

He turned and strode toward his house.

"Ian."

He stopped but didn't look back.

"Thank you. I appreciate your caring enough to try to fix me."

"I'm not trying to fix you, as you say, but to help you. That's what a person who cares does." He continued forward.

Why had she said it that way? Because that was her conscience talking. Her scars had become a scarlet letter she wore proclaiming her guilt.

Annie had spent Sunday at church then at her sister's until nightfall. That was the first day in months she hadn't seen Ian or his children at least once. And she was miserable.

Was that why she was rushing to dress this morning, to be at the house when the children woke up? To see Ian before he left for work?

When Annie walked into the kitchen to decide what to fix for breakfast, Ian had a cup of coffee in his hand and was staring out the bay window overlooking the patio and pool. He acknowledged her presence by glancing over his shoulder, then returned to sipping his drink. Since the drive to Dallas a few days before, a barrier stood between her and Ian. Annie had started it, but after that day, he'd added to it. Even the kids noticed. Joshua had said something to her on Saturday about his daddy being mad at her.

After checking the refrigerator for the ingredients for pancakes, she turned toward Ian. "What time will you be home this evening?"

"Early. The agency is sending out a couple of applicants for your job this afternoon. I'd like you to have the children gone from three to five."

"I'm sorry Mary Franklin didn't work out for you."

"She's too young. Barely out of high school. Although I see why you think she'd be good, she doesn't have enough experience."

"Yesterday at church I ran into Mrs. Addison. All the kids in the family she used to work for are in high school. She's been taking a month's break, but now she's ready to move on to a new family. I mentioned you and your children. She's interested."

"Fine. Have her come this afternoon at five with her résumé."

"I'll let her know, and I'll keep the kids away from the house until six."

"Sure." He started for the hallway. "Whatever you think. I'm going to work now."

"But I haven't fixed breakfast yet."

"I'll grab something on the way."

Ian disappeared down the hall. For a moment Annie felt as if a part of herself had walked out of the room. She shook that idea from her mind and concentrated on getting the pancakes ready, then she went to see if the children were up yet.

Later that afternoon when Annie settled on a bench near the playground area at Sooner Park, she felt tired—even after the day of rest on Sunday. Mrs. Addison was arriving at the house at five, so Annie had packed an early dinner for the kids.

She'd have the children eat in a couple of hours. Maybe then she could take her mind off the interviews taking place, especially Mrs. Addison's. She would be perfect for the family, similar to what their aunt had been like. And to satisfy Ian, she wasn't nineteen but in her late forties with a ton of experience, having been a nanny for twenty-five years. He would probably hire her on the spot.

Why am I so depressed by the prospect? I'll be able to leave soon and put my life back on track.

Annie checked her watch over and over, and the hours seemed to crawl by. Keeping an eye on four children required a lot of her concentration, but obviously not enough. All she could think about was leaving in a couple of days.

Jasmine waved to her from the top of the slide while Jade ran toward Annie and plopped on the bench beside her. Jade waved her hand in front of her face. "Hello? Water, please."

Annie dug into the cooler she'd brought and passed a bottle to the young girl. "Having fun?"

"Yes, there are even a couple of friends from school here."

Annie scanned the children, hoping Kayla wasn't one of them. She didn't want Jasmine's afternoon ruined.

"Is Dad joining us for our picnic?"

"No, he has business to take care of. I made him something and left it in the refrigerator."

"He's been upset lately." Jade slanted a look toward her.

Annie tensed. "He must have a lot on his mind."

"Are you going to have the surgery? All of us were wondering. I figured it didn't work out and that made him sad."

Annie had wondered when one of them would ask. "I haven't decided."

"Then, you can have the surgery. Great!" Jade clapped her hands. "But then, why is Dad upset? He was so excited when he went to Dallas with you."

Out of all of Ian's children, Jade was the one who was the hardest to keep anything from. "I can't answer that. You'll have to talk to your dad."

She twisted toward Annie. "Is he mad at you?"

Ian had requested she not say anything about leaving to his kids, and she hadn't. She wouldn't break her word, but looking into Jade's inquisitive expression, she didn't know what to tell the child. She panned the playground again, locating Joshua and Jasmine right away. When Annie couldn't see Jeremy, she stood up. "Just a sec, Jade. Where is Jeremy?"

"He's on the monkey bars."

Annie took a few steps to the right and spied the boy swinging from one end to the other with Rex near him. She sat back on the bench where she had a good view of him.

Jade scooted down to Annie. "You care about us."

Although it wasn't a question, Annie answered, "Yes, of course. You're all special to me." *Then, why am I leaving?*

"Is Dad?"

More than she wanted to admit to Jade—even herself. "Yes."

Jade beamed. "Good." She threw her arms around Annie, kissed her on the cheek then hopped up and raced back to play.

Stunned, Annie touched her cheek. Jade reminded

her of herself before the fire: sports oriented and full of life. But the fire had changed her in more ways than physical.

Rex trotted toward her and sat in front of Annie, whining. She glanced at Jeremy still hanging from the monkey bars. "Is something wrong?"

Rex barked.

Annie jumped to her feet. Rex had done this before, and Jeremy had had a seizure not long after. She hurried to the boy. The dog ran to Jeremy and barked insistently. The boy peered at Rex, then Annie and let go of the bar, dropping to the ground.

"Sit on the grass for a few minutes and play with Rex," Annie instructed.

"But I wanted to do the big slide next. Why is he barking?"

"I'm not sure, but I think he senses something. If that's the case, being on the grass would be safer for you."

"But—"

"Please, Jeremy."

With his forehead wrinkled, he trod out of the pool of small, round pebbles under the playground equipment and sank to the lush grass. "How long do I have to stay here?"

"I'm not sure. Awhile." Annie took a seat next to him and checked the ground to make sure there were no objects in the vicinity that could hurt Jeremy.

Jeremy lay back on the grass and began playing with Rex. Within a few minutes, he stiffened and began shaking. She turned him on his side and swiveled her attention between him and his siblings. Rex placed himself right next to Jeremy and licked his face. Sixty seconds later the boy became aware of his surroundings and put his arm around the dog.

"You okay?" Annie relaxed.

He nodded, still dazed a bit. "How did he know?" Jeremy asked when he sat up and petted Rex.

"The more he is around you, the better he's getting at sensing stuff. There's a connection between you two."

"Good boy. I love you, Rex." Jeremy buried his face against the dog's neck.

A lump in her throat made it difficult for Annie to say anything. Seeing the boy and dog together lifted her spirits. She'd set out to help Jeremy especially, and now he had some help. He wasn't alone.

But I am.

After interviewing two disappointing candidates for the nanny position, Ian sat across from Mrs. Addison. On paper she looked good, but…

She isn't Annie.

Ian had tried to help Annie, and instead she was running away as though she had to pay for her innocent mistake the rest of her life. It broke his heart, but he knew he couldn't force her to accept the truth. Now he needed a nanny to replace Annie, but so far no one had come close to her.

"Do you have any questions about the job, Mrs. Addison?"

"Annie had nothing but good things to say about you as an employer. I'm not sure why she's leaving, but this job sounds like a nice match for me. I had a nephew with epilepsy and know how to deal with a seizure. I didn't realize dogs could help with them. I'll have to tell my sister about that. Do you have any more questions for me?"

"No, you've given me all the information I need. And your references are impressive." Tired of the process, Ian pushed to his feet. "I'll let you know after I finish my interviewing."

Mrs. Addison clutched her purse and rose. "I'd hoped I could meet your children, but it's awfully quiet in the house."

"They went on a picnic with Annie." Ian glanced at his watch and noted they'd be home soon. He wanted to make sure the candidate was gone before then. He started toward the foyer.

Mrs. Addison followed. "I look forward to hearing from you, Mr. McGregor."

After he shut the door on his last applicant of the day, Ian wanted to bang his head against the wood. He didn't want to do this again. He never thought he would fall in love after Zoe's death. She'd been his life for years, and they'd been happy. Then her being wrenched from his arms had left him shocked for months, really years, until Annie had popped into his life and shaken it up. Shaken his whole family up.

Earlier Ian noticed that Annie had left him a plate with a sandwich and fruit salad. He went into the kitchen, took the food from the refrigerator, sat at his large table and ate. The silence taunted him. As he ate his chicken salad on rye, he stared at the schedule that Annie had put up to help the family keep activities straight. Something that simple had been an enormous aid for him and even the children. When he glimpsed the dogs' water and food bowls, he grinned at the difference Rex and Daisy had made in everyone's life, but especially Jeremy's. Ian had his eldest son back, and he had Annie to thank for that, too.

The sound of the utility room door opening and then footsteps pounding proclaimed his family had returned. Annie was back. For a second his heartbeat raced, then he remembered she would be leaving soon. He ate the last bite and headed for the sink as they all poured into the kitchen.

The first thing Joshua said was "Where's Daisy?"

"Out in the backyard." Ian gestured in that direction. Annie hadn't come in.

"Annie went to her apartment and said she'd be back in a few minutes. Dad, next time we need to take Daisy, too," Jade said while Joshua and Jasmine ran out the back door.

"Someone will have to keep up with her on a leash the whole time."

"We can take turns." Jade walked through the kitchen to the hallway.

"How did it go with you and Rex?" Ian asked Jeremy, who was feeding his dog.

"I had a seizure, but I'm okay now. It wasn't long, and Rex knew about it before it happened." Jeremy straightened from filling Rex's bowl with dry dog food.

"How do you know Rex knew about it?"

"He went and got Annie. She had me sit on the grass. Good thing because I was swinging on the monkey bars." Jeremy talked about the incident as though it was nothing out of the ordinary.

"How long ago?"

His son shrugged. "Probably two hours."

"How did the other kids at the park react?"

"Fine. A couple wanted to know about Rex, and I told them what he did. They were amazed."

And so was he. Ian knew some service dogs noticed a seizure coming on. In a short time Rex and Jeremy had become close. They did everything together, and Jeremy loved having his dog tag along.

Within minutes Rex wolfed down his food, and he followed Jeremy to the den. Ian thought back to when Jeremy had fought him about having a service dog. A lot had changed.

And the woman coming into the kitchen had been instrumental in it.

"How did the interviews go?" Annie asked after looking around for any children.

"They all showed up."

"Wasn't Mrs. Addison great? The kids at church love her. She teaches a third-and fourth-grade Sunday-school class."

"She was nice."

"That's all? Did you hire her?"

"No, I didn't hire anyone today."

"But you're going to call her back and ask her, aren't you?"

Ian plowed his fingers through his hair. He hadn't thought much about it until Annie had brought it up. If he could avoid...

"Ian?" Annie stepped a few feet closer.

Too near. "I'm not going to hire any of the women tonight."

"What was wrong with Mrs. Addison?"

"Too old."

"First Mary was too young, and now Mrs. Addison is too old. I can't believe it. Either would be a great nanny." She opened her mouth to say more, then closed it.

"My kids are active. I know there are days you get tired. I certainly do. Keeping up with them requires an experienced hand."

"Between what ages?"

"Twenty-five and forty."

The back door opened, and Jasmine and Joshua came inside with Daisy. Annie glared at Ian while Jasmine fed the dog.

Joshua remained. "Daisy was so happy to see me." Then, as if he sensed the tension in the kitchen, he looked between Ian and Annie. "What's wrong?"

"Nothing you need to worry about, son. We'll be in my office. Jeremy is in the den." Ian walked into the hallway, glancing back to make sure Annie was coming, too.

When he reached his office, he leaned against his desk, too agitated to sit. He clasped its edge and waited for Annie's response.

After shutting the door, she pivoted. "What are you doing? You've turned down two perfectly good nannies. Are you doing this to keep me here?"

Anger surged through him. Ian gritted his teeth and waited to calm down before he answered. "I'm looking out for my children's best interests. What are you afraid of, Annie? Loving a man?"

"Why do you want to change me?"

"Why are you blaming yourself for your mother's death when no one else does?"

She gasped, her eyes wide. "That's low. That isn't something I share with others."

"But you did with me. Why?"

She started to say something but shook her head.

"Annie, it's because you feel something for me beyond employer/employee and even friendship."

"But you don't think I'm good enough for you the way I am."

Ian shoved off the desk and closed the space between them. "That is not why I contacted my friend. If you choose not to have the surgery, that's your decision, and I'll respect it."

"You say that, but when I told you I didn't want it, you went to your friend without my knowledge. So obviously my appearance bothers you more than you'll admit, maybe even to yourself. You're a plastic surgeon—you want people to be as beautiful as possible."

For a moment her words halted him. His mind went blank. Was she right? Not a chance. "Annie, I don't see your scars. I see you. I started caring before I even knew about your scars."

"I don't believe you. You're lying to yourself, Ian. And I think my staying would only complicate the situation. Believe me, I don't want to leave your children. They mean a lot to me."

"Obviously not enough to stay. This will devastate them." *And me.*

"That's why I wanted someone like Mary or Mrs. Addison to take my place."

"No one can do that. I think you're scared. Acknowledging your feelings for me means you can't move on in a few years like you've been doing. You've always been able to put a certain distance between you and the family. You're afraid to give love a chance."

"That isn't true." Annie stiffened, her fists curling and uncurling at her side. "Ian, I'm giving you my two weeks' notice."

Kneading his neck, Ian tried to quash the hurt and pain that filled every part of him. "I think it's best, then, for my children not to come to depend on you any more than they already do. You can leave right away, if that suits you."

Looking stunned, Annie whirled around and threw open the door as she stormed from the office.

Ian started after her but stopped in his tracks when Jasmine and Jade blocked the entrance, horror on their faces. Behind them were Jeremy and Joshua. *They must have heard everything we said.*

Somehow Annie held back the tears as she drove to the church. She had stopped at Amanda's house, but no one had answered. She needed a refuge in which to think and decide what to do next. She needed the Lord to comfort her, guide her.

Annie noticed some cars in the parking lot, but she prayed no one was in the sanctuary. When she entered the church, she found a pew in front but off to the side, shrouded in shadows.

For a long moment she sat silently. Then emotions flooded her, and she quietly cried. She wasn't yet ready to say goodbye to the children—she wanted to make the transition to a new nanny as easy as possible—but Ian had told her to leave *now.*

If that suits you.

Those words made her pause. Ian had tried to keep her. She'd been the one who'd insisted on going. Tension prickled from her neck down her spine. When she massaged her tight muscles, she felt the rough texture of her scars.

Mom, I miss you so much. I could use your words of wisdom right now. Help me.

"Annie, are you all right? I saw you come into the foyer and waved."

She turned tear-filled eyes on Emma, who stood a few feet from her.

Ian gathered the children in the den on the couch and sat across from them.

"Why is Annie leaving us?" Jasmine asked, then burst into sobs.

Jade held her twin and patted her back. "I thought Annie loved being here. What did we do wrong?"

"It's me. I drove her away with my seizure today. I didn't mean to have it at the park," Jeremy said sadly.

Joshua remained quiet, staring at his lap, then he looked up. "I'll do everything Annie wants if she'll stay."

"Who are Mary and Mrs. Addison?" Jade asked.

"Two women I interviewed to take Annie's place."

"How could you?" Jasmine shot to her feet and ran from the room.

Jeremy moved to the floor in front of the couch and held Rex. Joshua joined him.

"Fix this, Dad," Jade said fiercely.

Ian's desire to fix the family was what had started

this. That and making the mistake of falling in love with Annie. "I wish I could."

"There's no choice. You have to."

How do I make someone fall in love with me when she's decided she's not worthy of love?

"May I sit with you?" Emma asked, and took a seat next to Annie before she could answer. "I feel as though we've gotten to know each other lately with Rex. I hate to see someone in pain. I felt as though I needed to come in here and see you. What's wrong?"

For a long moment Annie couldn't even find the words. She'd have to tell Emma everything, even about the fire. When Annie began explaining about her scars, it flowed from her like a flood.

"So what I'm hearing is that you blame yourself for your mother's death."

"I *was* at fault."

"Okay, let's say what you did led to your mom dying."

Her throat full of unshed tears, Annie nodded.

"You think you need to spend the rest of your life paying for that mistake?"

"Yes."

"Why? Who said that? Certainly not the Lord."

"What do you mean?"

"I saw how you were with the McGregor children. You have a gift and a lot of love inside you. God sent you there when they needed you most."

"You've been talking to Amanda."

"Yes, I wanted some background so I could help Jeremy and Rex bond."

Annie folded her hands together and rubbed the back of one.

"You've spent fourteen years mourning your mother's death and keeping yourself apart from others emotionally. I don't believe God asked you to do that. I think you decided you had to without asking Him."

"How can you say that?"

"Because I did the same thing. When my first husband died, I blamed myself. I was the reason he was on the ladder he fell from. My husband now, Jake, helped me to see the error of my thinking. It's okay to forgive yourself, Annie. God did a long time ago. That's the beauty with Him. All we have to do is ask Him from our hearts."

It sounds so easy. But I know it isn't.

"Do you have feelings for Ian?"

"Yes. I haven't let myself feel anything for a long time. I don't..."

"Embrace them. They are a gift from the Lord. He wants you to be happy."

Was that possible?

When Annie returned to Ian's house, it was ablaze with lights, a beacon in the dark. The kids were usually in bed by now. Had Jeremy had a bad seizure? She hurried through the breezeway and into the utility room and kitchen. Her heartbeat pounded a mad staccato against her rib cage. She charged into the hallway, paused to check the den. Empty.

At Ian's office she peeked in and saw him sitting in his chair, staring at his desktop. The forlorn expression on his face rent her heart into pieces.

"Is something wrong? Jeremy? One of the other children?"

Ian peered up at her, and he erased the look from his face. "I didn't hear you come in. The kids are okay. I need to go up and tell them good-night, but I don't know how much sleep they'll get."

"They overheard us?"

He nodded.

"I'm sorry. I wish they hadn't."

"Oh, well, they needed to know, and I would have stewed over how to tell them." Ian sat forward, resting his elbows on the tan blotter. "Have you decided to leave now?"

Annie heard defeat in his voice. Without saying a word, she strode to him and leaned against the desk next to him. He swiveled his chair to look at her.

"I've decided to leave—never."

He blinked.

"How can I leave the man I've fallen in love with? Especially when he told me he loved me?"

For a few seconds Ian's face was blank, and then a grin broke through. "You aren't joking, are you?"

"Never about something this important. Ian, you've been right all along. I didn't think I had a right to be happy. I was afraid of feeling anything good. But I love you and the children. I can't imagine my life without you."

Ian jumped to his feet and drew her into an embrace. "You're sure?"

"I went to my church, talked with Emma and came away feeling like a new woman. God forgave me long ago. I just had to forgive myself. If I didn't, I would be hurting a lot of people I care about—including you, your family and mine."

Ian put his hand on her cheek. "Annie, I don't care what you decide about the surgery."

"I believe you."

Ian bent his head toward her and kissed the scars on her neck and cheek, then trailed more to her mouth. When he stopped he said, "This has been the worst and best day of my life. I won't let you forget how much you mean to me, Annie."

"Let's go tell the children. I have to make everything right with them."

Ian looked over Annie's shoulder and laughed. "I don't think you have to."

All four children along with two dogs poured into the room and surrounded her and Ian with laughter and hugs. *I've finally found what I always wanted. Thank You, God.*

Epilogue

"Shh. They're here. Hide."

Coming down the hall, Annie heard Jeremy's words a few seconds before she and Ian entered the den. "I guess my sister hasn't brought them home yet," she said, playing along with the kids wanting to surprise them by hiding.

Ian wrapped his arms around Annie. "Hmm. That gives us more alone time. What do you think we should do?" He kissed her loudly on the mouth.

"Yuck," Jeremy said while the other children, along with Amanda, jumped up and said, "Surprise!"

Jeremy had to help Annie's sister stand up. She was eight months pregnant and big. As Amanda waddled toward them, the children swarmed Ian and Annie, all wanting to know about the honeymoon. Ian actually blushed, then told them about the places they'd visited in Key West.

Amanda hugged Annie then whispered in her ear, "You look great. I see married life agrees with you."

Annie pulled back, chuckling. "How were the kids?"

"Perfect, except…"

Everyone looked at Amanda.

"Except what?" Ian asked.

"They threw me a baby shower."

Annie settled her hands on her waist. "You did that without me?" She tried to look angry.

"It was a trial run," Jasmine said. "We're gonna do another one next week with everyone, including you."

"That is if the baby doesn't come early." Amanda laid her hand over her stomach.

"He'd better not. I have my last laser treatment next week in Dallas. I can't miss the baby's birth." Annie snuggled into the crook of Ian's arm, so glad she'd finally done something about her scars. They were still there, but less obvious, and her prosthetic ear was so realistic looking. But the best part was that Ian had left the decision to her, emphasizing that he thought she was beautiful as she was. Annie knew, without a doubt, he loved her no matter what.

Amanda cleared her throat. "Kids, let's go in the kitchen and get dinner ready."

"But—" Joshua sputtered to a stop because Jade had put her hand over his mouth.

"We're gonna help Amanda. All of us, Joshua." Jade tugged on her brother's arm, pulling him toward the hallway.

After the children left with Amanda, Ian went to

the den doorway, looked up and down the hallway then shut the door. "That's just in case they decide to eavesdrop again."

Annie nestled within his embrace. "Our kids don't eavesdrop. They told me they were just keeping themselves informed about what was going on in the family." *My new family.*

Ian kissed the tip of her nose, then settled his mouth over hers, pressing her against him. When he nibbled her ear, she shivered.

"I love you, Mrs. McGregor."

Annie leaned back slightly and looked up at him, running her fingers through his hair. "I might have been a little slow to grasp that, but I know now. And I love you." She pulled his head down so she could kiss him again.

* * * * *

Mikey's fingers contracted. "Suppose I told you that the
hotel I own is actually a casino," he said slowly, "and it's
in Las Vegas?"

Bernie's eyes widened. "You own a casino in Las
Vegas?" she exclaimed. "Wow!"

He laughed, surprised at her easy acceptance. "I run it
legit, too," he added. "No fixes, no hidden switches, no
cheating. Drives the feds nuts, because they can't find
anything to pin on me there."

"The feds?" she asked.

He drew in a breath. "I told you, I'm a bad man." He
felt guilty about it, dirty. His fingers caressed hers as they

neared Graylings, the huge mansion where his cousin lived with the heir to the Grayling racehorse stables.

Her fingers curled trustingly around his. "And I told you that the past doesn't matter," she said stubbornly. Her heart was running wild. "Not at all. I don't care how bad you've been."

His own heart stopped and then ran away. His teeth clenched. "I don't even think you're real, Bernie," he whispered. "I think I dreamed you."

She flushed and smiled. "Thanks."

He glanced in the rearview mirror. "What I'd give for just five minutes alone with you right now," he said tautly. "Fat chance," he added as he noticed the sedan tailing casually behind them.

She felt all aglow inside. She wanted that, too. Maybe they could find a quiet place to be alone, even for just a few minutes. She wanted to kiss him until her mouth hurt.

Don't miss
Texas Proud *by Diana Palmer,*
available October 2020 wherever
Harlequin Special Edition books and ebooks are sold.

Harlequin.com